"I could kiss you."

Extending his arms, David winked at her. "Come and put one right here." He pointed to his mouth.

Devon shook her head. "Just kidding."

"Oh, so the pretty lady is a tease."

"No, David. I'll show you I'm not a tease."

She stood up and walked over to him, her arms going around his neck as she went on tiptoe. His head came down as if in slow motion, and his mouth covered hers in a tender joining she didn't want to end. It wasn't a kiss filled with unbridled passion but one that seemed to heal her, sweep away any doubt that she'd been wrong for agreeing to become involved with him.

ACCLAIM FOR THE
CAVANAUGH ISLAND NOVELS

MAGNOLIA DRIVE

"I would recommend this wonderful story to anyone that truly loves a good second-chance love story."
—HarlequinJunkie.com

"Upon returning to Cavanaugh Island, readers will be entertained with the history and culture of the Lowcountry of South Carolina. Characters finding love the second time around are an added bonus. There is also the pleasure of a story told in language that flows."
—*RT Book Reviews*

"Rochelle Alers is a very descriptive writer and she made Cavanaugh Island come to life for me...There is a very interesting plot to this book and it is much more than a romance."
—OpenBookSociety.com

HAVEN CREEK

"Alers does not disappoint the romantics among us: *Haven Creek* is powerfully uplifting for the soul."
—USAToday.com

"4½ stars! Believable and satisfying, on all levels. Sit back and enjoy!"

—RT Book Reviews

"Appealing, mature protagonists, a colorful cast of islanders, and a rewarding romance that realistically unfolds add to this fascinating, gently paced story that gradually reveals its secrets as it draws readers back to idyllic Cavanaugh Island."

—Library Journal

"An excellent love story...Huge messages throughout this book made for a very loving and interesting summer read."

—PublishersWeekly.com

SANCTUARY COVE

"4½ stars! With this introduction to the Cavanaugh Island series, Alers returns to the Lowcountry of South Carolina. Readers will enjoy the ambiance, the delicious-sounding food, and the richly described characters falling in love after tragedy. This is an excellent series starter."

—RT Book Reviews

"I truly and thoroughly enjoyed the book. I found it a wonderful, warm, intriguing romance and was happy to find a new author to read."

—Jill Shalvis, *New York Times* bestselling author of *Simply Irresistible*

"Carolina Lowcountry comfort food, a community of people who care, and a wonderfully emotional love story. Who could ask for more? *Sanctuary Cove* is the kind of place you visit and never want to leave."

—Hope Ramsay, bestselling author of *Welcome to Last Chance*

"Soaked in an old-fashioned feel, Alers's hyper-realistic style...will appeal to readers looking for gentle, inexplicit romance."

—*Publishers Weekly*

"The author writes in such a fluid way that it captures the readers' attention from the word go...A sweet, charming romance, *Sanctuary Cove* is a quick read you will remember."

—FreshFiction.com

"*Sanctuary Cove* is a gripping, second-chance-at-love romance...real and truly inspiring...I highly recommend it!"

—NightOwlReviews.com

Also by Rochelle Alers

The Cavanaugh Island Series

Magnolia Drive
Home for the Holidays (novella)
Haven Creek
Angels Landing
Sanctuary Cove

Cherry Lane

A Cavanaugh Island Novel

Rochelle Alers

FOREVER

NEW YORK BOSTON

Forever
Hachette Book Group
1290 Avenue of the Americas
New York, NY 10104

www.HachetteBookGroup.com

Printed in the United States of America

First Edition: May 2015
10 9 8 7 6 5 4 3 2 1

OPM

Forever is an imprint of Grand Central Publishing.
The Forever name and logo are trademarks of Hachette Book Group, Inc.

The Hachette Speakers Bureau provides a wide range of authors for speaking events. To find out more, go to www.hachettespeakersbureau.com or call (866) 376-6591.

The publisher is not responsible for websites (or their content) that are not owned by the publisher.

Do not exploit the poor because they
are poor and do not crush the needy
in court.

—Proverbs 22:22

Cherry Lane

Chapter One

The brilliant afternoon sunlight shimmered off the numerous steeples and spires dotting Charleston's skyline. And despite the fatigue weighing her down from more than five hours of flight delays and layovers, Devon Gilmore found herself in awe of the sight that gave the Holy City its nickname.

Reaching for her handbag, she took out enough money for the fare and tip for the taxi ride from the airport to the city's Historic District. She felt some tension ease as the taxi drove down the broad tree-lined avenues and pulled up to the historic Francis Marion Hotel. When she'd complained to her friend Keaton Grace about the frigid snowy New York City weather, he'd suggested she come to the Lowcountry for several weeks, and this visit was exactly what she needed right now. As much as she loved the bright lights and bustle of New York City, she was ready for a change. And going to Chicago to see her parents had been an utter disaster.

The taxi driver came to a complete stop at the same time

the bellhop rushed over to open the door for her. "I'll get your luggage, ma'am."

"Thank you." She'd brought her large black quilted Vera Bradley spinner and matching roll-along duffel and stuffed them so full she could hardly lift them. The first order of business would be finding an outfit for the party Keaton had convinced her to attend this evening.

Devon placed a hand over her flat belly. She wasn't showing yet, but it wouldn't be long before her baby bump became visible. She took a deep breath. Even the air here smelled different—clean and sweet. Like a fresh start.

Devon wasn't particularly in a party-going mood, but she'd promised Keaton she'd go to his girlfriend's birthday party out on Cavanaugh Island. He'd reassured her that it was only going to be close family and friends. Maybe the distraction would do her good, especially the way her life was unraveling at the seams right now.

She slipped into a skirt and managed to zip and button it without too much difficulty. The waistband was tighter and tonight would probably be the last time she would be able to wear it for a while. Sitting on the chair at the table that also doubled as a desk, Devon reached for her cosmetic bag. Flicking on the table lamp, she took out a small mirror with a built-in light. She stared at her reflection, noticing that although her face was fuller, there were dark circles under her eyes. Opening a tube of concealer, she squeezed a small dot on her finger and gently patted the liquid beneath each eye, and blended it to match her natural skin tone.

When she initially found herself facing an unplanned pregnancy, Devon realized she had two options: give up the baby for adoption or do something no other woman in her family had ever done—become an unwed mother. It had taken a lot of soul-searching, but in the end she decided she would keep her baby. After all, she was already thirty-six. And her job as an entertainment attorney afforded her a comfortable lifestyle.

What she refused to dwell on was the man whose child she carried. They had slept together for more than a year, and at no time had he given her any indication that not only was he involved with another woman but he was also engaged to marry her. She sighed, straightened her shoulders, and promised herself she would try to have some fun at this party.

An hour later Devon got out of the taxi in front of the Tanners' three-story Colonial. She walked up four steps to exquisitely carved double doors flanked by gaslight-inspired lanterns. A larger matching fixture under the portico and strategically placed in-ground lighting illuminated the residence. She'd just raised her hand to ring the doorbell when she heard the low purr of another car pulling up.

Turning around, she saw a tall man get out of a late-model Lexus sedan. He paused to slip on a suit jacket, and she couldn't help admiring the way the fine fabric fit his lean frame and broad shoulders. As he walked her way he deftly adjusted his emerald-green silk tie. Golden light spilled over his sculpted dark face and neatly cropped hair.

"Are you here for the party?" he asked her.

The sound of his soft, drawling voice elicited a smile from Devon as she lifted her chin, staring up at him through a fringe of lashes. Not only did he have a wonderful voice, but he also smelled marvelous.

"Yes," she answered.

He smiled, drawing her gaze to linger on his firm mouth. "I had no idea Francine had such gorgeous friends."

Devon lowered her eyes as she bit back her own smile. The compliment had rolled off his tongue like watered silk. She wanted to tell him he was more than kind on the eyes, but she'd never been that overtly flirtatious. "Thank you."

The tall, dark stranger inclined his head. "You're quite welcome." He rang the bell and then opened the door. Stepping aside, he let her precede him. "You must not be from around here because folks on the island usually don't lock their doors until it's time to go to bed."

"I'm a friend of Keaton Grace. I just got in from New York."

"Ah, well that explains it." He extended his hand. "David Sullivan."

A beat passed before Devon took his hand. "Devon Gilmore," she said in introduction. Truly, she was Devon Gilmore-Collins, but just like her mother, she'd been raised to uphold the vaunted Gilmore tradition. And given her current state of being unwed and pregnant, her mother was no longer speaking to her.

"Well, it looks as if you two don't need an introduction."

David released Devon's hand. "Happy birthday, Red," he said to the tall, slender woman with a profusion of red curls framing her face. Angling his head, he kissed her cheek. Then he reached into the breast pocket of his suit jacket and handed her an envelope. "And Happy Saint Patrick's Day, too."

The redhead patted David's smooth cheek. "Thank you. Everyone's here," she said. Turning, she offered Devon her hand. "I'm Francine Tanner."

Devon shook her hand. "Devon Gilmore," she said, smiling. "Thank you for inviting me to your home."

Francine's green eyes crinkled as she returned Devon's smile. Her eyes matched the silk blouse she'd paired with black slacks. "Any friend of Keaton is always welcome here. He had to go upstairs and should be back at any moment." She looped her arm through Devon's over the sleeve of her suit jacket. "Come with me. As soon as Keaton returns he can introduce you to everyone before we sit down to eat. And David, I want to warn you that my father is making Irish coffee again this year. If it were up to him he would celebrate Saint Patrick's Day every day."

Devon gave Francine a sidelong glance. "Is that good or bad?"

Francine laughed. "It all depends on your tolerance for alcohol. Yours truly learned a long time ago to pass, but most folks who've drunk Daddy's Irish coffee swear it's the best they've ever had."

David stared at Devon as she walked with Francine through the entryway and into the family room, his gaze lingering on her shapely legs. Pushing his hands into the pockets of his suit trousers, he followed Devon and Francine into the house. His gaze swept over Morgan and Nathaniel Shaw sitting together and talking quietly to each other, while Jeffrey and Kara Hamilton stood at the open French doors, she gesturing to the birds that had gathered to eat the seeds that had fallen from a feeder attached to a pole on the patio. Everyone was wearing green. Nearly every resident on the island celebrated the holiday even if they didn't claim a drop of Irish blood.

Mavis Tanner was the first to notice him. "David," she crooned softly. "Thank you for coming. I know how tied up you've been lately with Bobby's case. If that lying heifer had her way, the poor boy would've spent at least twenty-five years in prison."

Lowering his head, he pressed a kiss on Francine's mother's salt-and-pepper twists. Until yesterday, David hadn't been certain he'd be able to attend the party. His last case had gone to trial and he'd spent every waking hour in an attempt to keep his client from going to jail for a crime David knew he did not commit. At the last possible moment before the case went to the jury for deliberation, the prosecution's eyewitness recanted, claiming she'd lied in an act of revenge because the defendant had rejected her advances. After the judge dismissed the charges, David went home, turned off his phone, and slept for twelve uninterrupted hours.

"Well, now the witness is locked up for perjury. I'm just glad I was able to make Red's party."

Mavis rested a hand on his jacket sleeve. "You may as well go over to the bar and let Frank light you up with that concoction that can definitely pass for hooch."

David lowered his head until his mouth was only inches from Mavis's ear. "You can be honest with me, Miss Mavis. Are you certain it isn't hooch? I heard Old Man Kennedy has a still hidden behind the shed where he butchers and smokes his hogs and sells the stuff only to a few folks that know how to mind dey mout."

He hadn't realized he'd spoken in dialect until the words were out. Even though he had a law degree, there were times when David couldn't totally escape slipping in the Gullah dialect of African descendants who'd passed down the language from one generation to the next. He knew if his mother heard it she would've been mortified. The thought made him smile. Edna Sullivan, grande dame of Charleston's African American social circle, was very conscious not to lapse into the dialect she'd grown up with.

Mavis rolled her eyes. "Please don't start me lying, because you'd have to charge me with perjury, too. I'm too old to sit in jail, even though the color orange would go quite nicely with my complexion," she said jokingly.

David's laugh caught the attention of his cousin Jeffrey Hamilton, who was also the sheriff of Cavanaugh Island. With their six-three height, dark complexions, warm brown eyes, and cleft chins, the familial resemblance between the two men was evident.

Although he'd been raised in Charleston, David always felt more of a kinship with his relatives living on the island than those on the mainland. Perhaps it had something to do with their unpretentiousness. There were a few exceptions, but most of the islanders were down to earth, more trustworthy, and usually just more willing to help one another out than the people on the mainland.

Jeff gathered David in a rough embrace, pounding his back. "Congratulations on getting Bobby Niles off. You're a helluva lawyer, cuz. It would've been a damn shame if Bobby had to spend the next two decades of his life locked away for something he didn't do."

David peered over his cousin's shoulder, meeting Devon's eyes. It was apparent she'd overheard Jeff. He pounded Jeff's back before easing out of his bone-crushing grip. His cousin outweighed him by almost thirty pounds and it was apparent the former Marine wasn't aware of his own strength. "It would've turned out differently if Larissa hadn't recanted her testimony."

Jeff lifted his dark eyebrows a fraction. "That's BS and you know it. I was in the courtroom during your closing argument and from the expression on the faces of the jury, most of them were going for a not-guilty verdict."

David wanted to tell Jeff he wished he'd been *that* optimistic.

"Here's the man of the hour!" shouted Frank Tanner, as he walked across the room with two clear mugs filled with hot black coffee, Irish whiskey, and granulated sugar, topped off with whipped cream. Frank gave David one of the mugs, lifting the other one in a toast. "Congrats, Counselor. Now I know who to call if the sheriff decides to lock me up for speeding."

Jeff smiled and shook his head. "I should lock you up for buying moonshine from Old Man Kennedy and trying to pass it off as Irish whiskey." Everyone laughed, including Frank.

David had always liked Francine's father. The red hair from his youth was now completely gray, but his large gray-green eyes were still striking. The former Pittsburgh Steelers' defensive end–turned–restaurateur had been a local hero back in the day. And he told anyone who stood still long enough to listen that his two greatest accomplishments were becoming a father and keeping off the fifty pounds he'd lost after his football career ended.

David took a sip of the drink, then blew out a breath. "I'm going to have to agree with my cousin. This stuff *is* lethal. Delicious, but definitely lethal."

Frank took a deep swallow from his own mug, a rush of color darkening his face until it took on a cherry-red shade. "Da-a-a-yum!" he gasped. "I didn't realize it was *that* strong."

"I told Daddy that he should let Keaton make the drinks, but he wouldn't listen to me," Francine drawled.

Devon saw Keaton Grace enter the family room just in time to hear Francine's pronouncement. "No, baby, you don't want me to tend bar. I've always had a very heavy hand whenever I mix drinks."

Devon knew Keaton was being truthful. He was an incredible cook but a complete failure when it came to mixing drinks. She'd had a lot of male friends in the past, but none more loyal or dependable than Keaton.

A hint of a smile tilted the corners of her mouth when she noticed the longing stare Keaton gave Francine. Only a blind person couldn't see the tenderness in his gaze. It was a gesture she'd shared with Gregory Emerson countless times. She closed her eyes for several seconds and when she opened them she saw Keaton walking toward her.

"Don't get up," he said softly, hunkering down and kissing her cheek. "You're as pretty as the first time I saw you in college."

Devon lowered her eyes, hoping no one overheard him. She met Keaton at New York University when she was a first-year law student, while he was enrolled in the graduate program at the Tisch School of the Arts. They'd become good friends and after graduating he became her first client, and eventually she became his agent and business manager. She had to admit that time had been more than kind to Keaton. Except for a faint sprinkling of gray in his cropped black hair, he could pass for a man much younger than forty-one. His dark olive complexion, high cheekbones, lean jaw, and large, deep-set brown eyes made for an arresting face.

"Thank you. How's the studio coming along?" As an independent filmmaker, Keaton had moved from Los Angeles to set up Lowcountry Productions.

"They just laid the foundation for the soundstage last week and now they're framing it."

"Have you settled into your home?" she asked.

"Yes and no," Keaton replied. "I moved out of the Cove Inn a couple of weeks ago. Right now I'm sleeping on a blow-up mattress and I have a card table with a folding chair as a desk to work on my latest script. The decorator estimates that most of the furniture will be delivered early next month. Thankfully all of the kitchen appliances are in, so I can cook for myself."

"Sounds like you're incredibly busy, but I'm so proud of you."

He kissed her cheek. "Thank you—that means a lot. I'm sorry we won't have as much time together as I originally thought when I invited you here."

"There's plenty for me to do on my own. Don't even worry."

"We'll talk more later," Keaton promised. "Right now, I'd better go help play host."

Keaton accepted a mug of Irish coffee from Francine's father, grimacing after taking a sip. "Oh shee-eet!" he gasped. Laughter and guffaws filled the room when he clutched his chest. "I'm sorry, ladies. I didn't mean for it to come out like that."

Mavis frowned at her husband. "I told you they were too strong."

Frank, grinning like a Cheshire cat, blew Mavis a kiss. "Now that everyone's here, I think we should get the introductions out of the way before we go into the dining room and eat. Keaton, please introduce your guest."

Keaton's gaze swept around the room. "Ladies, gentlemen, it gives me great pleasure to introduce Devon Gilmore, my agent and business manager." He smiled at Francine. "You can introduce the others to Devon."

Francine ran a hand through the curls falling over her

forehead. "The one passing off the nitroglycerin for Irish coffee is my dad, and the beautiful woman with the twists is my mother." Devon laughed with the others. "Grandma Dinah, who along with my mother cooked everything for tonight's gathering, will be along shortly. She just went upstairs to get dressed."

Devon acknowledged each person with a smile and a nod when Francine introduced her to Jeffrey Hamilton and his wife, Kara, and Morgan Shaw and her husband, Nathaniel. Francine winked at David. "Next is David Sullivan, but it appears you two already know each other."

Chapter Two

Devon couldn't stop the rush of heat suffusing her face as everybody turned her way with questioning looks. She wanted to tell the others she'd just met David, but decided to let them draw their own conclusions.

Frank put an arm around Mavis's waist. "Does anyone need a refill before we sit down to eat?"

Mavis gave her husband a glance. "Sweetheart, it's time we eat while we're still able to see how to pick up a fork."

The words were barely off Mavis's tongue when David extended his hand to Devon. Placing her hand on his out-stretched palm, she permitted him to pull her gently to her feet. He tucked her hand into the bend of his elbow. She didn't want to read too much into the gesture; maybe he just wanted to make her feel less conspicuous that she wasn't a part of a couple. But it still felt good to be tucked against him.

She couldn't imagine David not being able to find a date, because everything about him radiated breeding and class—qualities every Gilmore woman looked for in a suitable partner. For a brief moment she wondered how her mother would react if she showed up on her doorstep with David on her arm. Would it make her condition more acceptable?

Devon's jaw dropped slightly when she walked into the formal dining room, feeling as if she was watching an episode of an antebellum *Downton Abbey*. Prisms of light from two chandeliers shimmered on the silver and crystal place settings. The table was covered with a delicately crocheted cream-colored cloth and green liner and accommodated seating for twelve. A hand-painted vase overflowing with white roses, tulips, and magnolias served as an elaborate centerpiece. A mahogany buffet server held a bevy of chafing dishes from which wafted the most delicious mouthwatering aromas.

Devon found her place card, fortuitously right next to David's. She got a little thrill in her belly when he pulled out a chair for her. Whoever said chivalry was dead was definitely wrong, she mused. It may be considered old-fashioned in other parts of the country, but the practice was alive on Cavanaugh Island. All the women sat, while their men lined up at the buffet table to fix them a plate.

She'd lost count of the number of times men in New York lowered their heads and feigned sleep rather than get up on the bus or subway to give a woman their seat. And forget about holding a door or helping a woman into or out of her coat.

"I'll bring you a plate," David offered. "Is there anything you can't eat or don't like?"

A slight shiver of awareness swept over Devon at his proximity. David was being so kind, but it wasn't the same as having someone who knew you inside and out bring you a plate of food. Gregory, bastard that he was for cheating on her, would've known that she always took extra gravy and disliked rhubarb. Although an inner voice told her that her ex-lover wasn't worth her tears or angst, moving on wasn't easy. After all, he'd given life to the tiny baby growing inside her. A tentative smile trembled over her mouth.

"No allergies, and I'll eat just about anything. Thank you so much, David."

"No problem." He put a comforting hand on her shoulder and squeezed. Devon swore she could feel the heat right down to her toes.

Morgan caught her eye from across the table. "How long are you going to be here?" Morgan asked her.

"Probably for a month." She didn't tell the beautiful, tall, dark-skinned woman with the dimpled smile that she wanted to stay until northeast temperatures no longer hovered around the freezing mark. Although she'd grown up in Chicago and had managed to survive countless frigid winters in New York City, Devon felt somehow this year was different. Despite wearing multiple layers, she still found herself chilled to the bone.

"Where are you staying?" Morgan asked.

"I have a suite at the Francis Marion, but I'm hoping to move to the Cove Inn by Wednesday, so I can be closer to Keaton when we have to go over legal issues. I've always been a hands-on attorney when it comes to Keaton." Devon had shepherded his career from the time he wrote scripts for daytime soaps to his becoming an independent filmmaker.

"You can stay here with us," Francine chimed in. "I have an extra bedroom in my apartment."

Mavis shook her head. "She can stay down here with

me and Frank. We have six bedrooms in this house, and that's not counting my mother-in-law's and Francine's apartments."

Devon was in a quandary. As tempting as the invitation to sleep in the Tanners' historic home was, she didn't really feel up to living with strangers. But she also didn't want to insult them by turning down their Southern hospitality. "I don't want to impose."

Mavis waved her hand. "Child, please. There's no imposition. We have the room, so you just move yourself out of that hotel tomorrow and come and stay with us. And I'm not going to take no for an answer."

Devon sat there, hands clasped together in her lap, as she attempted to bring her emotions under control. People she'd met for the first time had welcomed her into their home, while her own mother had slammed the door in her face.

Smiling, she blinked back tears. She couldn't believe she was going to start crying when she'd earned a reputation for being a no-nonsense, hard-nosed, take-no-prisoners attorney. It had to be the hormones. "Please let me think about it. I promise to let you know after the weekend."

A slight frown appeared between Mavis's eyes. "I'm going to hold you to that promise."

Francine pressed her palms together as her eyes sparkled like polished emeralds. "Even if you decide not to stay with us, I still want you to join Kara, Morgan, and me for our Monday afternoon get-together at Jack's Fish House. It's the only time we can get to see one another because I work at the salon Tuesday through Saturday, Kara just became a new mother, and Morgan is busy with her architectural and interior design company."

This was a proposition Devon could easily agree to, to

connect with women her own age. "What time should I meet you?"

"Twelve noon," Kara said, smiling.

Devon returned the sheriff's wife's warm, open smile. She was scheduled to pick up a rental car the following morning, so she'd have the independence she needed to do some sightseeing on her own.

Five minutes later, she looked down at the plate David set in front of her. He'd selected fried chicken, red rice and sausage, collard greens with cornmeal dumplings, and a slice of corn bread. "There are also sweet potatoes, ribs, Gullah fried shrimp, perlow rice, and barbecue trotters and turkey wings," he informed her.

"Thank you. This looks delicious. I'll make certain to save enough room for seconds," she said as she spread her napkin over her lap. Devon was amused that he'd referred to pig's feet as trotters. The Gilmores eschewed pig's feet, ears, chitterlings, cheeks, and other parts of the pig they deemed scraps. It wasn't until she moved to New York and visited several Harlem soul food restaurants and sampled sloppin' trotters and chitlins for the first time that she wanted to call her mother and let her know the scraps were to die for.

As David returned to the buffet, she wondered if he was always so buttoned up. Of all the men there, he was the only one wearing a suit. But then she was forced to look at herself, realizing she was the only woman wearing a skirt. Maybe it had something to do with their both being attorneys.

Devon turned down Frank's offer of a sparkling rosé and noticed that Kara and Morgan did the same. Kara was probably nursing, but was Morgan pregnant too? It would be so nice if she could talk to another woman going through the same thing.

At that moment, Dinah Tanner entered the dining room, and the men rose to their feet to greet her. The petite, slender woman had short, graying strawberry-blond hair and wore a leaf-green shirtwaist dress. "Everyone please sit down," she said, waving her hand in dismissal.

Frank pulled out a chair for his mother. "Do you want me to fix you a plate, Mama?"

Dinah smiled up at her son. "No thank you, Francis. I'll get it later."

Frank tapped his water glass with a knife. "I'd like to thank everyone for coming to help celebrate my baby's birthday." He ignored Francine when she pushed out her lips. "I know she doesn't like it when I refer to her as my baby, but that's who she'll always be to me. This birthday is very special, not only because I'm sitting here with the women who've made me the happiest man on Cavanaugh Island, but also because there's a man sitting at my table whom I'm honored to think of as a son." He raised his glass in Keaton's direction. "Keaton. Welcome to the family."

Morgan looked at Francine, then Keaton. "Are we missing something?"

Reaching into the pocket of his slacks, Keaton took out a ring, prisms of light from the chandeliers reflecting off the large blue-white center diamond, while holding it up for everyone to see as he rounded the table and dropped to one knee beside Francine. The blush covering her face came close to matching her hair color.

"Milady," he said in a dead-on aristocratic British accent. "I knew when I entered the tavern and saw you for the first time what I had been missing. Your beauty, your wit, and a well-turned ankle caused me many sleepless nights. I must admit you were quite a challenge, but as someone used to giving and not taking orders, I am willing to offer you my title and protection if you would become my wife."

Devon gasped along with the others sitting at the table. She never would've expected Keaton to fall for the redhead she'd glimpsed at Jack's Fish House when she'd come to Sanctuary Cove in early January. When she'd teased him about being into redheads, he revealed he'd seen Francine perform in an off-Broadway play many years ago.

Francine's smile was dazzling. "Milord, I did not reject your advances straight away," she said in an Irish brogue, "but I had to make certain you were not toying with my affections. Me mum and me da raised me to be a lady despite our lowly station. You have proven yourself noble. Therefore, I will marry thee." Keaton slipped the ring on her finger. "I love you, milord."

Keaton smiled. "Fancy that, maiden, because I love you, too."

Applause went up from everyone, as Devon struggled not to cry tears of joy.

"Bravo!" Dinah yelled loudly.

"I knew it, I knew it," Kara crowed.

One by one everyone stood up to kiss Francine and hug Keaton. "When's the wedding?" Devon whispered in Keaton's ear.

"Probably sometime in June. We decided not to set an exact date until after I introduce Francine to my folks. We're going to fly up to Pittsburgh midweek for a few days."

She kissed his smooth cheek. "I'm so happy for you."

Keaton kissed her forehead. "Thank you, Devon."

Frank clasped his large hands together. "Let's eat."

Devon and the others sat down again, picked up their utensils, and began eating. "I overheard Mavis inviting you to stay with her," David said in a quiet voice. "If you don't feel comfortable living in someone's home I can get you a room at the Cove Inn tonight."

She blinked once. "What are you going to do? Have management boot some elderly couple so I can get their room?"

Throwing back his head, David laughed. "Nothing that drastic," he said, sobering quickly. "My firm reserves several suites for out-of-town clients. They seem to prefer the laid-back atmosphere of the island to some of the Charleston hotel chains."

Devon's eyebrows lifted slightly. Her internal antennae had just gone up. In the past, if a man did anything for her, he usually wanted something in return. It was either money or free legal advice or representation; however, it was never something for nothing. Now a man she'd met less than an hour ago had offered to put her up at the Cove Inn in his business-related suite. What, she thought, did he want from her?

"Why would you do that for me?"

David gave her a long, penetrating stare. "You're a friend of Keaton's and Keaton is a friend of Francine's, and Francine happens to be someone I'm quite fond of. And down here we're serious when it comes to friendship."

Perhaps she'd been too critical during her last trip to the island when she told Keaton that Cavanaugh Island was a nice place to visit but doubted whether she'd want to come too often. Much to her chagrin, this was her third trip to the island in the past three months. The first had been for business and the last two personal.

"I appreciate the offer, but I don't mind staying at the hotel for a few more days."

"The offer stands just in case you decide to change your

mind." David paused. "Your significant other doesn't have a problem with you being away for a long time?"

Again, Devon was unprepared for David's direct questioning. She would love to watch him in a courtroom cross-examining a witness. "I suppose he would if I had a significant other."

She angled her head, staring up at him through lowered lashes, unaware of the seductiveness of the gesture when he expelled an audible breath. "Do you have an office here on the island?" she asked, deftly directing the topic of conversation away from her.

David ran a forefinger down the stem of his wineglass. "Not yet. I'm currently a partner in a Charleston firm with my father and his fraternity brother. I decided several months ago to open an office in Haven Creek."

"That sounds exciting. Congratulations. Where exactly is Haven Creek?"

In between forkfuls of rice and chicken, David gave her a brief historical overview of the towns that made up Cavanaugh Island. "All of them are incorporated with their own mayor and town council. Sanctuary Cove is the largest of the three, with a thriving downtown business district. Angels Landing is entirely residential, and Haven Creek is where the artisans and farmers live."

"What made you decide to set up an office there?"

"There are several vacant stores for rent in their business district, and because most of the folks who live in the Creek are self-employed, many of them don't have the money to pay the fees of mainland law firms."

"How do you expect them to pay you?" Devon asked.

David angled his head. "Probably with a hog or a few chickens as barter," he teased, deadpan.

Pressing the napkin to her mouth, Devon smothered a laugh, her body shaking as David patted her back in a comforting motion. She touched the napkin to the corners of her eyes. "That's something I'd love to see."

"What's that?"

"Your office filled with farm animals and bushels of produce."

He chuckled. "Maybe the next time you come down you'll get to see it."

As soon as he spoke, David realized what his words really meant. He wanted to see Devon again. He stared at her delicate profile, his eyes tracing the softness of her jaw and the length of lashes feathering the tops of her cheekbones. Without warning, she turned to look directly at him and he noticed the color of her eyes had changed from a clear gold brown to a grayish green that reminded him of a field of heather he'd photographed when he'd toured the French countryside.

For several seconds David drank in the stunning, natural beauty of the woman sitting a hairbreadth away. His gaze lingered on her hair, which was pinned into a loose twist on the nape of her neck. Under the light from the chandelier it appeared raven black, and he wondered if it was her natural color or if she dyed it. If her complexion had been lighter than tawny brown, the contrast between her skin and hair color would've been more startling.

"Maybe I will," she said in a quiet voice. "So you're only going to serve the indigent?"

David glared at Devon, frowning. His mood took a sudden turn, and he didn't bother to disguise his annoyance. He didn't want to believe she was so arrogant that she would belittle the people of Haven Creek. "I didn't say they were destitute," he practically spat out.

"I just meant that starting a business can be so hard. It takes a lot of courage...not to mention capital."

Leaning back in his chair, David gave Devon a sidelong glance. "Where did you grow up?"

"Chicago," she replied. "Then law school at NYU."

David wondered how long it would take for her to become bored with the laid-back attitude of Cavanaugh Island after living in such large cities. "You live in New York?" She nodded. "As a big-city attorney you must see a lot of clients with a myriad of legal problems."

Devon shook her head. "I don't work for a firm. I have only three clients, and I like it that way. It's just Keaton, a pro football player, and a pro basketball player."

"You aren't looking for more business?"

"Not right now. Believe me, being their agent and business manager keeps me busy enough. Besides, I'd rather keep a low profile."

This bit of information puzzled David. "Why, Devon?" he asked.

"That's the way I prefer doing business. I'm comfortable enough financially that I don't need to do more. I give back by tutoring students studying for the bar, pro bono."

"How do you deal with athletes with overblown egos who can't seem to stay out of trouble?" He frowned. "If it's not drugs, then it's domestic violence or baby-mama drama."

"I deal because that's what I'm paid to do," Devon stated firmly.

"Do you ever tell them that just because they're making millions it doesn't excuse their bad behavior?"

"I'm their lawyer, not their mama. If their mamas and

daddies don't check them, then I'm not going to. Do you have something against athletes making money?"

David grunted under his breath. "Of course not. It's just that they should be treated just like everyone else—not given a pass because they make millions. If some high school kids from here were to be charged with drug possession or a DUI, they wouldn't be let off with a fine or a slap on the wrist. They would be cut from the team and their dream of becoming a professional athlete would disappear like that." He snapped his fingers for emphasis.

"I agree completely. It's one of the reasons it's important to me to try to help my clients manage their money, too. It's estimated that sixty percent of NBA players are broke five years after their retirement."

"How do you help them?"

"One client, who will remain nameless, has five babies from four different women, all within the span of three years, and is forced to pay out most of his salary for child support. Unfortunately his baby-mamas' drama caused him to lose a multimillion-dollar sports gear endorsement."

David whistled softly. "Didn't anyone ever tell him about using protection?"

"He has a latex allergy," she whispered. "But after a while he was having a problem paying his bills, so I finally convinced him to downsize his lifestyle. He sold his Lamborghini, Ferrari Testarossa, and Rolls-Royce Phantom, then moved from a huge mansion to a two-bedroom condo in San Juan. His friends weren't too happy when they had to find someplace else to hang out. A few of them were living with him year-round."

"That's really downsizing. How did you manage it?" David couldn't help being impressed.

"I'll admit, it's pretty exhausting. Whenever these young athletes get into trouble, which is more often than not, I drop everything and clean up their mess. One of the reasons I don't work for a firm is because I always have to be available to them."

David blew out a breath. "I don't envy you. How did you get so involved in money management?"

She paused. "I also have an MBA."

David wondered if Devon's clients realized how valuable she was to them and their futures. He had to admire her tenacity. Being a sports agent wasn't for the faint of heart and there weren't many women in the business. She had to be particularly remarkable to earn a reputation strong enough that she could afford to go out on her own and maintain such a select clientele.

Reaching into the breast pocket of his jacket, he took out a silver monogrammed business card case and handed Devon a card. "I could use a good consultant *if* you decide you like the Lowcountry enough to want to move here."

She stared at the card for several seconds. "I'm not licensed to practice in South Carolina."

David pumped his fist under the table. She hadn't turned down his offer outright. "That wouldn't be a problem. You can act as a consultant until you decide whether you'd want to join my firm. I'll take care of all of the cases going to trial until you pass the state's bar."

Devon slipped the card into the pocket of her jacket. "The only thing that would force me to move south is the weather. Growing up in Chicago and living in New York has tested the limits of my patience when it comes to cold and snow."

He leaned to his left, their shoulders touching. "You don't

have to worry about that down here. I can't remember the last time it snowed."

She nodded. "That's good to hear."

"I'm going up for seconds. Would you like me to bring you something else?" She gave him a bright smile that reached her luminous eyes.

"No thank you. I'm still working on what I have here."

David returned to the buffet, silently applauding his good luck. He'd come to the Tanners' to celebrate Francine's thirty-fourth birthday, never expecting to meet his friend's fiancé's friend and attorney. Once he'd made the decision to open his own office, he knew it would take a while to build a clientele, so initially he wouldn't need a partner or an associate. But he could utilize the services of a consultant and Devon's admission that she had only three clients and could be away from her home for weeks at a time meant her life wasn't bogged down with responsibilities or obligations that would prevent her from relocating.

He'd given her his card and made the offer. Now he would have to wait and see if a big-city attorney would be willing to relocate to the Lowcountry to become a small-town country lawyer. And Devon had the experience, intelligence, and poise to make the firm viable. In other words, she was the total package.

Chapter Three

⌒

Even at the end of the evening, Devon wasn't ready to leave David's company, so she was thrilled when he offered to give her a ride back to Charleston instead of her calling a cab.

Again showing off his gentlemanly manners, he opened the passenger-side door to his Lexus, waiting until she was settled before heading to the driver's side. He took off his jacket, leaving it on the rear seat, and slipped behind the wheel. He punched the Engine Start button, then turned his head and caught her staring at him.

She smiled. "I really appreciate your driving me back to the hotel."

Several seconds passed before he shifted into gear and maneuvered out of the driveway. "I'm going back to the mainland, so it's not an imposition. Besides, I'm the only one who lives there."

"Did you grow up on Cavanaugh Island?" Devon asked as she stared at the beams from the headlights. She still hadn't gotten used to driving along the island roads in complete darkness. The only lighted areas were in the business districts.

"Nah. I've always lived in Charleston," David replied.

"So how are you connected to the island?"

"My mother grew up in the Cove. Jeff's grandmother is my mother's aunt. I used to hang out here during the summer when a lot of my friends went to either Boy Scout or sleep-away camps. The beach was the playground and the ocean the Olympic-size pool. Once we were teenagers Jeff and I would go out with some of the fishermen trolling for crabs and oysters. We'd bring back our catch, build a fire on the beach, and cook them." David gave Devon a quick glance. "How did you spend your summers?"

Devon chided herself for broaching a topic where she would have to reveal details of what she thought of as her atypical childhood. She knew some children would've loved to change places with her and her brother to live on an estate with a staff that included a chauffeur, cook, and house-keepers where all of their needs were met *and* every hour, minute, and second of her life was accounted for.

It continued at the prestigious boarding school where generations of Gilmore women were taught the academics and social instruction that would prepare them to take their place in upper-class society.

"It wasn't as exciting as yours," she said. "We alternated years spending a month in the States with going abroad."

"Traveling abroad is not what I'd think of as boring."

Devon closed her eyes for a brief moment. "When you're a kid and you're traveling with your parents it can be, because you can't see things that would interest you if you were an adult or even a college student." Her mother had planned their itinerary down to which cities and museums they would tour and which restaurants they would dine in. Even when her father would suggest taking a route off the beaten path, Monique Gilmore would throw a hissy fit and Raymond Collins would acquiesce rather than engage in a verbal confrontation with his wife.

"Your parents are teachers?" David asked.

She nodded. "My father is a college professor and he made it a practice never to teach summer courses."

"What about your mother?"

Devon wanted to tell David that, although she held a teaching degree, she never pursued a career because marriage and motherhood had become her priority. "Right now she does a lot of volunteering, while serving on the board of several charitable organizations."

David's inky-black eyebrows lifted a fraction with her disclosure. "She sounds like my mother. Mom worked for the Charleston public schools as a librarian for thirty years. She retired about ten years ago. She's so busy volunteering that I have to make an appointment just to see her."

"Good for her," Devon remarked, "because some people retire, then sit around doing absolutely nothing."

"That would never be Edna Sullivan." He gave Devon another quick glance. "Are you an only child?"

The silence inside the vehicle was deafening before she said, "No. Why would you ask me that?"

"I find you somewhat aloof. Maybe *poised* is a better word to describe you," David explained. "Most folks I've met who are only children are usually a little reserved."

She wanted to tell him she had been raised to be reserved and any behavior deemed outgoing was frowned upon and considered gauche. A wry smile twisted her mouth when she thought about her upbringing. By the time she was ten, Devon was able to quote verbatim what it meant to be a Gilmore woman. They were poised, intelligent, educated, feminine, and self-reliant, but not necessarily in that order, and they were expected to marry men with comparable qualities.

"I was an only child for six years before my brother was born." A younger brother sentenced to spend the next seven years of a fifteen-year sentence in federal prison for robbing a bank at gunpoint, while holding a customer hostage for several hours before he finally surrendered. "What about you? Do you have any brothers or sisters?" she asked David.

"I have a younger sister, but I rarely get to see her. Leticia's a corporate flight attendant for an international businessman. One week she's in Beijing or Singapore, and then the following week she might send me an email from New Zealand. Last year she tried to get me to take time off and go with her to Dubai, but I was involved in a case that had gone to trial."

Devon sat up straight, her eyes dancing with excitement. "That was one time I would've asked the court for a two-week recess and gone with her. Or gotten another lawyer to cover for me."

David chuckled under his breath. "I was seriously thinking about it."

"But why didn't you go?"

"It was a case where the jury had been sequestered, so the judge never would've agreed to a recess."

"You're probably right," Devon agreed. "After passing the bar I clerked for a judge who was also a Marine reservist and he ran his courtroom like a drill sergeant. I felt sorry for the prosecutors and defense attorneys whenever he told them he wanted to see them in chambers. The first time I witnessed one of his tongue-lashings I got up to walk out and he yelled at me not to move. After court recessed for the day he apologized to me for his outburst, explaining he wasn't going to tolerate theatrics in his courtroom from anyone. He smiled, saying he was the exception."

"Did you continue to clerk for him?"

She nodded. "Yes, because I then realized he was all bark and no bite. At least where I was concerned. I worked for him until he was deployed to Afghanistan. He served for a little more than a year, and when he returned he left the bench and went to head a Fortune Five Hundred company's legal department."

"Did you clerk for another judge after that?" David asked.

"No. By that time I'd gone back to school for an MBA and I'd also taken on Keaton as a client. I was teaching business and Intro to Law as an adjunct professor when a student who'd overheard me counseling another student about which courses he should take to get into law school asked if I'd represent her brother. He'd been approached by NBA scouts to go pro right out of high school. I recommended he go to college, but his family really needed the money, so I took on my second client when I negotiated his contract for an obscene amount of money for an eighteen-year-old."

"Is he the one with the latex allergy?"

Devon cut her eyes at David when he smiled at her. "You would remember that, wouldn't you?"

"That's because his excuse is lame. There are nonlatex condoms on the market."

"I guess you would know," she countered.

Increasing his speed, David took the ramp leading to the causeway, merging into traffic heading toward Charleston. "Every man who's sexually active should know that."

"Are you speaking from past experience?" As soon as the question slipped off her tongue, Devon wanted to retract it. Where, she thought, had that come from?

"Yes, I am," he said quickly, "although I don't have an allergy to latex."

"I'm certain you've had your share of quirky clients," Devon said, knowing talk about condoms and sex would lead to a discussion she wasn't quite ready for.

Attractive lines fanned out around David's eyes when he smiled. "A few. I had one client who changed her story every time I sat down to consult with her. She'd come in with either black eyes, bruises on her face and throat, or scratches on her arms. First she claimed her husband had assaulted her, but she hadn't reported him to the police. Then she said she hit him first so he had to defend himself. When the truth finally came out, she admitted she'd hit herself in the face with a wooden spoon, tied a scarf around her neck and pulled it as tightly as she could without losing consciousness, and torn out handfuls of hair because she wanted to punish her husband for cheating on her."

Devon wanted to laugh, but the situation was much too serious for levity. "Wow! That's really extreme and a tad crazy. Did they end up staying together?"

"Believe it or not they did. I asked her if she wanted me to handle her divorce and she said she had to think about it because she was truly in love with her husband. I advised her to give him an ultimatum. Either he stop cheating or she was going to divorce him. She had the upper hand because she was a very wealthy woman and she'd made him sign a prenup. The slacker didn't want to give up the high life, so he finally gave up chasing other women. And to make certain he stayed faithful, she hired a private detective to follow him."

Devon grunted softly. "I can't believe she had to go to that extreme just to get him to stop cheating. Instead of physically hurting herself, all she had to do was threaten to divorce him."

"I agree. But apparently she wanted people, her friends in particular, to see that he was an abusive husband."

"She'd rather ruin her face than kick a cheat to the curb? And private detective or not, there's still no guarantee that he won't cheat on her again." There came another measure of silence. "Can you answer one question for me, David?" Devon asked in a quiet voice.

"I'll try."

"Why do men cheat?" She knew she'd caught him off guard with the question when his fingers tightened around the leather-wrapped steering wheel.

David's expression had become a mask of stone when he said, "I could ask you the same question, as to why women cheat."

His answer spoke volumes and Devon knew he'd been on the receiving end of either a cheating wife or girlfriend. "I suppose neither of us will be able to answer that question."

"Did he cheat on you, Devon?"

She had to decide whether to skirt the question or tell David the truth, and decided on the latter. "He didn't cheat on me as much as he did on his fiancée. I had no idea he was engaged to marry another woman."

"*Bastard*," David said softly. "Are you all right?" There was genuine concern in his voice.

"It took a while, but I'm good," she confirmed.

And she was. Once she'd accepted her fate, she was very, very good. She'd alternated between crying and cursing Gregory, while contemplating whether she wanted to give up the baby for adoption. However, in a moment of serene sanity she could imagine going to the playground and watching her son or daughter laughing while coming down a slide or screaming for her to push him or her higher while sitting in a swing.

The only dilemma facing her was where to raise her child. New York City was a wonderful place to work and live, but Devon had second thoughts about raising a child there. A city park or playground could not compare to living in a house with a backyard jungle gym. Sitting on a park bench wasn't the same as sitting on a front or back porch watching her child frolicking in the grass.

And she'd also asked herself if she was willing to continue to live in the Northeast, where during and after a snowstorm streets in some neighborhoods were impassable for days. Maybe, she mused, it was time to move again. This time for good.

Devon had been so lost in her thoughts that she hadn't realized David had turned onto King Street and stopped in front of the hotel. The evening was warm enough for people to sit outside at bistro tables.

She unbuckled her seat belt as he got out of the car and came around to assist her. Placing her hand on his outstretched palm, she smiled when his fingers closed over hers and he gently pulled her to stand. Standing on the sidewalk close to him suddenly made Devon aware of his height. She stood five-five in her bare feet, and even with three-inch pumps David was almost a full head taller.

Tilting her chin, she gave him an open smile. "Thank you again for driving me back."

"No problem. Do you need me to walk you to your room?"

She found David the quintessential gentleman, enjoyed talking with him, and for a reason she couldn't fathom, Devon didn't want her time with him to end. Under another set of circumstances she would've invited him to relax with her in the Swamp Fox bar over cocktails while listening to piano jazz music. But at this time in her life she couldn't afford to become involved with a man—even one as close to perfect as the man standing so close to her she could feel his body's warmth and inhale the lingering scent of his hauntingly sexy masculine cologne.

"No thank you. I believe I can find my way," she said teasingly. A slight gasp escaped her parted lips when he leaned down and kissed her cheek.

"Good night, Devon."

"Good night, David," she whispered, struggling to breathe normally. He'd only kissed her cheek, the gesture lasting mere seconds, but somehow Devon couldn't help thinking something momentous had just happened.

She was still standing in the same spot when he returned to his car and drove off. Turning on her heel, Devon smiled at the doorman when he opened the door to the hotel lobby. "I hope you're enjoying your evening, miss."

Devon's smile said it all. "I am." And she was. Everything about her evening was nothing short of perfection, from Francine's birthday celebration to the delicious cuisine and the people who'd come together in the Tanner dining room. She hadn't expected to meet David Sullivan or be seated next to him, or have him offer to drive her back to the hotel.

She liked him. A lot. However, she knew nothing about her liking him could go beyond friendship. Not as long as she carried another man's baby under her heart.

Chapter Four

$\backsim$

David's head popped up when he heard soft tapping on the door to his office. Taking off his glasses, he pinched the bridge of his nose. He welcomed the distraction because he'd been perusing open case files for hours.

Working nonstop had helped him not think about Devon. It'd been three days since Francine's birthday gathering and he'd found it almost impossible not to think of Devon whenever he got into his car. The lingering scent of her perfume was a constant reminder of the most sensual woman he'd had the pleasure of interacting with. He'd accused her of being overly poised only because it was a trait he wasn't familiar with in young women nowadays. Women of his mother's and late grandmother's generations exhibited poise as if it were a badge of honor. And Devon's graceful bearing wasn't something she could turn on and off like a faucet. It was a learned composure that had come from years of training.

He'd noticed she was very controlled, as if she feared opening up about herself. David hadn't expected her to tell him her life story, yet a sixth sense told him she was reluctant to talk about her brother. He also wondered why she'd decided to spend a month away from her home if she wasn't attempting to avoid someone or something.

"I think it's time for a coffee break, DJ."

A smile tilted the corners of his mouth when he saw his assistant with a mug of steaming coffee. Angela Burton had an uncanny gift for reading his mind, making certain he was always on schedule, and keeping him relatively sane. He'd hired the single mother of three adolescent boys one week after making partner four years before, and not once had he regretted his decision to select her over two much more experienced candidates.

Pushing back his chair, David stood and came around his cluttered desk. He took the mug from Angela's outstretched hand. "Thank you." He gestured to the chair beside his desk. "Please sit down." Waiting until she was seated, he sat down again. For an instant he thought he detected fear in her smoky gray eyes, but it vanished when he smiled. "I suppose you're wondering why I asked you to bring me all my open cases."

"I must admit I was curious."

David knew what he was about to disclose would shock Angela as much as it probably would the others at the firm. The only exception would be his father and the other senior partner. David Sullivan Sr. would inform the staff at their weekly Monday luncheon meeting that Sullivan, Matthews & Sullivan would revert to Sullivan & Matthews.

His gaze shifted back to Angela. "I'm leaving the firm."

Angela's jaw dropped. "Why? What happened?"

"Nothing," David said in a quiet tone. "I've decided to open my own firm in the Creek, and if you're willing, I want you to come with me as my office manager. I know you want to become a paralegal, so if you're willing to take the courses, I'll cover the tuition, but only with the proviso that you'll work for me for the next three years."

Clapping a hand over her mouth, Angela stared at David as if he'd taken leave of his senses. "You're kidding," she whispered through splayed fingers.

He smiled and shook his head. "No, I'm not."

Angela lowered her hand. "Does Mr. Sullivan know about this? About your wanting to take me with you?"

David's smile vanished at the reminder that he was still seen as a subordinate, an associate rather than a partner at the firm. "He knows I'm leaving, and everyone else will know after today's staff meeting. My wanting you to come with me has nothing to do with my father. This is just between you and me."

Combing her fingers through her hair, Angela closed her eyes. "Yes, David," she whispered. "I'm honored you want me to come with you." She opened her eyes. "And I promise to work for you until I'm eligible to collect Social Security."

His eyebrows rose in amazement. It was the first time since they'd begun working together that Angela had called him David. "A lot of things can happen in twenty years," he said teasingly.

"True," she drawled, "but I'm looking forward to it."

David sobered. "I'm going over my open cases to recommend which of the associates should get which." He glanced at the desk clock. "I'm not going to be at the staff meeting because I'm scheduled to meet with a rental agent at noon to see several vacant spaces."

Angela stood up. "I'll buzz you when it's time for you to leave."

David nodded, smiling. "Thanks." There had been a few times when he'd become so engrossed in what he was doing that he'd forgotten that he had a meeting outside the office. Knowing how much he detested tardiness, Angela had taken the initiative to remind him when he should leave in order to keep on schedule.

He blew out an audible breath when she walked out, closing the door behind her. He hadn't been *that* certain Angela would accept his offer to continue to work with him. He'd heard through the office grapevine that she wanted to become a paralegal, but she couldn't afford the tuition. She'd married young and soon had three rambunctious boys who spent more time in detention than they did in class. Her husband walked out on her, blaming her for their sons' troublesome behavior, but there were rumors he had been sleeping with a woman who worked at his trucking company. Although he'd turned his back on his family, he'd continued to support them financially until he was arrested and jailed for trafficking in drugs.

Everyone on the island rallied around Angela and her sons, who'd moved back to Haven Creek to live with her parents. The elderly couple had passed away a few years later, leaving her the home where she'd grown up. However, even without the responsibility of paying a mortgage, she'd had to take a number of part-time jobs to make ends meet. After she'd begun working for the law firm and all her sons enlisted in various branches of the armed forces, Angela's life settled into a more stable routine. It was the perfect time for her to start a new venture. Not only did David need someone he could trust to keep his office running smoothly, but Angela deserved to realize her dream—and he would make certain she did.

*   *   *

Stepping out of the shower, Devon reached for a bath towel, tucking it around her body. She decided to become a tourist again, this time on Cavanaugh Island. After picking up the rental car, she'd parked in a lot close to the hotel and spent Saturday and Sunday setting out on foot for a walking tour of Charleston's Historic District. David's revelation that Haven Creek was home to artisans and farmers had piqued her curiosity. She wanted to see the farms and shops before heading over to Sanctuary Cove for lunch with Francine, Kara, and Morgan at Jack's Fish House.

As she sat, massaging a moisturizer over her face, then a scented cream over her body, Devon's mind drifted back to Friday night. She couldn't recall when she'd enjoyed herself that much and what shocked her was, with the exception of Keaton, all those present were strangers to her. She was also pleasantly surprised at how open she'd been with David when revealing that the man she'd been sleeping with was engaged to another woman. And when he'd referred to her as being aloof when she knew she was anything but.

Underneath her somewhat reserved demeanor was a party girl struggling to break free of the invisible chains that had repressed her natural desire to become a free spirit. As a child she hadn't been permitted to run barefoot through the sprinklers or to laugh uncontrollably about something silly because it wasn't behavior becoming of a Gilmore girl.

When David mentioned his clients paying their fees with chickens and hogs, she, being a very visual person, couldn't stop laughing. And it'd felt good to laugh because she'd cried enough these past weeks to last her the rest of her life. After her last crying jag she swore it would be the last time she would dissolve into an abyss of self-pity.

Yes, she mused, interacting with David was good. She'd enjoyed discussing their clients, and even if he didn't like some of the antics of her bad-boy clients, he had applauded her efforts to protect their financial futures. They hadn't agreed on everything, yet there was one thing she knew they had in common: They were willing to go the distance to protect the people they represented.

Smiling, Devon slathered cream on her legs and feet. She planned to spend at least a month in the Lowcountry, and during that time she was certain she would run into David again. There was something about the dapper attorney that made her want to get to know him better. And a month was more than enough time for her to conclude whether she wanted to continue to live in New York or relocate.

Her cell phone rang—someone calling from the Cove Inn. "This is Devon Gilmore-Collins." Whenever she made reservations, she used her legal name because that's what appeared on her driver's license and credit cards.

"Ms. Collins, this is the reservation desk at the Cove Inn. I'm calling to let you know a guest moved out earlier than scheduled and we now have a suite with a private bath and kitchen available for you. If you still want to stay with us, you can move in any time after three o'clock today."

She smiled. Checking into the inn would solve her dilemma of declining the Tanners' offer to stay with them. It wasn't as if she wasn't grateful for their hospitality, but unlike Keaton, they were strangers to her and she didn't want to be beholden to anyone.

"Please hold it for me."

"Then should we look for you later on today?"

"Yes." She had to pack and contact the front desk at the Francis Marion to let them know she would be checking out.

Devon had just finished getting dressed in a pair of cropped khaki-colored linen pants and a white linen shirt when her cell chimed a familiar ringtone. She tapped the speaker feature. "Good morning, Keaton."

"Hey you," he said. "Are you ready to go back to the Big Apple yet?"

She smiled. "Believe it or not, I'm actually enjoying the slower pace down here."

His deep chuckle came through the speaker. "What did I tell you? Before you know it you'll have a Gullah accent of your own."

"Let's not pack the moving boxes yet, mister."

"It's only a matter of time, my friend." Keaton's deep laugh rumbled through the phone. "I was actually calling to see if you want to come see the house today. I've decided to take a break from the script because all the scenes and dialogue have conspired to mentally beat me down."

"So you decided to listen to me when I told you to slow down?"

"Yes, I did, Counselor. Are you coming?"

"I'd love to," Devon responded. She glanced at the bedside clock. It was almost eight, which meant she had at least four hours before she was scheduled to meet the women at Jack's for lunch. "I've got lunch with Francine, Morgan, and Kara. But I could swing by after, if that works for you."

"I'll be here."

"See you later," she said, then ended the call.

As she got ready to leave, she couldn't help giving

Keaton's teasing more serious thought. Could she leave New York? No doubt about it; she had some thinking to do...and she wasn't just planning for herself anymore. With seven months before her baby was due, it was time to make some decisions.

Chapter Five

Every time Devon came to Cavanaugh Island, she felt as if she'd entered an alternate, more primordial universe. She drove past towering ancient live oaks draped in Spanish moss and palmetto and cypress trees growing so closely together they provided a natural canopy from the sun's heat.

The island's rhythm was set on slow. People walked slowly, talked slowly, and drove even slower. But it was quiet—no honking horns, no wailing sirens. Just birdsong and the quiet purr of the car's engine. In the downtown business district, shopkeepers were busy sweeping and hosing down sidewalks, while a few were setting out tables on which to display their merchandise.

Outside of the downtown, Devon spent nearly fifteen minutes driving past fruit, vegetable, hog, and poultry farms before she got out of the car, walking over to a one-story raised cottage and staring at a number of chicks and ducklings splashing in a wading pool behind a fenced-in yard; a large gold hound lay nearby, eyeing the antics of his feathered neighbors. He bayed loudly until a woman came out of the house, wiping her hands on an apron.

"Mornin'. Can I help you?"

Devon gave the dour-faced woman with a graying bun and pale blue eyes a warm smile. "Good morning. I'm just looking at your chicks and ducks."

The woman grunted. "They're more work than they're worth. Are you looking to buy some eggs?"

"No," Devon said quickly. "I happen to like baby chicks." One year she had brought home two baby chicks during her school's Easter recess. "Do you sell chickens?"

"No. I raise chickens and ducks for their eggs. I sell them to a restaurant in Charleston. There's nothing like fresh eggs for breakfast. If you're looking to buy chickens, then you have to check out Herman Davis. He has a chicken farm on the other side of the creek." The older woman wiped her right hand on her apron, extending it and smiling for the first time. "I'm forgetting my manners. I'm Peggy. My momma and daddy named me Margaret, but everyone round these parts calls me Peggy."

Devon shook her hand. "And I'm Devon."

Peggy's eyes narrowed. "Ain't that a boy's name?"

"It can be either a girl's or boy's name." She wanted to tell Peggy that she liked her name. "I'm just visiting and decided to do a little sightseeing."

Peggy dug the toe of one of her bright red Crocs into the dirt at the same time she pushed her hands into her apron pockets. "There's not much to see around here except farms." She gave Devon a critical squint as her mouth tightened into a thin line. "Are you one of those snowbirds who comes down here for the winter?"

"No," Devon answered truthfully. "I'm visiting a friend who moved to Sanctuary Cove several months ago."

"Are you looking to move here, too?"

"I'm not sure," Devon answered truthfully for the second time. "Why?"

"I thought maybe you're one of those folks working for those greedy-ass developers wanting to buy up properties so they can put up them gated communities with golf courses. And if that happens, then after a few years we won't be able to pay the taxes on land that has been in our families for more than a hundred years. Take this place here. My great-granddaddy bought this land before the Spanish-American War and built this house with his own two hands. It may not look like much, but it's mine free and clear."

Devon smiled, hoping to alleviate the woman's anxiety that she was a land speculator. "I can assure you that I don't work for a developer. But if I do change my mind and decide to buy property down here, it'll probably be in Charleston or here on Cavanaugh Island."

The tension tightening Peggy's mouth eased. "I happen to know of a large renovated vacant house for sale on Cherry Lane. That's the road just behind my house. The owners gutted the interior several years back, putting in new floors and updating all the kitchen appliances. A year later they did the siding to give it an instant old-house feel, replaced the shutters with new ones, and put in a wrap-around porch with a door that leads into another entrance to the kitchen. It's a real nice house for someone who can afford to buy it."

"Why is the house vacant?" Devon asked Peggy.

"The couple who lived there, the Wickhams, decided it

would be better if they moved closer to their kids. I was sorry to see them go because our children used to play together."

"How large is large?" Devon asked.

"I believe it has at least five bedrooms. Do you have any children?" Peggy questioned.

Devon smiled. "Not yet. Why?"

"Because there's a lot of space for kids to run around. As I said, my kids used to run out the back door and over to the Wickham house and play for hours. I'd holler across the road for them to come home whenever it came time for them to eat. But if you're really serious about looking at the house, then go to the Cove and talk to the folks at Duryea Realty. They have an office off Moss Alley."

Devon was familiar with Duryea Realty because they'd represented the owner of the property she'd closed on for Keaton. She didn't need five bedrooms for herself, the baby, and an office, but the extras could be used for guests. Then without warning she thought of her brother. Ray had served eight years of his fifteen-year sentence and once paroled he would need someplace to live. As a convicted felon, he would likely have a hard time finding employment, but Devon planned to do everything in her power to help him restart his life.

She forced a smile she didn't feel at that moment. Thinking about her brother was always a downer. "I'll keep that in mind," she told Peggy. "I won't keep you any longer, but it's been nice talking to you."

Peggy smiled. "Same here."

Returning to her car, Devon reversed direction, returning to the downtown business district. She still had more than an hour before she had to be at the restaurant, and she couldn't stop thinking about what Peggy had said about the house with plenty of space where a child could run around and play. The more she thought about relocating, the more she could see it as a reality.

There were signs prohibiting vehicles from stopping, standing, and parking on Oak Street. She left the car in an area set aside for shopper parking. Cobblestone streets, bricked sidewalks in a herringbone design, and black-and-white-striped awnings shading storefronts gave the main thoroughfare a quaint and picturesque look.

Strolling along the sidewalk and peering into shop windows, she lingered at one advertising handmade quilts. Seeing the quilts reminded her of the time she'd spent with her paternal grandmother, who'd patiently taught her to knit, quilt, and crochet. Grandma Arlene claimed real quilts were always pieced by hand and not a machine. Glancing at her watch, Devon decided to go into the Nine Patch Quilt and look around.

The bell over the door tinkled melodiously when she walked in. A young woman with neatly braided hair and a tiny gold nose ring greeted her with a smile. Her parted lips revealed a set of braces with sparkly red-and-white brackets. "Mornin'."

Devon smiled. "Good morning."

"I'm Keziah, so if there's anything in particular you'd like to see, just let me know."

Devon stared at the unfinished quilt, stretched over a frame, stamped with children in native dress from different countries around the world. "Do you have any crib blankets?"

She'd asked the first thing that came to mind. Devon realized she'd morphed into motherhood mode. Her obstetrician had reassured her that she should be able to carry to term and deliver a healthy baby, although since she was thirty-six she was now in the high-risk category. However, there were tests she would have to undergo in the coming weeks to rule out fetal abnormalities and sickle-cell anemia because both she and Gregory were of African descent.

"Yes. Would you like to see machine or hand stitched?" Keziah asked.

"Both," Devon said. Although she could hand stitch her own quilt, she still wanted to see the quality of the work. Keziah led her to a corner of the shop where stacks of crib quilts were labeled.

"Many of the quilts we carry are hand stitched by local women, so if you see one with a name attached with a tiny safety pin you'll know it's not factory made. They also carry a higher price tag than the others."

The bell over the door tinkled again and two women filed in. As Keziah went to greet them, Devon looped the strap of her leather tote over one shoulder and sorted through stacks of quilts with patterns she recognized as tumbling blocks, baskets, flying geese, and broken dishes. She examined one stitched in a rose wreath on a quilt top of pale yellow and lime-green blocks. The hand-stitched workmanship was exquisite. Devon noted the price tag. It was slightly overpriced, but then she had to factor in the time it took to sew the tiny stitches. She lingered in the section with pattern books and magazines for knitting and crocheting baby clothes. She decided to buy the hand-stitched crib blanket, several magazines, and enough yarn to crochet a crib blanket and knit several hats and sweaters.

Keziah, chatting quietly with the two women who were sitting at the quilt draped over the frame, demonstrated a particular stitch as Devon approached the counter with her merchandise. Waiting patiently until she got the saleswoman's attention, she said, "I'm going to take all of this."

Keziah ran her hand over the quilt. "You have a good eye for quality."

Devon nodded. "The handiwork is flawless."

"You quilt?"

She nodded again, handing the saleswoman a credit card. "Yes. My grandmother taught me."

"Many young women nowadays don't even know how to thread a needle, let alone quilt," Keziah said as she swiped Devon's card. "I come from five generations of quilters. A few of my great-great-grandmomma's quilts hang in several museums throughout the South. She pieced quilts with secret codes that were used by the conductors of the Underground Railroad."

Devon recalled stories about quilts hanging out of windows or on clotheslines whose patterns and stitching provided an ingenious method of communication for those escaping slavery for freedom in either the Northeast or Canada. "You must be very proud that someone in your family was instrumental in impacting the course of history."

Keziah ducked her head and flashed a modest smile. "It does feel good." Reaching for a sheet of tissue paper, she wrapped the folded blanket, tied the bundle with narrow green-and-yellow grosgrain ribbon, and then slipped it into a shopping bag with the shop's logo. The magazines and yarn were placed in another bag. "If you're interested in the secret story of quilts and the Underground Railroad, then you should come by the shop around seven the first Tuesday of each month. My mother hosts a meet and greet where she lectures about the history of African textiles. The talk usually lasts about an hour, including a slideshow. After that we serve light refreshments. We also teach quilting free of charge, but only if the materials are bought here." She leaned closer. "Those two women are retired nurses," she whispered, "who are quilting a wall hanging they plan to donate to the children's wing of the mainland hospital where they worked for years."

"That's very generous of them," Devon whispered back.

One thing she'd discovered about the people in the region was that they were very forthcoming with information. They were willing to talk to strangers, whereas people in New York were in too much of a hurry to stand still long enough to carry on conversations—especially with strangers. Cradling her purchases, she thanked Keziah and promised she would return for her mother's lecture.

Devon made a mental note of some of the other shops she wanted to visit when she returned to Haven Creek. After placing the shopping bags on the rear seat, she got into the compact car. She felt the familiar sensation in her belly indicating she had to eat something. Reaching into the cavernous depths of her tote, she took out a protein bar and a bottle of water. She took her time consuming the granola-and-fruit bar and drinking the water.

The pangs of hunger temporarily assuaged, she punched the Engine Start button, but before shifting into gear she spied David's dark blue Lexus maneuvering in reverse into the spot next to hers. Their eyes met, and as if on cue they shared a smile. The seconds ticked as he got out and opened her driver's side door, offering a hand to help her from the car. He was impeccably dressed again, this time in a light gray suit, robin's-egg blue shirt, dark gray silk tie, and polished cap-toe oxfords in a hue resembling aged cognac.

David lowered his head, brushing a light kiss on her forehead; she closed her eyes, savoring the scent of his spicy masculine cologne. Her smile widened, bringing her gaze to linger on his perfectly aligned startling white teeth before she focused on the cleft in his strong chin. The dapper lawyer was the epitome of tall, dark, and very handsome.

"Hello again," she said in greeting.

"Hello to you, too," he drawled. He pointed to the bags on the rear seat of her car. "I see you've been shopping."

Devon nodded. "I've done more sightseeing than shopping."

He gave her a long, penetrating stare. "How are you enjoying the Lowcountry?"

"I really like it."

"Better than New York City?" he teased.

She knew what he was alluding to. Would she join him at his new firm in Haven Creek? Although the offer was tempting, she wasn't sure she was ready to work at someone else's firm after being independent for so long. "Let's just say it has a few advantages over the Big Apple."

David gave her a questioning look. "Only a few, Devon?" She smiled, bringing his gaze to linger on her parted lips. "Maybe we can discuss the merits of the Big Apple and the Holy City at another time," David said. He blinked slowly. "Do you have anything planned for this Sunday? A bunch of us are getting together at my place to watch the March Madness games."

Her smile was dazzling. March Madness always found her in her local sports bar with the neighborhood regulars rooting for their favorite college basketball teams.

"Are you certain I won't be viewed as an interloper?"

David shook his head. "Of course not. Keaton and Red are coming, along with Morgan and Nate. Jeff hasn't committed because he may have to work Sunday. Even if he can't switch his shift with one of his deputies, Kara said she's coming, if only for a couple of hours."

Devon's association with Francine, Morgan, and Kara was still too new for her to think of them as girlfriends, even though she'd thoroughly enjoyed interacting with them Friday night. "If that's the case, then count me in. I'm going to need your address."

He held out his hand. "Grab your phone and I'll program in my address, cell, and home numbers. I'll also need your number so I can get in touch with you."

Devon retrieved her phone from the tote in her car and handed it to David. He gave her his and they quickly entered their personal information. She studied the address when he returned her phone. He lived in Charleston's Historic District. "What time should I come?"

"Anytime after noon."

"Do you need me to bring anything?"

A hint of a smile softened David's mouth. "Yes. You," he said after a pause.

Devon detected a trace of laughter in his voice. "Other than me, there *has* to be something else you'll need."

Crossing his arms over his chest, he cradled his chin on his left fist; his smile was now as intimate as a kiss. "No, there isn't."

"Look, David, I was raised never to go to someone's house empty-handed, so I'm going to bring a little something that I'm certain the others will enjoy."

"You cook?" he teased, smiling.

She narrowed her eyes at him. "Very funny. Why would you think I don't know how to cook?"

He lifted his shoulders under his suit jacket. "I just

thought most young women nowadays prefer making reservations to cooking."

Devon flashed a sexy moue. "You can't lump me into that category because I can cook. And quite well," she added, blowing him a kiss.

His smile grew wider. "It sounds as if the beautiful lady has issued a challenge—one I'm willing to accept. I'll concede to you bringing something."

She inclined her head. "Thank you. I'll probably have to come over at least a half hour earlier than the others to heat it up."

"Come anytime you want. I'll be home."

Devon glanced at the time on her cell phone. She had less than fifteen minutes to get to Jack's Fish House. "I have to go or I'll be late for a luncheon meeting. I'll see you Sunday before noon."

David moved forward, opening the car door for her. Once she got settled in, he leaned down into the open window and winked at her. "I can't wait to taste your dish."

"I promise you won't be disappointed," she countered. There were several dishes she'd perfected and she had to decide which one she would bring. Fortunately, she had several days before she had to reach a decision.

"Thank you, Devon."

She returned his smile. "You're welcome, David."

Devon backed out of the lot, taking furtive glances up at the rearview mirror to find David standing where she'd left him. His image grew smaller and smaller until he disappeared from her line of vision.

And for the second time in less than a week she wondered why David had come to the Tanners' alone.

Chapter Six

———◯———

Devon pulled into one of the few remaining spots in the parking lot at Jack's Fish House. It was exactly twelve noon when she walked into the restaurant to find Francine waiting to be seated. The redhead hugged her. "I'm glad you made it. Kara and Morgan are on their way."

A waitress, carrying menus, approached them. "If y'all follow me I'll show you to your table."

They walked through the bustling restaurant back to a corner table. Most of the diners were men, with the exception of a few women who were seated together. The waitress removed the RESERVED sign, placing four menus on the deeply scarred tabletop that had been hewn from the trunk of an oak tree. "I'll be back directly with water, sweet tea, and biscuits," she said to Francine, speaking so quickly Devon had to listen intently in an attempt to understand what she was saying.

Waiting until the woman was out of earshot, Devon whispered, "It sounds as if she's speaking a foreign language."

Francine smiled. "Linguists refer to the Gullah language as English-based Creole. Early scholars mistakenly referred to it as broken English. What they'd failed to recognize was the strong influence of African languages."

Devon stared at the woman who'd gotten Keaton to fall in love with her within a matter of weeks *and* commit to a future together. Her gaze lingered on the emerald-cut solitaire diamond ring on Francine's left hand. With the sprinkling of freckles across her nose and her curly red hair secured in a ponytail, Francine looked more like a college coed than a woman who'd just celebrated her thirty-fourth birthday. Devon found everything about her appearance natural and refreshing.

"Do you speak Gullah?" Devon asked.

"No. But I do understand it."

Devon rested a hand on her throat. "Oh, before I forget. Please let your mother know I appreciate her offer to let me stay with her, but I got a call from the Cove Inn that I can move in later this afternoon."

Nodding, Francine said, "I'll let her know. How have you been enjoying the Lowcountry?" she asked, not pausing to take a breath.

Devon hesitated, then said truthfully, "I like it a lot."

"Enough to move down here?"

Devon went completely still, wondering how much Keaton had told his fiancée about her. "You're the third person today who's asked me if I like the Lowcountry. First it was Keaton, then David, and now you."

With wide eyes, Francine stared at her, seemingly in shock. "You spoke to David?"

"Yes. I ran into him in Haven Creek."

Francine chewed her lower lip. "You can tell me to mind

my own business, but I have to ask. Are you two seeing each other?"

Caught off guard, Devon held her breath for several seconds. What, she thought, made Francine believe she and David were a couple? Being seated together and his driving her back to Charleston did *not* mean they were in a relationship.

"No." Her voice was low, controlled. "Why would you think that?"

"Awkward," Francine whispered under her breath. "I only asked because I've seen David with other women in the past, and Friday night was the first time I got to see him laugh. I mean really laugh without censoring himself. Most times he's so intense that he makes folks uncomfortable."

"Maybe he was more relaxed because he'd proven his client's innocence."

Francine shook her head. "It wasn't the first time David has won a case, so it has to be you, Devon."

Hazel and green eyes met and fused. "I hope you're not trying to hook me up with David."

"No! It's just that the two of you look so perfect together. It helps that you're both lawyers. Even your names are similar. David and Devon."

Devon couldn't help smiling. "The names would be perfect if we were fraternal twins." Her smile faded as she stared at the various initials carved into the tabletop. She didn't want to talk about her and David. "Did Keaton tell you that I'm pregnant?" she asked, then noted the lack of surprise on Francine's face.

"No, because he didn't have to tell me," she admitted. "I happened to be in the room when you called him. When he said congratulations and then said he would be there for you I'd assumed you told him you were pregnant."

"So you've never discussed me?"

Francine shook her head again. "Not at any great length. Of course I know you're his agent and that you guys met while in college, but nothing personal."

Leaning back in her chair, Devon laced her fingers together, wondering how much she should divulge to Keaton's fiancée about her current circumstances. She'd trusted him with her secret, and instinct told her she could trust Francine, too. "I plan to become a single mother. I dated a man for more than a year not knowing he was engaged to another woman."

Francine leaned closer. "When did you find out?" she whispered.

Devon's hands went from the tabletop to her lap. "Not until I discovered I was pregnant."

"Does he know about the baby?"

"No. I'd planned to tell him in person, but that never happened." She told Francine about her and Gregory's I-95 romance. "Most times he would come up from Virginia to see me."

"Where does he live in Virginia?" Francine asked Devon.

"Newport News. When I told him I needed to talk to him about something important, he promised me he'd come to New York the following weekend. Well, it never happened, and when I tried calling him I discovered he'd blocked my number. Then I did something I promised myself I would never do, and that was chase after a man. I flew down to see him."

Francine rested a comforting hand on Devon's back. "You weren't chasing him. The man had gotten you pregnant."

She bit down on her lower lip. "I thought I had to tell him because what if he found out later I'd had his child and he sued for joint custody? But when I got to his house, his aunt told me he was staying at his parents' place because his father had had open-heart surgery. Then she went on to inform me that Gregory and his fiancée had postponed their Valentine's Day wedding until after his father's health improved."

Francine smothered a curse under her breath. "Where was the fiancée all this time when he was seeing you?"

"She was in Japan studying for a graduate degree in Asian studies. If I'd known I never would've gotten involved with him." Devon didn't tell Francine that Gregory's aunt had boasted that her nephew's future bride's father had been a celebrated civil rights attorney and was currently the longest-serving African American congressman from the Magnolia State, whose influence was certain to make Gregory's dream of becoming a politician a reality.

"That sneaky, egg-sucking, lowdown dog," Francine said between clenched teeth.

Devon laughed despite the seriousness of the topic. "I called him a bunch of names that definitely cannot be repeated in polite company. I went into a funk for several weeks because not only was this baby unplanned but I'd also told Keaton a long time ago that I never wanted children."

"Why did you change your mind when you have choices?"

"Abortion isn't an option for me. I did wrestle with the idea of giving up the baby for adoption." She paused when the waitress came back to deliver some water to the table. "I know there are millions of unmarried women who are raising their children alone, but I grew up listening to my mother preach to me that no Gilmore woman ever had a child out of wedlock. She literally slammed the door in my face when I told her I would be the first, and it was her rejection that strengthened my resolve to have this baby. I'm thirty-six, financially stable, and have options a lot of women in my predicament don't have. And having Keaton as a friend has kept me strong and sane."

Devon was taken aback when Francine hugged her tightly. "I want you to remember you have Keaton and you have *me*."

Devon returned the hug, her eyes filled with unshed tears as her chin quivered. "Thank you. Now, please stop hugging me if you don't want me blubbering all over you."

Francine released her. "I should be the one thanking you, because if you hadn't suggested that Keaton form his own production company he never would've come to Sanctuary Cove."

Devon reached into her tote for a tissue and dabbed the corners of her eyes. Moisture spiked her lashes, turning her eyes a mossy green. "That's because you two were destined to be together." Keaton had told her about seeing Francine in an off-Broadway play almost ten years before and that he was transfixed by her riveting performance. He had never expected to see her again when he walked into the Beauty Box to find her working in her mother's salon.

The seconds ticked by as Francine stared into space. "Do you believe in destiny?"

Devon's eyebrows lifted. "I believe that some things are meant—" Whatever she was going to say died on her tongue when Morgan rushed over to the table. Pushing back her chair, Devon stood up and hugged her. "It's nice seeing you again," she said to the architect.

"Same here," Morgan said. She sat down opposite them.

"Where are the biscuits? Right now I'm hungry enough to inhale every morsel of food in this place." Reaching into her handbag, she took out a small plastic bag with several rice cakes. "I hate these things, but they manage to stave off hunger until I can eat a meal."

"You're pregnant," Devon said. What should've been a query came out like a statement. Morgan nodded as she chewed. "If you don't mind my asking, when are you due?"

"The first week in September."

Devon had already confided her pregnancy to Francine, and now she felt comfortable enough to tell Morgan. "And I'm due the last week in September."

Morgan's jaw dropped as she stared at Devon, her expression mirroring utter shock. "You don't look pregnant."

Devon laughed softly. "I can still wear my regular clothes for now, but it's the girls that are taking center stage." She patted her chest. "I'm already wearing a larger bra cup."

A shadow fell over the table. "I'm sorry I'm late," Kara said as she hugged everyone. She'd pinned a campaign button stamped with ALICE PARKER FOR MAYOR on her jacket lapel. Like Francine, she also wore her hair in a ponytail. "Austin was sleeping and I didn't want to wake him up, so I had to use the breast pump so Gram can feed him when he does wake up." She blotted her forehead with a tissue. "What did I miss?"

A pause followed Kara's question and Devon took the initiative when she said, "Morgan and I were talking about being pregnant at the same time."

Kara clapped a hand over her mouth to muffle the scream threatening to escape. "Congratulations! I can't believe David didn't mention anything about becoming a father."

Devon went completely still and she stared at Kara as if

she'd taken leave of her senses. "Why does everyone believe I'm involved with David Sullivan?"

"Because you two looked like such a great couple Friday night," Morgan said in a soft tone. "Even Nate mentioned it to me and he's not one to gossip or spread rumors."

Devon expelled a breath of exasperation. "David is not my baby's father." Devon decided to let Kara and Morgan draw their own conclusions about her child's paternity. Single women still frequented sperm banks if they wanted a child from an anonymous donor.

"And I'm going to be the auntie," Francine announced proudly.

All conversation stopped when the waitress set down a pitcher of sweet tea and a platter of fluffy golden biscuits.

Taking a pad and pencil from the pocket of her apron, she nodded to Francine. "What can I get for you, Red?"

Francine didn't bother to open her menu. "I'll have shrimp and grits. I'd also like an order of fried okra, hush puppies, and green tomatoes for the table before you bring out the other dishes. And please don't forget to give us the lunch portions."

Kara studied the menu. "A bowl of gumbo with a side order of perlow rice, please."

"What will you have, miss?" the waitress asked Devon.

She quickly scanned the menu. "I'm going to try the stewed shrimp and gravy with white rice."

Morgan closed her menu. "And I'll have oxtails and gravy over white rice."

Waiting until the waitress walked away, Devon asked, "Do you ladies eat like this every Monday?" She was grateful for the interruption, if only to steer the conversation away from her and David.

"Yes," the three women chorused.

"It sounds like a lot, but the lunch portions are halved," Morgan explained.

Devon moaned under her breath when she bit into a biscuit; it literally dissolved on her tongue. "Omigosh! Omigosh!" she repeated. "These are delicious."

Kara swallowed. "I never get tired of eating Miss Luvina's biscuits."

Morgan nodded, holding up a biscuit. "Folks talk about not using lard, but these wouldn't taste the same without it."

Devon took a sip of water. "I believe in everything in moderation."

Francine, Kara, and Morgan held their glasses aloft. "Moderation," they said in unison, dissolving into laughter.

Devon joined them, touching her glass to theirs while experiencing what it felt like to be a giggly adolescent laughing at any and everything. There was something about the three women that drew her to them, while it hadn't been the same with some of the women she'd interacted with in New York. First of all, these women were happily married or engaged, so there was no competition to land a husband. But even besides that, there had always been distance in her relationships. Never would Devon have thought to open up about her personal life so quickly. But these women made it easy to share, made it easy to laugh. Instead of feeling judged, she felt welcomed.

Between bites of fried okra, hush puppies, and fried green tomatoes, the conversation segued to the upcoming Sanctuary Cove mayoral election. Devon recognized the passion in Francine's and Kara's voices when they talked about the possibility of electing the Cove's first female mayor.

Morgan rolled her eyes upward. "Even though I don't live

in the Cove, I'm praying Alice will win tomorrow. It's sad that Cavanaugh Island is so far behind the times that we don't have any female elected officials. All of the mayors have been men, as well as the members of the town councils."

"New York City didn't have a woman mayor when I lived there," Kara said quietly.

"They still don't," Devon chimed in. "When did you live in New York City, Kara?" she asked.

"I lived there for thirteen years before I moved here two years ago. I'd left Little Rock to attend college, then stayed on when I got a position as a social worker for one of the city's child protective services agencies."

Devon's curiosity was piqued, and she wondered why the social worker had chosen to come to the island. "Why did you decide to move here?"

Kara met her eyes. "I wasn't given much of a choice. It all began with a certified letter from Sullivan, Matthews & Sullivan requesting my presence at the reading of the will of Taylor Patton."

Devon listened intently, stunned, when Kara revealed the man she'd believed was her father wasn't her biological father. "My mother and Austin Newell grew up together and had planned to marry once she graduated college. She met Taylor Patton when she was a student at Spelman, while Taylor was at Morehouse. One night during spring break, they slept together, but it wasn't until after she'd graduated that Mama discovered she was pregnant. She called Taylor's house, leaving a message for him to call her back. Then she wrote him, and her letters went unanswered," Kara continued, capturing the attention of everyone at the table. "Mama was unaware that his mother made certain to intercept the phone call and her letters. She finally had to tell Austin she couldn't marry him because she was carrying another man's child, but instead of turning his back on her Austin married her. I was born Kara Newell instead of Patton.

"It was apparent Taylor knew of my existence, because when he died he left me a house listed on the National Register of Historic Places, two thousand acres of land, also with landmark status, cash, bonds, vintage cars—all with the proviso that I restore Angels Landing Plantation and live in it for five years, otherwise the land would be divided among the Landing Pattons, relatives, some who were willing to sell to developers. Rather than give away what the locals claim was my *birthright*, I commissioned Morgan to oversee the restoration, fell in love with and married the local sheriff, and now I'm the mother of a beautiful son. And if you were to ask me if I miss Little Rock or New York, the answer would be a profound no. I love living here, and when my son is ready to attend school he will be in a class where the teacher-student ratio is no more than one to eight. In other words, our public school functions like a private one. Thanks to my husband and his deputies, crime is practically nonexistent, but I have to admit that it did take a while before I was able to get used to leaving doors unlocked. So, now you know why I decided to put down roots on Cavanaugh Island."

"Damn, Kara," Francine drawled softly. "You sound like the mayor's community affairs spokesperson."

Kara rolled her eyes at the hairstylist. "Don't act like you don't know, Francine. You've lived in New York and I've heard you say you like it here better."

"That's because my family's here," Francine countered.

"Your family and your *boo*," Morgan teased. Francine blushed to the roots of her hair while everyone at the table laughed uncontrollably. The frivolity ended when the waitress arrived with their orders.

Devon groaned under her breath after she swallowed a forkful of shrimp and rice. "Why does everything here taste so good?"

"That's because it's Lowcountry cooking, city girl," Francine teased.

It was Devon's turn to blush as she focused on her plate. "I've eaten at good soul food restaurants in New York, but this is exceptional."

"That's because it's made with Gullah luv," Morgan said, smiling and flashing dimples in her round face. "Some folks call it cooking from the heart, while others just call it luv. When you hear someone say 'e put e foot en um dis time' or 'dey a lot of luv in dis food,' then you know they're giving you a compliment."

Kara touched the corners of her mouth with a napkin. "Can you cook, Devon?"

Devon's head popped up. "Yes."

"Who taught you?" Francine asked.

Devon knew what she was about to disclose would probably make the other women view her differently. "I attended a boarding school where, in addition to the academics, we were taught to cook and sew. And dance," she added when they stared at her in disbelief. "In my family a Gilmore woman is expected to graduate college, marry well, know how to cook and plan a formal dinner party, and have a child within the first two years of marriage. And the child should have a live-in nanny, which will allow his or her mother enough time to fulfill her social obligations."

Francine stared at her. "Should we assume that you're not a traditional Gilmore woman?"

"As an unmarried pregnant thirty-six-year-old woman? Hardly."

Devon thought about what Kara had revealed about her mother trying to contact the father of her baby. Their lives were similar because she'd also tried to tell Gregory that she was carrying his child. He hadn't come to see her as promised, blocked her telephone number, and hadn't been at his town house when she'd gone to see him. Her last resort had been to write or email, but after thinking about it she'd decided to let it go.

Morgan set her fork next to her plate. "Are you going to take maternity leave after you have the baby?"

"I don't work for a firm."

"Who do you work for?" Kara asked Devon.

"I work for myself. I'm an agent for NBA and NFL players. And of course there's Keaton. I negotiate their contracts and handle all of their endorsements."

Crossing her arms under her breasts, Morgan gave her a steady stare. "That means you're free to live anywhere you want." Devon nodded. "If that's the case, then why not move down here? Not only will you be close to Keaton, but you'll also have us to babysit if you want a day off."

"Who's going to babysit your baby?" she asked Morgan.

"My sister had twins last year, so her career is on hold until they're old enough to go to school. She says looking after one more baby shouldn't send her to the loony bin. Thankfully I can make my own hours now that I have a partner."

"I can also help out," Kara volunteered. "Right now I'm a stay-at-home mom. Jeff is talking about having another baby once Austin is potty trained, but I'm trying to hold off until the house at Angels Landing Plantation is fully restored so we can have more room."

"Where are you living now?" Devon asked Kara.

"Jeff's grandmother's house here in the Cove."

Again Devon felt slightly overwhelmed by the outpouring of generosity from strangers she hadn't known a week ago. Although she didn't need money, she did need friends and a support system now that the fragile bond she'd had with her parents seemed broken beyond repair.

"I'll definitely think about it," she said. "Thank you guys so much for all your kindness and support. I know it's a lot to ask, but I'd appreciate it if what I've just told you about my having a baby doesn't leave this table."

Kara made a sucking sound with her tongue and teeth. "Let me school you on something, Devon. Any and everything we talk about at our Monday afternoon Lowcountry Ladies Luncheon is never repeated. Not even to our men." She placed her hand, palm down, on the table. Francine covered Kara's hand, Morgan followed suit. Kara lifted her eyebrows questioningly. "Well, Devon. Are you in or out?"

She smiled and rested her hand over Morgan's. "I'm in." Reaching into her tote, Devon took out her wallet. She had to leave to meet Keaton, then return to Charleston and check out of the hotel. "Lunch is on me."

Francine held on to Devon's wrist. "Don't even try it. You're our guest today, so your money is no good here."

"I'd like you to make an exception for me. Please." She wanted to tell the three women that eating and talking with them had changed her life in a way they would never understand.

Francine shared a glance with Morgan, who nodded. "We'll make an exception only if you promise to join us next Monday."

"I promise," she said without hesitating. Placing several

large bills on the table, she pushed back her chair and stood up, Francine, Kara, and Morgan also coming to their feet. "I have to leave now," she said, hugging each one.

"You left too much money," Morgan called out.

"Whatever is left over after the tip you can put toward next week's bill."

Devon wended her way through tables and out of the restaurant, feeling freer than she had in years. Just talking about what it meant to be a Gilmore woman made her aware that she'd sentenced herself to an emotional prison. She'd become an overachiever in order to prove that she didn't need to rely on her family's name or money or marry into a well-to-do family to be successful. She earned more money with a stroke of a pen than some people did during their entire lifetime. Yet none of her success impressed her parents—particularly her mother, because Monique claimed she'd shamed the family when she refused to marry a man whom Devon found profoundly repulsive.

Her mantra had become "My life, my way," and that was what she intended to do. Live life on her terms.

Chapter Seven

❧

It took Devon less than fifteen minutes to tour Keaton's renovated farmhouse. Four second-story bedrooms had French doors that opened out onto a veranda, decorative ceiling fans, fireplaces, sitting areas, and en suite baths. New wood floors and central heat and air-conditioning were welcome additions to the house that had been in the same family for generations. She was partial to the enclosed back porch, which she found to be the perfect spot to begin and/or end the day.

Several workmen had just completed roofing the guesthouse that would become the home of Keaton's housekeeper. Devon had never hit it off with Mrs. Susie Miller. The woman guarded her employer's privacy like a Secret Service agent hovering over the president. And whenever Devon flew to Los Angeles to meet with him, the middle-aged woman always gave her the stink-eye. She hadn't understood Mrs. Miller's possessiveness until Keaton told her about a young actress he'd dated who'd taken her own life by swallowing a bottle of sleeping pills after he'd stopped seeing her. What Mrs. Miller hadn't known was that she and Keaton had always been friends and Devon wasn't looking for anything more.

Perched on a tall stool at the cooking island in the updated kitchen, Devon watched as Keaton blended a smoothie. Although he didn't have any furniture in the other rooms in the house, the stainless steel kitchen was functional, with copper cookware suspended from a rack over the island and a fully stocked refrigerator/freezer. As the son of chefs, Keaton learned to cook at a very early age, and whenever he announced to his friends he was cooking, Devon had not hesitated to climb the five flights of stairs to join the others crowding into his minuscule Manhattan apartment.

Resting her elbows on the black granite countertop, she laced her fingers together. "How's Mrs. Miller?"

Keaton glanced at her over his shoulder. "I spoke to her the other day and she says she can't wait to leave L.A."

Devon smiled. "Did you tell her you're engaged to be married?"

He nodded.

"What did she say?"

"She told me it's about time."

"She's right, you know."

Keaton set the smoothie and a straw on the countertop in front of her. "I'm really looking forward to starting a family."

Devon took a sip of the icy concoction, her eyes meeting Keaton's. He'd added banana to the mixture of yogurt and fresh berries. "You really love her, don't you?"

Keaton sat opposite her. "If you're talking about Francine, then the answer is yes."

"She's delightful. I'm glad you found someone whom you want to spend the rest of your life with."

"It's going to happen with you, Devon," he said after a comfortable silence. "You'll find someone who will love and appreciate all of you."

She took a long swallow of the chilled concoction. "I know I've been acting a little weird lately, but I don't need you to feel sorry for me, Keaton. I went through the 'why me?' and 'why now?' but I'm done with that. There's no doubt my decision to have this baby will definitely change my life. I've worked hard to get where I am today, and while I'd told myself I never wanted children, I'm beginning to think getting pregnant is the best thing that has ever happened to me."

Keaton gave her a puzzled look. "Why do you say that?"

"It's no longer all about me. Even though I loathe the concept of what it means to be a Gilmore woman, I've been living my life as one. Once I started earning six figures a year, I decided I didn't want to live in Washington Heights or Chelsea. It had to be Central Park West, Carnegie Hill, or Lenox Hill, because that's what a Gilmore would want. If the apartment didn't have views of the Manhattan skyline, Central Park, or the East River, I rejected it." She bit down on her lower lip. "Can you believe I actually thought about buying a twenty-four-hundred-square-foot penthouse with a nine-hundred-square-foot private rooftop terrace for six million dollars?"

Shaking his head, Keaton whispered, "That's crazy!"

Devon smiled. "Exactly! If I had bought the property, I'd have ended up broke as a convict. That's when I realized I had to stop thinking like a Gilmore woman."

"Not all convicts are broke," Keaton teased playfully.

"Do you ever watch *American Greed*? Even the best scammers end up broke *and* in jail."

"You're right about that," he said.

"I rest my case." Devon paused. "I think it's time I share my good fortune with someone else other than myself. And that someone will be my son or daughter. This is not to say I haven't made mistakes, but I don't intend to repeat them with my child. All I want right now is to carry to term and deliver a healthy and happy baby."

Keaton angled his head, giving her a lengthy stare. "Everything's going to work out well for you."

That's what she prayed for. "How's the writing going?" she asked, changing the topic. "I saw your executive office on the back porch."

Lines fanned out around Keaton's eyes when he smiled. "You hatin' on my office?" he teased.

It was Devon's turn to smile. "I don't think so."

"How was your lunch with the girls?"

Devon lowered her eyes for several seconds. "It was interesting."

"How so?"

She ran her forefinger down the length of the glass. "I can't believe how open and friendly they were. It's been only one afternoon but I feel as if I've known them practically all of my life. They're like the sisters I never had. Believe it or not, they offered to babysit once I have the baby. That never would've happened with the women I hang out with in New York."

"If they offered to babysit, then you'll have to live nearby to take advantage of all of this unexpected help," Keaton teased.

The seconds ticked by as Devon met Keaton's eyes. She tucked a wayward strand behind her left ear that had escaped the twist on the nape of her neck. She studied the man who'd become more than a friend. He was like an older brother. There wasn't anything she wouldn't do for Keaton, and she knew he would do the same for her.

However, Devon knew he was uncomfortable about the fact that she'd given up trying to contact Gregory. But she'd argued that she'd done everything she could to contact him, short of camping out on his doorstep, which would prove embarrassing to him and his fiancée *and* was certain to thrust her into the spotlight for newshounds to dissect her life.

"You're right, and I've seriously considered relocating. I could easily live in New York for the rest of my life, but I keep asking myself whether I really want to raise a child there. If I buy a house, then I could relax on the back porch and watch my baby play in the backyard instead of bundling them up and taking them to a playground. I also want enough land where I can put in a flower and maybe an herb and vegetable garden. Then I have to think of neighborhood schools. Don't look at me like that, Keaton," she admonished when he gave her a questioning glance. "What's wrong with becoming a domestic diva?"

He patted her hand. "Nothing. It's just that I hadn't figured you for the domestic type."

"Neither had I until I found out I was going to be a mother." Devon told him about meeting the woman in Haven Creek who told her about the vacant house on Cherry Lane. "I'm going to try to keep an open mind when I see it."

"Do you want me to come with you?" Keaton eagerly volunteered.

"No, that's okay."

"Why not? You came with me to see this property, so I'd like to return the favor."

"I'm certain everyone on this island knows that you and Francine are engaged to be married and I don't want folks gossiping about seeing us together looking at houses. There's already enough talk about me and David going together."

Keaton smiled. "I noticed that, too."

"Noticed what?"

"That you two did look like a couple."

She shook her head. "That's where you're wrong. We are *not* a couple."

He gave her a skeptical look. "What are you?"

"*Friends*, Keaton."

Keaton scratched his stubble, the sound reminding her of fingernails on a chalkboard. "If you say so."

Devon wasn't about to get into a debate with him about her association with David. It was as if everyone wanted her and David together. She stood up; he rose with her. "I have to head back to Charleston now and check out of the hotel."

"Are you still planning to stay until the middle of April?"

"If I find a house, I'll stay long enough to close on it before I go back to New York to list the condo and clean it out. I also have a doctor's appointment the third week in April, so if I'm coming back then it won't be until May."

"Do you think you'll have a problem selling the condo?" Keaton asked Devon. He walked alongside her as they left the kitchen and the house through a side door near where she'd parked her car.

"No," she said confidently. "I spoke to the manager in the sales office and he claims there's a waiting list for a one-bedroom in my building." Fortunately she didn't have to wait for the proceeds from the sale of the condo in order to buy a house on the island. She hugged Keaton before slipping behind the wheel of her rental. "I'll call and let you know if I like the house."

Ninety minutes later Devon folded her body down to a cushioned chaise on the veranda outside her Cove Inn suite. When checking in, the desk clerk told her the antebellum mansion-turned-inn was filled to capacity with tourists and snowbirds. Crystal chandeliers suspended from twelve-foot ceilings, marble floors, antiques and exquisite reproductions, and curving twin staircases leading to the second floor transported her back to a time when women wore gloves and hooped skirts and carried fans to ward off the intense heat and insects. An elevator had been installed off a narrow hallway to assist guests and bellhops with luggage and packages.

The bedroom to which she'd been assigned was furnished with a mahogany queen-size four-poster bed, matching armoire, and chest-on-chest. There was a spacious sitting area and an alcove with a desk, chair, and workstation.

The bathroom, a welcome respite from the tiny one in the Francis Marion, had a claw-foot tub and shower stall. The galley kitchen contained a full-size refrigerator, dishwasher, eye-level microwave, and a stove. Cabinets were stocked with glassware, dishes, and pots and pans. Devon's appreciation of her new lodgings escalated when she contemplated occasionally preparing her own meals. The suite also included a living room and a dining area with a table and chairs seating four.

The Cove Inn's services included a buffet breakfast, lunch, and sit-down dinner. She had the option of choosing an early seating at six, the later at seven-thirty, or room service. Guests were invited to linger in the formal parlor to listen to prerecorded music while sampling a variety of cordials between the hours of eight thirty and ten thirty. During the daytime hours, the parlor doubled as a meeting room for board games and watching movies on the large, wall-mounted flat screen.

The owners of the inn had adopted a policy of environmental consciousness wherein the housekeeping staff changed linens and bath towels every third day. An on-site laundry service was also available for anyone choosing not to take their clothes to a local Laundromat and dry cleaner.

Crossing her bare feet at the ankles, Devon closed her eyes. There had been a time when she would've felt guilty sitting around doing absolutely nothing. Now she had to grasp every minute of nothingness until the baby came. For the past three years she'd tutored four law school graduates in her office Monday through Thursday for three hours to prepare them to pass the bar exam. Fridays were usually devoted to meeting her friends for after-work mixers either in Greenwich Village or at the South Street Seaport. During the summer months, she joined them on board a yacht, eating, drinking, and listening to live jazz while sailing along the Hudson River under the stars. The weekends were set aside for Gregory whenever he came to New York to meet with a client or for a little R & R. They got to see each other an average of twice a month, and there were a few times when he'd invited her to come to Newport News to spend the weekend with him.

A light breeze swept over her exposed skin, but she wasn't yet ready to leave the veranda; she opened her eyes. Instead of river views she now had an unobstructed view of the ocean. Her cell phone vibrated. Glancing at the display, she picked it up. It was the real estate agent returning her voice-mail message. The call lasted less than two minutes. He would meet her at ten the following morning and show her the house on Cherry Lane.

It wasn't until the lingering heat from the day faded completely that she swung her legs over the side of the chaise and reentered the suite, deciding to order room service instead of eating with the other guests. There would be plenty of time to acquaint herself with them in the coming days. Reaching for the binder with the directory of businesses, places of worship, and public buildings in Sanctuary Cove, she flipped to the page advertising the Cove Inn and perused their menu. Picking up the house phone, she dialed the number for room service, ordering baked chicken, steamed carrots, sautéed spinach, and milk.

"Would you like dessert, Miss Collins?" the woman asked.

"What do you have?"

"Tonight we have sweet potato pie, pecan pie, lemon pound cake, and homemade peach ice cream."

She groaned inwardly. If ice cream were an illegal substance, it definitely would become her drug of choice. "I'll have the ice cream."

"Your dinner will be delivered within the hour."

Devon glanced at her watch, hoping she wouldn't have to eat another protein bar before dinner arrived. She was down to two bars and knew she had to replenish her supply. She also had to stock the refrigerator with bottled water. Sitting down at the desk, Devon reached for a pen and pad, jotting down items she needed from the local supermarket. Unconsciously, she pressed her fingertips to her forehead above her left eye, mulling over what she wanted to bring to David's house. Although he'd insisted he didn't need anything, she still didn't want to show up empty-handed.

Scrolling through her contacts, she found David's number and tapped Send Message: How many are you expecting for your March Madness Sunday soiree? Devon didn't have to wait long for him to reply to her text.

David: Around 20. Why?

Devon: I need to know how many you're entertaining before I buy the ingredients for my dish. She planned to make an assortment of pot stickers with a spicy Asian chili sauce.

David: I'm looking forward to sampling it. BTW are you free for dinner tonight?

She stared at his questioning text. Why? she mused. Was he asking her out?

Devon: I just ordered room service.

David: What about tomorrow?

Now he'd piqued her curiosity. Did he want to discuss a case with her or...Her thoughts trailed off because she didn't want to think he was even remotely romantically interested in her. But the only way to find out was to go out with him.

Devon: I'm free.

David: Will you have dinner with me?

Devon: Why?

David: I'm working on a case and I'd like you to look over my notes and give me your opinion.

Devon: You want my professional opinion?

David: Yes.

Devon: Are you going to give me a hint about the case?

David: It involves a female client.

Devon: Don't you have female lawyers on staff you can confer with?

David: No. That's one of the reasons I'm leaving.

Devon's thumbs stilled. It was the twenty-first century

and she couldn't believe a firm, even a small one, didn't have
at least one female lawyer.

Devon: What time do you want to meet?

David: How's 7?

Devon: Make it 6. Now that she was going to bed earlier
than she had in the past, she'd begun eating dinner at six
rather than seven or even as late as eight.

David: Okay. I'll meet you in your hotel lobby at 5:30.

Devon: I'm at the Cove Inn now.

David: Then I'll pick you up there.

Devon: Casual or dressy?

David: Casual. See you tomorrow.

Devon: Good-bye.

David: It's not good-bye but later Madam Counselor.

Devon: Later Counselor. ☺

Hearing that their dinner would be casual was a nice
change from how she grew up. Her father would sit at the
head of the table in a suit and tie, and her mother with coiffed
hair and perfect makeup would sit at the opposite end like a
queen lauding over her subjects. Devon, wearing her Sunday
best, would fidget nervously in fear she would spill something on the one-of-a-kind dress her mother had ordered from
her personal dressmaker. Her brother had rebelled against
their rigid, stifling lifestyle at an early age, drinking and dab-
bling in drugs by the time he was twelve. She'd taken a little
longer, but she'd made it clear she was done when she refused
to marry the man her parents had chosen for her. What would
they think if they could see her now?

Chapter Eight

❧

David lay across the leather sofa in his office, an arm
flung over his face. He'd turned off all the overhead lights
and dimmed one of the lamps on the table next to the sofa
to the lowest setting. The clock on the credenza behind his
desk chimed nine o'clock and he knew he should get up and
go home, but he couldn't stop thinking about the case he
wanted Devon to look over for him.

His reason for asking her to dinner was twofold. He
wanted her professional opinion on a case one of the partners didn't want to take on, but more than that, he hadn't
wanted to wait until Sunday to see her again. And talking to
her in the parking lot in the Creek while staring at her in the
brilliance of the warm spring sunlight was akin to looking
at her for the first time. Everything about her bare face was
natural, feminine, and wholesome and drew him to her like a
bee to a flower. Even the woman he'd dated for far too long
hadn't had that effect on him.

David had given up analyzing his five-year relationship

with an oral surgeon, because he blamed himself more than Petra for continuing to date her when she'd been open about wanting him to marry her. But at that time he wasn't ready to settle down to become a husband and a father.

He opened his eyes, staring up at the ceiling. Thinking about his past relationship and what he was beginning to feel for Devon was not going to solve his current dilemma. He'd insisted to the other partners they take on the discrimination case, but they believed they couldn't win it because of their client's assertion she'd been discriminated against based on her dress size. However, David felt there was something else the woman was hiding. He lowered his arm when he heard tapping on the open door. Swinging his legs over the side of the sofa, he sat up.

"I saw the light and I thought you would've gone home by now."

David reached over and turned up the bulb on the table lamp. "I could say the same about you," he said to one of the associates who'd just celebrated his third year at the firm.

Everyone called Trevor Lincoln the boy wonder because he'd graduated high school at fifteen, college at eighteen, and law school at twenty-one, and passed the South Carolina bar with a near-perfect score. Tall, slender, and blue-eyed with sun-streaked blond hair, Trevor was the poster boy for a California surfer. He'd spent eight years working for a law firm in Columbia, the state's capital; after reuniting with a former college classmate, he moved to Charleston to be close to her, but less than six months later they decided to split up.

Trevor sat. "I needed to catch up on my billing."

David knew that was something he wasn't going to miss: calculating billable hours. "Did you finish?"

Trevor exhaled an audible breath. "Finally. Why are you hanging out here so late?"

Sandwiching his hands between his knees, David stared at the toes of his highly polished shoes and replayed Trevor's question in his head. "I was looking over that discrimination case we discussed at last week's meeting and trying to figure out a way to approach a full-figured woman about her weight."

Grimacing, Trevor ran a hand through his hair. "Good luck with that." Clearing his throat, his expression changed as his eyes met David's. He pushed to his feet. "I'm going to miss working with you."

"Same here, Trevor. But let's not get maudlin. I'm not leaving for several weeks. And once I'm up and running, you're always welcome to come by and see the new digs. After that, we'll catch up over drinks at Haven Creek's Happy Hour."

"I'd like that. Speaking of drinks. I'm going to stop by the Dugout for a couple of beers before I head on home. Want to join me?"

David also stood up. "Sure. Are you still coming over Sunday for March Madness?" he asked.

Trevor was the only one, other than Angela, with whom he'd formed a close association outside the office. And like Trevor, he didn't have anyone at home waiting for him. It'd been that way for the past two years. Although he and Petra hadn't lived together, they had managed to see each other several times a week when he wasn't working on a case or if she wasn't teaching or attending dental conferences. Now he lived his life by his leave and once he opened his firm, his professional success or failure would rest solely on his shoulders.

Trevor grinned like a Cheshire cat. "I wouldn't miss it. As soon as I get my jacket I'll meet you in the parking lot."

"Pretty isn't it?" Michael asked Devon. The Realtor had picked her up in front of the Cove Inn at exactly ten o'clock, and they were just turning onto Cherry Lane.

"It is," she said, unable to pull her gaze away from the beauty of the passing landscape. The trees that had given the narrow road its name were in full bloom with white-and-pink cherry blossoms. Tiny flowers littered the ground like colorful confetti. The wildflowers growing alongside the stone bridge dividing North Haven Creek from South Haven Creek reminded her of a Monet landscape. The only thing missing were the water lilies.

Devon smiled, returning the wave of an elderly woman sitting on a porch while several toddlers chased one another on the front lawn. She imagined her own child running barefoot in the grass while she watched from the porch of her home, and all doubt as to whether to make the decision to move to the Lowcountry fled like clouds after a tropical storm. Nothing but blue skies from here on out.

"Do you have other listings on Haven Creek?" she asked the agent after a comfortable silence. He'd told her the selling price of the vacant house set on a quarter of an acre, then reassured her it was negotiable. Devon wanted to tell the agent the purchase price was far below what she'd expected to spend. Although she had no intention of lowballing him, she had to factor in the cost of possible repairs, despite the fact that Peggy had been forthcoming about the renovations on the Wickham property.

Michael gave her a quick glance. "I have several vacancies in the business district, but only two residential listings.

The Wickham property is one, and the other is a house that needs so much work that it should be demolished." He turned onto a stone-covered road and drove up to a classic Creole house with a wraparound porch. "Here we are."

Devon waited for him to cut off the minivan's engine and come around to help her down. She loved the design. The hipped roofline reminded her of French and Caribbean architecture, which was mimicked by Louisiana plantation homes with their raised foundations. She glanced up at the three perfectly placed dormers, which seemed to balance out the squat roofline. The shutters were a rich forest green, the siding of cedar shakes was made of vinyl in ecru, and the antique-white trim afforded the home an old-house feel.

"It's larger than many of the other homes I've seen in the Creek," she remarked.

Michael unlocked the front door. "It's approximately thirty-two hundred square feet. Mr. Wickham worked for one of the big insurance companies on the mainland. He and his wife had four kids—two sets of identical twins—and they wanted each of the kids to have their own room. Come on in and look around."

Devon glanced around the entryway, noting the small stained glass window through which pinpoints of color reflected on the parquet floor designed in a herringbone pattern; she held her breath for several seconds before letting it out slowly at the same time her lips parted in a smile. The spacious entryway widened to a living room with a fireplace. She glanced up, noting the capped-off wires where a ceiling fixture once hung. She walked into the dining room, leaving footprints on the dusty parquet floor; it, too, claimed its own fireplace. Tall windows brought the outside in with a view of the backyard. There was more than enough space for a playground and outdoor furniture and a vegetable and flower garden.

"What do you think so far?" Michael asked.

"It's very nice." The three words were filled with an excitement Devon found difficult to repress. And she did like what she'd seen. However, she still needed to tour the rest of the rooms before reaching a decision as to whether she would buy the house.

"I'll be outside on the porch, so take your time looking around."

Devon continued her tour, discovering a room between the dining room and kitchen, which would be perfect for an in-home office. It was large enough for a workstation, bookcases, and a love seat. Even before seeing the upstairs bedrooms, it was the bricked-in kitchen with a pantry, a nearby bathroom with a shower, vanity, and commode, and an adjoining mudroom that sold her on the house. She stood in the middle of the kitchen staring at a wood-burning fireplace and the imported stove she recognized as the same one installed in her parents' kitchen. Considered the Rolls-Royce of stoves, La Cornue CornuFé 1908 was famous for its style and high performance. Her mother's stove was ivory with copper trim, while this one was gleaming black and brass.

Devon could envision herself spending hours cooking in the homey kitchen, whether on the stove or in the wood-burning fireplace. The cooking island, with double stainless steel sinks, a granite and butcher-block countertop, provided more than adequate space for food preparation, while the pantry had floor-to-ceiling shelves to stock foodstuffs for months. A door led from the kitchen directly onto the rear of the wraparound porch, which meant she could cook and keep an eye on the happenings outside. Her mind churning with ideas, she decided the mudroom with a slop sink could also double as the laundry and utility room.

She left the kitchen through a back staircase to the second floor, stepping out into a wide hallway with tall facing windows at opposite ends. Devon walked in and out of empty bedrooms, opening and peering out the windows in each one. The master bedroom claimed a fireplace and full en suite bathroom and overlooked the front of the house from the dormers. A door connected the master bedroom to a smaller bedroom, which she knew could be used as a nursery. The other three bedrooms, located at the rear of the house, had bathrooms with shower stalls, commodes, and vanities. There was also a full second-floor bathroom.

Keaton had teased her about being a domestic diva and that's what she planned to become. She would decorate her home, bake cookies, knit, and sew while awaiting the birth of her baby. Devon blinked back happy tears when she fantasized about celebrating her baby's first Christmas in her new home. Covering her mouth with her hand, she struggled not to cry. It still bothered her that she cried so easily now when it'd never been like that in the past. She managed to bring her fragile emotions enough under control to descend the staircase and walk out to the porch. Michael rose to his feet at her approach.

"You can lock it up now."

"What do you think?" the Realtor asked her.

"I want it." Devon surprised herself with her quick decision. She couldn't afford to spend a lot of time house hunting, because she wanted each passing month to be less stressful than the previous one.

Michael gave her a stunned look. "You do?"

Devon almost laughed at his expression. It had central air and heat and more than enough outdoor space for recreation and entertaining. She even thought of inviting Francine, Kara, and Morgan over for their Monday luncheon once she'd settled in. She also had to order furniture from Williams-Sonoma and Restoration Hardware, which had become her favorite shops for home furnishings.

"Yes. It's perfect for what I need. I want to go to contract, and after I have an engineer check it over and a title company do a search to find out if there are any liens against the property, I'll be ready to close on it."

"Do you need me to recommend an engineer?" Michael asked.

"No, thank you. I know someone locally who'll recommend one." She would ask David who he'd suggest when she saw him later that evening.

"Have you been preapproved for a mortgage?"

"Yes," Devon half lied. She planned to contact her personal banker and arrange for him to cut a bank check.

Michael smiled. "Well, let's get back so we can draw up the contract, and hopefully within another six weeks you'll be able to call Haven Creek home."

Chapter Nine

Devon peered at her reflection in the mirror over the bathroom vanity as she picked up a sable brush, dipped the tip into a pot of bronzer, tapped off the excess, and applied it in light strokes over her forehead, checks, and chin. Her lips parted in a smile when she examined the subtly applied makeup. A light dusting of bronzer, mascara, and lip gloss had transformed her bare face to glowing. She'd changed twice, then decided on a pair of black stretch slacks and a matching tunic sweater. And instead of her favorite flats, she slipped her bare feet into a pair of leather wedge-heeled peep-toe booties.

It seemed as if it'd taken her forever to select something to wear before she reminded herself it wasn't a date or a formal affair but a dinner meeting. David wanted to confer with her about a case, and she wanted to ask if he would handle her house closing. Yet somehow she wanted it to be a date, because David was so wholly different from the men in her past. Not that there had been that many with which to compare him. Now that she knew for certain she was going to relocate, Devon felt as if the heaviness weighing her down had been lifted. She could reconcile her past in order to move forward.

She drew a wide-tooth comb through her hair as she recalled the student she slept with as a college freshman, and another one in law school whom she actually believed she loved enough to marry—if he proposed. Then there were men she'd dated but refused to sleep with because they always wanted something from her. This prompted her to swear off men for months at a time. There had been a time when she'd gone nearly a year before agreeing to date again.

Gregory had appeared in her life when she truly needed a male friend. Keaton was three thousand miles away in Los Angeles, and while he occasionally lent an ear to her to vent, it was always by phone. And for all of her confidence, she'd begun to question why she couldn't find a man willing to accept that she wanted nothing more from him than companionship. Then things changed the first time she and Gregory slept together.

Their physical involvement filled an emptiness Devon hadn't known was there. Their relationship was straightforward, uncomplicated. There were no declarations of love or promises of marriage. They'd always practiced safe sex, aside from a single encounter when Gregory had not stopped to slip on a condom. Devon hadn't panicked because she'd believed it was the safe phase of her menstrual cycle, but nature threw her a vicious curve and in the end she found herself facing an unplanned pregnancy.

She exchanged the comb for a hairbrush, smoothing the ebony strands off her face and braiding her hair into a single plait. If anyone were to see her, they would think she was losing her mind, but she couldn't stop smiling when thinking about the house on Cherry Lane. It'd taken her less than an hour to decide to buy it. It had taken her almost three months before she decided to buy the condo, after seeing so many she'd almost forgotten where they were located and what they looked like. She'd told the agent it was going to be her first big-ticket purchase and she wanted to be certain that when she purchased the condo she planned to spend many, many years there. Her plans now included selling her condo, shipping the furniture to South Carolina, decorating the house, finding a local ob-gyn, and preparing for the birth of her son or daughter.

Devon checked her face for the last time. Walking out of the bathroom, she glanced at the clock on the nightstand as she picked up a black cashmere shawl and small cross-body designer purse that had been a Christmas gift from her client's mother. Although she'd asked the woman not to give her anything, her request seemed to fall on deaf ears, because every year she got either a handbag or jewelry. She left the suite and rode the elevator down to the first floor. The doors opened and she nodded to a couple clutching a number of shopping bags as they stood aside to let her exit the car.

David, sitting in a chair behind a potted palm, watched Devon as she strode across the lobby. He smiled. Her black body-hugging outfit surpassed casual. It was downright sexy, as was her walk. A single braid had replaced the sophisticated twist, the curling end falling over her left shoulder. She looked younger, fresh, and very approachable.

Rising to his feet, he went over to meet her. "Hi, beautiful." David knew he'd startled her when she gasped. However, she recovered quickly, tilting her head and giving him a warm smile.

"Hi yourself," she whispered breathlessly. She stared at his blue-and-white pin-striped shirt with a white collar and matching cuffs and navy-blue silk tie. "A tailored suit is not casual," she teased, smiling.

He offered her his arm and he wasn't disappointed when she slipped her arm over the sleeve of his suit jacket. "I came directly from the office and didn't have time to go home and change. I promise to ditch the tie."

Her fingers tightened on his arm. "You don't have to. It's very nice. What I can do is go back to my room and change."

David covered her hand with his, tucking it into the bend of his elbow. "Please don't. What you have on is perfect for where we're going."

"Where are we going?" she asked as he steered her out of the hotel and into his car.

"I made a reservation at Magnolias in Charleston."

David had tried to convince himself that his interest in her was solely for business, yet his heart knew otherwise. Yes, he wanted her to join his firm *and* he also wanted to date her. But combining business with pleasure was rarely a good idea. He'd learned that the hard way in law school.

Almost as if she could read his mind, Devon's soft voice broke into his thoughts. "I'd like to retain your services."

He gave her a quick glance. "For what?"

"I'm buying a house in Haven Creek. Can you recommend an engineer to make certain everything is in working order? And I'm also hoping you'll handle a title search."

Fingers tightening on the leather-wrapped steering wheel, David clamped his jaw to keep from laughing. It'd been his fervent wish—no, prayer—that Devon would consider relocating to the Lowcountry. What a blessing!

"Congratulations. Where's the house?"

"It's on Cherry Lane. The owners were named Wickham. Do you know them?"

He shook his head. "I'm not familiar with them."

Devon shifted on her seat, giving him a long stare. "I thought you knew everyone on Cavanaugh Island."

David tapped his horn when he recognized the driver coming in the opposite direction. The man waved, returning the tap. "I grew up in Charleston, although I still have relatives in the Cove. Each of the towns has its own school from grades K to eight. They only combine for high school."

"Are you saying the kids in the Cove don't hang out with those in Angels Landing or Haven Creek?"

"Not until high school. Now, back to you becoming a resident of the Creek. Do you have a preapproved mortgage?"

"I don't need a mortgage."

That bit of information confirmed what Devon had told him about the commissions she earned from her clients affording her a substantial income and a comfortable lifestyle. "If that's the case, then closing on the property should go quickly. Have you gone to contract?"

"Yes. Michael Duryea is handling the sale."

"I'll call him tomorrow."

"Thank you, David," Devon crooned.

He winked at her. "You're welcome, Devon."

"Be sure to bill me for your services."

His smile vanished. "That's not going to happen."

"Why not?"

"Please don't give me attitude, Devon."

"I'm not giving you attitude," she countered.

"Yes, you are, if you have your fists at your waist," he said, chuckling softly when she dropped her hands. "What if we barter services?"

She blinked slowly. "How?"

"After you read it and give me your opinion on the case I have on the backseat, we'll call it an even trade." David left the town limits of Haven Creek behind as he accelerated to the on-ramp leading to the causeway.

Devon shook her head. "I don't think so, Counselor. My giving you an opinion definitely doesn't equal—"

"Please don't say it, Devon," David said, interrupting her. "Your opinion may result in my client winning a discrimination suit totaling six or even seven figures, which means you've just been overruled."

"Is this the way it's going to be when we work together? You overrule me and I'm supposed to remain silent?"

Smiling, he maneuvered smoothly into the flow of traffic heading toward the mainland. "Is this your way of telling me you're willing to join the firm?"

"No, it isn't. I was just throwing out the possibility."

David knew he had to choose his words carefully or he would alienate Devon. He needed her experience and her extensive knowledge of contracts, and he needed a female attorney. He'd discovered female clients were more comfortable talking with a woman when it involved rape, sexual assault, and domestic violence.

His latest client was suing her employer because she believed she'd been passed over for promotion a number of times because of her weight, and when he sought to take a deposition from her she refused to answer some of his questions, leaving him in a quandary as to whether to represent her.

"I'm glad you're at least considering the possibility of coming to work with me. Please forgive my impertinence."

Devon smiled when their eyes met for several seconds. "You're forgiven, and I accept your apology."

"Thank you, Dee." David felt her withdraw as she went completely still. "What's the matter?"

"Nothing."

He gave her a sidelong glance. "Are you sure you're all right?"

"Yes," Devon said, although David wasn't convinced.

"Look, Devon, if we're going to work together, we're going to have to learn to trust each other. I don't need to know your private thoughts, but I should know enough about you so if I say something out of line you're not going to go for my throat."

"I go for the knees first as a warning. The throat is usually the last resort." There was a hint of laughter in her voice.

"Point taken," David replied lightly. "If you don't want me to call you Dee because your ex called you that, then I won't."

Devon stared out the side window. "It has nothing to do with an ex, and you may call me Dee if you want."

He'd just pulled into a parking space near the restaurant when she said, "There's something you need to know about me before you decide to put my name on your firm's letterhead."

David tapped the button, turning off the engine. Unbuckling his seat belt, he turned to look directly at her. "Whatever it is, it can't be that bad."

"I'm pregnant."

Devon watched David close his eyes and go completely still, as if temporarily paralyzed. He opened his eyes and turned his head to look at her as if he'd never seen her before. "Does the father know?"

She unbuckled her seat belt, shifting to face him. "No."

"You're not going to tell him." His question sounded like a statement.

Devon sucked in a big breath, then let it out slowly. "I tried to tell him." She told David about her attempts to contact Gregory, without mentioning his name, to let him know she was carrying his baby. "I've gotten used to the fact that I'm going to have to go it alone when it comes to having this baby."

Reaching for her hands, David laced their fingers together. "You're not going to be alone. You'll have Keaton and Francine. And you also have my numbers, so if there's anything you need, I want you to call me, regardless of the hour."

She smiled through the tears welling up in her eyes. "You may regret saying that."

David gave her fingers a gentle squeeze. "I never say anything I'll later regret. At least not with my friends," he added.

Devon rested her head on his shoulder. "Thank you for being so understanding."

He pressed his mouth to her hair. "I should be the one thanking you, Dee. When I'd hinted at you moving here and working with me it was wishful thinking."

She raised her head, trying to make out his features in the diffused light in the parking lot coming through the windshield. "I want you to understand my wanting to tell my ex he was going to become a father had nothing to do with getting him to marry me. He was aware that I never wanted to get married. I suppose that's why he was attracted to me. I made it easy for him to have a fiancée and, as they say, a chick on the side."

"You're far from side chick material, and if your ex couldn't figure that out then he was a fool."

"Do you know how good you are for a woman's ego?"

David's expression changed, becoming a mask of stone. "I don't say things just to boost someone's ego. You're a young, beautiful, and very successful attorney, and you are kind enough to help others, whether volunteering to tutor or coming to a friend in need. " He kissed her forehead. "Let's go inside because it's almost six."

In that instant Devon felt closer to David than any man with whom she'd been involved, and that included her first lover. She'd glimpsed something special about him from their initial meeting. She didn't know if it was his soft, drawling voice or that he knew exactly what to say to put her at ease. Whatever it was indicated she'd made the right decision concerning the two most important events in her life thus far: having a baby and moving south.

She didn't want to get ahead of herself where she and David were concerned, but wondered if she could possibly have a future with him. Although startled that the thought had flashed through her mind, Devon decided to embrace it.

Chapter Ten

~

David sat across the small table in the restaurant watching Devon peruse Cynthia Humphries's file. He'd ordered appetizers of pan-fried chicken livers with caramelized onions, country ham, and Madeira, and egg rolls stuffed with collard greens, chicken, Tasso ham, red pepper purée, spicy mustard, and peach chutney, cautioning their waiter to alert the chef to leave out the wine. Now he knew why Devon hadn't drunk any alcohol at Francine's birthday dinner party.

Devon took a sip of water. "I can see why you have the impression she's not being forthcoming."

The tea light under a glass chimney cast a warm glow over Devon's features. David's eyes caressed the delicate bones in her lovely face. He'd been truthful when he told Devon she was beautiful. "You can see in the transcript that I'd asked her the same question several different ways and her responses were always evasive."

"Do you think she lied?"

He shook his head. "I'm not sure, but I can't go forward if she did."

Devon closed the folder. "She claims she weighed the same when she was hired, so it didn't prevent her from getting the job. And she's received favorable evaluations but been passed over for promotion twice?"

"Yes," David confirmed.

"So why after four years would her weight become an issue? I think there's something else compelling her to sue her former employer." She pulled her lower lip between her teeth. "Do you want me to talk to her? She may feel more comfortable talking to a woman about her weight than a man."

David whispered a silent prayer of gratitude. "Would you?"

Devon smiled, her eyes turning a rich mossy green. "Of course."

"I'll see if she's available to come to my office tomorrow." Reaching into the breast pocket of his jacket, David took out his cell phone and tapped the client's number, speaking quietly and nodding. "Please hold on." He placed his thumb over the mouthpiece. "She's not available until Friday and only in the evening."

"Make an appointment that's convenient for her," Devon said.

He removed his thumb. "What time do you want to meet?" David stared at Devon. "She can't come until nine."

"That's okay," Devon confirmed.

"Okay, Cynthia. I'll see you Friday night at nine. Ring the bell and I'll let you in." David ended the call and returned the phone to his jacket. "Thank you, Dee."

Reaching across the table, she placed her hand over his. "You're welcome."

David didn't want to question the universe as to why Devon had come into his life when it was in transition, and he'd found it a little unnerving that her life was also in flux. He couldn't begin to imagine what she'd gone through when she tried contacting her unborn baby's father only to encounter a series of roadblocks. She'd disclosed she'd never wanted children or marriage, yet she'd decided to become a single mother. Had she changed her mind because she was still in love with her ex?

The waiter arrived with their appetizers, setting the plates on the table. Waiting until he walked away, David picked up a fork. "May I serve you?" he asked Devon.

Their gazes met, fusing as a slow smile softened her features. "Please."

The appetizers were followed with Bibb and field greens salads and entrées of grilled Atlantic salmon with asparagus and blackened catfish with dirty rice. They kept each other entertained with stories about the idiosyncrasies of their college and law professors. David couldn't stop laughing when she imitated her tort professor who moonlighted as a Shakespearean actor. The witty man had conducted his lectures as if he were onstage, his vocal range fluctuating from soprano to baritone depending upon which character he'd identified with on any particular day.

"One week he was Beatrice from *Much Ado About Nothing*, then without warning he morphed into Orlando, the romantic lead of *As You Like It*. Despite his eccentricities— or maybe because of them—his classes were always well attended." She paused to take a sip of water. "Most of his students went to see him perform in the annual production of Shakespeare in the Park held at the Delacorte Theater in Central Park."

"Did you go see him?" David asked.

Devon nodded. "Yes. And he was very good."

"My law school experience wasn't quite as theatrical as yours," David began, "even though William and Mary had its share of oddball professors, including one who invited us to his home for wings and beer. I left many a Friday night tanked up on beer and feeling as if I could fly because I'd eaten so many wings."

Devon's eyes danced with amusement. "That is crazy!"

"What's crazy is that I gained twenty pounds and couldn't button any of my slacks."

Resting her elbow on the table, Devon cupped her chin on the heel of her hand. "Did you ever lose the weight?"

David nodded. "I started running. I began with a mile until eventually I was able to run five miles a day."

"Do you still run?"

"Not as much as I would like to. We have a health club at the office, and if I get in early enough I'll do a couple of miles on the treadmill or lift some weights, but not with any regularity. I was thinking of installing an in-home gym, which would allow me to work out before and after work."

"Why don't you join a sports club?" Devon asked.

"I've never been attracted to sports clubs. You're in great shape. Do you work out?"

Devon shook her head. "The only workout I get is walking. If you live in Manhattan you'll spend half your life walking, especially if you're going crosstown."

"What's the farthest you've ever walked?"

Her expression stilled, becoming almost somber. "It was on nine/eleven. I'd gone to Brooklyn to visit a friend and I had to walk across the Brooklyn Bridge to Manhattan. The subways weren't running, so I walked uptown to Eighty-Sixth Street to stay with an ex-roommate because I was too traumatized to be alone. We sat on her sofa, watching television for hours without saying a word. The realization of what had happened hit us at the same time and we started crying and couldn't stop. I stayed with her for two days because the soles of my feet were blistered from walking in heels."

David covered her hand with his. "I think everyone remembers where they were on the day the towers fell."'

"Sitting in her apartment and seeing the smoke, the fire, and people running for their lives haunted me for a long time."

Suddenly David was sorry he'd asked the question because he hadn't expected the answer would conjure up horrific memories for Devon. "Are you ready for dessert?"

Devon pressed a hand to her middle. "I can't eat another morsel."

"What if we share?"

She dropped her eyes before his steady gaze. "Okay. But only if we share."

Dinner ended with dessert, he paid the bill, and then hand in hand they walked to the parking lot. The return drive was accomplished in twice the time it took to drive to Charleston because David drove very slowly; he didn't want his time with Devon to end.

Devon sat on a rocker on the porch of the Cove Inn while David had settled into one beside her. She rested a hand over her belly. "I knew I ate too much."

Stretching out his legs and crossing his feet at the ankles, David closed his eyes. "Don't forget you're eating for two."

She smiled. "That may be true, but I really didn't need dessert."

"We shared it, so it barely counts."

"True." She hadn't been able to decide whether she wanted the vanilla bean crème brûlée or warm strawberry shortcake and had eventually ordered the shortcake. She covered her mouth with her hand to smother a yawn. "I know I should go inside and go to bed, but I can't move."

David stood up. "I'll carry you."

Devon panicked. "No!"

Crossing his arms over his chest, he angled his head. "You don't look heavy."

She pushed to her feet. "It doesn't matter, you're not carrying me."

He took a step, bringing them less than a foot apart. Cradling her waist, David pulled her close to his chest. "I'll carry you around to the side entrance. That way no one will see us."

Going on tiptoe, Devon kissed his cheek. "Good night and thank you for a wonderful dinner."

"The only thanks I want is for you to allow me to play superhero tonight. When we were kids, Jeff always made me play the sidekick because I was younger and smaller. I never got to play Batman or Superman."

Tilting her chin, Devon stared up at him. "If you had a cape, then you were a superhero."

"Are you saying the cape is the key to superpowers?"

She nodded.

"Who told you that?"

She smiled sweetly. "No one. But everyone knows it's all in the cape. Even Wonder Woman wore a cape on special occasions."

Lowering his head, David pressed a light kiss to the corner of her mouth. "We'll continue this in-depth discussion about superheroes at another time."

"David Junior. It's been a month of Sundays since I saw you last."

David smothered a groan when he recognized the voice. Rachel Dukes told anyone who stood still long enough to listen how she'd invested her life's savings and poured out her blood, sweat, and tears to restore the Cove Inn, an eight-thousand-square-foot, twenty-two-room mansion that had once been the winter residence of a Charleston-based cotton planter before the Civil War, to its original magnificence.

"Good evening, Miss Rachel." He turned to find the petite woman standing a short distance away. Rachel and her sister, Rose, were direct descendants of one of the first Gullah families who'd settled the island. Rose Dukes-Walker, owner of A Tisket A Basket, wove sweetgrass baskets, a tradition that would forever link the continent of Africa with the American Southeast.

"Oh...I'm sorry. I thought you were alone," Rachel stuttered.

David's right hand shifted from Devon's waist to her back. "I was just saying good night to my girlfriend."

Rachel's dark eyes narrowed suspiciously as she peered closely at him. "I didn't know you were keeping company."

He knew he'd put his foot in his mouth when he said Devon was his girlfriend. He'd only said it to protect her from what would become fodder for island gossip. The familiar adage of what you do in the dark will be revealed in the light was always in full effect on Cavanaugh Island. Rachel could casually mention she saw him kissing one of her guests and before the next sunrise it would be repeated like a chain letter.

"You know I don't like to flaunt my business," he said.

Rachel placed a finger over her mouth. "I promise I won't tell anyone."

David smiled and nodded, although he doubted she would keep her promise. "Thank you, Miss Rachel."

The innkeeper patted the coronet of snow-white braids pinned neatly atop her head. "Why don't you two come into the parlor and join the other guests for after-dinner drinks?"

Devon, speaking for the first time, said, "No thank you, Miss Rachel. Perhaps another time." She leaned into David. "We'll talk later."

"Okay, baby."

He watched her walk off the porch, open the door, and disappear inside. His gaze shifted to Rachel, who'd watched him watching Devon. "Have a good evening, Miss Rachel."

Rachel nodded. "Same to you."

David's cell rang two minutes after he pulled out of the inn's parking lot. Devon's name and number appeared on the navigation screen. Tapping the steering wheel, he activated the Bluetooth feature. "Yes, girlfriend?"

"Why did you tell Miss Rachel that I'm your girlfriend?"

"It was the only thing I could think of at that moment."

"We're not really dating, David."

"Why are you getting so bent out of shape?"

"I'm not getting bent out of shape. It's just that I don't want people believing we're a couple when we're not."

"Folks are going to believe what they want to believe, Devon, and there's nothing you or I can do about it. Would it bother you if we become a couple?" There was a swollen silence after he asked the question. "Dee? Are you still there?"

"Yes, I'm here."

"You didn't answer my question."

A soft sigh caressed his ear through the speaker. "No, it wouldn't bother me at all."

David couldn't stop the smile spreading across his features. "If that's the case, then 'Good night, sweetheart, well it's time to go,'" he sang, mimicking the Spaniels' classic doo-wop hit.

"Hey, you sound really good," Devon said.

"That's because I love doo-wop."

She laughed softly. "I'd expect you to be old-school rap, not doo-wop."

"I guess you can say I was born in the wrong decade."

"If that were the case, then you'd be too old for me," Devon teased. "And I'm not looking for a sugar daddy."

David nodded, although she couldn't see him. "And I've never been a cradle snatcher."

"On that note, I'm going to say good night. And thank you for dinner. I really enjoyed myself."

"I enjoyed it, too. When do you want to do it again?" he asked.

"Wednesday. I have to decide what I want to cook, then go grocery shopping."

"Heeey! So the girl wants to show me she has skills before Sunday's soiree."

"Don't hate, David. I told you I can cook."

"We'll see," he teased. "What time should I come by Wednesday?"

"Any time before seven."

"I'll see you then."

"Good night, David."

"Later, Dee."

Tapping another button, David tuned the radio to a station featuring cool jazz. He hadn't meant to refer to Devon as his girlfriend, but thankfully it hadn't backfired. His attraction to her intensified every time they shared the same space. He knew it was a combination of a physical and an emotional pull, but it was also a need to protect her. Whether she realized it or not, she was going to need a friend or friends before *and* after she had her baby. However, he found it odd that he'd spent almost three hours with Devon and not once had she mentioned her parents or sibling. Most women in her condition would've reached out to their families for emotional support.

David looked forward to their dinner date and the time when they would be able to officially announce they were a couple. David tapped the wheel again, tuning the radio to a station playing upbeat hip-hop. He sang and nodded his head along with the Chris Brown club hit "Turn Up the Music." Although partial to doo-wop, he preferred contemporary club music like Flo Rida's "Wild Ones" and Rihanna's "We Found Love." It'd been a while since he'd gone to the Happy Hour, and if he went again he wanted to take Devon with him. It was the only club on Cavanaugh Island that offered live and prerecorded music, food, and exotic cocktails catering to the twenty-five to forty crowd.

It'd been two years since he'd been in a relationship with a woman, and now that he'd met Devon he was glad he'd waited.

Chapter Eleven

❧

Devon sat on the veranda waiting for sunrise, a blanket wrapped around her body to ward off the early-morning chill. She'd spent a restless night tossing and turning until she finally left the bed to sit outside. She didn't want to believe she'd agreed to become involved with a man while she was carrying another man's baby.

There were things she remembered about last night and she realized she'd become someone she didn't like very much: a Gilmore woman. She'd been rude and condescending, and like Monique, when she criticized David for wearing a suit and tie and took him to task because he'd referred to her as his girlfriend when all he wanted was to protect her from small-town gossip. Pulling her knees to her chest, she closed her eyes. Being pregnant had changed her, turning her into a shrew.

Don't mess with your blessings, grandbaby girl. Devon heard her grandma Arlene's voice as clearly as if she were sitting next to her. If she were still alive, her father's mother would remind her that she had enough resources to live comfortably, the career she'd always wanted, and friends who'd promised to be there for her. David asking her to join his firm gave her the opportunity to practice law, and if she decided to continue to tutor for the New York Bar, she could do it either online or through video conferencing.

A knowing smile parted her lips when she thought of David. "I'm not going to mess with my blessings, Grandma," she whispered.

The hoot of an owl punctuated the eerie silence. Devon opened her eyes, taking in the awe of the nighttime sky brightening to a new day. The island was slowly waking up as the twitter of birds joined the owl's hooting. It was as if the nocturnal bird of prey didn't want to go to sleep. She closed her eyes again, falling asleep, and when she woke up the sun played a game of hide-and-seek with darkening clouds. The couple from a neighboring suite had joined her on the veranda, drinking coffee while talking quietly with each other.

Devon slipped off the chaise and returned to the bedroom. Twisted sheets and a jumble of pillows were obvious signs of her restlessness. She straightened the bed before crawling back into it and pulling the sheet and a blanket over her nightgown. Her last thought before sleep claimed her again was the image of David holding her hand and promising she wouldn't have to go through her pregnancy alone.

The weather changed dramatically, the sun disappearing behind dark storm clouds, and by early afternoon the skies opened up with a steady driving rain as temperatures plummeted from a high of sixty-five degrees to the midforties. Devon ventured outside despite the storm, eager to take in more of downtown before going to the local supermarket.

Instead of walking to the downtown business district, she drove.

A large banner across Main Street heralded Alice Parker, the winner in Sanctuary Cove's local mayoral election. Devon smiled. Cavanaugh Island had its first female elected official. It was truly a historic event. And she was about to buy a house here.

Devon figured she'd be able to move into her home on Cherry Lane before the Memorial Day weekend. Unlike Keaton's house, which needed major renovations, hers required little or no improvement—just ripping up carpeting, refinishing floors, and repainting. She knew how she wanted to decorate the house, but she planned to consult with Morgan at Dane and Daniels Architecture and Interior Design when it came to furniture.

Devon fantasized about the meals she would prepare in the rustic kitchen; the thought of grilling on the fireplace grate elicited a wide smile as she pulled into the area set aside for shopper parking. Using the fireplace meant she could grill all year regardless of the weather. Her ideas for her new home gave her a giddiness she hadn't experienced in a while. She wanted to plant a vertical garden with herbs and vegetables on an outside wall and put in a rock and flower garden with an array of wildflowers.

She had accepted that her life was going to change with a child totally dependent on her, and she had to be mentally ready for the challenge. Instead of on occasion coming home from a club at two in the morning, it would be two a.m. feedings. Devon knew it wasn't going to be easy in the beginning, but failing as a mother wasn't an option.

Pulling the hood of her bright yellow slicker over her head, she got out of the car and sprinted through Moss Alley, fittingly named because of its ancient oaks draped in Spanish moss. The aroma of baked goods wafted to her nose as she rounded the corner. The muffins, cookies, and pastries in the showcase window of the Muffin Corner beckoned her to come in and sample their goodness. Unable to resist the delicious-looking confections, she opened the door and walked in, a tiny bell over the door announcing her presence.

A woman came from the rear of the shop, flashing a gap-toothed grin. "Welcome to the Muffin Corner. I'm Mabel Kelly. Is there anything I can help you with?"

Pushing back her hood, Devon returned the smile of the short, stocky woman with a flawless, smooth, dark complexion. Several gray-streaked braids had escaped the white bouffant cap covering her hair. "I'm just looking."

"There's never a charge for looking."

After eating the strawberry shortcake the night before, Devon knew she definitely didn't need any more sugary foods. Her gaze shifted to a tray labeled COOKIE OF THE DAY. She pressed her finger to the showcase. "Are those oatmeal cookies?"

Bending slightly, Mabel reached for a cookie measuring an inch in diameter and handed it to Devon. "Yes."

She took a bite, chewing slowly. It had the texture of a soft cookie, but the taste reminded her of biscotti: slightly sweet, with chopped dates and golden raisins. "It's really good."

Mabel chuckled softly. "It's become a favorite for folks who are health conscious and don't like a very sweet cookie. They eat them instead of those overpriced protein bars because Iris makes them without using any processed sugar. If you eat protein bars, then four cookies equal one bar with less than half the calories."

"I like the sound of that. I'll take four."

Mabel completed the sale, placing the box of cookies in a small shopping bag with the Muffin Corner logo. "Thank you and please come again."

Devon dropped the bag into her tote. "I'm sure I will." Pulling up her hood, she left the bakery and headed in the opposite direction. When she visited Sanctuary Cove for the first time—before she returned to close on Keaton's property—she hadn't had time to tour the business district. It wasn't New York City's Fifth or Madison Avenues with high-end department stores and boutiques. There were no strip malls with row after row of stores and fast-food restaurants, but mom-and-pop shops catering to the immediate needs of those living in the town. Other than the Muffin Corner and Beauty Box, there was a supermarket, florist, liquor store, pharmacy with a post office, variety store, bank, ice cream shop, and bookstore.

A woman holding the hand of a small child emerged from the doctor's office several feet from the Parlor Bookstore; the little boy's face was red and streaked with tears. "My throat still hurts, Mama."

"Dr. Monroe says after I give you medicine the hurt will go away."

Devon watched the interchange between mother and child. Those living on the island were fortunate to have direct access to a resident doctor in the event of a medical emergency. She walked into the doctor's office and asked the receptionist for Dr. Monroe's business card.

"Do you want to make an appointment to see Dr. Monroe?" the woman asked.

"I . . . actually I don't need to see Dr. Monroe for a medical problem. I'm pregnant and I'd like him to recommend a local ob-gyn."

"I can get that information for you." Tapping several keys on her computer, she printed out a single sheet. "All of them have offices in or close to Charleston. Dr. Monroe highly recommends the first two on the list."

"Thank you so much."

"Good luck."

The smile parting Devon's lips reached her eyes. "Thank you again."

She continued walking along the street lined with palmetto trees, stopping at the florist. A man with a shaved head, a massive chest, and a colorful dragon tattoo on the side of his neck glared at her. There were tattooed Asian characters on each of his fingers.

"What can I do for you?"

Hold up, biker dude, Devon thought. If he sought to intimidate her with his angry stare, then he was sorely mistaken. Living in New York, occasionally riding the subway, and being confronted by panhandlers had toughened her up so that she didn't scare easily.

"Is it too late to deliver flowers to Charleston?"

"Where in Charleston?"

Devon reached into her tote, took out her wallet with David's business card, and handed it to Knuckles. "I'd like to send a bouquet of flowers to this person."

"We can do it, but it's going to cost you extra because we usually make deliveries between the hours of ten and two."

"I don't mind paying extra if it's going to get there today," she countered.

"Our normal delivery charge is twelve dollars. This will cost you an extra twenty."

Devon clenched her teeth in frustration. She'd told the man she didn't mind paying the extra charge. "That's not a problem. I'd like to send Mr. Sullivan a bouquet of a dozen yellow roses." She glanced around the shop at the flowers in the refrigerated case. "I'd like to include a few yellow tulips, lilies, and freesia."

He jotted down her order on a pad. "You sending yellow flowers to a man?"

"That's exactly what I intend to do," Devon retorted.

An elderly woman appeared from the rear of the shop, wiping her hands on a towel. "May I help you, miss?"

"I got it, Mom."

The woman extended her hand. "I'm Tammy. You must be new around here."

Devon shook her hand, feeling the roughness on her fingertips. "I am."

Tammy picked up the pad, reading what her son had written down, then noted the business card. She whistled softly. "So this is going to one of those big-shot lawyers on the mainland. I hear they're good, but they're a little too high priced for folks around here."

Devon wanted to tell her that would soon change when David opened his office in Haven Creek. She waited as Tammy itemized the bill for the bouquet, then included the charge for delivery. "Please add the cost of a vase," she told Tammy as she slid her credit card across the counter. "And I'd like to include a card with the flowers."

"Do you want a greeting card or the little ones folks usually attach to a bouquet?"

"A little card will do." Devon struggled with what to write on the card. She didn't want anything that sounded too romantic. Finally the words came to her: *Thank you for being you. Dee*

Her breathing stopped for several seconds, then started up

again when she saw the incredibly beautiful arrangement of sunny yellow flowers in a curving glass vase. "You're definitely an artist," she said, smiling at Tammy's son. He'd added several sprigs of baby's breath to break up the yellow.

The man smiled for the first time. "I'm a licensed tattoo artist. If you want some ink, then I'm your man."

"No, thank you."

"Well, if you ever change your mind, just let my mother know. I have a studio over in Goose Creek. I'm just helping out here because Pop is getting over the flu. I'll make sure these flowers get over to Mr. Sullivan before five."

Devon thanked him and walked out into the rain. She intended to make one more stop before returning to the Cove Inn. She had to shop for groceries. Visiting the bookstore and the Beauty Box would be left for another day.

"DJ, you need to come out here and see something."

David pressed the intercom button on his telephone console. "What is it, Angela?"

"Just come out and see."

Taking off a pair of black horn-rimmed glasses, he massaged his eyelids. "I'm in no mood for games, Angela. Either you tell me what you want me to see or hang up." He'd spent all night tossing and turning. With Devon moving to the Lowcountry, it was as if the planets in his personal universe were all aligned perfectly...until she mentioned she was having a baby.

"The florist from the Cove just delivered a vase of flowers for you."

David came to his feet, staring at the closed door. "Please bring it in."

"I can't, DJ. It's too heavy."

Rounding the desk, he walked across his office and opened the door. Angela sat in the alcove outside the office grinning at him like someone possessed. She gestured gracefully to the bouquet of flowers on the credenza as if she were presenting a game-show prize.

"I do believe this is a first for you."

David was momentarily speechless, an expression of complete surprise freezing his features. The assortment of yellow flowers was breathtaking. "It is," he said quietly once he recovered his voice. Several clients had sent cases of champagne or wine as gifts, but never flowers. He plucked the envelope off the cellophane.

"Aren't you going to take them with you?" Angela asked when he turned to go back to his office.

"No. Both of us can enjoy them if they're left out here."

"Someone must really like you because they're gorgeous."

David wanted to tell his assistant to stop prying. He closed the door and opened the envelope, a smile ruffling his mouth as he read the neat cursive. Reaching for his cell phone, he tapped in Devon's number. After the fourth ring it went to voice mail. "Dee, this is David. Please call me back."

His dark mood lifting, he sat down again to review the living will section for a new client's estate planning. Trevor had left the file with Angela less than an hour ago, even though he'd promised to have it on his desk at nine in the morning, not four in the afternoon. It was the first time the boy wonder had not met a deadline, and David wanted to tie up all of his cases before leaving.

He'd noticed Trevor appeared distracted when they'd gone to the popular sports bar only blocks from the office. The associate had ordered a second drink when he hadn't finished his first and David was forced to repeat himself as Trevor sat staring into space.

He didn't know what was going on in Trevor's personal life, but if he planned to make partner, he had to complete his assignments and submit them on time. Even when his own personal life unraveled after the breakup with his longtime girlfriend, David had never let it affect his work.

The cell phone vibrated. He picked it up. The caller wasn't who he expected. It was his cousin's wife. "What's up, Kara?"

"Do you remember Dawn Ramsey?"

"Wasn't she your maid of honor?"

"Yeah. She's coming down for a month and I'd like to bring her with us when we come to your house for March Madness on Sunday."

"No problem. The more the merrier."

"Thanks, cuz. Wait, don't hang up, David."

"What's up?"

"I know we talked about christening Austin at the end of May, but if Dawn is going to be here for a month, then what do you think if we christen him before she goes back to New York?"

"I don't have a problem with that." Jeff had asked David if he would be his son's godfather.

"Let me check with the secretary at the church to see when Reverend Crawford is available."

"No problem. Let me know the date and time and I'll be there."

"Thank you, David," Kara crooned in singsong.

He smiled. "You're welcome, cuz." David ended the call, his smile still in place. For the past three years, every other Sunday afternoon at his house during March Madness had become an annual event. The first time he'd suggested hosting the get-together, Petra refused to participate because she didn't like or understand the game of basketball. When he tried to explain the game to her, she covered her ears and rolled her eyes upward.

Slipping on his glasses, David picked up the section outlining designated beneficiaries, losing track of time and glancing up only when Angela knocked lightly on the door to let him know she was leaving for the day.

He peered at her over the reading glasses. "I thought you'd gone home already."

"I wanted to stay and finish up some paperwork. Remember I have a dental appointment in the morning, which means I won't get here until about noon."

He nodded. "Good night."

"Don't work too late." It was the same thing she said to him most nights.

"I won't," he said. David glanced at his watch. It was after seven, and Devon hadn't returned his call. When he dialed her cell again, it went straight to voice mail.

An uneasy feeling settled in his chest. *What if…No, no, no.* No doubt he was overreacting and she was fine. But he knew he wouldn't be able to relax until he heard her voice.

After dialing the number to the Cove Inn, he asked to be connected to Devon's room. Again the phone on the other end rang incessantly until it connected to the suite's messaging system. He hung up without leaving a message. Maybe he was worrying about nothing, but he doubted she would be out at night, in the rain, on an island with unlit roads.

Twenty minutes later, David pulled into the inn's visitor parking area. He'd exceed the island's unofficial twenty-mile-an-hour speed limit to get to the Cove Inn in half the time it would normally take to make the drive. Some of his anxiety eased when he spotted Devon's hybrid. By the time he climbed the porch steps and walked into the lobby he was back in control.

David didn't recognize the desk clerk on duty. Rachel made it a practice to hire students from local colleges. "Good evening. Could you please ring Miss Rachel and let her know David Sullivan would like to speak to her."

The young man with spiked hair flashed a practiced smile. "I'm sorry, but Miss Rachel just went into the dining room."

"Then I'll wait here while you go and give her my message. Now please, Kenneth," he drawled facetiously, noting the name badge pinned to the clerk's vest.

David paced back and forth in front of the mahogany counter. He didn't have to wait long. Rachel gave him a questioning look. "What's the matter?"

Cupping her elbow, he escorted her away from the desk, so the clerk couldn't eavesdrop on their conversation. "I tried calling Devon, but she's not answering her cell or the phone in her suite. I know she's here because I saw her car in the lot. I need you to open her door so I can make certain she's all right."

"Of course, son. You should've called me directly and I would've checked on her for you. Follow me. I take the elevator because these old knees ain't what they used to be. Can you believe I used to run track? One year I even competed in the Penn Relays."

"I never knew that," David said absentmindedly as he held the door to the elevator to let Rachel precede him. The door closed and the car rose smoothly to the second floor.

Rachel continued to talk about her racing achievements

as they walked the carpeted hallway to Devon's suite. Rachel knocked, and when she didn't get an answer, she reached into the pocket of her jacket, took out the master cardkey, and inserted it into the slot. After the light changed from red to green, she pushed the door open.

"She's all yours."

"Thank you, Miss Rachel."

Closing the door softly, David entered the suite. The living and dining areas were dark, as was the kitchen. David flicked on lights as he made his way into the bedroom. One lamp on the nightstand was turned to the lowest setting. Then he saw her. Devon lay in bed, on her back, her chest rising and falling in an even rhythm. Waves of relief swept over him. She hadn't answered the phone because she was asleep. Now he felt foolish. He'd panicked prematurely.

He took a backward step, nearly losing his balance when he almost slipped on the magazines scattered about the floor. He smothered a curse at the same time her eyes opened. Wide-eyed, she sat up, seemingly in slow motion.

Her hands were shaking. "David?" His name came out in a breathless whisper.

He nodded. "Yes."

"What are you doing here?"

David couldn't pull his gaze away from the swell of her breasts in the revealing tank top. His gaze moved up to her unbound hair falling to her shoulders. She wasn't just sexy; she was sensual, voluptuous.

"I was worried about you—you weren't answering your phone. Plus, I came to thank you for the flowers and to take you back to my place so I can make you dinner. If you don't want to come home with me, then I'll go pick up something from the supermarket and fix it here." He knew he was rambling. Something he rarely did. It was either talk or think about the hardening flesh between his thighs.

Moving off the bed, she closed the distance between them. In bare feet the top of her head was level with his shoulders. David swallowed a groan. Devon was standing so close he could feel her body's heat and inhale the lingering scent of her perfume. He held his hands in front of his fly to conceal his erection.

"I must have fallen asleep after getting back from the grocery store," she said. "What time is it now?"

He checked his watch. "It's seven fifty. How about I make you dinner?"

She massaged the back of her neck while rolling her head from one side to the other. "You'd cook for me?" He nodded like a bobblehead doll at the same time she shook her head. "I can't believe you, David."

"What can't you believe?"

"You let yourself into my suite, woke me out of the first sound sleep I've had all day, and now you want to commandeer my kitchen."

"You like it, don't you?" he asked with a grin.

"Like what?"

"Someone looking after you. Caring about what happens to you."

Chapter Twelve

$\backsim$

Devon wanted to deny that she didn't need David looking after her, but she knew it was a lie. All her life she'd prayed for the strength to rebel against her structured upbringing, and when she eventually found the freedom to determine her own future she guarded it jealously. She was free to choose her own career path, who to become involved with, and where she wanted to live. Now, if she allowed David to take care of her then she would have to relinquish some of her hard-won independence that had caused her to lose her family.

"Why do you want to take care of me?"

His eyes moved slowly over her face. "Remember what I told you about friends?" She nodded. "Down here, not only do we look after our friends, we also take care of them. And I'm also willing to run interference when folks realize you're pregnant and assume I'm the father."

Her eyes grew wider. "Why would you do that?"

"Why not? After all, you agreed we are going to be a couple."

She didn't want to think he had an ulterior motive, because there was no way she would become physically involved with him—not as long as she was carrying another man's child. "I seem to recall you just suddenly announced I was your girlfriend. Did I ever actually agree?" she teased.

"Oh, but how could you resist?" He threw his head back, full of charm. He took her hand in his and kissed the back of it. "Now come with me to the kitchen, my fair lady, and show me what you want to eat."

"I thought I was going to cook for you tomorrow night."

"You can still do that if you want, but tonight I'm the head chef."

She pulled her hand out of his loose grip. "I have to take care of a few things first." Devon didn't want to tell him that whenever she felt pressure on her bladder she couldn't delay getting to a bathroom. Turning on her heel, she practically ran out of the bedroom, David following close behind as she closed the door to the bathroom in his face.

"You didn't give me your answer," he shouted at the door.

"About what?" she shouted back.

"That you'll call me if you need help settling into your house or for any other emergency that may come up."

Devon sighed in relief. She'd made it just in time not to embarrass herself. "Yes, David."

She wanted to tell him she didn't need him as much now as she would after she had the baby. Devon knew she would have to hire a plumber or electrician to take care of repairs in the house, but she would need a man's help when it came to rearranging furniture. She was a little obsessive-compulsive when it came to a room's balance and symmetry. She'd also become a feng shui expert. Every spring she cleared her apartment of clutter because she believed it blocked her chi and compromised her well-being.

The door opened slightly. "Can I come in so we can shake on it?"

"David Sullivan, don't you dare come in here!" His mocking laugh came through the slight opening. "It's not funny."

"I'm going, baby."

She closed her eyes when she heard the endearment. It was the second time David had called her baby, and she wondered if it was a slip of the tongue.

She washed her hands, then brushed her hair until the curls were smooth and secured them with an elastic band. Twice a year she had her hairstylist apply a texturizer to relax her naturally curly hair, but she now had to forgo it because her obstetrician had cautioned her not to use any chemicals on her hair. She lingered in the bedroom long enough to slip on an oversize T-shirt over her tank top, straighten the sheets and blankets, and pick up several magazines that had fallen off the bed.

She walked into the kitchen to find David peering into the freezer drawer, which was filled with meats and frozen foods. He'd removed his jacket and tie, hanging them on the back of one of the dining area chairs. Her gaze lingered on his slim waist and hips in a pair of trousers that were the perfect fit for his tall, slender physique. *Dapper* and *fastidious* were two words that came to mind if she had to describe him. With his lean, dark chiseled face, balanced features, and sexy cleft chin, he'd be a perfect candidate for the cover of a men's fashion magazine.

David glanced over his shoulder at her. "You have quite a stockpile of food. Don't you like the meals they serve here?"

Devon rested a hip against the countertop. "I don't mind the buffet breakfast and lunch. Dinner is another matter, because it's sit-down and most of the table conversation is about grown kids and grandchildren, of which I have neither. It's either cook for myself or order room service. And I'm not saying the food isn't good, but I'm trying to eat healthfully."

David closed the freezer drawer and turned to face her. "You have the ingredients to make chicken piccata. You also have linguine, so I should be able to whip something up in less than thirty minutes."

She pressed her palms together and whispered a silent prayer of gratitude. The man who'd appointed himself her protector knew how to cook. "When you said you'd make dinner I thought it would be something like grilled franks or peanut butter and jelly sandwiches," she teased.

"That's cold, Dee."

"I'm sorry. So I've hooked up with a Renaissance man."

"Not really," he said humbly. "If I hadn't gone into law I definitely would've become a chef."

"You and Keaton share that in common. He comes from a family of chefs. By the way, he's an incredible cook."

Reaching into an overhead cabinet, David took down a glass, rinsed it in the sink, and filled it with unsweetened almond milk. He handed Devon the glass. "Maybe one of these days he and I will share cooking duties."

"Do you do a lot of entertaining?"

David rolled back his shirt cuffs. "No. March Madness is it. I usually spend all day Saturday prepping what I plan to serve on Sunday."

"I take it you like basketball."

"Love it," he confessed. "The day my dad bought a basketball hoop for my twelfth birthday and set it up in the backyard I thought my world couldn't get any better. I'd shoot hoops rain or shine, summer or winter. Most of the boys in the neighborhood would hang out at my house because I had the best hoop. It all came to a crashing halt when a couple of the boys got into a fight and one threw a rock and broke a window. They scattered like mice when you turn on the light, and after that my mother banned them from the property. Once I entered high school I discovered I had other interests."

"Like girls?" Devon teased.

David winked at her. "Nah. I discovered them before I got to high school."

Her jaw dropped. "Please don't tell me you were sleeping with girls in middle school."

"No comment."

"If I have a boy and I find out he's sleeping with girls when he's that young I don't know what I'd do."

"You'd sit his little randy ass down and let him know if he doesn't use a condom, then you're going to wait until he falls asleep and then turn him into a eunuch."

Devon laughed so hard her ribs hurt. "Is that what your mother said to you?"

"You're damn skippy. Dad was pretty cool, but it was my mother who put the fear of God into me and my sister. After a while we realized she was blowing smoke and let whatever she had to say go in one ear and out the other."

Devon drained the glass, then plucked a banana off the bunch on the countertop. "Where did you learn to cook?" she said, as he palmed a lemon. She wanted to know more about the man moving confidently about the kitchen opening cabinets as if he knew exactly where she'd stored jars of herbs and spices, canned goods, and boxes of cereal and pasta.

"I try to take a couple weeks off during the spring or summer and go to either Italy or France for cooking seminars. I took a course on which wines to pair with cheese, seafood, pork, duck, sauces, poultry, beef, lamb, and game. Once you have your baby, I'll make a special meal for you, beginning with a cheese platter, artisan bread, and a salad of bitter chicories. Then I'll serve you a duck confit with a glass of either a dry Riesling or a Chilean Pinot Noir."

She watched him rinse the thin, boneless chicken breasts, then blot the excess moisture with a paper towel. "That sounds delicious. You are really full of surprises, aren't you?"

He gave her a wide smile. "Speaking of surprises, what if I tell you that you may be able to close on your house within three weeks?"

Devon clapped a hand over her mouth. "That's more than a surprise," she said through splayed fingers. "What did you do?"

"I called your Realtor and he faxed me the specs on your house. I have a contact at a local title company who promised to make you a priority. I also got in touch with an engineer who will make certain the house is structurally sound and that the plumbing and electrical pass inspection. He'll give you a report of his findings if you to need to make repairs or upgrades."

Devon lowered her hand. "I could kiss you."

Extending his arms, David winked at her. "Come and put one right here." He pointed to his mouth.

She shook her head. "Just kidding."

"Oh, so the pretty lady is a tease."

"No, David. I'll show you I'm not a tease."

She stood up and walked over to him, putting her arms around his neck as she went on tiptoe. His head came down as if in slow motion, and she inhaled his moist breath before his mouth covered hers in a tender joining she didn't want to end. It wasn't a kiss filled with unbridled passion but one that seemed to heal her, sweep away any doubt that she'd been wrong for agreeing to become involved with him. Devon quivered at the sweet tenderness of the kiss and at that moment she longed to take off her clothes and lie with him. It was with a great deal of reluctance that she ended the kiss, her breasts heavy, her nipples distended and tingling.

With wide eyes, David stared down at her as if he'd never seen her before. Devon rested her cheek on his chest, counting the rapid runaway beating of his heart. It was more than apparent he hadn't been unaffected by the kiss. "Now do you believe I'm not a tease?" she whispered against the fabric of his crisp shirt.

He pressed his palms against her back. "I may need another demonstration before I can answer that question."

She chuckled softly. "I give only one demonstration per day."

David kissed the top of her head. "Stingy are you?"

Tilting her head, Devon met eyes the color of rich, dark coffee. "You have to work up to more than one a day," she teased.

His eyebrows flickered. "What do I have to do to earn multiple kisses?"

She pulled her lower lip between her teeth as she mulled over David's question. "I don't know. I haven't come up with a strategy yet." The shocked expression on his face was priceless.

David tightened his hold on her body, pulling her closer until her breasts were crushed against the hardness of his chest. "You lied," he whispered. "You *are* a tease. An incredibly gorgeous tease and a temptation who, just being who she is, makes me want to spend time with her. I've laughed more with you than with any other woman I've been involved with."

"Is that a good thing, David?"

The corners of his firm mouth lifted slightly. "What do you think, Dee?"

She scrunched up her nose. "I think it is. Were you ever married?" The question was out before she could censor herself.

David dropped his arms and walked back to the sink. "No."

"Why not?"

"I haven't met the woman I'd like to spend the rest of my life with."

Devon took a bite of the banana. "So, you do date?"

"I do. But it has been a couple of years since I've been in a committed relationship."

"What happened?" Devon asked.

"I dated someone for five years—"

"That's a long time," she interrupted.

"She felt so too. A week before I was going to take her away and propose, she told me she'd met someone else. I later learned she'd been sleeping with several other men at the same time."

Devon shook her head. "That is so wretched."

"It was a good reality check that I'd taken her for granted. I'd made partner and I wanted to wait a couple of years to get the experience I needed to set up my own firm. It wasn't until she left that I realized it was very selfish of me to ask her to wait when she wanted to marry and start a family."

"Are you over her?"

Devon wanted to know if he still had feelings for his ex, because the more time she spent with David, the more she felt an invisible magnetism pulling them together. Was it destiny that put all the right pieces in place for her to find him?

David took so long to answer her question that Devon thought he hadn't heard her. "Now I am," he admitted in a low, quiet tone.

Devon felt a chill sweep over her body when his gaze moved from her face to her chest. The smoldering flame in his eyes caused a slight throbbing between her thighs. The hormonal changes in her body had heightened her libido and elicited erotic dreams that woke her in the throes of multiple orgasms shaking her from head to toe.

"Let's promise each other that from this point on we never mention our exes again."

She closed her eyes for several seconds. "I promise."

Smiling, David inclined his head. "I second that."

Devon decided to change the topic. Like David, she didn't like dredging up her past. "If I'd known we were going to have an Italian meal, I would've put up some dough for bread."

"You make your own bread?"

"I do," she drawled confidently. "I'm not quite a domestic goddess, but I can cook, bake, and sew."

"My grandmother used to say a woman had to learn to cook if she wanted to land a husband. But you just sit and relax. Enjoy it now, because once you have little Debbie or

Johnny you'll have your hands full with changing diapers and trying to catch up on your sleep."

She smiled when he mentioned little Debbie. It was too early to confirm the sex of her baby, but Devon prayed for a girl. It would be easier for her as a single mother to raise a girl than a boy. Sons needed fathers in their lives to teach them how to become men.

"Are you speaking from experience?"

David stared at her as if she were a stranger. "I just remember Aunt Corrine used to fuss with Kara about getting up early and making breakfast for Jeff at six in the morning when she should've stayed in bed, because once she had the baby she'd barely have time to make her own breakfast."

Devon remembered Kara rushing to get to Jack's because she had to use a breast pump to express milk for her son's next feeding. "I don't mind sitting, but I need to do something with my hands, like knitting or quilting."

"So you really are a Martha Stewart?"

"Not quite. But I am looking forward to cooking in my new home." She told David about the rustic kitchen with the brick walls and a wood-burning fireplace. "I haven't decided whether to replace floor bricks with wood floorboards."

"What about the walls?"

"I want to keep the brick. They may need cleaning, but other than that they add a lot of character to the space."

Her voice filled with excitement and anticipation, Devon gave David a room-by-room description of the house she planned to call home as he put up a pot of water for linguine. She saw his cooking skills firsthand as he prepared the chicken piccata, linguine tossed with fresh minced garlic and virgin olive oil, and a mixed citrus salad with thinly sliced red onion and escarole and vinaigrette.

She set the table in the dining area with plates and serving pieces and when they sat down together it seemed so natural, as if it was something they did often. She swallowed a fork-ful of linguine. It was delicious. "Next time I'm cooking."

David lifted a glass of water. "I'll drink to that."

It was minutes after eleven when Devon practically pushed David out the door. They'd cleaned the kitchen to-gether, then retreated to the living room. They lay on the sofa together watching *Pretty Woman*. "I'll see you Friday night for the interview with Cynthia."

Holding her face between his palms, David kissed her forehead. "Remember, we're going to see each other tomor-row."

Devon held on to his wrist. "Oops. I forgot about that. Thank you for making dinner."

He kissed her again, this time on the mouth. "Good night."

"Good night," she whispered as he turned, walked out, and closed the door. "We really are a couple," she said aloud.

Chapter Thirteen

Devon sat across the table from the young woman, noting her full hips, wavy light brown hair, peaches-and-cream complexion, and large coffee-brown eyes. Cynthia Humphries was a beautiful young woman.

Devon positioned the tape recorder so it would record both voices. "Miss Humphries—"

"Please call me Cynthia."

Devon paused, smiling. "Okay, Cynthia. Mr. Sullivan asked me to interview you because he thought you'd feel more comfortable talking with a female attorney." She noticed Cynthia rubbing her forefingers over her thumbs. She was obviously nervous. "I've gone over your file and discovered you have two degrees in education and another in computer science. That's quite an accomplishment for a young woman who has yet to celebrate her thirtieth birthday."

Cynthia dropped her gaze, staring at her fidgety fingers. "I like learning."

Devon knew if she got Cynthia to talk about herself,

rather than hurl questions about her being discriminated against, she probably would be more unguarded. "But you decided not to be a teacher?"

Cynthia met Devon's eyes for the first time. "After I completed student teaching, I realized I wasn't cut out to be a classroom teacher, so I became a consultant and trainer."

"What made you study computer programming?"

An attractive blush crept over Cynthia's face. "I've always been a computer geek." She paused, picking up the glass of water on the coaster and taking a sip. "When I went online and saw a job posting for an assistant researcher for an independent publisher of children's and educational textbooks, I knew I was the perfect candidate based on their specifications and my education and experience. I updated my résumé and emailed it to them.

"A week later I got a phone call from someone in HR asking me to come in for an interview. Unfortunately I'd just had foot surgery and couldn't walk or drive, so I suggested they interview me in a video chat. It went well and I had a second video interview the following week. Because I was seated, all they saw was me from the chest up. The publisher called me the next day offering me the job. We discussed salary and benefits and he told me I could start pending medical clearance from my doctor."

"Did anyone follow up the call with a letter stating your start date?"

"Yes. They sent me a packet by certified mail with the forms I needed to complete for health insurance coverage and payroll deductions and the company's policy and procedure manual. I had to sign and return the page indicating I'd read the handbook."

"What title were you given when you were first hired?"

"Assistant researcher."

"What was your supervisor's reaction when you showed up at the office for the first time?"

"He was unable to hide his shock when I introduced myself as Cynthia Humphries. It took him about two minutes before he told me to wait in the reception area. The office manager came out twenty minutes later and gave me some bullshit story about having to move my office because of a leak. She said workmen were scheduled to come in to rip up the carpet and replace ceiling tiles."

Devon leaned over the table. "Why did you believe it was a lie?"

"How long does it take to make repairs to a twelve-by-twelve office? Definitely not three years. They put me in a cubbyhole next to the mailroom and whenever I had to confer with my supervisor I had to walk halfway around the office to see him. I knew I wasn't imagining his revulsion because he never looked me in the eye."

Although full figured, Devon found Cynthia well groomed. Her black sheath dress was perfect for her curvy figure. "How was your relationship with other employees?"

"It was good. We ate lunch together in the office lunchroom and every couple of weeks we'd hang out on Fridays for happy hour."

Lacing her fingers together, Devon gave Cynthia a long, penetrating stare. "So it was only your supervisor who seemed to have a problem with your appearance?"

"Yes, Miss Gilmore."

"Do you have proof of this?"

Cynthia closed her eyes. "I overheard someone saying that Mr. Gantt couldn't bear to be in the same room with me because I reminded him of a beached whale."

"If we were to subpoena this person, would they be willing to testify under oath that he said this?"

Cynthia opened her eyes, blinking back tears. "I doubt it, because there might be reprisals from upper management." She sniffled and sucked in a breath. "I've always had a problem carrying most of my weight below my waist and I've tried every diet in existence. I'd lose a few pounds, then pack them back on when I was stressed out. I've been the brunt of every fat joke imaginable. I know Mr. Gantt would've never hired me if I'd had an in-person interview."

Devon wanted to tell Cynthia she was right if the man really did harbor an intense dislike of overweight people. "Tell me about your being passed over for promotion."

"After the company expanded the digital department, they posted a position on what we call the community board for a programmer. My supervisor, who'd been promoted to head that department, would have to approve the candidate for the position. Although I didn't expect to get the position, I still applied. I got the customary thank-you-for-applying rejection letter and let it pass. However, I continued to get raises and favorable evaluations."

"Why didn't you leave?" Devon asked her.

"I needed the money because I'd just bought a condo. Meanwhile, I'd been working at home coding a curriculum program for homeschooled children in grades K through twelve. Companion books and teacher guides would accompany each subject for every grade. There was another posting for a programmer a year later for which candidates had to submit samples of their projects."

"You gave them the software for your homeschool curriculum?"

A wry smile twisted Cynthia's mouth. "No. I gave them

something else. I wasn't ready to shop the curriculum project because I knew a tech company would offer a lot more than a promotion with a raise. They rejected my submission and I was again passed over for a promotion. Each time they would hire someone from outside the company when they professed to hire from within in order to boost morale. That's when I decided I'd had enough and quit."

"If you left of your own accord, then why are you suing them for discrimination?"

"Because someone at the company sent me an anonymous letter with the news Johnston and Jennings Publishing was selling my program to schools and colleges."

A frown appeared between Devon's eyes. "Why isn't this detailed in your original deposition?"

"Because I met the informant earlier today. That's why I didn't want to talk with Mr. Sullivan until tonight."

Devon carefully schooled her expression not to reveal her excitement. If Cynthia's former employer was selling her program, then she was entitled to a portion of the sales. "How did this person know it's your program?"

"She overheard them bragging about it in a closed-door meeting. Mr. Gantt said I did them a favor by resigning because they got their money's worth out of the fat cow. She said they were laughing about keeping Baby Huey in the corner. She was so angry she couldn't remain silent any longer because J and J had fostered a culture of not promoting their female employees as quickly as they did the men."

Reaching into her oversize handbag on the table, Cynthia took out a large plastic box filled with computer disks. "Here's what J and J Publishing is selling." She pushed another box with a half dozen disks across the table. "They've condensed eighteen disks into six."

"How did they get your prototype?" The silence following Devon's questioning was deafening.

Chewing nervously on her lips and rubbing her thumbs, Cynthia sniffled again. "There was a company rule against fraternizing, but I kind of liked this guy who worked in the digital unit and I would occasionally flirt with him over lunch. One day I told him about my coding but warned him not to tell anyone. Then…"

Devon shook her head. She knew instinctually what had happened, because all over the world some man was taking advantage of a woman for his own personal gain. "He seduced you and eventually you let him see it." The tears filling Cynthia's eyes overflowed, running down her cheeks to her chin. Devon flicked off the tape recorder. Rounding the table, she sat next to Cynthia. "Don't cry, honey. We're going to make those bastards pay."

The floodgates opened as Cynthia wept openly against her shoulder. "He said things to me no man has ever said. He called me beautiful… said that… that he wanted to spend the rest of his life with me. I didn't want to tell Mr. Sullivan that it was the first time I'd slept with a man because I didn't want him to think—"

"Mr. Sullivan is your attorney and it's his responsibility to protect your interests, not judge you," Devon said, cutting her off. Now she knew why Cynthia hadn't told David the entire story. Devon took a tissue from the box on the desk and blotted Cynthia's face. "I want you to answer one question for me."

"What is it?" Cynthia whispered, reaching for another tissue and blowing her nose.

"Did you copyright your software?"

She nodded. "I researched intellectual property rights and

discovered they are the foundation of the software industry."

Devon pumped her fist. In their haste and greed, J and J Publishing had underestimated Cynthia Humphries. She patted the woman's back. "Go to the restroom and fix your face. Mr. Sullivan will take over now."

Cynthia hugged Devon so tightly she thought she was going to strangle her. "Thank you, Miss Gilmore. I feel so much better."

"You're pretty and very smart. Don't ever let anyone define who you are."

Waiting until Cynthia disappeared behind the door to the restroom, Devon picked up the recorder and walked out the conference room and into David's office.

David stood up when Devon walked in. His admiring gaze moved slowly from her hair, which was in a sophisticated twist, to her black double-breasted pantsuit and matching patent leather pumps. The single strand of pearls around her slender neck matched the studs in her ears. She'd morphed effortlessly from tourist to attorney. He'd had to cancel their Wednesday dinner date when a client called him after he was arrested for assaulting his sister's abusive boyfriend.

Smiling, she handed him the tape recorder. "Everything you need to sue the hell out of J and J Publishing is on this tape." She gave him a brief overview of her interview with Cynthia. "Are you familiar with computer law and intellectual property protection?"

David's hand tightened on the small instrument. Devon had done in less than half an hour what he hadn't been able to do in two hours. "No, but we have someone on staff who is. I can't believe you got her to talk."

"It's all about girl power."

It took all of David's self-control not to hug her. Several attorneys were working late and he didn't want to risk one walking in on them. She had arrived five minutes before Cynthia and he'd escorted her to the conference room as he would a client.

"I owe you, Dee."

"No, you don't," she said quietly. "This firm owes it to that young woman to make it right, and I'm willing to bet her that former employer will settle rather than go to trial, because it could prove quite embarrassing for one of their executives once women's groups are made aware of his views about full-figured women. You'll also need to get the names of the people who can back up her testimony before drawing up subpoenas."

"I'm going to make this case a priority," David promised.

"Do you think you will settle it before you leave?"

"I'm not going to give it a time limit. I'll continue to work the case until Cynthia gets her dignity back."

Devon rested a hand on his shirtsleeve. "That's good."

"Don't you want to go for drinks to celebrate?" he asked when she scooped her tote off the chair beside his desk.

"Ask me again next year around this time and I'll take you up on your offer." She blew him an air-kiss. "I can find my way out."

Cupping her elbow, David steered her out of the office. He'd forgotten she couldn't drink while pregnant. "I'm going to walk you to your car."

"David, please go and talk to your client."

"She's not going anywhere." He reached for her hand. "You agreed to let me take care of you," he whispered in her ear, "so let me play superhero, because right now I'm the one with the magic cape."

She giggled softly. "Who are you tonight? Batman or Superman?"

David reached over Devon's head, holding open the door leading to the parking lot. "Spider-Man."

"But he doesn't wear a cape."

"Don't hate on Peter Parker. Cape or no cape, he's a real cool dude."

"Please don't tell me you're a comic book junkie."

"I *was* a junkie. I still have my collection packed away at my parents' place. One of these days I'll take you there and show it to you."

Devon stopped short, causing him to almost trip over her. "Your parents' place?"

"Yes, my parents." She pressed a button on the Prius door handle, and David opened the driver's side door for her. "I'm certain they'll adore you."

"No, David!" Devon protested. "Our friends and the whole town are already going to assume you're my baby's father."

"So let them."

"But even your parents?"

"Do you actually think they aren't going to hear about us?" David asked her. "And I'm willing to bet my mother will want to meet you sooner rather than later."

"I'd rather it be later," Devon said under her breath.

David shifted to the right, stopping her from getting into the car.

"I'll tell them you don't want to use the baby as leverage to get me to marry you."

"I'm certain they didn't raise you to become a baby daddy."

"They didn't," he confirmed. "But as they say, times have

changed. Shotgun marriages are a thing of the past. What about your parents? Do they know you're pregnant?"

"Yes, but I don't want to talk about them. I'll call you tomorrow for an update on Cynthia."

"Call me before eleven, because after that I'll be out of the office." He moved aside, watching as she got into the car. He closed the door, smiling.

Blowing him another kiss, she started the engine and drove away, leaving him staring at the lights on the rear of the hybrid vehicle.

David didn't have to have the IQ of a rocket scientist to know Devon's relationship with her parents wasn't warm and fuzzy. Were they disappointed with her decision to become a single mother? Under the façade of being a strong, independent woman, he suspected she wasn't as secure as she seemed.

A man with whom she'd had a relationship abruptly shut her out of his life, leaving her to uncover his duplicity when she was most vulnerable. A pregnant woman—whether married, single, or in a relationship—shouldn't have to go it alone. David knew folks would talk when they suspected Devon was carrying his child. However, he would be better prepared to combat the gossip than Devon. Turning on his heel, he retraced his steps and walked into the conference room, where Cynthia stood staring at paintings depicting fox-hunting scenes. "Miss Humphries?"

She turned around. Her lips parted in a smile. "She was awesome."

He knew Cynthia was referring to Devon. "Yes, Miss Gilmore is quite remarkable." He pulled out a chair. "Please sit down." Waiting until she was seated, he took the chair at the head of the table and set a legal pad and pen in front of her.

"We can sue J and J for sexual discrimination and for stealing your software program, but I'll need you to work with me. You have to tell me everything."

Cynthia nodded. "I can do that. How much do you think we'll be able to get?"

"How much would a tech company offer for your software?"

Cynthia exhaled an audible breath. "Maybe ten to fifteen million."

David's smile matched hers. "Okay. We ask for fifteen million for the theft of the software and between two and five million for sexual discrimination. But first I'll need the names of people who will testify on your behalf." He pushed a pad toward her.

"Will there be a trial?" she asked, as she made a tidy list on the page.

"I'm going to suggest they settle because trials can be long and very costly." And David doubted whether the heirs to Johnston & Jennings Publishing wanted the 150-year-old family-owned multi-award-winning children's book and textbook publishing house's reputation tainted by scandal. He glanced at the names on the pad.

"Do you need anything else from me, Mr. Sullivan?"

"Not at this time, Miss Humphries. I'll be in touch if I need anything." Cynthia stood, and he rose with her. "I'll see you out."

Chapter Fourteen

Richmond, Virginia

A ringtone punctuated the silence in the ostentatiously furnished living room. A sweep of false lashes fluttered as the young woman reclining on a butter-yellow silk-covered chaise glanced up from her smartphone. "Mr. Emerson, you may go in now."

Gregory Emerson forced a smile, meeting the sea-green eyes of the barely legal wife of an aide to the governor, who'd spent the last fifty minutes filing and buffing her nails and texting, totally ignoring him after he'd driven nearly one hundred miles from Newport News to the state capital for a rare Saturday meeting. She wasn't even gracious enough to ask if he wanted water or coffee.

"Thank you, Mrs. Hanson."

A door opened and Charles Hanson stuck his head through the opening. "Come on in, Emerson. Sorry you had to wait but I couldn't get one of the governor's very generous constituents off the phone."

Chuck, as he was referred to in the press, was all teeth and hair. His porcelain veneers looked like the Mentos that Gregory's mother used whenever she attempted to mask the smell of alcohol on her breath, and Chuck's coiffed, dyed black hair was a return to the greaser comb back. Even his black tracksuit was retro. Appearance notwithstanding, the man had earned a reputation as a brilliant political strategist. He had the Midas touch. Every candidate he supported won.

"Sit over there," Chuck ordered as if Gregory were a dog following commands.

Gritting his teeth, Gregory sat on a worn leather armchair as the aide dropped to a matching chair opposite him. The space where Chuck conducted business reminded him of a study hall at a venerable university. The oak tables, built-in bookcases, and leather seating arrangement were totally incongruent to the occupant with the flamboyant personality of a Vegas showman. He stared at the man who'd recently married his fourth wife, a woman half his age, and it was apparent his plastic surgeon had pulled the skin on his face so tight Gregory marveled that he could actually see out of the slits passing for eyes.

"How's the governor?"

Chuck rubbed his palms together. "He's well but he's also concerned about Congressman Earley Guilford. That's why he wanted me to meet with you. I'm going to give it to you straight, no chaser. Guilford confided to the governor that he's going to announce his retirement in the coming months due to failing health. We went through names for his replacement and yours came up on top of a very short list."

Sinking lower in the chair, Gregory whispered a silent prayer of gratitude. He'd studied hard and worked even harder to achieve success and apparently it'd paid off. "Please tell the governor I'm grateful he's even considering me to replace Congressman Guilford."

Chuck waved a hand. "Cut the bowing and scraping, Emerson. You may be a brilliant litigator, but if you want a career in politics, then you have to be convincing and persuasive and not kowtow to anyone, and that includes our governor. If he detects a modicum of weakness in you, then there's nothing I could do or say to get him to change his mind once you're cut from the list."

Gregory's jaw hardened as he clenched his teeth. He may be many things, but weak didn't figure into the equation. Now, if the political strategist had accused him of being too arrogant or even overly ambitious, he would've readily agreed with him. "Point taken," he said, the two words filled with defiance.

"If the governor appoints you to serve out the remainder of Guilford's term, then we need to know if there's anything in your past that would hinder you from being elected in your own right."

"Like what?" Gregory questioned.

"Like drugs, DWIs, or getting arrested for soliciting a hooker."

"Wouldn't you know that already if my name is on your short list? Should I assume you've already vetted me?"

Chuck sat up, an expression of shock causing him to attempt to open his eyes wider as a hint of a smile parted his lips. "You're right. We have vetted you, but there are some things known only to the person that we're unable to ferret out."

Now that he'd gotten Chuck's attention, Gregory decided to show the condescending man he was more than qualified to serve out the venerable congressman's term and win the upcoming election on his own. "No drugs, not even a parking citation."

"What about women?"

"What about them?" Gregory countered.

"We know you're engaged to the daughter of the representative from Mississippi, but what about the women in your past? Would they be privy to some indiscretion that would derail a possible run for the office in November?"

Gregory shook his head. "I don't think so."

"Think, man, about the women you slept with when you were in high school, college, and even law school. Did you screw any of them without using protection? Did you get any of them pregnant? Did any of them ever mention they'd aborted your baby?" He fired off the questions in rapid succession.

The seconds ticked by as Gregory closed his eyes and tried recalling all of the women he'd slept with. There were so many that he couldn't remember their names or faces. A fist of fear squeezed his heart when he remembered the time he and Devon had been so caught up in making love that he hadn't used a condom.

"I slept with one woman—once—without using protection."

"What happened, Emerson?"

"I don't know."

"What the hell do you mean you don't know?"

"We stopped seeing each other."

"Did she break up with you?" Chuck's tone was blatantly accusatory.

"No. I stopped seeing her because my fiancée returned from Japan."

"You were fuc—screwing one woman while engaged to another?"

Bracing both feet on the floor, Gregory leaned forward. "Don't get sanctimonious with me, Hanson. You're the one who has been married four times, and I'm willing to bet you're not finished."

Chuck slapped his thigh. "That's what I need to see from you! Thanks for showing me you have a pair of balls, because you're going to need them once you begin campaigning. Now, tell me about this woman who made you so temporarily insane you forgot to wrap up your meat."

Although he wasn't physical by nature, Gregory curbed the urge to reach over and choke the man. "Her name is Devon Collins, but she goes by Gilmore professionally."

"When was the last time you saw her?"

"Early January."

"And you haven't had any contact with her since that time?"

"No."

Chuck stared at the floor, seemingly deep in thought. "Have you set a date for your wedding?"

"Not yet. We'd planned to marry on Valentine's Day, but we had to postpone it because of my father's heart attack."

"Marry the woman before the Easter recess, because Guilford plans to announce his retirement right after they reconvene. The governor will wait a week before appointing you. The voters look more favorably on a married man than a footloose bachelor."

"I know my fiancée is planning on having a big—"

"This is not about your fiancée," Chuck interrupted. "It's about your future, and I'm willing to bet the little lady wouldn't mind forgoing a big wedding if she can one day live in the governor's mansion. She knows how to play the political game, Emerson, because of her father." He rose to stand. "That's all for now. I'll be in touch."

Gregory, realizing he'd just been dismissed, stood up and walked out, nearly bowling over Chuck's Barbie doll wife, who apparently had been listening outside the door. "Don't bother to see me out."

It wasn't until he started up his late-model, top-of-the-line Mercedes-Benz sedan that he was able to process what had just occurred. His fiancée had made it happen. When he and Michelle began dating, she'd asked him what he wanted for his future and when he told her he wanted a career in politics, she said she could make it happen because of her father. She'd hinted that the governor of Virginia and her father attended the same law school and would occasionally reunite when both entered fund-raising golf tournaments that supported their favorite charities.

He wanted to call Michelle and tell her the good news, but he decided to wait. They would celebrate over champagne while planning their spur-of-the-moment wedding.

Chuck opened the door that was concealed artfully within the floor-to-ceiling bookcase. "Did you get it all?" he asked Jake Walsh. When he'd first glimpsed the brilliant investigator, Chuck did a double take because he looked exactly like the French painter Toulouse-Lautrec.

Jake sat at a table with state-of-the art video equipment. "Every facial expression and syllable," he confirmed.

"I want you to check out this trick Emerson was balling. Find out everything you can about her and report back to me. Let's hope he didn't knock her up."

"What if he did, boss?"

Chuck patted his stiff hair, checking to see if any strand was out of place. "Then I need you to take care of it, Jake."

Of all the candidates he was responsible for getting elected, he hated the current governor the most. The pompous bastard actually believed he occupied the governor's mansion because of his perfect face, hair, and charisma. Widowed a decade before, he'd become a most sought-after bachelor, while he treated those in his inner circle like slaves. Chuck had lost count of the number of times he'd stepped in as his boss's fixer, shielding him from scandals before his indiscretions went public. Finding a candidate to replace Guilford would be his last selfless act for the governor, who'd confided to him he would not seek re-election because his party had selected him as a possible vice presidential candidate; he'd promised to take Chuck with him if or when he went to the nation's capital. The man didn't know Chuck wouldn't go with him even if he occupied the Oval Office, because his strengths were in local and not national politics. He preferred to be a big fish in a little pond rather than a little fish in a big pond.

Chapter Fifteen

$\backsim \!\backsim$

Devon left the bed before dawn to discover someone had slipped a single sheet of paper under the door. At first she thought it was an invoice, but when she read and reread the bold type she felt her knees shake. There was a German measles outbreak at the inn. The local health department had been notified and all guests and employees would receive ongoing updates.

She didn't want to panic. Devon wasn't certain whether she was still immune to rubella and she knew contracting the disease during pregnancy could put her baby at risk for fetal malformation. Making her way to the door, she opened it, placed the DO NOT DISTURB placard on the doorknob, and closed it, making certain to flip the security bolt.

After taking a shower, she felt more in control. She couldn't risk staying at the inn or on the island while the health emergency was in effect. Reaching for her cell, she tapped David's number. She knew she woke him up when he emitted a long sigh before greeting her.

"Yeah," he drawled.

"David, I'm sorry to wake you up, but I can't stay here."

"What's the matter?"

His voice indicated he was awake and alert. Devon told him about the health warning. "I know I was vaccinated as a kid, but I haven't been checked for immunity since then. And—"

"Pack a bag," he said, cutting her off. "You're going to stay with me until the health crisis is over. I'll be there... by six thirty. I'll call you when I get to the parking lot. Use the side entrance rather than the front door."

Twenty seconds after David hung up Devon was galvanized into action. It'd taken a single telephone call for her to replace Keaton with David as her go-to person in a crisis. Once Keaton moved from New York to Los Angeles, and although separated by three thousand miles, he was always a phone call away; now that she'd decided to move to Cavanaugh Island, they would once again live a short distance away from each other. However, Devon had to respect Francine's place in Keaton's life and although she would always think of him as a friend, their friendship would have to take a backseat to their business relationship.

As she filled a large quilted bag with enough clothes to last her at least a week, Devon refused to acknowledge how much she'd come to depend on David. She, who'd always believed she didn't need a man for anything, had called one who'd promised to take care of her and shield her from gossip once her pregnancy was evident.

You're a friend of Keaton's and Keaton is a friend of Francine's, and Francine happens to be someone I'm quite fond of. And down here we're serious when it comes to friendship. Whenever she attempted to come up with an answer for why he wanted to take care of her and not some other woman, she remembered his words as clearly as if he'd just spoken them to her. What would make him risk his reputation by pretending he was the father of her unborn child and possibly hinder his chances of meeting someone with whom he could possibly fall in love and marry?

The possibilities crowded her mind when she thought of the likelihood that he wanted to show his ex he'd moved on with another woman. Pump your brakes, Devon! her inner voice chided. Analyzing her relationship with David always upset her emotional equilibrium, and with the unexpected mood swings from pregnancy she wondered if she would ever be in control again. Why couldn't she just accept what he was offering and not look for an ulterior motive? He needed a female attorney and she needed his protection.

Devon hoped that when she moved into her new home some if not all of the anxiety and uncertainty she was experiencing would subside or disappear completely.

David managed to shower and dress in record time, and once behind the wheel of his car, he literally put the pedal to the metal. He wasn't concerned about being stopped by the Charleston PD because he was familiar with most of the officers on the force. It wouldn't matter if he was caught speeding on the island because his cousin was the sheriff and Jeff knew he would have a good reason for exceeding the island speed limit.

He'd opened the trunk and was out of the car at the same time Devon walked out of the side entrance, which guests used when the front doors were locked at eleven o'clock every night. Taking long strides and closing the distance be-tween them, David took two bags from her loose grip. He rested his free hand on the small of her back.

"Did you run into anyone?" he asked, storing her bags in the trunk.

"No," she said as he opened the passenger-side door for her. "I took the back staircase instead of the elevator."

Rounding the sedan, David sat next to Devon. He couldn't decide which Devon he liked better, the under-stated, sophisticated urbanite or the one without makeup. "Did you eat?"

She nodded. "I had yogurt with sliced fruit."

Shifting into Reverse, he maneuvered out of the lot. "You need more than yogurt. I'll make breakfast for you once we get back to my place." He rested his right hand on her knee. "Have they identified who has the measles?"

"No. The notice stated a measles outbreak but didn't in-dicate whether it's a guest or a member of the staff."

"You're probably immune, but you still don't need to take unnecessary risks in your condition."

Devon put her hand on his. "I hope you don't mind that I called you this morning."

Never had David wanted to shake someone as much he did her at that moment. He didn't know any other way to tell her that he'd meant his promise to look after her. He'd heard some men claim that pregnant women were sexy, and he had to agree with them. Everything about her, from her round face to her full breasts and rounded hips, radiated temptingly ripe lushness. And he'd never get enough of her slightly tilting her head while staring up at him through her lashes, the gesture so damn seductive he'd come to look for it.

"Did it bother you?" she repeated.

David pulled his hand from under hers. "I don't intend to answer that because you may not be ready to handle the truth."

There came another moment of silence. "Why don't you tell me and I'll let you know whether I can or can't?" Her voice was soft, coaxing, and challenging.

David's expression closed, as if he was guarding a secret. "I like you the way a man likes a woman." He glanced at her and she stared back wordlessly. "I knew you wouldn't be able to accept it."

Devon took a quick breath. "That's not true. I can accept the fact that you like me because the feeling is mutual. You're definitely one of the good guys. Not too many men would be willing to do what you're doing. Accept another man's responsibility—even if it's only temporary."

"It's not about gratitude or tit for tat, Dee. It goes far beyond my getting you to agree to come work with me."

"In other words, you want a relationship."

He smiled. "There you go."

"Are you asking to become friends with benefits?"

A tense silence filled the car again. The muscles of David's forearms hardened as he gripped the leather-wrapped wheel. "If that's what you think, then I'll drop you off at the nearest Charleston hotel."

She exhaled an audible breath, her nostrils flaring delicately. "I need to know where we're going with this."

Turning the wheel sharply to the right, David maneuvered off the asphalt onto a grassy area. Shifting into Park, he unbuckled his belt and turned to face Devon, draping his right arm over her headrest.

He was close to losing his temper and couldn't say what

he really wanted to say. "What type of men are you used to dealing with? Just because I tell you that I like you, it doesn't mean I want only sex from you. That's something I can get at any time from any woman willing to drop her panties *and* with no strings attached." David ignored the rush of color darkening Devon's face. "I'm sorry if I shocked you," he continued, his voice softer, more conciliatory, "but I find it easier to meet a woman in a bar, buy her a couple of drinks, then go back to her place for sex than to have a meaningful relationship. I've met some women who believe either I'm gay or there's something wrong with me because I prefer getting to know them better before sleeping together. I'm not saying I don't like sleeping with a woman, but it can't always be slam bam thank you ma'am."

Devon blinked slowly. "You prefer a platonic relationship to a physical one?"

"That's not what I'm saying, Devon, so please don't try to twist my words. Maybe I'm old school, but I enjoy courting a woman. We date and over the course of time we learn what we like, don't like, and if we have anything in common. I much prefer an emotional commitment before moving onto something more physical."

"How long did you date your ex before you slept together?"

David turned his head, staring through the windshield. "I thought we agreed not to bring up our exes again." He didn't want to talk about his past now.

"My bad," Devon said. "Forget it."

He shifted into Drive, maneuvering off the grass onto the paved road. "My bad, because I did promise to feed you."

"David?"

"Yes, babe?"

"Please put your seat belt on."

"Okay, Mama."

A smile flitted across Devon's lips when he reached across his body with his right hand and secured the belt. "I don't think I want my child to call me mama. It sounds somewhat old-fashioned." She held up a hand when David glanced at her. "I know you're old-fashioned."

"Old school," he teased. "What do you want him to call you? Devon?"

She scrunched up her nose. "No way! My child will not call me by my name. That is much too grown."

"Kids nowadays are grown. It's no more Miss Sally or Mister Sam, but Sally and Sam."

"Or worse," Devon interjected. "I've heard little kids cuss in front of their parents as casually as asking for a Happy Meal."

"That's because they see and hear things they shouldn't. When I was growing up I was told constantly to stay out of grown folk's business. And if I overheard something I shouldn't, then I better not repeat it or my grandmother would make me clean out the pigpen. She knew I used every trick in the book to avoid getting into the pen because a sow chased me after I'd picked up one of her babies. I refused to eat bacon or ham until Grandpa butchered that ornery swine for Christmas dinner."

"You can't blame her, David. She was just protecting her baby."

"True, but you also don't bite the hand that feeds you, and one of my chores was to feed the pigs."

Devon rolled her head from side to side. She moaned

softly when David's fingers massaged her shoulder muscles. "I don't think I could eat a pet."

"Big Babe wasn't a pet but food. She was ham, bacon, ribs, trotters, pig tails, hog jowls, and chitlins."

"In other words, from the rooter to the tooter."

"Let the choir say amen," David drawled with a wide grin.

"Amen!" Devon sang out, her contralto resonating throughout the car.

David gave her an incredulous look. "Whoa, girl. You can really blow."

"I used to sing in my school's glee club and the church gospel choir."

"One of these days I'm going to take you to the Happy Hour in the Creek for karaoke night. They used to offer prizes for the best male and female singers, but it got too competitive, so the owners did away with it."

"So the Creek isn't just about farms and craft shops."

He shook his head. "No. The Creek is an interesting place to live. Of the three towns, it's the most laid-back."

"Should I expect folks to hold hands and sing 'Kumbaya'?" Devon teased.

"Did you know that *kumbaya* is Gullah for *come by yuh*? Translated it literally means 'come by here.'"

"There's so much I don't know about the Gullah and their language."

"Live here long enough and you'll begin to eat, think, act, and maybe even talk like one. By the way, do you have any Southern roots?"

"I do on my father's side. His folks were from Tennessee. My mother is Scotch Irish and African American. My paternal grandmother used to say I was her little gumbo—a little bit of this and a little bit of that."

"And the combination is exquisite." The compliment was out before David could censor himself. "And I'm certain you'll have a beautiful baby."

"I just want a healthy baby," she murmured.

David felt Devon withdraw without moving, aware that he had to be careful not to cross the line by delving too much into her past. He had to remind himself that Devon wasn't a client or an opposing witness he had to examine or cross-examine. She was a woman he'd promised to protect, the woman with whom he found himself opening his heart at the risk of falling in love again once he'd fulfilled his vow to be with her throughout her pregnancy.

"I usually don't work Saturdays, but I have to go into the office this morning to carry out the reading of a will, so you're going to be on your own until I get back home. The fridge and freezer are filled, and if there's anything you need, let me know, and I'll bring it back when I return."

She gave him a warm smile. "Thank you for asking, but I don't need anything. I brought some knitting with me and that's enough for me to keep busy. Knitting baby sweaters, hats, and booties goes quickly because they're so small."

David went still. Could she, he wondered, actually take into consideration that he'd want to be her baby's father? He'd never slept with a woman without using protection because he knew he hadn't been ready to take on the responsibility of becoming a father. However, with each passing birthday, the realization that he wanted a family grew stronger and stronger. The number forty then gained greater significance on his wish list, the number indicating the threshold for his personal accomplishments.

Like many men, he wanted his own biological children,

yet it wasn't paramount for him to acknowledge fatherhood. He'd known couples unable to have children of their own, and he'd had to handle the legal work for them to adopt children, and those children were loved and protected as if they shared DNA with their adoptive parents. And he'd known men who'd fathered children with a number of women only to walk away to live their lives according to their own rules. David and his father occasionally bumped heads on certain issues, yet they were of one accord when it came to family. The only time a man was excused from taking care of his family is when he is six feet under.

He winked at her. "I had to ask, Mama. Once I come back I want to start prepping for tomorrow's get-together."

Closing her eyes and pressing a hand to her belly, Devon smiled. "I think I'm getting used to being called mama." She opened her eyes, meeting David's. "Would it bother you if I called you daddy?"

"I don't have a problem with it." And he didn't. He knew a lot of women who called their husbands or boyfriends daddy. It wasn't a specific title but a term of endearment.

"Speaking of prepping food. The smaller bag in the trunk is filled with what I plan to fix tomorrow for appetizers, so as soon as we get to your house it needs to go into the fridge."

Gripping the wheel with one hand, David saluted her with his right. "Yes, ma'am!"

By the time David exited the causeway the sun was up and Charleston had come awake with those waiting at bus stops or walking or driving to work. Devon stared at the pastel houses of Rainbow Row on East Bay Street. She recognized Broad Street from her walking tour of the city's Historic

District that now seemed so long ago. She found time in the Lowcountry slowing to almost a crawl. Two days seemed like a New York week.

David parked along the cobblestone street in front of a row house with iron balconies and Italianate cornices. She unsnapped her belt. "How old is your house?" she asked him, staring at his unshaven jaw. In his haste to get to her, he'd showered but hadn't shaved. His relaxed-fit jeans, pullover sweater, running shoes, and stubble were a welcome change from his normal formal attire. The look made him appear much more approachable.

"It was built and expanded before the Civil War."

"Does it have landmark status?"

David released the lever for the trunk. "Yes. Most of the houses in this district have landmark status."

Devon waited for him to retrieve her bags and open the passenger-side door for her. Gaslight-inspired streetlights lined the brick sidewalk. She had an affinity for old homes and accompanying period furnishings, unlike her modern condo, which was filled with contemporary pieces. Rather than sell her furniture, Devon planned to decorate the house using an eclectic decorating style, mixing contemporary, art deco, and colonial reproductions.

She didn't know what lay behind the door to the Greek Revival–style home, but when she stepped inside she found herself slack-jawed. The parlor, filled with obvious antiques, beckoned her to come and relax. Double-hung windows were tall enough to walk through and twelve-foot-high ceilings and heavy cornices supported the pocket doors that closed the space off from the rest of the house.

"I feel as if I've stepped back in time," she said, her voice filled with awe.

"Come upstairs and I'll show you your room. *Mi casa es su casa*, so make yourself at home." He gave her fingers a gentle squeeze.

"You may regret saying that if I move in and stay until my house is ready."

Bringing her hand to his mouth, he kissed the back of it. "That sounds like a wonderful plan. Living with me would lessen your risk of catching something from transient strangers."

Devon felt as if she'd just come down with a case of foot-in-mouth disease. She didn't want to send mixed signals that she wanted them to live together. For her, living together translated into a lifetime commitment, something she couldn't entertain at this time. It was as if she'd placed her life on hold, and other than buying a house she wasn't able to make any life-changing decisions until late September.

"Do you offer rain checks for sleepovers?"

"Sure. Why?"

"I'll take you up on your offer when I have the floors done, because I won't be able to stay in the house once the contractor puts down the polyurethane. The former owner carpeted the bedrooms, but I plan to have them ripped up. That's when I'll see if they need to be refinished."

"So you know exactly how you want to decorate your home?"

Nodding, Devon said, "I have a good idea about what I want, but I intend to ask Morgan about ordering certain pieces I'd like to use in the bedrooms."

"Once Angels Landing Plantation is restored, the design world will definitely take notice of Dane and Daniels Architecture and Interior Design."

David led her up a curving staircase to the second story and down a carpeted hallway, stopping in front of a door near a window overlooking the backyard. "You're here and I'm at the top of the stairs on the left. You have your own bathroom and there's a jib door that leads out to a second-story balcony." He set her bags inside the bedroom, angled his head, and brushed a light kiss over her mouth. "I'll see you downstairs."

Chapter Sixteen

~~~

Devon sat across the table from David in the kitchen with maple floors and a planked ceiling, enjoying a breakfast of fresh-squeezed orange juice, grits, scrambled eggs, turkey sausage, and buttered toast. He'd muted the small flat screen set on the countertop under a row of shelves with a collection of blue Depression glass.

"How did you put this together so quickly?" she asked him. "I couldn't have been upstairs more than twenty minutes."

David touched a napkin to the corners of his mouth. "I have an electric juicer, and the sausages are precooked. The grits took the longest because no self-respecting Southerner would ever make instant."

She lifted her eyebrows. "Is there a difference?" Lowering his head, David pinched the bridge of his nose, seemingly deep in thought. When his head came up, Devon noticed the slow smile parting his lips. "What's the matter?"

"The matter is I should buy a box of instant grits and cook

them for you, but it would be sacrilegious to even bring them into my home."

"I've cooked instant grits," Devon said, defending her own cooking efforts. "They're not too bad if you put butter and eggs on top of them."

David pointed at her plate. "Do they taste like those you're eating now?"

"No, but—"

"No *buts*, Madam Counselor. It's either yes or no."

She decided she was going to let David sweat a bit. Of course his grits were better, but she wasn't ready to wave the white flag and surrender. "I'll let you know after I finish them."

Pushing back his chair, he stood up. "I'm going to brew a cup of coffee while you..." His words trailed off when her cell phone rang.

Devon retrieved the phone she'd left on a serving cart, a slight frown furrowing her brow when she saw the name of her building's management company. "Excuse me, David, but I have to answer this." She tapped the phone icon, listening intently when the man asked if she was serious about selling her condo. "Yes, I am."

"One of your neighbors wants to buy your apartment and knock down the adjoining wall to expand his." He didn't have to tell Devon who wanted her apartment, because a well-known artist had hinted about needing more space for a studio and art gallery.

"If he meets my price, then I can move out before the end of next month." Devon listened, stunned when the agent quoted an outrageous figure that was nearly one and a half times the amount she'd paid for the unit. "I'm not in New York right now. So Mr. Tobin will have to give me time to come back and pack up everything." Not only did she have to arrange to box up her clothes, books, and other personal items, but she also had to get an appointment with a Charleston-based ob-gyn and rent a storage unit in Charleston to store her possessions in until she moved into the house on Cherry Lane.

"When do you think you'll be back?"

"I don't know. I have some business to take care of before I return to New York."

"I'm only asking because Mr. Tobin wants to let the workmen know when they can start. He wants to use a Cinco de Mayo theme for a May fifth showing."

"Please let him know that although I understand his need for things to move quickly, he also has to understand that I have to put things in place before I move out."

"I'll definitely let him know, Miss Gilmore."

"Thank you, Mr. Stanish. I'll be in touch once I get back." Devon ended the call, her eyes meeting David's when she returned to the table. "I guess you heard my side of the conversation."

He took a sip of coffee. "You have a buyer for your condo."

"Yes. And he wants me to move out like yesterday."

"What are you going to do?"

Closing her eyes, Devon blew out a breath. "He has to wait until I close here. Once I know the house is mine, then I'll go back and sell the condo."

Setting down his coffee cup, David rose and rounded the table, easing Devon to her feet. He put his arms around her waist, pulling her close. "You don't need to stress yourself out about trying to be in two places at the same time. If you want to go to New York and pack up your place, then I'm willing to take care of what you need to close on the house down here."

Anchoring her arms under his shoulders, she held on to him, savoring the heat from his hard, slim body. Tilting her head back, she studied his face, feature by feature, committing each to memory. "What would I do without you? Even though I know I need to unload the condo, I hadn't planned to go back to New York until the middle of next month. I'll hire a company to pack up the apartment, so instead of it taking more than a week, it'll just be a few days. All the paperwork for the sale can be done either electronically or overnighted."

What she didn't say was that she didn't want to leave David. Not now. A hint of a smile touched the corners of his firm mouth as he stared at her under lowered lids. She didn't want to question why he'd come into her life at a time when she needed him most because it had to be karma. Once events were predestined, they had to be played out until they were manifested.

"Everything's going to work out okay, and I want you to remember I'm here for you if ever you need something," David said in a soft tone. "You may not want to believe it, but you're one of the strongest, most confident women I've had the pleasure of knowing."

David cradled her face, seemingly trying to see the uncertainty that crept in when she least expected it. Over and over she'd told herself she could do this, she could go it alone as so many other women had done throughout the ages. When she'd contacted Gregory to tell him she was pregnant it wasn't to trap him; she didn't need his money as much as she did his emotional support.

Although she'd slept with Gregory, she'd never revealed

the names of her clients and it'd been a source of contention between them. He also wanted to know how much she earned, and her comeback was that only the IRS was privy to that information.

Going on tiptoe, Devon nuzzled David's ear, her tongue tracing the outer edge. She knew she was wading into uncharted territory with David, yet she was beyond caring. She'd been introduced to him exactly a week ago, yet it seemed as if they'd met in another lifetime. He was an amalgamation of all the positive traits of the men she'd known; he wasn't perfect but he also wasn't very far from it.

She felt him go completely still as her mouth continued its exploration, pressing light kisses along his jaw. "I'm glad you are here for me," she whispered against his slightly parted lips, inhaling and tasting the coffee he'd just drunk.

Without warning, Devon was lifted off her feet as David's mouth devoured hers in a marauding, smothering kiss that stole the breath from her lungs. Her arms went around his neck, holding him tightly for fear that if he let her go she would collapse on the floor like a rag doll.

Her hands cradled his head and as he deepened the kiss, her lips parted of their own volition, allowing his tongue to plunder the recesses of her mouth. A groan escaped her when she felt his erection, the hardness eliciting a rush of erotic pleasure that shot waves of desire down her body and settled between her thighs. Her libido went into overdrive as she struggled to get even closer. The sound of David's breathing penetrated the fog of desire threatening to swallow her whole, and she managed to extract her mouth from his, her breasts rising and falling with each breath she drew before she begged him to make love to her.

* * *

David noticed that all traces of green in Devon's eyes had disappeared, leaving them a deep gray. He lowered her slowly, setting her on her feet. He hadn't expected her to kiss him, while his hard-on was just as unexpected.

He hadn't lied when he told Devon he liked courting; however, in a moment of madness, he wanted to sweep her up in his arms, carry her up the staircase to his bedroom, strip her naked, and make love to her until he was sated. And it didn't matter to him that she carried another man's baby in her womb.

"I'm sorry I—"

"Please don't apologize," Devon whispered, placing her fingers over his mouth and stopping his words.

Reaching up, he held her wrist. "I don't want to take advantage of you"

"You didn't. I kissed you first."

He smiled. "And I kissed you back."

Her expression softened, becoming almost angelic. "I'm glad you did."

David palmed her face, his eyes communicating what he couldn't tell her. He didn't want to believe he was falling in love with Devon. Beauty and intelligence aside, everything about her appealed to him. He knew she was strong, and yet her occasional displays of vulnerability fired all his protective instincts and tugged at his heart. If instructed to jot down a list of qualities he wanted in a woman, there would be only one word on the page: *Devon*. He'd stopped asking himself why her and not some other woman; why her and not another woman who would come to him unencumbered.

She rested her cheek on his chest. "I'm going to clean up the kitchen so you can get ready to go to work."

David ran a hand up and down her back, luxuriating in the warmth of the body molded to his. "I didn't invite you here to do housekeeping."

"You shouldn't argue with Mama. It's not good for the baby."

Easing back, he glared at Devon. "You don't play fair, do you?"

With wide eyes, she returned his stare, her expression mirroring confusion. "What are you talking about?"

They engaged in a stare-down, but David wasn't easily fooled. "You're really good, babe. You should've been a prosecutor or trial attorney, because you're an incredible actress. How many more times are you going to play the 'it's not good for the baby card'?"

She affected a sexy moue. "As many times as I need to to get my way."

David kissed her hair. "Well, you're not going to get your way this morning. I'll take care of the kitchen, because I still have time before I have to leave."

Devon nodded. "Once you're finished, I'm going to defrost the meats I need for the pot stickers."

"How did you learn to make Chinese food?" David asked as he began clearing the table.

"I shared an apartment with two other law students—one Chinese and the other Latina. We alternated Sundays cooking for one another. After a while we traded recipes. I've perfected pot stickers and steamed buns filled with either chicken, pork, or duck, and occasionally shrimp."

Crossing his arms over his chest, David held his head at an angle, unable to believe he'd found a woman who liked to cook as much as he did. "What else can you make?" he asked, taking an empty plate from her as she stood up to help him.

"Pork or crab dim sum, barbecue spareribs, sesame prawn toasts, and crispy shredded beef. That's just the Chinese. What's on your menu for tomorrow?"

"Wings, guacamole, skewered lamb and beef, deviled eggs, chili, shrimp cocktail, and sweet-and-sour meatballs. I'll also make up a cheese platter with stone-ground crackers and artisan breads."

"What about fruit, David?"

Turning on the water in the sink, he rinsed dishes, glasses, and pots before stacking them in the dishwasher. "What about it?" he asked.

Devon stood beside him. "Don't you think a fruit bowl would be nice to offset the heavy richness of some of the food?"

Wiping his hands on a terry cloth towel, he opened a drawer under the countertop and took out a pad and pen, handing it to her. "Write down what you want me to pick up from the supermarket."

She walked to the table and sat down again. "Do you have spareribs?"

David nodded. "I have at least a half dozen slabs in the freezer in the other kitchen."

"What about chicken liver?"

Throwing the towel over his right shoulder, David crossed his arms while leaning against the countertop. "What do you plan to do with the liver?"

"I'd like to make sautéed Cajun chicken liver wrapped in bacon. It's a little spicy but goes well with beer and white wine." Devon glanced up from writing. "I'm going to need sesame seeds for the toasts and wonton wrappers for the dim sum."

"Anything else, Mama?" he teased, winking at her.

"That all depends on whether you're going to make Southern-style ribs or Chinese."

"What if we make both?"

She nodded. "Sounds good." Devon wrote down a few more items on the page. She ripped the sheet off the pad, handing it to him. "I think that does it."

David dried his hands on a towel before walking over and easing Devon to her feet. He cradled her head, his eyes making love to her face. "We're going to make a helluva couple."

Devon anchored her arms under his shoulders. "We're already an amazing couple."

Burying his face in her hair, he inhaled the scent of coconut clinging to the soft curls. David was astonished at the sense of completeness he felt at that moment, and the harder he tried to ignore the truth, the more it nagged at him. He'd promised Devon he would be with her during her pregnancy, but he wondered if he would be able to walk away from her after she had the baby.

"You're right about that." He pressed a kiss to her forehead. "I have to shave and get dressed. I should be back sometime this afternoon, so if you get hungry you can call out for delivery." Reaching into the pocket of his jeans, he took out several large bills. "Menus to nearby restaurants are in the drawer next to the dishwasher. Otherwise you can defrost something from the fridge or freezer in the downstairs kitchen."

"I'll be okay," Devon countered, waving away the money. She kissed his cheek. "Now go to work. I'll be here when you get back."

He brushed a light kiss over her mouth. "You promise?"

"Yes, love. I promise."

His eyebrows lifted questioningly at the endearment. "Am I really your love?"

A rush of color suffused her face. "Do you want to be?"

Now David knew what a witness on the stand felt like, sworn to tell the truth and nothing but the truth, while a little slip of a woman with whom he'd found himself completely enthralled had just asked him if he could be her love. What she didn't know was that he wanted that and more. Much more. And the more was marriage.

"Yes, I do." That said, he turned on his heel and walked out of the kitchen.

Devon was still standing in the kitchen staring at the space where David had been. Picking up a glass, she filled it with water from the front door of the refrigerator. Where had that come from? she asked herself as she sipped the water. The four-letter word had rolled off her tongue as if she said it all the time. There was something about him that had unlocked her heart, while knocking down the wall she'd put up to keep men from getting close to her because she feared surrendering her independence. All her life she'd struggled to determine her own future, and she'd believed she'd succeeded—until now. The tiny life growing inside her had forced her to make changes she never would've considered before. As a big-city girl, she looked forward to living in a small town where people looked out for one another.

And for more than half her life she'd told herself she never wanted to marry or have children, but life had a way of proving her wrong. She was going to have a baby *and* she wanted a husband, and the only man she could possibly consider marrying was David Sullivan. The smile parting her lips reached her eyes as she tried imagining herself as David's wife and law partner. She knew she would succeed because, like everything else she'd attempted, she didn't mind sacrifice and hard work to achieve her goal.

Fifteen minutes later, humming under her breath, she walked out of the kitchen and headed for the staircase. Holding on to the banister, she climbed the stairs, coming to an abrupt stop when she spied David standing at the top staring at her. He'd shaved and exchanged his jeans and sweatshirt for a suit and tie.

"That was quick," she remarked.

"Electric shaver," he explained, smiling.

Devon stepped off the last stair and onto the landing, the familiar scent of his aftershave wafting to her nostrils. She rested a hand on his shoulder. "You look very nice."

David nuzzled her ear. "Thanks. I wish I could stay home with you this morning."

"There will be plenty of other Saturday mornings when we'll be able to stay home together." Devon stared at him with a longing that came from a place she hadn't known existed. "I think you'd better leave now before I beg you to do something that would keep you here all afternoon."

David returned her stare, his gaze moving slowly over her face and down to her breasts before returning to meet her eyes. "I'd promised myself that if we did get involved with each other that I wouldn't touch you until after you had the baby. But...but if we continue like this, then I'm going to have to break that promise."

Devon closed her eyes, asking herself if she could do this. Could she sleep with a man she'd met exactly one week ago? Her body screamed yes while her mind said maybe. "You won't get an argument from me."

He blinked once. "Are you sure, Devon?"

She nodded. "I'm very sure."

Reaching for her hands, he dropped a kiss on her fingers. "I suppose we're going to have the shortest courtship and engagement on record, because I'm not going to sleep with you until we're married."

"Married!?"

He kissed the end of her nose. "Yes, married. We'll talk about it later on tonight before we go to bed." He flashed a sheepish grin. "I should've said before *you* go to sleep."

For the second time that morning, Devon found herself staring at his departing back. Minutes later, she didn't remember walking down the hallway to her bedroom or sitting on the comfortable club chair, where she lost track of time staring out the window. What she couldn't forget was David's pronouncement that he wouldn't sleep with her until they were married.

How she wished her grandmother was still alive, because she needed to talk to her. "I need you, Grandma," she whispered aloud. Devon wasn't going to delude herself into believing she was madly in love with David, but she knew with time she could easily grow to love him.

Never at that moment had she felt more alone. She missed her grandmother *and* she missed her brother.

Chapter Seventeen

Devon got into bed and positioned several pillows behind her back and shoulders. Reaching over, she picked up a skein of yarn and the tiny cap she looked forward to completing before going to sleep. She'd spent the morning sitting on the veranda outside her bedroom knitting, then retreated to the kitchen to make lunch. She was still in the kitchen watching CNBC when David returned home in a funk. He barely acknowledged her when she greeted him. He finally opened up, revealing that the reading of the will hadn't gone well, and that he'd had to step in as referee to stop several of the attendees from assaulting one another.

His dark mood lifted once they began prepping the dishes for the following day, and she saw firsthand his culinary skills when he expertly wielded a knife like a professionally trained chef. They wound up spending more than four hours in the kitchen chopping, mincing, and marinating, and she filled dough with finely chopped chicken, beef, and pork for five dozen pot stickers and three dozen dim sum.

David defrosted twenty pounds of spareribs, trimming off the fat and giving her half to marinate overnight. She'd sampled his chili, truthfully declaring it was the best she'd ever eaten. Working side by side with him in the kitchen was something she'd never shared with any other man, which bonded her to him.

Her fingers stilled when she heard a light tapping on the bedroom door. "Come in." Her breath caught in her chest when David walked in wearing only a pair of light blue pajama pants. Although slender, his upper body was extremely toned. He rounded the bed and slipped in next to her. He smelled of soap and peppermint mouthwash. It wasn't until he shifted slightly and she saw his shoulder that she noticed a tattoo of the scales of justice. So, she mused, the outwardly conservative attorney had body ink.

He pointed to the tiny knitted cap in her lap. "It's a strawberry!"

Devon nodded, smiling. When finished, the red cap dotted with black for seeds and the top with green leaves and a rolled brim would resemble a strawberry. "I couldn't resist making it when I saw the pattern. I also have a pattern for a pumpkin cap. If they come out all right I'm going to make a couple for Morgan's baby."

"You're really something."

An expression of confusion replaced her smile. "What are you talking about?"

David ran a finger down the length of her nose. "I had no idea you were so multitalented. You sing, cook, knit, and you're an incredible attorney."

Devon couldn't stop the heat warming her cheeks. She was never comfortable when she was on the receiving end of compliments. "I just have a lot of varied tastes."

"Varied or not, you're still very talented. I'm willing to bet your parents are very proud of their daughter."

"You would lose that bet if you really knew the truth." The words were out before Devon could form a different reply. If they were going to become involved with each other, then he needed to know about her relationship with her parents.

Stretching his right arm over the mound of pillows, he pulled her close to his side. "I'm here if you want to talk about it, but I will respect your wishes if you choose not to."

Shifting slightly on her side, Devon buried her face against his throat. "I owe you the truth if we're going to have an honest relationship. I've been estranged from my parents for years—my mother in particular. The year I celebrated my sixth birthday I was told what was expected of me as a Gilmore girl. I was expected to graduate college, marry well, and have at least two children. I was enrolled in a prestigious boarding school from which generations of Gilmore women had graduated. Social deportment was weighted equally with academics, and by the time I graduated I could speak fluent French and Spanish and plan a menu and set a table for a formal dinner party. And when I came home during school recess and holidays the lessons continued, because dinners at my house were always formal, with the live-in chef conferring with my mother about what she wanted to serve and kitchen staff standing by at our beck and call.

"If my dad's mother hadn't come to live with us after Granddaddy passed away, I know I would've had a breakdown from the intense pressure of living up to my mother's standards. I managed to survive when my brother either didn't or couldn't. He was expelled from so many schools that my mother decided to hire a tutor to homeschool him. By the time he was nine he was raiding the liquor cabinet, began smoking weed at twelve, and then graduated to heroin and cocaine before turning sixteen. He never finished high school, and when my parents cut him off he started robbing people and corner stores to get money to support his habit."

"He didn't come to you for money?" David asked.

"He'd called asking me to meet him at a particular place, but when I got there he was nowhere to be found. Meanwhile, I was going through my own battle with my parents because they'd arranged for me to marry an older wealthy widower once I graduated college. I'd met him a few times, and just his looking at me made my skin crawl. When Grandma Arlene found out what her daughter-in-law had planned she took me aside and asked me what I wanted. I told her I wanted to be a lawyer. She encouraged me to take the LSAT and to apply to law schools on either the East or West Coast. That way I would be far enough away from my overbearing, controlling mother's influence. The day I got the acceptance letter from NYU Grandma Arlene gave me her life's savings, which included the money she'd received from her husband's death benefit. It was the first time in my life I had to pinch pennies. The money wasn't enough for tuition and books, so I applied for student loans and waited tables on the weekends. I made a lot in tips whenever I waited on a table of men." She blushed. "I'd learned a little subtle flirting translated into generous tips.

"When I told my parents I was leaving to move to New York to attend law school, all hell broke loose. My mother went into hysterics and had to be sedated, while my father lectured me about being ungrateful and said that my mother only wanted the best for me. I told him she wasn't thinking of my happiness and that arranged marriages were asinine and archaic. Meanwhile, my brother was in and out of rehab, and the last time I saw him he told me he'd met a woman and was moving in with her. Unfortunately he couldn't stay clean and she put him out. He called me to let me know he was living in a men's shelter and that our grandmother was sending him money from her Social Security check so he could get his own apartment." Devon paused, her eyes filling with tears when she thought about the demons that had held her brother in their savage grip so he couldn't stay clean.

"Why didn't he go back home?" David whispered in her hair.

"When I asked him that, he said he couldn't be what our mother wanted him to be, so he preferred living on the street to living in a Lincoln Park mansion with servants waiting on him hand and foot. Her plan was for him to become a doctor like her father." Devon told David that her mother's family once owned the largest meat-packaging plant in Chicago in the 1920s, then went into trucking after the stockyards closed.

"So she had her children's lives planned out for them."

"That's because her mother had planned her life for her. I went to see my folks earlier this month to tell them they were going to become grandparents and my mother slammed the door in my face because no Gilmore woman had ever had a child out of wedlock."

"That's crazy," David spat out. "Doesn't she realize women can choose to marry or not marry?"

"Not according to Monique Gilmore-Collins. Her own mother had an affair with the chauffeur's son, who at the time was in medical school, and once her parents discovered she was carrying his baby, they arranged for them to be married. It was better she marry a young black doctor than to embarrass them when they had to explain why their unmarried daughter had a mixed-race baby."

"People and their stupid shit," David said under his breath. "What happened with your brother?"

Devon bit down hard on her lower lip until she felt it pulsing. Talking about her brother being locked away was never easy. "He's in prison serving a fifteen-year sentence for bank robbery. Instead of giving up, he held a customer and her child hostage before surrendering. I offered to defend him, but he opted for a public defender. He refuses to see visitors, won't take my calls, and all of my letters have been returned. It's as if he's cut himself off from everyone."

Pulling back, David stared at her. "How long has he been in?"

"Eight years. I keep telling myself prison is the best place for him because at least he can't abuse drugs while incarcerated. I'm in touch with the warden at the prison, who tells me that he's a model prisoner and doesn't see a problem when it comes time for him to be paroled. Ray got his high school diploma and is now taking college courses, so I suppose something good came out of his going to prison."

"Do you think he'll contact you once he's paroled?"

David was asking her a question she'd asked herself over and over. "I don't know. But I told the warden to contact me when it comes time for his release, because I want him to stay with me until he decides what he wants to do."

"From what you've told me about the house on Cherry Lane, you'll have more than enough room to put him up. But if he feels he needs to be in a city environment, then he can always stay here."

David's suggestion shocked Devon and she stared at him, virtually tongue-tied for a full minute. "Why would you offer him your home?"

"If he's going to become my brother-in-law, then why shouldn't I open our home to him?"

She put up a hand. "Wait a minute, David. You're talking about Ray becoming your brother-in-law when I haven't said I'm going to marry you."

His eyebrows lifted questioningly. "I thought we decided that we're getting married."

Devon shook her head. "*We* can't decide on anything until *we* talk about it."

David smiled, arms outstretched. "You have the floor, Counselor."

Her gaze lingering on his cleft chin, Devon carefully formed her thoughts. She didn't want to start a new life with a man with unanswered questions. "I'd like you to answer a few questions for me." He nodded. "Don't you believe a man and woman should be in love if they're going to marry each other? And why me? Why do you want to marry a stranger when you dated a woman exclusively for five years?"

"Maybe it's because I didn't know what I wanted until I met you." David gave her a long, penetrating stare. "And I do believe in love. But I hope you'll come to love me as much as I want to love you."

"What's stopping you from loving me?"

"You, Devon. You put up barriers to protect yourself, but you should ask yourself from what. And then you talk about us meeting a week ago. Would it make a difference if we dated a year or two before deciding to tie the knot?"

She paused as she chewed the inside of her lower lip. "I don't know."

"How long did you date your ex?"

Devon ran her hands over her head in a nervous gesture. "We met in law school and became friends. He was in his last year and I was a first-year student. He graduated and moved back to Virginia. Then we ran into each other a little more than a year ago and after a month we became lovers."

"Had he moved to New York?"

"No."

"How often did you see each other?" David asked, continuing with his questioning.

"Maybe once or twice a month."

"Well, I'll be dammed," he whispered. "You see this dude twice and sleep with him for the first time, meanwhile we've seen each other more than that in one week. And not once have I attempted to make love to you or will I make love to you until we're married. What I want to do is court you until the day you become Devon Sullivan or Mrs. David Sullivan, and hopefully that will be enough time for us to get to know each other better and possibly fall in love."

Devon's forehead creased with worry. "I still can't wrap my head around the fact that you want to marry woman who happens to be pregnant with another man's child."

A frown settled into his features. "Why are you bringing up something I've already accepted? I told you I'm willing to take care of you and the baby, but you haven't told me what you want from me."

For the very first time in a very long time Devon found herself at a loss for words. "It's not about what I want, but what I need."

"And what do you need?"

"Stability for me and the baby. I need to give my child what I didn't have, and that is a loving home. I don't want him or her locked away in a boarding school only to come home on holidays or to a house where the atmosphere is as cold as a frigid Chicago winter night. You want me to marry you and I'll accept your proposal on one condition."

He stared at the silky robe she'd thrown over a chair in the corner, and when his eyes swung back to her they were burning with a tenderness that made her heart turn over. "What is it you want from me?"

"I want your word that you'll promise to help me raise our son or daughter to believe we wanted them rather than needed them because society expects us to have children."

David smothered an audible sigh. What Devon was asking wasn't the impossible. If he was falling in love with her, then he knew he would love anything that was a part of her. Burying his face against the column of her silken neck, he said, "I promise on the graves of my Gullah ancestors that I will protect you, our home, and our children." His head popped up and he stared lovingly at her before capturing her mouth in an explosive kiss. The kiss ended quickly because he found himself becoming aroused. Shifting slightly, he put some space between them.

There was a hint of a smile curving the corners of her mouth. "I think you're getting ahead of yourself when you talk about having more children."

He winked at her. "We can't have just one—unless you're carrying twins."

"I doubt it."

"But what if you are?"

Light from the bedside lamps reflected off the green

glints in her luminous eyes. "Then you can claim two dependents instead of one."

Throwing back his head, David laughed loudly. "Spoken like a true financial planner." He sobered. "Now that we've discussed it, do you think you can give me your answer now?" An angelic expression softened her features and he knew her answer even if she were rendered mute at that moment.

"Yes, David. I will marry you."

"Thank you." The two words were filled with an emotion so powerful that David felt as if he was strapped into one of the world's fastest roller coasters, racing headlong along tracks with continuous loops.

Devon was right about him dating another woman for a long time, but proposing marriage to Devon when they'd met a week before. He hadn't realized it at the time, but he'd been marking time with Petra until he met Devon. There were other women after Petra, but none held his interest long enough to form a relationship. And he never could've imagined what Devon had to go through as a child living in a suffocating environment where her very life had been planned out for her from the moment she drew breath. Thanks to her grandmother, she'd escaped, but her brother hadn't been so lucky. David knew she'd sacrificed a lot not having her parents in her life, and although he knew he wouldn't be able to right the wrongs of the past, he wanted to make certain not to repeat those mistakes.

She was a thirty-six-year-old woman who'd taken care of herself and could continue to take care of herself and her child, but there were times when the most self-reliant, independent woman needed a man in her life to protect her and her children. He'd offered to marry her, and therefore he would become her life's partner and protector.

"When do you want to marry?"

Her query broke into David's thoughts. Sitting up, he pointed to her cell phone on the bedside table. "Please give me your cell." She handed it to him and he tapped the icon for the calendar. "What about May first? That's a Saturday."

Devon peered closely at the phone. "That gives us about five weeks." She met his eyes. "Do you think we'll close on the house before we get married?"

"It doesn't matter. We'll live here until it's furnished and decorated the way you want."

"What are you going to do with this house?" Devon asked.

"We'll keep it. We can live in the house in the Creek during the week and come here on weekends or whenever we decide to entertain."

Devon's smile reached her eyes. "I like the idea of having a city *and* a country home."

David kissed her forehead. "There you go. You have to decide whether you want to get married in a church or have a judge marry us."

Unconsciously her brow furrowed. "It really doesn't matter. It's not as if I'm going to invite my relatives."

Cradling her face between his hands, David rested his forehead on hers. "Why don't you try calling your parents and offer the olive branch. I'm certain they'll want to see their only daughter married."

"No!"

"Why not, Dee?"

"Please don't push it, David. I'm not ready to forgive my mother for destroying my brother's life."

"You talk about your mother. What about your father? Didn't he have a say in how you were treated?"

Devon clamped her jaw tight and stared straight ahead. It was the first time David had witnessed her stubborn side. "Are you familiar with the expression *petticoat man*?"

"Quite," David confirmed. "Petticoat, frock tail, or panty man. I believe they're all labels for a wimp."

"Well, Daddy *is* the ultimate petticoat man, and my grandmother, before she passed away, blamed herself for making him so weak. She miscarried three babies before she had him, and to say she spoiled him would be an understatement. I never saw my father challenge my mother about anything. I'd sit there praying he would say something, but it never happened. The one time I asked him why he let my mother get away with browbeating her children, his response was that he wanted peace in his house, not constant turmoil. Well, there was turmoil and either Daddy chose to ignore it or he was in denial." She offered him a wry smile. "Now you know all the sordid details about my past."

"A past we will not dredge up again." David would've preferred Devon contact her parents once more, yet decided not to dwell on it. There would be time after she had the baby to bring it up again, because he couldn't imagine her parents not being excited about becoming grandparents for the first time. He went completely still when he heard a familiar sound. "Was that your stomach rumbling?"

Devon pressed her palms to her belly. "Guilty as charged."

"Do you want something to eat?" He'd made her chicken saltimbocca, brushing the inside of a split ciabatta roll and filling it with pesto, sliced grilled chicken, fontina, prosciutto, and chopped fresh sage, which he cooked in a panini press until the sandwich was golden and crisp; he'd also put together a salad of fresh spinach, sliced hard-boiled egg, mushrooms, and julienne pickled beets tossed with a home-made herb dressing.

"I just ate less than two hours ago."

He rested a hand on her belly over the blanket. "I thought pregnant women eat all the time."

She placed her hand over his. "Not this pregnant woman. I eat only when I feel hungry, and I usually prefer five small meals to three big meals."

David pressed his mouth to her bare shoulder. "How much weight have you gained?"

"At my last visit I'd gained four pounds."

"That's not much."

Devon smiled. "It's enough. And please don't look at me like that," she said when he squinted at her. "Believe me, I'm not dieting."

"How much weight has your doctor recommended you gain?"

"At least twenty."

"You're how far along?"

"I'm close to the end of my first trimester. And if I gain at least two pounds each month, then I'll reach my goal of twenty pounds. I have to make an appointment to see a local ob-gyn because I won't get back to New York in time to keep the next one there." Devon told David she'd gotten the names of doctors from the nurse at Dr. Monroe's office and planned to call one on Monday.

"Is it too early to know what you're having?"

She nodded.

"Do you want to know beforehand?"

"Yes. Only because it's going to take a while for me to come up with a name for a boy or a girl."

"Why don't you play it safe and come up with a name for either sex, like Meredith, Morgan, Sydney, or even Devon."

Shifting on her side, she gave him a long stare. "One Devon in this family is enough."

"So, you're warming to the idea that we'll become a family?" David asked, smiling.

She reached for his hand, threading their fingers together. "I love the idea that we'll be a family." Her fingers tightened on his. "Speaking of family, what will your mother think about you marrying a woman you just met?"

Suddenly his face went grim. "What my mother thinks has nothing to do with us being together. But I'm willing to bet that when she hears you're expecting a baby, she'll act a little silly because she's been beating her gums about wanting grandchildren for so long that Leticia and I have learned to tune her out."

A momentary look of discomfort settled into Devon's features. "I don't like being duplicitous. Pretending this baby is yours when it isn't."

A muscle in David's jaw flicked angrily as he glared at her. "Would you say that if we adopted a child together?"

"No. Legally we'd be the child's mother and father."

He counted slowly to ten as he formed his words carefully. David didn't want to say something that would make him come off like her mother—wanting to control her and dictate every phase of her life. He wanted to replace the last man in her life who'd abandoned her when she needed him most, and hopefully get her to trust again. He extracted his hand from hers, placing it over her belly.

"From this point on and going forward I want you to think of this child in your womb as mine. We won't be able to stop folks from talking or counting on their fingers when our son or daughter is born, but that won't matter because it will be a Sullivan."

Devon, closing her eyes, breathed an audible sigh. "Would you want our *son* to be named after you?"

"Oh hell no! Two David Edgar Sullivans in the family are enough," he said, laughing. "Folks either call me DJ or Junior and I hate it."

"I happen to like your name."

I like it too, but three generations of Davids is really pushing it. Whatever name we choose for our son or daughter, we have to make certain it doesn't begin with a D."

"If we have a girl, then I'm thinking of something beginning with an A that would honor my grandmother Arlene."

"What about Alexis, Ashley, or Anaïs, after the writer Anaïs Nin?"

Shifting on her side and resting an arm over David's midsection, Devon closed her eyes. "I like it."

"Which one?"

"Anaïs."

"What about a boy?" His question was answered with a soft snore. Within seconds Devon had fallen asleep. When they'd shared dinner at the Cove Inn, she'd admitted that although she hadn't been plagued with nausea, she experienced recurring fatigue. Disengaging her arm, he pulled the sheet and blanket over her body and slipped out of the bed. Despite the fact that he wanted her to be the last person he saw before he fell asleep and the first he saw when he woke, David knew he had to be patient.

Leaning over, he kissed her hair, turned off the lamp, and walked out of the bedroom, closing the door behind him.

Chapter Eighteen

〜

Devon speared a bacon-wrapped chicken liver with a fork, holding it out to David. She'd taken the pan out of the oven and let it cool down before transferring them to a platter. "Let me know if you like it."

He took the appetizer off the fork and popped it into his mouth, his eyes opening wider as he chewed slowly. "Da-yum! That is incredible!" His jawed dropped. "Whoa! I just felt the burn in the back of my throat."

"I told you it was a little spicy." She'd woken up earlier that morning to find herself alone in bed. After showering and shampooing her hair, she went downstairs to find David in the enclosed galley porch where they would entertain their guests, setting up tables with chafing dishes and warming trays. He turned on the large flat screen resting on a table facing a seating grouping with black leather sofas, chairs, love seats, and side tables. He'd turned on the television, but muted the sound. A large ice-filled cooler with cans of beer;

bottled water; and apple, orange, and cranberry juice sat in a corner.

Devon had begun thinking of her and David in terms of *us* and *we* because it made what they planned to do more palatable. If someone had predicted that she'd agree to marry a man she'd known a week, she would've declared him or her insane. She'd heard of stories of couples meeting and marrying within days only to remain married for years, but she'd never believed she would be counted in that statistic.

She never thought herself in love, so what she was beginning to feel for David was shockingly surprising, because she'd made it a practice to shut down emotionally whenever someone attempted to get too close. Her relationship with Gregory had worked well. Seeing him once or twice a month served to keep her emotionally detached from him. His coming to New York to see her didn't always end in their making love. Gregory loved New York museums, restaurants, and theater, and having Devon accompany him was an added perk.

However, her feelings for David were rapidly changing. She enjoyed their verbal interchanges and cooking together; she'd even enjoyed sitting with him and watching a movie she'd viewed many times. She found him forthcoming but not overbearing. Francine thought him intense, but Devon had discovered he was the exact opposite—laid-back and easygoing.

Cradling her face, David brushed a kiss over her lips. "Spicy and delicious like you." He glanced around the room. "I think that does it."

Covering his hands with hers, Devon leaned into him. "Everything looks wonderful."

"I couldn't have done it without you."

"Of course you could." Her shopping list had included jars of scented candles, which she placed in the fireplace and along the mantel. A vase held a profusion of tulips, crocuses, and daffodils that she had found sprouting in his backyard garden. The candles and flowers added a softer touch to the otherwise totally masculine space.

A slight shiver raced through her when David looked at her, his eyes moving slowly over her face. His expression was one she hadn't seen before and she wondered what he was thinking. Had he had second thoughts about marrying her or accepting her child as his?

"Are you sorry?" she asked, speaking her thoughts aloud.

"About what, darling?"

His calling her darling took her slightly aback, and she chided herself for not trusting him. "I was just wondering if you were regretting asking me to marry you."

He frowned. "Where is all this coming from, Devon? I told you before I never say anything that I'll regret later. Did I do or say anything between now and last night that would make you think I'd go back on my word?"

She shook her head. "No. It's just that you were staring and the look on your face frightened me because—"

"It's going to take a while before we get to know each other well enough to know what's going on in the other's head," he said, interrupting her. "Maybe we'll never get to know each other that well, but I can reassure you that I haven't changed my mind about marrying you. In fact, I was going to ask you whether you would go with me tomorrow morning to shop for an engagement ring."

Devon stood there, totally shocked by the unpredictable man to whom she'd pledged her future. He wasn't content to marry at the local courthouse but apparently wanted all the bells and whistles that went along with courtship, an engagement, and a wedding ceremony.

"Don't you have to work tomorrow?"

"No. I'm taking off Mondays and Fridays for a few weeks."

"Okay," she said, trancelike.

"I called my mother before you got up and told her I'd met someone special, and she said she can't wait to meet you."

A flicker of apprehension eddied through Devon. For someone who was always in total control when negotiating business, she felt a momentary wave of panic. "Did you tell her about our plan to marry?"

"No. I'll wait until I see her in person."

"Are you looking to have a big elaborate wedding?"

David shook his head. "No. I wouldn't mind if we have a judge marry us. We could hold the ceremony and reception in the private room of a restaurant or hotel here on the mainland, because it's too late to book a venue at a catering hall."

"What about witnesses?" she asked.

"I'd like to ask Jeff to stand in as my best man."

"If you're going to have a best man, then I'll need a bridal attendant. Maybe I'll ask Francine and have Keaton give me away."

David smiled, his perfectly aligned teeth showing whitely in his face, which appeared even darker because of the stubble. "Now, that sounds like a plan."

"When do you want to let folks know about the wedding?"

"Let's wait until I put a ring on your finger." Reaching out, he pulled her close to his chest, lowered his head, fastened his mouth to the side of her neck, and breathed a kiss there. "Do you want me to hire a wedding planner to make things easier for you?" He raised his head, smiling.

"I don't think that's necessary." A powerful relief replaced the doubt as Devon's smile matched his. They had at least five weeks if they were to marry May 1, which meant they had time to send out invitations.

"If we're going to go shopping for rings, then it would have to be early in the morning or after two because I'm having lunch at noon with Francine, Morgan, and Kara."

David kissed her again. "Don't worry, baby. We can go as soon as the store opens and if we're lucky, you'll be able to show it off to your girlfriends at lunch."

"What about your mother?"

"I'll call her later and see if she'll have lunch with me. I'll have to tell her about the baby and that she'll get to meet you at another time."

Devon wound her arms around his waist. His telling his mother that she was pregnant would make it easier for her when she eventually met the woman. Rising on tiptoe, she curled into the contours of David's body and kissed him with a hunger that belied her outward calm. The realization she could trust him swept over her like the power of the water falling over Niagara Falls.

"Thank you," she breathed against his parted lips. Crushing her to him, David pressed his mouth to hers, deepening the kiss until both were breathing heavily. His hands were busy pushing up the hem of her blouse and covering her heaving breasts. She heard a strange sound before realizing she was moaning, a rising passion threatening to swallow her whole. The chiming of the doorbell echoed throughout the house, breaking the sensuous spell binding them together.

"I think I'd better go and see who's at the door," David whispered, seemingly struggling to catch his breath.

Devon nodded numbly. She adjusted her white man-tailored blouse, smoothing the front down over her breasts and slightly rounded belly. When she woke that morning, she discovered her belly was no longer flat. The loss of her waistline had been so gradual that at times she found it hard to believe that a baby was growing inside her. Maybe it was a good thing she would marry sooner rather than later; she didn't want to look at photographs years from now of herself in her wedding dress sporting an obvious baby bump.

David opened the door to find Jeff, Kara, Nate, Morgan, and Kara's former New York roommate Dawn Ramsey standing on the front steps. The two men carried large crates filled with cans of beer. "Y'all know I always have beer," he said, opening the door wider. He lowered his head and kissed Kara and Morgan. Reaching for Dawn's hand, he kissed the back of it. "Welcome back to the Lowcountry."

The petite natural blonde with a Peter Pan haircut, sky-blue eyes, and a peaches-and-cream complexion blushed attractively. "Thank you."

Jeff shouldered his way past his cousin. "Now, you know you can never have too much brew when watching basketball or baseball."

Nate, renowned throughout the Lowcountry as a master carpenter, nodded. "No lie, bro. And you know we like hanging out at your spot because right now you're the only one with a real man cave."

"Right now it's not looking manly because Devon decorated it with candles and flowers."

Kara and Morgan shared a look. "Devon's here?"

David stared at the women. "Yeah. In fact, she helped me cook."

"Break out your dress suit, Nate," Jeff drawled, "because I smell a wedding coming up. This is the first time since my cousin has started hosting March Madness that he's allowed *any* woman in his kitchen."

"Is there something you're not telling us, cuz?" Kara asked, questioning her husband's cousin.

David winked at her. "You'll find out soon enough, Miss Busybody social worker."

"Ah, sookie, sookie," Morgan crooned. "It sounds like someone's got bitten by the love bug."

David motioned with his head. "Y'all go in the back, because I know Mo is ready to get her eat on," he teased.

Morgan rolled her head on her neck while cutting her eyes at him. "If you think you're insulting me about eating so much, then you've got another thing coming. I ain't shy when it comes to feeding my face because this baby eats nonstop." She rubbed her belly for emphasis.

Nate let his wife precede him as they followed David to the rear of the historic house. "I told Mo if she doesn't stop eating we'll be bankrupt before the end of the year."

"Quit lying, Nathaniel Shaw," the architect threw over her shoulder.

"Uh-oh!" David and Jeff crooned in unison.

"Now you know she's pissed if she calls you by your government name," David teased. He always enjoyed the good-natured teasing between the two couples. That was something he'd never experienced with Petra because in spite of her partying lifestyle she was always very uptight with him.

He took the crates of beer, storing them in the pantry, then joined his guests. Kara introduced Dawn to Devon before she and Morgan greeted Devon with hugs and air-kisses. It was obvious they'd accepted her as a friend.

Morgan held a hand to her throat. "Now, this is what I'm talking about. I like the flowers and the candles."

Jeff frowned. "It looks sissified."

"Sissified or not," David said, "I happen to like it."

"You taking up for your woman?" Nate teased.

"You're damn skippy, bro," David retorted. "Don't you take up for Mo?"

Kara held up her hand. "You guys ought to stop the posturing. The room looks nice and the food smells delicious."

"Kara's right," Morgan said, peering at the trays of food lining two six-foot-long cloth-covered tables. "I hear the pot stickers calling my name."

Devon looped her arm through Morgan's. "Sit down and I'll bring you plate. The only thing I'm going to warn you about is the chicken liver roll-ups are a tad spicy."

"Yours truly has a cast-iron stomach. So far I've been able to tolerate spicy."

David selected two large plastic cups from a stack on the table with plates and cutlery, filling them with beer, then handed them to Jeff and Nate. Like himself, the two men wore jeans, sweatshirts, and running shoes. The doorbell chimed again.

Keaton walked into the room carrying a case of wine. "Francine is parking the car," he explained, handing off the box to David. "I hear you're an aspiring chef, so the case contains a mix of red, white, and rosé."

"I wouldn't call myself a chef."

Keaton rested a hand on David's shoulder. "That's not what I heard."

Francine strutted into the room in a pair of skinny jeans and high-heeled booties. She kissed David's cheek. "I left the door unlocked because I don't know who else is coming."

He returned the kiss. "How's it going, Red?"

She smiled. "It's all good." Francine spied Devon, took several steps, and hugged her. "Hey. I like your hair like that."

David agreed with Red. He also liked Devon's hair curly, framing her face, and falling to her shoulders in sensual disarray. "You guys should eat before the game starts. I'm going to put this wine away."

Francine held on to Keaton's hand, pulling him over to the table. "David, when did you start making Chinese food?"

"I didn't. Devon made it."

"Cuz, you have a keeper here," Jeff announced loudly.

David glanced at Devon. A blush crept up from her neck to her hairline. It was obvious she was embarrassed by his cousin's pronouncement. However, he knew all the innuendos and teasing would end abruptly once they announced their engagement.

Francine filled her plate with pot stickers, dim sum, shrimp toast, and ribs. "What I miss most about not living in New York City is Chinese takeout and bagels."

"I agree," Kara concurred. "But don't forget pizza. There's nothing like New York pizza."

Dawn picked up a plate, eyeing the different hot and cold dishes. "The reason I moved from upstate New York to the city was because of the restaurants."

Within the next half hour the house was filled with David's friends and co-workers and their dates. Angela came with a man she'd been dating for several months, and the men who came solo appeared to be actively looking for single females in attendance. David, aware of their motives, made certain to remain close to Devon, all the while resting his hand at the small of her back.

His associate's intent was more than obvious when Trevor spied Dawn, zeroing in on her like a heat-seeking missile. The professional dancer appeared receptive as they sat together talking quietly. David had never been keen on matchmaking, but he was glad Kara's friend had come, because Dawn interacting with Trevor would help him get over the breakup with his girlfriend.

A scroll rolled across the lower portion of the screen announcing the local health alert was canceled because a college student confirmed to have come down with rubella was now in quarantine. Within seconds of tip-off, everyone claimed a seat. The second round of the Big Dance had begun.

Chapter Nineteen

~~⌒~~

Devon sat on a stool in an upscale jewelry boutique watching the jeweler measure her finger. She'd managed to recover from the prior day's frivolity by going to bed earlier than usual. Even after turning off the TV, some of David's former high school buddies lingered. Over breakfast he told her that they didn't leave until it was close to midnight. Kara and Jeff had left earlier than the others because she had to feed her son, while Trevor had offered to show Dawn around downtown Charleston before driving her back to the island. Devon had taken a liking to Angela, who'd whispered she was better for David than his old girlfriend, which made her wonder what type of woman she had been to have turned off so many people.

She felt David's body heat when he stood behind her. She glanced up at him over her shoulder. "Don't you think I should get a half size larger in case my finger swells in the heat?" She normally measured five and a half.

"What do you think, Mr. Cage?" he asked the jeweler.

The jeweler glanced up over a pair of half-glasses. "It all depends on the band and setting. I'll have her try on a six, and if there's some wiggle room without the ring slipping over her knuckle, it should be okay if her finger swells a little."

Devon wanted to tell the man she was pregnant and that alone might compromise whether she would retain fluid. So far she'd been very careful about her sodium intake. She'd lost count of the number of loose stones she'd looked at, and her dilemma was whether to select a round or princess-cut diamond.

"I think I like the princess cut."

The jeweler picked up the stone with what resembled tweezers, placing it on a platinum band with micro pavé diamonds running halfway around the shank. Her eyes met David's and he nodded. Once the stone was set the ring would be magnificent.

"I like it," she said.

Mr. Cage smiled at David. "Your fiancée has exquisite taste. The center stone is almost flawless. I'll set it while you watch, then after I clean it you'll have the honor of putting it on her finger."

They watched as the jeweler meticulously set the center stone, then placed the ring in a strainer and dropped it in a small container that emitted a blast of steam. He rubbed it with a soft cloth before handing it to David.

David held Devon's left wrist as he slipped the ring on her hand. It went on easily over her knuckle. "It's a little loose."

"Loose, but I don't believe it will slip off," Mr. Cage said.

Leaning closer, David touched his mouth to hers. "Do you like it?"

She met his eyes, smiling. "Yes. It's beautiful."

"So are you," he whispered in her ear. "We're also going to need bands."

Mr. Cage ran a hand over his straight black hair. "Do you want a band to match the ring so your bride will have a wedding set, or do you want separate matching bands?"

"Matching bands," Devon said.

"A wedding set *and* matching bands," David countered.

Tiny lines fanned out around the older man's eyes. "What if I bring you both, then you can decide together."

"Don't say it," David warned softly when she opened her mouth.

She gave him a direct stare. "You don't even know what I was about to say."

"Yes I do…" His words trailed off when his cell rang. "Excuse me, baby."

Waiting until David had walked a short distance away to answer his phone, Devon leaned over the showcase. "Mr. Cage, I'd like to get my fiancé a wedding gift. What do you suggest?"

"How about a watch? I have some nice ones near the front of the shop. I know that he's a lawyer, so a designer fountain pen is another option. We have those in stock, but we usually don't put them out on display."

"I'll be back at another time to look at them," she whispered.

David ended his call and together they decided on wide plain platinum bands. He settled the bill and they left the boutique holding hands as they walked to where he'd parked his car. "I told my mother I'd meet her for lunch, so I'll drop you off at the Cove Inn, where you can pick up your car. Are you coming back to Charleston or staying at the inn tonight?"

Reaching up, Devon placed her left hand on his face as bright sunlight reflected off the precious stones on her finger. "I'll come back only for tonight so we can celebrate our engagement. You promised not to sleep with me until we're married and I promised not to live with you until we're married." She saw him flinch as if struck across the face. David had hinted at her living with him, but she knew their living under the same roof for the next month would prove too tempting—at least for her.

Reaching into the pocket of his slacks, David took several keys off a ring. "Here are the keys for the front and back door." Leaning closer, he whispered the code to disarm the security system in her ear. "I'm not certain when I'll be back because I have to see the contractor later on this afternoon about when he's going to start renovating the office."

"How will you get in if I'm not there?"

He smiled, taking her elbow as they crossed the street. "I have another set at my mother's house."

Devon sat in David's car staring through the windshield, still trying to fathom how she'd experienced more changes in her life in one week than she had in years. Within the span of ten days, she'd decided to buy a house and relocate, gotten engaged, and set a wedding date. Life in the Lowcountry moved slower than the fast pace of New York City, yet hers was still in Big Apple mode.

He drove her back to Sanctuary Cove, leaving her in the inn's parking lot and waiting until she got in before he reversed direction to drive back to Charleston. When she arrived at Jack's ten minutes after noon and found Kara, Dawn, Morgan, and Francine waiting at their usual table, she quickly greeted each woman before sitting down next to Dawn.

"Sorry about being late," she said in apology as she picked up a menu.

Francine put up a hand, shielding her eyes. "Please don't tell me I'm seeing what I think I'm seeing on your finger, girlfriend."

Devon placed her left hand on the table, fingers outstretched as the four women gasped. "Yes, you are."

Dawn caught her hand, bringing it closer to her face. "That center stone has to be at least two carats. My brother is a jeweler," she explained when Devon stared at her.

"If you tell me David Sullivan put *that* on your finger then I'm going to scream at the top of my lungs," Morgan threatened.

Flashing a sheepish grin, Devon stared at the scarred tabletop. Dawn was right about the carat weight. The total weight for the ring was just shy of three carats. She had no idea how much David paid for the engagement ring because he and the jeweler had negotiated the price in private. "I'd rather you not scream, but yes he did."

Kara shook her head in amazement. "Jeff had to know what David was up to because he said he could smell a wedding coming up."

"When did he say that?" Devon questioned, wondering if David had discussed proposing to her with his cousin.

"Yesterday. He said David never allowed any woman in his kitchen, so you have to be very special," Kara explained.

Devon lifted her eyebrows. "I don't know about special, but I think of him as extraordinary, because how many men would be willing to marry a woman knowing she's carrying another man's child?"

"My father did," Kara reminded her.

"And you think it's all about your baby?" Morgan asked.

Devon shrugged her shoulders. "What else can it be?"

Francine shook her head. "I've known your future husband a lot longer than you have, so I know him better, and if you believe David is just being altruistic then you must have your head in the sand. Anyone who's not blind could see that he's in love with you."

"I agree with Fran," Morgan said. "I noticed that yesterday. He couldn't keep his eyes *or* his hands off you."

Devon wanted to tell the women that she was the one who had to struggle to keep her hands off David. If he hadn't wanted to wait until after they were married to make love, she would've already jumped his bones.

"Talk about marking his territory," Kara said teasingly. "Every man there knew exactly who you were with."

"Have you set a wedding date?" Francine asked.

Devon nodded. "We're looking at May first." All conversations stopped when the waitress set a plate of biscuits on the table, along with a pitcher of ice-cold water, before taking their orders. Once she was out of earshot, Devon told them about her plan to buy a house on Cherry Lane in Haven Creek.

Morgan nearly choked when she took a sip of water. "We'll be neighbors! I live in South Haven Creek and Cherry Lane is just over the footbridge in North Haven Creek."

Devon felt Morgan's excitement. "That means our children can grow up together."

"I don't know." Dawn sighed audibly. "I must not be living right, because I can't find a man willing to commit to save my life."

"You have to come down here to find one," Kara teased. "Look at me. I was down here less than a month when I started dating Jeff, and a few months later we were married."

Francine gestured to Dawn. "You looked real cozy with David's co-worker yesterday. And didn't he drive you back to the Cove?"

Dawn's eyes sparkled like polished blue topaz. "Yes, and Trevor is really nice. He told me he's never been to New York, so I invited him to come up whenever he has some time and I'll show him the Big Apple."

Kara smiled at her former roommate. "I've been trying to get Dawn to move down here and open a dance studio. I told her I'm even willing to give her the money to get it up and running."

Dawn sighed. "It sounds tempting, but I keep thinking I'm going to miss the excitement of living in the big city."

"That's what I thought when I came down here earlier in the year," Devon said. "Now that I've been here more than a week, I loathe having to go back to New York to unload my condo."

Dawn smiled at Devon. "That's because you have your man here."

"Amen!" chorused Morgan and Kara.

Their orders arrived quickly and the five women concentrated on eating. It was only the second time Devon had joined Morgan, Kara, and Francine for their weekly Lowcountry Ladies Luncheon, realizing the first time wasn't a fluke; she felt a kinship with them that was missing with the women she'd known in New York. However, everyone seated at the table was connected in some way: Morgan and Francine had attended the same high school, Kara and Dawn were former roommates, and when she married David, she and Kara would share a bond because they'd married cousins.

The conversations swirling around the table included the details for Francine's June wedding and Kara and Jeff's son's christening. "Dawn and I have an appointment to meet with Reverend Crawford at one thirty, so we're going to have to leave soon," Kara announced.

Morgan glanced at her watch. "I have to be back at the office by two because Abram has an appointment to see a client over on Mount Pleasant."

Dawn stood up as Kara and Morgan left money on the table. "See you guys next Monday, same time, same place," Devon said as everyone exchanged hugs. She sat down again. "Once the house is decorated, I'm willing to host the Lowcountry Ladies Luncheons. Not only will it give me something to do, but we'll be able to laugh as loud as we want without folks giving us the stink eye."

Francine gave her a skeptical look. "I doubt if you'll have that much time on your hands."

"I'll have enough," Devon retorted. "I plan to assist David with some of his cases, but that's not going to occupy all my time. However, I do want to put in a vegetable and flower garden, which again doesn't require around-the-clock tending." She paused, staring directly at the redhead. "I've been thinking about buying a few laying chickens so I'd always have fresh eggs on hand. What do you think?"

Francine chuckled. "For a city girl you've gone completely *Little House on the Prairie* on us. Whenever my grandmother bakes a cake she has me drive her over to the

Creek to buy eggs from the chicken farmers. She claims a fresh egg tastes different from those you buy in the supermarket. So I say go for it."

"I want to ask you something else, but if you don't want to do it, I won't be insulted."

"You want me to be your maid of honor?"

Devon's jaw dropped. "How did you know?"

"Lucky guess," Francine said smugly.

A cold shiver snaked its way up Devon's back as something told her it wasn't just a lucky guess when she recalled Francine asking if she believed in destiny. "No, it's not a lucky guess, Francine. You knew somehow." It wasn't a question but a fact.

Averting her gaze, Francine smiled. "You're a lot more perceptive than many people who believe they know me. It's true that sometimes I can sort of see things before they happen."

"Does Keaton know?"

Francine nodded. "I had to tell him. Aside from my immediate family, only you, Keaton, and Mo know."

Devon leaned closer. "Are you good?"

"Do you want to know if you're having a girl or a boy?"

Again Devon felt a cold chill sweep over her as she quickly shook her head. "No. I can wait for the doctor to tell me. What you've just told me will go no further than this table. And yes, I'd like you to be my bridal attendant. I'm going to ask Keaton if he'll give me away, because my parents will not be attending my wedding." She held up a hand when Francine opened her mouth. "Please don't tell me anything about my parents."

Francine closed her eyes. "Okay, I won't."

"I don't want to interrupt Keaton when he's writing, so

when you see him please let him know I'd be honored if he would stand in as my escort."

"Of course. I still can't believe David's getting married. Mo and I were talking about him before you arrived. Seeing him laughing and joking was something neither of us could've imagined. This is not to say he hasn't always been a gracious host, but he was in rare form yesterday. Now, if he'd been like this after he broke up with Petra, I would've considered dating him, but then I wouldn't have fallen in love with Keaton."

"And I wouldn't be marrying David."

Francine pursed her lips. "I know why you're marrying David, but do you love him?"

The question gave Devon pause. She'd asked herself the same question since she'd agreed to become Mrs. David Sullivan, and the answer had evaded her. "There is a part of me that loves him. I find him to be the most kind, generous, and gentle man I've known. I keep telling myself he's perfect when I know there's no such thing as perfect but only what we perceive or want perfect to be. I know if I'd met him before I found myself in this predicament I would've fallen head over heels in love with him."

"I know you don't want me to read you, but I'm going to say this and then I'll shut up. You're going to fall in love with David even if you deny being in love with him and you're going to have more children. The two of you will live to see your grandchildren and maybe a great-grandchild—"

"Stop!" Devon pleaded. "Please stop, because you're frightening me." Now she was cold from her head to her toes.

Francine sat closer to her, rubbing her back in an effort to calm her. "It's okay, Devon. Now you see why I don't tell people about my gift. But I wanted you to know that everything is going to work out just fine."

It took several minutes before Devon regained her composure. She'd never had her palm, tarot cards, or tea leaves read, yet a woman who was to marry her client within three months had revealed her future. Francine had told her what Devon didn't want to see beyond her immediate future. David was good to her and good for her; however, something wouldn't permit her to open her heart to let him in, because there were times when she believed he needed someone who could love him the way he deserved to be loved. She'd chided Francine for telling her future, but it also served as an eye-opener. She had been given a second chance and Devon knew she would be a fool to squander it with doubt and distrust.

A hint of a smile softened her mouth. "Your secret is safe with me."

"Like attorney-client privilege?"

Devon smiled. "You've got it."

"Tell me what you're having for your wedding."

She told her what she and David had discussed. "Now you. Do you plan to have a formal wedding?" Devon asked Francine.

"Oh yeah. I told Keaton I want a wedding with the works. Weather permitting, we'll have the ceremony on the beach, then everyone will come back to the house for the reception. We have enough room to accommodate at least seventy-five if we open up the living and dining rooms and another room that was used as a small ballroom. The first time I got married it was at city hall, and that day will go down in infamy for me."

"I didn't know this will be your second marriage."

Francine rolled her eyes upward. "I was young and very, very stupid. Enough about the past. Now, when do you want to go and look at dresses?"

"I'll leave that up to you."

"This is **my day off**, so do you want to go now?"

Devon **reached into her** tote for her wallet. "Let's do it."

Chapter Twenty

～

David maneuvered into the driveway and parked behind his mother's vintage Mercedes-Benz. Edna Sullivan had bought the sedan for herself to celebrate her fortieth birthday, and after putting more than 150,000 miles on it, she refused to part with the twenty-five-year-old vehicle.

He unlocked the door to the stately white colonial and walked in. David found his mother in her sitting room, writing in a clothbound journal. Edna had begun keeping a journal at ten, and now at sixty-five the former school librarian had dozens of volumes chronicling her life. David and his sister had sworn an oath never to touch any of them until after her death. He'd always thought his mother to be a little melodramatic, but he knew there were probably things she'd recorded that would shock her children *and* her husband—if he happened to survive her.

Standing outside the space he'd always thought of as the rose room because of the drapes and matching wallpaper,

David whispered softly, garnering his mother's attention. "Good afternoon, Mother."

A slight frown appeared between Edna's eyes, temporarily marring her beautiful unlined face. "One of these days you're going to give me a heart attack sneaking in here like that."

David walked into the room, leaned over, and kissed his mother's coiffed silver curly hair. "You look very nice today." She wore a becoming leaf-green pantsuit with a black silk blouse and matching pumps. Edna was his aunt Corrine's niece and the resemblance between the two was remarkable. Both were tall and slender, with flawless skin the color of café au lait.

Closing the journal and rising to her feet, Edna hugged her son. "I just got back from chairing the Black and White Masque Charity Ball. I can't believe it's almost sold out. I know I promised to have lunch with you, but the committee members decided to order in."

Reaching for Edna's hand, David led her to a sofa covered with the same design as the wallpaper. "That's okay. I'll grab something later. Speaking of the ball, don't forget to save two tickets for me."

Edna gave him a sidelong glance. "If you don't mind my asking, who are you bringing?"

A beat passed. "My fiancée," he said in a calm voice.

"Your fiancée?" There was a trace of hysteria in Edna's voice. Resting a hand on her chest, she sucked in a lungful of air, then let it out slowly. "When did you get engaged? You told me yesterday that you'd met someone special, and now you tell me you're engaged. And why haven't your father and I met her? Who is she, David?"

David held up a hand. "Which question do you want me to answer first?"

"When did you get engaged?"

"This morning."

She nodded, blowing out her breath. "Who is she?"

Slumping against the plump cushion back, David stared at a low table filled with green and flowering plants in delicately painted glazed pots. "Her name is Devon Gilmore. She just moved here from New York."

"She moved here to marry you?"

"Yes."

Edna's eyebrows lifted a fraction. "You asked her to move or she volunteered?"

"We mutually agreed because of the baby."

Edna's mouth opened and closed several times before she managed to say, "Baby! What baby!?"

If the conversation hadn't been so serious, David would've laughed. Her shocked expression was priceless. "We're expecting a baby." The admission rolled off his tongue as if he'd said it countless times before.

It was Edna's turn to slump on the sofa. She closed her eyes. "Was it planned? Did you two plan to start a family?"

"No," he admitted truthfully.

"When's the wedding?"

"May first."

Edna sprang up like a jack-in-the-box. "May first! That's a little more than a month from now. How do you expect me to plan a wedding in a few weeks? I have to send an announcement to the newspapers. We have to find a venue, a caterer, and order a cake. I also need to contact her mother."

David gently eased her back down to the sofa. "The only thing you're going to have to do is show up and be your beautiful self, Mother. I'm thinking of holding the ceremony and reception at McLeay's Garden." He and the owner of the restaurant had attended the same high school. "Devon and I will apply for a license and go to a stationer before the end of the week for invitations. If we put a rush on them, they'll go out next week. Meanwhile I'll call everyone and tell them to save the date."

Having seemingly recovered from the shock that her son was getting married, Edna gave him a tender smile. "When am I going to meet my future daughter-in-law?"

"I know you said you don't feel like fixing Easter dinner, so I'll do it at my place. Maybe we'll make it a family affair and I'll invite Aunt Corrine and Jeff and his family. By the way, have you heard from Leticia?" David hadn't had contact with his sister in weeks.

"She emailed me the other day to let me know she was going to take time off and spend a couple of weeks in Paris."

"When you contact her again, let her know about the wedding and that I'd love for her to meet Devon."

Edna pressed her palms together in a prayerful gesture. "I can't believe I'm going to be a grandmother."

"Are you going to be Grandma or Nana?" David said teasingly.

"I don't know. You didn't tell me what Devon does for a living."

"She's a lawyer."

"Is she going to work with you?" Edna asked in a monotone.

"Eventually she will," David answered.

"Is she the reason you decided to desert your father?"

David clamped his teeth together. He didn't want to get into it or rehash the reason that he'd decided to set up his own firm. A volatile encounter with his father had resulted in his walking out of his parents' home literally biting his tongue to keep from spewing expletives. He was approaching forty years of age and felt he didn't have to account for his actions to anyone but himself. He could've easily joined another firm after graduating law school rather than come to work for his father, and there were occasions when he wished that he had. David Sullivan, Sr., had always been a hard taskmaster and he the obedient, dutiful son. However, it was no longer about pleasing his father but himself.

"Devon had nothing to do with my decision to set up my own firm. I'd decided long before I met her that I want to help clients who have to rely on public defenders who are overburdened with more cases than they can handle to offer them justice. It's not about the size of one's retainer or billable hours, Mother. It's about helping those who can't help themselves."

Edna gave him a direct stare. "I've never heard you talk like this."

"Because it's something we never discussed. I remember Nana giving me a card with a quote from Proverbs after I graduated law school and I've never forgotten it: Do not exploit the poor because they are poor and do not crush the needy in court."

Edna sat up straight, pulling back her shoulders. "My mother-in-law was always a little weird. I never understood why she'd give you cards, but refused to give you and Leticia gifts for your birthdays, Christmas, or graduations."

David smiled. "Weird because she was saving our gifts for when she was no longer here." His grandmother's estate had made him and his sister millionaires.

"She never wanted me to marry your father."

"Please stop, Mother. I didn't come here to listen to you talk about Nana." He knew his mother and grandmother hadn't seen eye to eye on a lot of things and had barely tolerated each other. He hoped he wouldn't have to relive that with his mother and Devon.

"Are you and Devon living together before you get married?"

"No. She's staying at the Cove Inn. Once we're married, we'll live in Charleston until we can move into the house in the Creek."

"The Creek?"

David pushed to his feet. "She's buying a house in Haven Creek."

"What about your place here?"

"We'll use it on weekends or when we want to entertain."

"I guess if she's buying a house, then she's not marrying you for your money," Edna said quietly.

"Maybe I'm marrying her for her money," David quipped. He didn't know Devon's net worth, but knew she was far from a pauper.

Edna's lips parted in surprise as she stood. "Oh my!"

"I'm not marrying her for money," he said quickly. "I'm marrying her because I'm hopelessly in love with her."

"So it's not about the baby?"

He'd asked himself the same question and the answer was always the same. "It's about Devon *and* the baby." He couldn't profess to love her and not love the baby.

"I'm glad you said that," Edna said. She held out a hand and David gently pulled her to her feet. She hugged David.

David didn't do or say things to garner compliments from his parents but to follow his own conscience. He kissed her scented cheek. "I hope you and Dad are coming for Easter dinner."

"We wouldn't miss it. Do you want me to bring anything?"

"No thank you." He unwound her arms from around his neck, kissing the backs of her hands. "I'll let myself out."

Sitting in his car, David scrolled through the navigation screen until he got to Jeff's work number. "Cavanaugh Island Sheriff's Department. How may I direct your call?"

"Winnie, this is David. Is my cousin around?"

"Hold on. He's in the back."

He'd made it a practice not to call Jeff at home because he didn't know his schedule. And if he was home, then he could be sleeping before ending or starting his shift. "Hey, cuz," he said when he heard Jeff's greeting.

"What's up, David?"

"Tell Aunt Corrine not to bother cooking for Easter because I'm inviting the family to my place for the holiday."

"You can count on us being there," Jeff drawled.

"I want you to make certain you take off May first."

"What's happening on that date?"

"I'm getting married and I want you to stand in as my best man."

"You're shittin' me," Jeff said after a pregnant pause.

David couldn't help but smile. He knew he'd shocked his cousin. "No, I'm not."

"Please tell me it's Devon."

"Guilty as charged."

"Hot damn! You really shock me, cuz. I thought I moved fast when I met Kara, but you've taken the prize. Why the rush? Is she in the family way?"

Knowing he couldn't lie to Jeff because it would be only a matter of time before everyone knew that Devon was pregnant, David said, "Yes, she is. And you should know we country boys don't waste time when we see something we want."

There was a noticeable pause before Jeff said, "No shit. Congratulations. I'm sure you know Kara was a couple of months along when we got married."

David smiled. "Anyone who bothered to do the math realized that."

"What do you want? Girl or boy?"

"It doesn't matter as long as he or she is healthy."

Jeff chuckled. "I hear you."

"I'll let you go, but look for invitations in the mail in a couple of weeks. And don't forget to tell Aunt Corrine about the wedding."

It was the second time in a week that David opened his home to entertain, but this time Devon found herself a spectator when he wouldn't permit her to help him cook. She set the table in the formal dining room with china, silver, crystal, and a vase of white mini calla lilies.

The days were passing so quickly she had to stop and think of what she'd done the day before. She and Francine had visited two bridal boutiques before she selected an A-line, silk duchesse satin gown with a square neckline, Empire waistline, cap sleeves, a gold-and-platinum embroidery embellishment, and a sweep train. The gown's design would perfectly conceal her expanding waistline, and the saleswoman informed her there was enough fabric to let out the garment if she did gain more weight, while recommending she come back a week before she was to be married if alterations were necessary. They also found a gown with a similar design for Francine in sea-foam green, which complemented her dark red hair. They'd lingered long enough at the boutique to select shoes.

Midweek she and David visited a stationer and ordered

wedding invitations. Instead of the ubiquitous wording with parents inviting guests to witness the nuptials of their children, they'd substituted their names: *Ms. Devon Juliana Gilmore-Collins and Mr. David Edgar Sullivan, Jr., request the honor of your presence at their marriage.* The printer had promised to expedite the order and by next week word would get out that one of Charleston's most eligible bachelors was no longer available.

Devon had also taken the time to shop for clothes to accommodate her changing body and to confirm an appointment with a Charleston ob-gyn. She'd called her New York obstetrician's office to send her a form to sign to release her medical records, which she had David notarize. They joked about the benefit of having two lawyers in the family. They'd applied for a marriage license and David had contacted a judge who'd agreed to officiate.

She walked into the kitchen, stopping short when she saw David take a roasting pan out of the oven, from which wafted the mouthwatering aroma of lamb encrusted with minced garlic and oregano. "That smells amazing."

He turned to give her a wide grin. "You look beautiful."

Devon flashed a modest smile. She'd flat ironed her hair and styled it in a loose braid. A white silk poet's shirt and a pair of black stretch pants with an elastic waistband and low-heeled black patent leather pumps and a light cover of makeup completed her look for meeting his parents for the first time.

"I know you said you're not too fond of lamb, but I hope you'll like this."

"If it tastes as good as it looks and smells, then I'll be forced to eat my words." Not only had David roasted the lamb, but he'd also baked a half bone-in ham studded with cloves and covered with crushed pineapple and glazed honey. She watched him carefully when he prepared couscous with dried apricots and raisins and slivered almonds because she loved Mediterranean cuisine. Stir-fried green beans with minced garlic and a mixed salad of field greens with an herb dressing rounded out his Easter Sunday feast.

She was standing with her arm around David's waist when the doorbell rang; they smiled at each other. Devon didn't know how he did it, but David was able to time his cooking to coincide with the arrival of his first guest. "I bet that's my mother and father."

Devon stood next to David as an older couple followed by a younger woman whom she assumed was David's sister strolled into the kitchen carrying shopping bags and a cake box.

She met his mother's eyes, wondering what she was thinking. She didn't have to wonder long, though, as Mrs. Sullivan smiled and extended her arms for a hug. "Aren't you adorable," Edna said in Devon's ear.

"Thank you. It's a pleasure to meet you, Mrs. Sullivan."

Edna pulled back and when she opened her eyes they were shimmering with unshed tears. "Mrs. Sullivan was my mother-in-law. I insist you call me Mother."

Devon nodded. It was what she'd called her own mother, but whereas Monique was emotionally cold and empty, David's mother was the complete opposite. Warmth and acceptance radiated from her. "Okay, Mother."

David looped his arm around Devon's waist. "Darling, the man standing there grinning like a Cheshire cat is my father and namesake. And the gorgeous woman with the cake box is my prodigal sis, Leticia, who didn't have the decency to let me know she was back in town."

Leticia, dressed in her flight attendant uniform, placed the box on the countertop. "FYI, brother love, I just got in from L.A. and I wanted to surprise you."

Extending one arm, David winked at her. "Well, you did. Come here and give your big brother a hug and kiss."

Leticia, ignoring David, closed the distance between them and reached for Devon's left hand. "Very nice!" she said, smiling. She pulled Devon close, forcing David to release her. "Welcome to the family. You don't know how long I've waited for a sister."

"Me too," Devon said truthfully as she returned Leticia's embrace. The flight attendant had the appearance of a high fashion model.

"Save some of her for me, Letty," David Senior drawled.

Seconds later Devon found herself crushed against Mr. Sullivan's tall, lean body. Looking at him was an indication of what David would be like in twenty years. The Sullivans were tall and very attractive, and their children had inherited their best features. "My wife tells me you're going to make us grandparents."

Devon closed her eyes and nodded. "It's true. David and I are expecting our first child at the end of September."

She didn't want to believe how easily the lie had slipped off her tongue; then she had to remind herself that although David wasn't the biological father, he was going to be the baby's father in every sense of the word.

"Do you know the sex?" Leticia asked as she shrugged out of her jacket and left it on the back of a stool.

"Not yet. I have an appointment for a sonogram next week, though."

Walking into the half bath off the kitchen, Leticia washed her hands. "Either way, I'm going to spoil the hell out of my niece or nephew. And soon as they're walking and toilet trained I'm going to take them with me on a trip to the other side of the world."

Edna took off the silk Hermès shawl she'd tied over her shoulders. "Don't you think Devon would have some say in that?"

Leticia emerged from the bathroom, drying her hands on a paper towel. "Of course she'll come with us."

"What about David?" Devon asked.

Cradling Devon's head, he planted a noisy kiss on her parted lips. "That's what I like. A woman who looks out for her man."

She felt uncomfortable with David's display of affection in front of his family. She gave him a warm smile. "Please let me go," she whispered under her breath. "I have to put out another place setting for Leticia."

"Who else is coming, brother?" Leticia asked as she opened the refrigerator and placed the box on a shelf.

"Jeff, Aunt Corrine, Kara, the baby, and a friend of Kara's who's visiting from New York."

"Austin must be big now. The last time I saw him he was—" Her words stopped with the chiming of the doorbell. "That has to be them."

Ten minutes later Devon cradled Austin in her arms, singing softly to the sleeping infant. He looked exactly like Jeff, including a slight indentation in his tiny chin. Then without warning he opened his eyes, yawning and smiling before going back to sleep. His eyes were a mysterious smoky gray. She couldn't wait to hold her own baby to her breast, feel his soft breath against her throat, and inhale the scent exclusive to newborns. In the past she'd avoided picking up or holding a baby, but now it felt so natural and comforting. She met David's eyes as he stared at her holding his cousin. The seconds ticked, becoming a full minute before she glanced down at Austin, shattering the soporific spell.

Kara took the sleeping infant from her. "I'm going to put him down because someone who will remain nameless likes to carry him around. And *his* name is not Aunt Corrine," she said, throwing her husband a *you know who I'm talking about* look.

Devon glanced at David's aunt, who was engaged in a lively conversation with her niece. He'd given her an overview of his relatives and told her Corrine had been a teacher in the Sanctuary Cove school district before becoming the town's first African American principal.

David, who had just finished slicing the lamb, handed the platter to his father. "Dad, could you please take this into the dining room?"

Jeff reached for the platter with the ham. "I'll take that."

One by one all the dishes were set on the table with seating for ten. Aunt Corrine, sitting at the head of the table facing Edna, was given the honor of blessing the table, and then David busied himself pouring wine while his sister filled water goblets.

The conversation was lively and colorful as Austin slept soundly in a portable playpen in a corner of the dining room. Leticia kept the assembly entertained with tales of her travels to exotic locales with her billionaire boss. Devon detected something in her voice that indicated her relationship with the international businessman went beyond employer and employee. It was probably why she was away for extended periods of time.

The thought had barely entered her mind when she found

herself the focus of attention as Edna asked about how her plans were progressing for the upcoming wedding. Between bites of fork-tender, expertly seasoned lamb, Devon gave everyone an update.

Leticia pressed the heel of her hand to her forehead. "I just remembered I'm scheduled to go to Brazil that weekend, but I'm coming, even if I have to drag Chris with me. We can always fly out the following morning."

"You're coming with your boss?" Edna asked, giving her daughter a look of disbelief.

"There's no way I'm going to miss my brother's wedding. If he doesn't like it, then he can find another flight attendant to take my place. Or better yet, he can fire me."

"I doubt he'll do that," Edna said quietly. "He depends on you too much to let you go."

David stared across the table at his sister. "Am I missing something?"

Devon nudged David's leg with her foot under the table. She wanted to tell him to mind his business, but there were too many people staring at them. "I'll make certain you get an invitation for two," she said quickly. Leticia pantomimed a thank-you when she nodded to Devon.

David's father cleared his throat. "I know Edna doesn't like it when I talk shop at the table, but I have to thank you, son. I got a call late Friday night from the legal department at J and J Publishing about a possible settlement in the Humphries copyright infringement and discrimination suit. How did you expedite the subpoenas so quickly?"

David had instructed the paralegal to prepare and file the subpoenas within twenty-four hours. "Don't thank me, Dad. It was Devon who got Cynthia Humphries to open up about how they treated her."

The elder Sullivan studied Devon with curious intensity. "You're kidding."

David smiled. "I wish I were."

David Senior massaged the back of his neck. "You know you're entitled to a portion of the settlement."

"Forget it, Dad. I didn't do it for the money." And for David it had never been about money but justice for his clients.

"How would you like to join my firm as an associate?" David Senior asked Devon.

"It's too late to hire Devon, because she belongs to *me now*," David said quickly, preempting whatever Devon wanted to say. "I told you a long time ago to hire a female attorney."

"Damn, cuz," Jeff said. "You don't have to act so possessive."

Corrine shot her grandson a knowing look. "Jeffrey, you know I don't abide cussin' on Sunday, yet you keeping doing it."

Jeff smiled at his grandmother. "After spending twenty years in the Corps, you're lucky I really don't let loose."

Corrine glared at Jeff. "Why can't you be more like David? I'm willing to bet he doesn't cuss."

"Hell yeah I do," David said, and everyone at the table burst into laughter.

Devon landed a soft punch on David's shoulder. He should've been ashamed teasing his octogenarian great-aunt. "He'll have to clean up his mouth once we have this baby, because I'm not going to tolerate a potty-mouthed kid when he's still wearing Pull-Ups."

"Preach, my sister," Kara intoned, waving her hand in the air as if testifying in church. "I told Jeff I'm going to put out a swear jar and charge him five dollars each time he curses."

David shook his head. "What happened to a quarter?"

"Inflation," Devon and Kara said in unison, then rose slightly to bump fists.

The good-natured teasing set the tone for the rest of the afternoon and early evening. Dinner was a leisurely affair and no one appeared anxious to leave the table. Kara excused herself and went into the living room to feed and change Austin, while David brewed a pot of coffee, cut and served the coconut layer cake, and offered cordials for those drinking alcohol. Devon decided to pass on the coffee and cordials but opted for a slice of cake with a glass of cold milk.

David commandeered the men to help clear the table and pack up leftovers in takeaway containers, while Devon and the women retreated to the former man cave, which she'd converted into a family room with family photographs and green and flowering plants in clay and colorful ceramic pots. A quartet of pink-and-white moth orchids, flanked by large pink-and-white pillars in glass chimneys, lined the fireplace mantel.

"This is nice," Edna remarked as she sank down to a leather chair. "I always thought this room needed a woman's touch."

Devon folded her body down into a chair and pressed a button on the side to elevate the footrest. She didn't tell Edna that even though she'd added the accessories she'd conferred with David to get his approval. If they were to become man and wife, there had to be mutual respect between them. Even though Monique Gilmore's blood ran in her veins, Devon was determined not to become her mother.

Chapter Twenty-One

~⌒~

David, sprawled on the oversize club chair with Devon, opened his eyes. The fire he'd lit in the fireplace was dying out while candles flickered behind chimneys on the mantel. After everyone had left, they'd retreated to the family room to unwind.

"Are you falling asleep on me, baby?" he asked Devon.

"I don't think so," she slurred.

He smiled. "Either you are or you aren't."

A beat passed. "I think I am, but it's too early to go to bed."

"Let me know when you want me to drive you back to the island."

Devon shifted until her hips were molded to his groin. "I'm still not ready."

David splayed a hand over her barely there baby bump. "Are you feeling all right?"

"I'm a little full, but I feel wonderful." She shifted again, trying to find a more comfortable position. "I like your family."

"They like you, too. Especially my mother and sister. Speaking of my sister, why did you kick me under the table when she was talking about bringing her boss?"

"Don't you think Leticia was a little over-the-top when she mentioned her boss?"

"You think there's something going on between them?"

"It may be woman's intuition, but I think so."

David smiled, pressing his mouth to the nape of Devon's scented neck. "Letty had a bad experience in college. She had a boyfriend who continued to stalk her after she'd split with him, which left her skittish when it comes to relationships."

"What happened to her stalker?"

"A few guys from the football team caught him and that's all she wrote. A couple of days later he dropped out, citing medical problems."

"Please don't tell me they gave him a beatdown."

"I wouldn't know because Letty never told me about him until after she'd graduated. She claimed she didn't tell me because she was afraid I might do something stupid."

Glancing over her shoulder, Devon stared at him. "Would you have done something stupid?"

David kissed her hair. "The only thing I'll say is that Letty has witnessed my dark side on occasion."

Devon shifted again, this time facing him. "I can't believe you have a dark side. Jeff, yes, because he's ex-military. But never you."

"Captain Oorah has changed since becoming a husband and father. But don't test him once he morphs into Sheriff Hamilton because he's all business. He's been known to pop and drop someone with a single punch if he gets in his face."

Devon trailed her fingertips over his jaw. "You should be

ashamed of yourself teasing your aunt Corrine. And I meant what I said about cursing around our child. I've heard kids as young as five or six cuss like there's no tomorrow, and if you were to tell them to tie their shoes they would cry like a baby because they wouldn't be able to do it."

David caught her wrist. "Don't worry about me using bad language in the house. I'll wait until either the baby's sleeping or I'll go outside and cuss until I run out of words." Devon rested her head on his chest and giggled. He buried his face in her hair, chiding himself for promising not to make love to her until she became his wife. The urge to be inside her was so strong he was helpless to stop his hardening sex. He knew Devon felt his hard-on when she went completely still.

"David?"

He heard the uncertainty in her voice when she called his name. "I know," he whispered in her ear. "I know I promised not to touch you but—"

"Can we do this?" Devon asked, interrupting him.

He smiled, not wanting to believe they would make love before exchanging vows. "Yes. I know I can because I love you."

The passionate confession was torn from somewhere that was totally foreign to David. Although he'd told a few women that he loved them, it wasn't the same as what he felt for Devon. He'd wrestled with his conscience when he wondered why she'd come into his life at this time. Why couldn't he resist her when every sense of reason told him to run in the opposite direction?

Devon studied the features of the man who'd managed to scale the wall she'd erected to protect herself from the heartbreak that had begun with her parents, then continued with her brother and finally Gregory.

She knew David wanted to make love to her, and she wanted to make love to him. "I want..." Devon couldn't bring herself to tell him what she not only wanted but needed.

David's eyes were steady as he asked her, "What do you want, Devon?"

She swallowed to relieve the dryness in her mouth. "I want you."

He blinked once. "How?"

An uncertain smile trembled over her lips. "I want you to make love with me." Devon was very conscious that she'd said *want* instead of *need* and *with* instead of *to*. Their coming together wouldn't be one-sided but joint. David had admitted he loved her, but Devon still was uncertain as to her feelings for him. There was a difference in loving someone and being in love with him, and what she wanted was to be in love with him.

David pressed a kiss over each eye. "Don't move."

Devon watched as he moved off the chair and extinguished the candles, then adjusted the fireplace screen around the dying fire. She sat up when he walked back to scoop her up in his arms, her arms going around his neck to keep her balance.

Everything appeared to move in slow motion as he carried her effortlessly up the staircase to the second floor. Instead of walking down the hallway to her bedroom, David shouldered open the door to his. The only illumination came from the ceiling light outside the en suite bathroom. She attempted to make out her fiancé's features in the diffused light when he placed her on the large California king bed.

She couldn't pull her gaze away from David as he pulled the hem of his shirt from the waist of his slacks, unbuttoned it, and dropped it on the floor beside the bed. Slowly, methodically, he removed his belt, shoes, socks, slacks, and finally his boxer briefs, leaving them in a pile on the floor. He was magnificent in every way.

The mattress dipped slightly when he placed one knee, then the other, on the bed. Lying beside her, David asked, "Are you okay?"

Devon smiled. "I'm good," she whispered. "In fact, I'm better than good." David hadn't even touched her intimately, yet she could feel the trickle of desire coursing throughout her body.

He took his time undressing her. Her shoes, slacks, blouse, and bra joined the garments strewn on the floor. The only remaining article of clothing was her panties. Within seconds she found herself completely naked and grateful for the lack of light because she hadn't wanted to witness David's reaction to her ripening body. It was only recently that she'd come to accept the gradual changes to her breasts and belly.

A muffled shriek echoed in the room when David leaned over and suckled her breast, the sensitive nerve endings in her nipples forcing her to rise off the bed. He cupped her jaw, preventing her from escaping his marauding mouth. David's teeth, nipping at her nipples, submerged her in a frightening erotic torture that made her feel as if she were drowning.

She flung an arm over her face when his hot breath charted a path from her breasts to her belly, searing the apex of her thighs much like the heat from a blast furnace. Delicious spasms made the sensitive flesh of her sex quiver, followed by a rush of moisture bathing her core. Devon wasn't given a chance to react to all the sensations taking her beyond herself when she felt his erection brushing against her inner thigh.

David kissed her neck. "Let's do this together." Reaching for her hand, he placed it on his erection. Her fingers closed around his heavy sex, then his hand covered hers as he positioned himself at her entrance. She gasped slightly at the penetration. She and David sighed in unison when he was fully sheathed inside her. The flutters that began with his penetration grew stronger. Her muscles contracted around his rigid flesh, pulling him in, holding him fast. Devon released his sex before squeezing him again and again. The walls of her vagina convulsed as a scorching climax hurtled her to a place she'd never been.

Supporting his upper body on his forearms, David didn't want to believe the incredible heat coming from Devon. Maybe because it was the first time he'd ever made love to a woman without using a condom, or maybe it was just the contact of flesh against flesh, and heat on heat. Not only was Devon tight, but she was on fire.

"Oh, baby, I—" Her mouth silenced him with a searing kiss that only heightened its intensity when her teeth sank into his lower lip. Her hips moved against his, and he was lost.

Her need, her hunger, was transferred to him and David answered. He moved slowly, deliberately, and each time he withdrew it was a little farther, and each time he pushed in, it was a little harder and deeper. He knew he had to be careful not to put too much pressure on her belly. However, Devon wrapping her legs around his waist was his undoing.

Sliding his hands under her hips, he lifted her off the mattress, permitting him deeper penetration. Moans and groans escalated, breathing quickened, and then the dam broke. Burying his face against the column of her neck, David came, his deep moans of ecstasy muffled in her ear.

Completely spent, he lay beside Devon, struggling to catch his breath. Reaching for her hand, he threaded their fingers together. "I hope I didn't hurt you."

She turned to face him. "No. Did I hurt *you*?" she teased, giggling.

He caressed her mouth with his. "Nah." He kissed her again, this time on the shoulder. "You're an incredible woman. In and out of bed."

"You're not so bad yourself," she slurred.

David knew Devon was falling asleep and he pulled the sheet and a lightweight blanket over their bodies. He eased her hips against his groin, and minutes after she fell asleep he joined her in a slumber for sated lovers.

Devon woke, totally disoriented. She knew she was in bed, but which bed and with whom? Reaching out, her hand came into contact with a hard shoulder, and when the familiar scent of a man's cologne wafted in her nostrils she realized she was in bed with David.

"Stop wiggling."

"I'm not wiggling," she whispered.

"Yes, you are, baby. If you keep moving I won't be able to go back to sleep."

She rolled over, facing him while resting a leg over his. "I'm ready for seconds."

He groaned. "You're hungry?"

Devon shook her head. "Not for food."

David went still as his breathing quickened. "You want me...?"

"Yes, darling. I want you to make love to me again."

He turned to face her. "Are you sure?"

Devon splayed her hand over his chest. "Are you up to it?" He took her hand, placing it between his thighs to feel his growing erection. She smiled in the darkened room. "I would say you are *up* to it."

There was no foreplay when David moved over Devon and joined their bodies in one sure, swift move. He was buried so deep they ceased to exist as separate entities. David's raw sensuousness took Devon beyond herself, leaving her moaning aloud in erotic pleasure as orgasms lapped over one another until her body vibrated with liquid fire.

A lingering ecstasy followed when she felt David quicken his movements until he, too, groaned, spilling his passion inside her. They lay together, spent, until he rolled off her body and then gathered her close. Breathing out an audible sigh, she closed her eyes and fell asleep and didn't waken until the sky brightened with the dawn of a new day.

Richmond, Virginia

Chuck, chewing on the stub of an unlit cigar, peered at Jake Walsh over a highball glass half filled with premium mash whiskey. Jake was the only person Chuck trusted with his secrets. "What did you find on Miss Gilmore? Or is she Miss Collins?"

Jake tented his fingers and gave his boss a direct stare. "Emerson's right. Legally she's Devon Collins, but for some reason she prefers Gilmore. My man found out that she lives in a high-rise on Manhattan's Upper East Side. The building has a doorman twenty-four/seven, which makes it almost impossible to get inside without being announced."

"Did he ask for her?"

Jake nodded. "He did, but when the doorman rang her apartment he got no answer."

"I need your people to get inside that building. Bribe a doorman. Better yet, bribe the building superintendent by offering him an early Christmas bonus. Or have someone pretend they're from FedEx or UPS delivering a package. We only have a week until Guilford announces his resignation."

Reaching for the cane leaning against a nearby table, Jake used it for support as he pushed to his feet. The decorative handle with the head of a snarling wolf made entirely of sterling silver felt cool under his hand.

He would give Chuck want he wanted, because once he accepted a case he always gave a client whatever he or she wanted. It had been that way for the past fourteen years.

Chapter Twenty-Two

◦◦◦

Devon lay on the examining table, her feet resting in the stirrups and her eyes staring up at the ceiling while the obstetrician performed an ultrasound. When she'd gotten up earlier that morning at the inn and called David to let him know she had a doctor's appointment, he'd insisted on coming with her. Once they arrived at the office, she noticed he wasn't the only man who'd accompanied his pregnant significant other.

Dr. Ingram peered at the monitor. "Ms. Collins, you're carrying one baby and it's a girl."

A daughter! She was going to have a little girl. Devon nodded, too overcome with emotion to speak as the doctor continued to take pictures. Tears welled in her eyes, overflowing and trickling into her hair. She wiped them away with the back of her hand.

Rising slightly, she met the young doctor's eyes. Dr. Kelly Ingram was a throwback to the seventies, with a straight waist-length ponytail, bare face, John Lennon–type glasses, a midi skirt, and clogs.

Twenty minutes later Devon and David sat together, holding hands, while Dr. Ingram discussed the results of the ultrasound. "Everything indicates you're carrying a healthy little girl. We'll have the lab results for the other tests in a week. I know it's early, but I'd like you to think about whether you want natural childbirth. If so, we do offer on-site Lamaze classes." She trained her gaze on David. "Dad, you'll be taught what you have to do to assist your partner."

David gave Devon's fingers a gentle squeeze. "I'll go along with whatever Devon wants."

Dr. Ingram pressed her palms together. "Good." She glanced down at the file in front of her. "You indicated here no nausea or headaches, but that you're bothered by cold weather. That could be due to anemia, which could be why you're experiencing fatigue. The receptionist will give you an additional three-month supply of vitamins and iron pills before you leave, and we'll make sure to check your blood work." She paused as she scanned the questionnaire Devon had completed, checking off what she ate and didn't eat. "I want you to increase your daily caloric intake. I don't feel you're gaining enough weight."

Devon blinked. "I'm eating a lot now," she said defensively.

"Dad, I want you to make certain she doesn't skip any meals."

"Don't worry, Doctor," David said. "I'll make certain she has a balanced diet." Devon shared a glance with him.

"Is there anything else you'd like to ask me?" Dr. Ingram asked. She paused when David and Devon looked at each other. "Are you familiar with the different sex positions you can use during pregnancy?"

David curbed the urge to clear his throat. He wasn't a prude, but he didn't want to talk about how he and Devon made love. Although her belly wasn't large enough to become cumbersome, they preferred lying on their sides front to front or spooning front to back, which allowed both of them to make love in a slow, relaxed way. "We don't have a problem making love."

"And I have a book that outlines different positions we can use that won't put pressure on my belly," Devon offered.

"That's good to hear," Dr. Ingram said. She closed the file and smiled at Devon. "I'll look forward to seeing you again in a month. See the receptionist before you leave and she'll set up the appointment."

Rising to stand, David cupped Devon's elbow. "Thank you, Dr. Ingram." He waited until they were in the medical building's parking lot, then pulled Devon close to his chest and buried his face in her hair. "You're going to have to show me your book with the naughty positions."

"That's not happening," she said, laughing softly. "I want to surprise you whenever I show you a new position."

He kissed her hair. "I happen to like surprises, and knowing we're going to have a daughter calls for a little celebration."

She opened her tote, handing him the sonogram picture. "Your baby girl is a thumb-sucker."

He studied the photo, smiling. Seeing the image made Devon's pregnancy even more of a reality, because she still wasn't showing much. "We don't have to worry about her teeth. If she needs braces, then we'll send her to Morgan's parents. They have a dental and orthodontic practice here in Charleston. They're responsible for straightening my teeth."

Devon nodded, smiling. "They must be good because your teeth are beautiful."

"Thank you. I know a quaint little out-of-the-way bistro that serves delicious homemade soup, salad, wraps, and paninis."

"I think I'd like that," she said, as she anchored her arms under his shoulders.

He eased back, staring at her upturned face as shafts of sunlight turned her complexion into burnished gold. "It's not far, so if you're up to it we can leave the car here and walk."

Going on tiptoe, Devon kissed his chin. "I don't mind walking."

Holding her hand, David led Devon out of the lot and down to a cobblestone side street lined with a number of sidewalk cafés. It was close to noon and many of the bistro tables were filled with people sitting under awnings, taking advantage of the warm weather to dine alfresco. He'd just seated Devon when he saw someone he hadn't seen in more than two years. Their eyes met and he hesitated before sitting down. He schooled his expression not to reveal what he was thinking at that moment. Since their breakup he hadn't run into her, although he knew she still lived and had a practice in Charleston.

"Hello, Petra," he said in greeting.

The oral surgeon flashed a friendly smile. "Hi, baby. How have you been?"

David stared at the tall, slender woman who wore designer garments under her lab coat even when seeing patients. At no time was she ever seen with a hair out of place or without makeup. She took great pleasure when people remarked how much she looked like supermodel Naomi Campbell.

"Very well," he replied. There was no inflection in the two words.

Petra's eyes shifted from him to Devon. "Aren't you going to introduce me to your *friend*?"

Cupping her elbow, David helped Devon to her feet. "Devon, I'd like you to meet Petra. Petra, this is Devon, my fiancée." He almost felt sorry for the woman whom he'd dated when her gaze went to Devon's ring. His own gaze went to Petra's bare left hand. He'd heard she'd gotten married and wondered if she and her husband were still together.

"Congratulations. When's the big day?"

"May first."

"Good luck." She surprised David when she took a step and kissed his cheek. "I never should've cheated on you. But it took marrying a cheat to realize how much I hurt you." Petra stared at Devon. "You're marrying a good man."

Devon looped her arm through David's. "I know. And that's why I love him."

Waiting until Petra walked away, David seated Devon again, then sat opposite her. She'd just told Petra what she hadn't admitted to him. Was she being truthful, or gloating because she'd succeeded where a woman he'd dated for years had failed? He decided not to put Devon on the spot about her declaration of love just yet.

Devon covered his hand with hers. "She's beautiful."

"She is," he remarked. "But she's not you."

He could see the blush on Devon's face as her gaze dropped to peruse the menu. There was no comparison when it came to Petra and Devon. Both were strikingly attractive women with successful careers, but that's where the resemblance ended. Devon was gentle, quiet, reflective, while Petra had been more forceful in her ambition. She was the first in her family to graduate college and claim the title of doctor.

He shook his head as if to banish all memories of the woman he'd believed he would eventually marry to stare across the small space at the one with whom he would share his life and future. He told himself Devon needed him when he knew nothing was further from the truth. Devon didn't need him as much as he wanted her love.

"Have you decided what you want to eat?" he asked.

"The beef barley soup looks good, but then I am partial to lentil. I think I'm going to try the *insalata caprese* because it's been a while since I've had tomato and mozzarella."

"What about your sandwich?" David asked.

She glanced up at him. "I don't know. What if we share a panini?"

David wanted to remind Devon that she didn't need to share anything with him, but decided it wasn't the best time and place to insist she try to eat the sandwich by herself. Dr. Ingram had recommended she increase her caloric intake and he'd promised he would monitor what and how much she consumed whenever possible.

"Okay. I'm going to order split pea soup and a panini with turkey, avocado, and cherry tomato chutney." The restaurant used *quesito*, a soft Mexican-style cheese with a mild creamy flavor that melted easily when heated.

Devon smiled. "That sounds delicious."

He'd just given the waitress their orders when his cell rang. Reaching into the pocket of his jacket, he took out the phone. A slight frown furrowed his forehead when he saw Francine's name come up on the display.

"This is David."

"Are you alone or is Devon with you?" Francine asked.

His frown deepened. "The latter. Why?"

"I want you to excuse yourself. Tell her you have to talk to a client. I don't want her to overhear what I'm about to tell you."

David felt as if Francine were talking in riddles. "Okay." He placed his thumb over the mouthpiece. "Excuse me, baby, but I need to talk to a client."

Devon waved her hand. "Go."

Pushing back his chair, Devon walked far enough away so Devon wouldn't overhear his conversation. "What is it, Red?"

"You've heard about babies born with a membrane covering their faces."

He nodded, even though Francine couldn't see him. David grew up eavesdropping on old folks and griots telling and retelling superstitions about how people born in a caul had the gift to discern the future. Some used their gift for good, while others used it to work witchcraft and cast spells that could either kill or drive someone crazy.

"Sure. Why?"

"I was one of those babies."

He found himself temporarily mute with Francine's disclosure that she was clairvoyant. How she had grown up in the Cove and kept her gift a secret for so many years was astounding since there was no such thing as keeping a secret on Cavanaugh Island.

"Why are you telling me this now, Red?"

"Because there was never a need to broadcast my business," she retorted. "Outside of my family, only you and Morgan know my secret. And I don't know how she did it, but Devon knows I'm psychic."

David didn't want to believe Devon had been that perceptive when he'd known Francine all of his life and not once suspected she had second sight. "Why me?" he repeated.

"Because I want you to protect Devon. She came to me in a vision a little while ago and I saw her surrounded in darkness. There was also a man in the vision, but what troubles me is that I couldn't see his face."

Fingers tightening in a death grip around the palm-size phone, David felt as if his blood had congealed in his veins. The outdoor temperature read sixty-eight degrees, yet to him it felt like sixty below.

"How accurate are your visions?" He so wanted to believe Francine was mistaken. Perhaps she'd imagined the woman was Devon when it could've been someone else.

"Don't dis my gift, David! I know what I saw."

"I'm sorry, Red. I...I'm just trying to wrap my head around all of this."

"Me being psychic or that someone may try to hurt Devon?"

"Both," he said truthfully.

"Hold on a minute, David. Yes, babe. I'm all right. I'll be out in a few minutes. Keaton's wondering what's taking me so long," she said softly. "I had to go into the bathroom so he wouldn't overhear me."

"Where are you?"

"I'm at Keaton's house. I had a break between customers so we're eating lunch together. Now, back to Devon."

"What exactly do you want me to do, Red?"

"Stay close to her."

"What happens when she goes back to New York? Will she be safe there?"

"I don't know," Francine admitted. "I saw palmetto trees

so I'm assuming the danger surrounding her is here. Are you going to do it, David?"

"What choice do I have, Red? Yes, I'll do it. After all, I do love her."

"And she loves you, David."

He wanted to tell Francine he was waiting patiently for Devon to tell him she loved him. "Yes, she does," he said, wondering if she'd told the redhead that she loved him. Why, he mused, was it easier for her to admit to other women that she loved him when it hadn't been that way with him?

"Thank you for hearing me out," she whispered.

"No, thank you, Red. Call me again if you have another vision."

"I will. Gotta go."

David disconnected the call, unable to believe what he'd just heard. Francine's warning that Devon was in danger from some faceless man nagged at him as he walked over and sat down again. He didn't want to believe or imagine someone wanting to harm Devon. A number of possibilities crowded his mind. Did it have to do with one of her clients?

A part of him wanted to dismiss Francine's warning as superstitious nonsense, but the Gullah in him would not permit him to ignore what could be real; it was the twenty-first century, but like many living in the Lowcountry he still held on to some of the old traditions that were brought to the New World by his African ancestors. And much as his mother refused to talk about the stories she'd heard growing up, David knew she never disrespected the men and women who were able to discern the spirit. Either they were feared or held in high regard by those who believed in their powers.

"Are you all right?" Devon asked.

David blinked as if coming out of a trance, forcing a smile he didn't feel. "I'm okay," he lied smoothly.

"You don't look okay," she countered. "Is there something you need to tell me?"

"No," he said much too quickly. "I just got some news I didn't expect."

"Is it something I can help you with?"

"No, sweetheart." He flashed a strained smile. "Have you selected paint colors for the house?" David asked smoothly, changing the topic. Devon's eyes danced with excitement whenever she talked about decorating the house.

She rested her chin on the heel of her hand. "I was thinking about painting the rooms on the first floor with a shade known as harbor mist. It's a soft bluish gray and would go well with the furniture I have on order."

David stared, an expression of complete surprise freezing his features. "You already ordered furniture?"

"Of course," Devon said smugly. "Do you think I was going to wait six to eight weeks for furniture when I can have it delivered right after the painters are finished?" Reaching into her tote, she took out her cell phone, handing it to him. "Tap the Photos icon and see what I ordered for the dining and living rooms. You'll also see what I want for the patio and front and back porches."

David couldn't help smiling. Devon had excellent taste. "I like what you've chosen for the in-home office." She'd selected a glass-topped desk supported by polished nickel sawhorse legs.

"I figured you wouldn't want to work in a space that is too sissified. Yes," she continued, "I can't forget what Jeff said about my emasculating your man cave."

"And you heard me defending your decorating skills." He

angled his head. "I'm certain the house will be a showplace."

"I don't want it to be a showplace. I want a home."

He heard the passion in her voice. Devon wanted for their child what she hadn't had growing up: a loving home. "I'm certain our home will be lovely." He scrolled to another photo. "What's up with the chicken coop?"

"I'm thinking about buying a few laying chickens so we can have fresh eggs."

David glared at her. "You're kidding, aren't you?"

"No, I'm not."

He shook his head. "No chickens, Devon. They're smelly *and* messy and require constant care. You can't go a day without cleaning out the coop, and if you don't fence in the yard, you run the risk of inviting critters looking for food. If you want fresh eggs, then buy them from the chicken farmers."

"Why would I buy them when we can have our own?"

"Look, baby. I don't mind a cat or a couple of dogs. Even a fish tank is okay, but I'm not going to put up with chickens. And don't give me that look because it's not going to work with me today, tonight, tomorrow, or even next year."

They engaged in a stare-down until Devon gave him a barely perceptible nod. "Okay. No chickens."

David had never denied Devon anything she asked for, but he drew the line when it came to live chickens. Spending time on his grandparents' farm had turned him off most farm animals. By the stubborn set of her jaw, he knew she wasn't pleased with his decision, but she had to realize they wouldn't agree on everything. The waitress arrived with their soup and he picked up his spoon. "Do you need to stop anywhere after we finish eating?"

"I want to stop at a boutique so I can get a dress for the Black and White Masque Ball."

He'd told her about the charity event scheduled the week-end before they were to be married. "Do you know where you want to go?"

"Yes. Fabulous Frocks on Church Street."

Reaching into his jacket, David took out a credit card case. "Do you need money?"

"No. I have a few cards on me."

He returned the case to his jacket pocket. "If it's all right with you I'm going to sit in the car while you shop."

"So, you're not going to be one of those hubbies who sits around holding his wife's handbag while she shops."

David was certain Devon heard his sigh of relief as the tension between them slowly slipped away. "Not hardly. I'm going to be a husband who'll drop his wife off at the mall, give her cash and credit cards, and then tell her to call or text me when she wants me to pick her up."

Devon picked up her spoon. "Coward," she said under her breath.

"Oh hell yeah. I'll never understand why it takes a woman hours to buy a single dress when—"

"That is so sexist," she said, cutting him off.

He swallowed a mouthful of split pea soup. "That is so true, baby."

"It took me less than an hour to select my wedding gown."

David went completely still. "You didn't tell me you have a gown." Their wedding plans were on track: They'd confirmed the venue, mailed out invitations, and picked up their marriage license, while his mother had offered to host the rehearsal dinner.

"That's because you're not supposed to see it until I walk into the restaurant."

"Where is it?"

"It's at the bridal shop. I have to go for a final fitting three days before the wedding."

He and Devon had agreed she would spend the night at Francine's house after the rehearsal dinner hosted by his parents, and she would come to the restaurant with Keaton, which meant he wouldn't see her until the ceremony. "Are you having any misgivings?" he asked.

A momentary look of discomfort flitted across Devon's face. "No way. I love you and I'm counting down the days till we finally become husband and wife."

David had waited for her to tell him that she loved him, and now that she had, he didn't want to believe it. "You love me?"

Devon's smile was bright as a rising sun. "Of course I love you. Do you think I'd marry a man I didn't love?"

He suddenly found himself at a loss as to how to respond to her question. "I don't know, baby. How ... what I'm trying to say is that I don't know you well ... that well to know what you're ..."

"Stop stuttering, darling." Reaching across the table, she grasped his free hand. "You don't know much about me and I don't know much about you, but think of the fun we'll have getting to know each other. And we'll have at least six months to get your firm up and running and prepare for a new baby."

It took a full minute before David regained control of his emotions. Then, without warning, his joy was overshadowed by Francine's prediction. "What do you say we get a jump on getting to know each other better?"

Devon released his hand, her brow furrowing in confusion. "How?"

"We only have another three weeks before we're married, so I want you to move in with me."

"David!"

"Devon!" he said, mimicking her.

They engaged in another stare-down but it held none of the negative energy of the preceding one. The seconds ticked past a full minute before Devon said, "You've got yourself a roommate until May first."

Leaning back in his chair, he whispered a silent prayer of gratitude. He didn't know what he would've done if she'd rejected his offer. David wanted to discount Francine's warning as hocus-pocus nonsense, yet he didn't want to disrespect a gift afforded a select few.

"After you pick up your outfit for the ball, I'll take you back to the Cove so you can check out."

Devon touched the napkin to the corners of her mouth. "The next three weeks are going to be hectic for us. This Sunday we have Austin's christening in the Cove. Next Saturday is the Charleston charity ball, and then the following Saturday is our wedding."

Devon was right. He'd canceled the NCAA championship game gathering because he'd committed to becoming godfather for Jeff and Kara's son on that day. His cousins and aunt were opening their home for a small celebration following the ceremony.

"I don't want you to stress yourself about anything. If we get to close on the house before May first, then we should be able to take a honeymoon."

"Have you forgotten that I have to fly to New York to sell the condo?"

"You can handle that without going to New York. I'll call a bonded company that will pack up your apartment and ship everything down here. And you can handle the sale of the condo electronically."

Devon tucked several strands that had escaped the twist behind her ear. "The moving company cannot get into my place unless I sign a form because management won't allow anyone without signed authorization from the owner access to the condo. And I also have to take care of some banking, and that's something that can't be done electronically."

"What if you do that midweek?"

"That's doable," she agreed. "Maybe I can schedule the moving company to come and pack up the apartment while I'm there. I'll make a reservation to leave here Tuesday and return on Friday. And I want that to be the last time I'll fly until after I have the baby."

"Do you get seasick?" he asked her.

"No."

"If that's the case, then we can take a seven-day cruise on a ship with no more than a hundred and fifty passengers. We'll sail out of Charleston, stop at a number of Lowcountry islands, and end in Jacksonville, Florida. I'll rent a car in Jacksonville for the drive back home."

Devon eyed him suspiciously. "Did you have all of this planned in advance?"

David chuckled softly. "Not really. My father took my mother on the same cruise after she retired and they couldn't stop talking about it. Maybe next summer we can take a second honeymoon to Europe or anywhere you've never been."

"What about the baby?"

He heard the panic in Devon's voice. "You can decide whether you want to take her with us or leave her with my mother. And don't forget, you'll also have several local babysitters with Morgan and Kara."

Devon waved her hand. "That's too far off for me to think about now. I know there's not much time, but make the reservation for the honeymoon cruise. The date for closing can always be rescheduled."

Rising slightly, David leaned over the table and touched his mouth to hers. "Thank you, Mama."

Devon kissed him back. "You're welcome, Daddy."

Chapter Twenty-Three

Devon sat on a pew in the sanctuary of Abundant Life Christian Church next to Morgan, watching David as he held little Austin. Reverend Malcolm Crawford poured water over the infant's head, intoning the verses that represented the washing away of original sin. The baby woke, wailing at the top of his lungs, tiny fists jabbing the air.

The minister dabbed the child's forehead with a towel, which only served to make him cry louder. David rocked Austin in an attempt to soothe him but to no avail. She and Morgan shared a smile when he finally handed his infant cousin to Kara. The ceremony ended with the parents, godparents, and grandparents posing for photos with the pastor and Austin being shifted from one family member to another, the professional photographer directing them where they should stand.

"Now you know who's going to have to get up in the middle of the night to walk the floor with your baby," Morgan whispered.

"There will be no walking the floor in my house," Devon whispered back. "I'm going to put my baby in a snuggly, sit in a rocking chair, and rock until we both go back to sleep."

Morgan laughed softly. "I kinda like that idea. Now I know what Nate can make for you as a baby shower gift."

"What's that?"

"A rocking chair. And don't be surprised if he also makes a bedside cradle for you. He made one for Kara, and she claims it's the best thing since sliced bread. All she has to do is lean over and pick up Austin to feed or change him."

"When is he going to find the time to make baby furniture for you and me?" Devon still hadn't visited Morgan's husband's workshop to see his handmade pieces.

"We're going to use the cradle that's been passed down through several generations of Shaws."

Reminded of the traditions in her own family, Devon felt a pang of regret. But with the birth of her daughter, she and David would begin their own traditions. "Have you selected godparents yet?" she asked Morgan.

Morgan nodded. "Fran will be the godmother, and Nate's brother Bryce has agreed to be godfather. Nate and I are godparents to his son. What about you? Have you picked who you want for your baby?" Morgan asked Devon.

She leaned closer to the architect, their shoulders touching. "I told David I wanted Keaton as godfather, and he said he'll probably ask his sister to stand in as godmother."

"I still can't believe David is getting married. I'm willing to bet there's going to be a whole lot of wailing and gnashing of teeth when the single women in Charleston find out he's off the market for good."

"Do you think David would've taken Petra back if she hadn't married?"

"Oh no-ooo!" Morgan crooned. "David is no masochist. I'm glad he met someone like you, Devon. You're what he needed to mellow him out."

Devon still hadn't seen the severity in David that Morgan and Francine complained about. She'd witnessed firsthand his stubbornness when he rejected her notion of raising chickens. She knew if she pushed it, she may have gotten him to compromise. However, she had to learn to pick her battles, and arguing about something she could readily purchase at one of the local farms or at a supermarket wasn't worth the angst.

"Heads-up, girlfriend. Your man is heading straight for us," Morgan whispered in her ear.

Devon sat up straight as David closed the distance between them. His tailored suit was the perfect cut for his tall, slender physique. He extended his hand, easing her to her feet. "Come, sweetheart. You need to be in the family photos."

She wanted to tell him she wasn't family—at least not for another two weeks—but with him pulling and Morgan's hand at the small of her back, she had no choice but to follow David. His arm went around her waist, pulling her to his body as the photographer took more frames in rapid succession. She relaxed enough to smile directly at the camera before tilting her head to gaze lovingly at David at the same time he met her eyes. There were several more flashes as the photographer took frame after frame of the assembly.

Kara handed her the baby, and Devon cradled Austin against her chest, smiling at the now calm infant staring curiously at her. He gave her a toothless smile, and she kissed his forehead, the photographer capturing the gesture for posterity. Holding the baby, feeling his slight weight and warmth,

Devon thought about all the times she'd professed that she didn't want to be a mother. Now she couldn't wait to hold her own baby in her arms.

She went completely still when Austin began rooting for her breast. "No, baby boy. I can't feed you," she crooned. Walking over to Kara, she deposited her son into her arms. "I think he needs to be fed."

"I'll feed him once we get back to the house." Cradling Austin's head in one hand, Kara stared intently at Devon. "Whenever I see you it's like looking in the mirror. We have the same face shape, eye color, and complexion. The only difference is our hair texture and color."

"You know what they say about everyone having a double."

"That's true. By the way, you may get to meet some of the infamous Angels Landing Pattons later on today. I really didn't want to invite them, but Jeff insisted because they're Austin's family. And down here family means everything. I get so tired of folks asking 'Who are your people?' as if that's the only thing that matters."

"Are you on good terms with them?"

Kara rolled her eyes. "Yes and no. Some of them are still pissed because I inherited the plantation, but a few seem genuinely serious about extending the olive branch." She scrunched up her nose, then sniffed the air. "Somebody needs changing. Excuse me, but I need to let Jeff know we have to get back home ASAP before the reverend is forced to fumigate this place."

Devon smiled. "David and I will see you later."

She thought about what Kara had said about family and an olive branch. She found it ironic that after all their battles, she was going to marry a man her mother definitely would've approved of after all. David was educated, from a good family, and financially stable. Devon closed her eyes. She was marrying the perfect man and no one in her family would witness what would become one of the most momentous events of her life.

A knowing smile curved her mouth when she thought about her new family. David, Jeff, Austin, Kara, Aunt Corrine, Edna, Leticia, and David Senior were now her family. She thought of Keaton as an older brother, and Morgan and Francine had become the sisters she'd always wanted. Yes, she mused, she had family and a support system that would always be there for her.

"What are you smiling about?"

She turned around to find David standing only a few feet away. Resting her palms on the lapels of his suit jacket, she gave him a gentle smile. "I was just thinking about how blessed I am to have you and your family."

He led her away from the others into a corner of the sanctuary. "They're *our* family."

When David echoed her thoughts Devon knew she'd finally exorcised the ghosts that hadn't permitted her inner spirit to soar. She'd spent so many years wallowing in what she hadn't been able to control as a child, and despite her overall success as an attorney, she'd failed herself when it came to her personal life. She hadn't had friends but associates—those she saw and socialized with whenever it was convenient for her. Even her law school roommates called her mysterious because she didn't talk much about herself. She'd never even let a man sleep over in her apartment, always opting for his place instead. Even when Gregory came to New York, she'd slept with him at his hotel.

"I can't wait to marry you," she whispered.

David grinned sheepishly. "We have the license, so why don't we ask Reverend Crawford to marry us now."

"And cheat your mother out of seeing her son married? I don't think so, darling."

He nodded. "You're right about that. Being the drama queen that she is, Mother would probably take to her bed and not leave until you have the baby. Once she can claim the title of grandmother, there will be no living with her."

Devon sobered as she pulled her lower lip between her teeth. "We've never talked about whether we're going to tell your parents that this baby isn't yours."

"I thought we agreed the baby is mine."

"It is, but not biologically, David. I feel bad that your parents might think you were irresponsible in some way."

A muscle twitched in his jaw. "My personal life is none of their business. Though I'm sure they'd be proud that if this were my baby, I'd be doing the 'honorable' thing by marrying you."

"But is that really what *you* want?"

"Why is it so hard for you to accept that I've accepted the baby you carry as mine?"

"I've accepted it, but—"

"No buts, baby," he said, cutting her off. "You've just been overruled. And the judge will not grant an appeal."

"Since when did you go from defense attorney to judge?"

"When I found out I was going to have a daughter. Because if some horny little punk even thinks of taking advantage of her, then he'll find out the hard way that her father is prosecutor, jury, judge, and executioner." He kissed her forehead. "I think it's time we head on out," he said in a quiet voice. "I promised Aunt Corrine she would go back to her place with us."

Devon suddenly realized David had become quite adept at avoiding arguments he didn't want to have. She still felt uncomfortable deceiving her future in-laws into believing she carried their son's child. Keaton, Kara, Morgan, and Francine knew the truth. It seemed underhanded that the baby's grandparents didn't. But it was apparent David knew his parents well enough to understand what they were willing to accept or reject. And at that moment she swore not to broach the subject again.

The drive from the church to the Hamilton home on Waccamaw Road took less than five minutes. Kara—who'd changed, fed, and put Austin down for a nap—assumed the role of hostess when she escorted everyone into the sunroom for a light repast, which resembled anything but. It hadn't taken Devon long to acknowledge that food and family gatherings were synonymous. You couldn't have one without the other.

She was introduced to several Patton women who were dressed to the nines in haute couture and had gifts and envelopes for Austin. All of them, regardless of their complexions, which ranged from golden brown to mahogany, had the same gray eyes, which Francine whispered to Devon they'd inherited from Oakes Patton—rumored to be the son of the mistress of Angels Landing Plantation and a male slave. They reminded Devon of the women in her family who despite being married still regarded themselves as Gilmores.

"One of these days I want you to tell me about the history of the island," she said to Francine.

Francine chewed and swallowed a shrimp she'd dipped into a piquant sauce. "You should ask Miss Corrine. As a griot, she knows more about the history of the island than Hannah Forsyth, the Cove's librarian and official historian."

Devon took a sip of lemonade, peering at David over the rim of the glass. He'd shed his shirt and tie and rolled back his cuffs. He and Keaton appeared to be deep in conversation. "How are the plans for your wedding coming?" she asked Francine.

The redhead smiled. "Good. Keaton's parents are coming in a week early to plan the menu with Mama and Grandma Dinah."

"Thankfully I don't have to worry about stepping on anyone's toes, because David and I selected what we wanted to serve from McLeay's Garden's banquet menu. There are a couple of dishes I wanted that weren't on the menu, but the chef claimed he wouldn't have a problem making them."

Francine held her eyes. "How do you do it, Devon?"

For a long moment, Devon stared back at Keaton's fiancée. "What are you talking about?"

"You always look so poised, as if you don't have a care in the world. Meanwhile, if I had only two weeks before I was to marry Keaton I know I'd be the ultimate Bridezilla. I still can't believe you walked into one bridal shop and within ten minutes knew they didn't have anything you wanted. Then less than an hour after we go into Fabulous Frocks, you try on a couple of dresses and you choose a gown just like that." Francine snapped her fingers.

"If I'd tried on more than two or three gowns, then you definitely would've witnessed a meltdown if I hadn't been able to choose among them. And there weren't that many to choose from that would camouflage a baby bump."

"You're small compared to Mo."

"Don't forget she's due at least three weeks before me." Devon took another sip of the fresh-squeezed lemonade, enjoying the feel of pulp on her tongue. "We're having a girl."

The warmth of Francine's smile reached her eyes. "What was David's reaction?"

"He likes the idea of having a daughter." She told Francine what David said about some boy trying to hit on his daughter.

Shaking her head, Francine said, "Talk about a double standard. I'm of the belief that men need daughters not only to soften them but as a constant reminder of what they've done to another man's daughter."

"Amen to that," Devon drawled. "It doesn't become a reality until it hits home."

"What are y'all talking about?" Morgan asked as she sat down between them.

"Fathers threatening to jack up a boy if he takes advantage of their daughter," Devon said.

Morgan, running her fingers through her short curly hair, sucked her teeth. "That's the same discussion I had with Nate when we found out we were having a girl. He said, 'Instead of shooting the little creep I'll stuff him in a wood chipper where they'll never find his body.' I was so creeped out that I wouldn't speak to him for hours."

Devon grimaced. "That is a little extreme."

Francine nodded in agreement. "That is surprising coming from Nate, because he's always so quiet."

"It's the quiet ones you have to watch," Morgan whispered. "They can be real hell-raisers."

The celebrating continued for another three hours, and when David suggested they leave Devon was more than happy to comply. She said her good-byes to everyone, wishing Dawn a safe trip back to New York. The petite blonde shocked her when she said she would be back in a couple of weeks because Trevor had asked her to be his plus one for

Devon and David's wedding. It was obvious another New Yorker had been bitten by the Lowcountry bug.

When they arrived at the house in Charleston, Devon resisted the urge to go to bed as early as she had in the past. Kicking off her shoes and leaving them on a mat inside the front door, she smiled at David as he searched through the mail piling up on the entryway table.

"I have to go through the mail, so don't wait up for me."

Devon dropped her tote on the chair flanking the table. "I'm going to sit up and watch the news for a while."

He gave her a questioning look. "Aren't you tired?"

"Not really."

He took a step, cradling her face and kissing her gently on the mouth. "I'll see you later."

Going on tiptoe, Devon deepened the kiss. "Later."

She felt the heat of his gaze on her back as she walked on bare feet across the living room. She stopped to retrieve a bottle of water from the refrigerator before retreating to the family room. Flopping down on a recliner, she reached for the remote and turned on the television, surfing until she came to an all-news channel. The journalist was recapping the week's political news when the images popping up on the screen caused the breath to freeze in her lungs.

A veteran Virginia congressman had stepped down because of failing health and the governor had appointed celebrated litigator Gregory Emerson to serve the remainder of the venerable politician's term. With wide eyes, Devon stared at Gregory hugging an attractive woman who'd been identified as his new bride.

She clapped a hand over her mouth to keep from screaming obscenities at the television. It was no wonder he'd blocked her calls. He must've known all along he would be appointed to serve out Earley Guilford's current term. Devon slowly lowered her hand. Gregory didn't have to worry about her trying to tamper with his newfound success. In fact, he'd done her a favor because she knew something the public didn't: Newly appointed congressman Emerson was a snake.

Devon flipped the channel and ended up watching the second half of a British film she'd seen before. She loved the magnificence of the manor houses, the costumes, and the accuracy of the distinct differences among the various classes that made up British culture.

When the movie ended, she turned off the television and stood up to stretch. And that's when she saw David standing in the doorway smiling at her.

"I came to see if you're ready to go to bed."

"Now I am," she said. He took several steps, then bending slightly, scooped her up in his arms. "What are you doing?"

He winked at her. "Playing superhero."

Devon buried her face between his neck and shoulder. "Who are you tonight?"

"Arthur Curry."

"Who's he?"

"Aquaman," David said with a wide grin. "Arthur Curry is his alter ego who is an Atlantean-human hybrid."

Devon kissed his ear. "You're really a comic junkie if you know the superheroes' alter egos."

"Was," he reminded her.

"What are you going to do with your collection?"

"Hold on to it for our son."

Devon tightened her hold on his neck as he mounted the staircase. "Are you that certain our second child will be a boy?"

David nodded. "Very certain."

She bit gently on his earlobe and suckled, making David gasp. "What makes you so certain?" she whispered.

His breath was coming quickly and Devon realized she'd just discovered another one of his erogenous zones. She knew he also had one at the base of his spine.

"Don't do that. Please." He gasped as if he'd run a long grueling race.

"Does that feel good, baby?" she teased, not releasing his ear.

David had discovered one thing about the woman he planned to marry and that was that she wasn't shy or reticent when it came to lovemaking. She'd denied being a tease, but all she had to do was look up at him from lowered lashes and he was lost. The first time she looked up at him at the table in Francine's house, he'd fallen under her spell, and he didn't want to escape it.

"Yes," he finally admitted. It felt more than good. Her moist breath in his ear was like a shot of adrenaline racing through his body and pooling in his groin.

Taking long strides, he pushed open the door to the bedroom, walked in, and didn't stop until he reached the bathroom. Somewhere between sanity and insanity he managed to undress himself and then Devon, their discarded clothes landing in a pile on the floor. He loved feeling her silken skin against his as he carried her into the shower stall and turned on the water.

"David, no!" Devon screamed as cold water rained down on her head and body. He adjusted the water temperature and she let out a soft moan.

"Is that better?" he whispered in her ear at the same time he positioned her to face the wall. She nodded. He smiled.

"Young lady, you're under arrest for soliciting and I have to search you to see if you're carrying any contraband, so put your hands on the wall and spread your legs."

Devon's shoulders shook with laughter. "Trust me, Officer, I'm not carrying any contraband."

He positioned his knee between her thighs, spreading them just enough so she wouldn't lose her balance. "I have to see for myself." Cradling his erection in one hand, he eased her hips back far enough so he was able to enter her. He'd never felt anything as good as her warmth surrounding him.

Devon was so tight, hot, and wet that he knew their lovemaking would be fast and explosive. With each thrust, her buttocks made a satisfying smack against his thighs, and he had to fight the urge not to come. Cradling her breasts, he squeezed her distended nipples until she moaned with pleasure.

Those sweet sounds were David's undoing and he couldn't hold back any longer, releasing his passion inside her at the same time her orgasm crested and pulsed around him. Collapsing against her back, he held on to Devon as if she were his lifeline. He turned her to face him, her cheeks flushed with high color, her eyes a brilliant green. She lowered her lashes and smiled.

The water continued to beat down as he cradled her face, and they shared a kiss so tender that no words were necessary. David loved her and he knew without a doubt that Devon loved him equally.

He reached for a bottle of her bodywash. "Don't move, baby. I'll wash you."

David poured some bath gel on a sponge and washed every inch of her body before she returned the favor and soaped him from neck to toe. The water had turned luke-warm when they finished. He played superhero once again when he wrapped her body in a bath towel and carried her into the bedroom. He took his time dabbing the moisture from her skin, becoming a sculptor as he drew the towel over her breasts and belly. Gently turning her to one side, he dried her back and legs and then turned her again to repeat the motions on the other side. Her eyes were closing and her breathing had deepened when he patted the remaining droplets clinging to his chest.

David returned to the bathroom to drape the towel over a rod and when he returned to the bedroom he found that Devon had fallen asleep. He slipped into bed, easing her to lie beside him. They would have only one more day together before she left for New York. He only hoped Red was right in that whatever danger shadowed Devon was based in South Carolina and not up north where he couldn't protect her.

Chapter Twenty-Four

Devon stood at the living room window, watching north-bound bumper-to-bumper traffic on the FDR Drive. Her gaze shifted to the lights on the many bridges linking Manhattan with the boroughs of Brooklyn, Queens, and the Bronx. Staring out at the skyline was something she would miss, but it was already hard to think of this apartment as "home." Not when she had so much more waiting for her back on Cavanaugh Island. Although she'd been away only a month, a lot had happened that would drastically change her life.

Her apartment felt empty in a way she couldn't quite explain. Opening her tote, she took out her cell phone and tapped David's number. "Honey, I'm home," she drawled in her best Ricky Ricardo impression.

"You're on the ground or you're actually home?"

"I'm standing in my living room taking in the Manhattan skyline."

"How high up do you live?" David asked.

"I live on the eighteenth floor."

"The view must be breathtaking."

Devon nodded, although he couldn't see her. "It is, especially when it's snowing."

"Speaking of weather, how is it?" he asked.

"It's still a little chilly."

There came a beat. "I miss you already, Mama."

Devon bit her lower lip. "I miss you, too. Okay," she said around a yawn. Suddenly fatigue washed over her like a strong wave as she struggled to keep her eyes open. Although she was taking the iron pills, she still felt tired. "I just called to let you know I arrived safely."

"I'm going to hang up because you sound as if you're falling asleep," David said.

Devon sighed. "I am."

"Good night, babe."

"Good night, David."

She managed to stay awake long enough to shower and brush her teeth. Within minutes of her head touching the pillow she fell into a deep, dreamless sleep.

Two days later, Devon watched the men from the moving crew pick up the last two cartons, while another carried a carefully wrapped painting her soon-to-be former neighbor had given her as a parting gift for vacating the condo and signing over the deed in what he claimed was record time. The entire contents of the condo were on a truck headed for a Charleston storage unit and she would head to a hotel for her last night in New York.

She had the doorman hail her a taxi to take her to a midtown hotel close to Times Square. She wanted her last memory of the city to be bright lights and bustling crowds.

Devon thought about calling some of the people with

whom she had socialized to invite them over for one last get-together, then quickly changed her mind when she remembered none of them knew she was pregnant. She strolled along the streets like so many tourists taking in the sights before returning to the hotel, where guests were milling around the lobby, restaurant, and bar areas. She went into the restaurant and ordered dinner instead of calling room service. It was as if she had to feel the invisible electricity just once more before returning to Cavanaugh Island to begin a new life. Her cell vibrated on the table and she glanced at the display. "Hey, Daddy."

There came a pause before David said, "It sounds as if you're at a party."

"I'm at the hotel restaurant. There's a hockey game on television and the hometown team just scored a goal. How was your last day at the firm? Are you all right, because you sound tired."

"I'm still a little hungover."

A frown appeared between her eyes. "Hungover from what?"

"We all went out to a local sports bar and turned out the place. Some of my former colleagues really surprised me once they had a few drinks."

"Did you find out about a clandestine office romance?"

"How did you know?"

"My grandmother used to say what's done in the wash always comes out in the rinse. Office parties with a lot of alcohol are notorious for uncovering who's been sleeping with whom."

"It's true. Are you still coming back tomorrow afternoon as planned?"

She forced a strained smile. "Yes. Barring delays, my

flight is scheduled to touch down at five twenty. Don't forget I have an appointment at the Beauty Box for eleven Saturday morning."

"I'm going to call Red, and if she can fit me in for a haircut and shave, then I'll go with you."

"Okay. If I don't talk to you later, then I'll see you at the airport."

"Bye. Love you, baby."

She smiled. "Love you, too."

Devon ended the call and after she put away her phone she noticed a man at a nearby table staring at her. She estimated him to be in his midthirties to early forties, and he had straight light brown hair brushed off his forehead. He was what she thought of as nondescript: brown eyes, pale complexion, and balanced features. A slight smile parted his lips as he raised a glass filled with an amber liquid in her direction.

She pretended she didn't notice the gesture as she opened the menu. She hadn't come back to New York to have some man hit on her. Once she decided what she wanted to order she glanced up again. The table where he'd sat was empty. Hopefully he'd gotten the message that she wasn't receptive and moved on to find someone more willing to share his company.

Devon gave the waiter her order and spent the next forty-five minutes eating and watching the hockey game on one of the many mounted televisions.

Chuck disentangled himself from his wife's arms when he heard the programmed ringtone. He picked his cell up off the nightstand, slipped out of bed, made his way into the bathroom, and closed the door.

"What do you have for me, Jake?"

"We got a hit. My man spotted Devon Collins coming out of her building with two bags. She got into a cab and it looks like she's staying at the Times Square Marriott Marquis."

"Why would she check into a hotel when she owns a condo?"

"I don't know. Maybe she went there to meet a man."

Chuck stared at his reflection in a wall of mirrors. He didn't know why he'd agreed to let his wife install floor-to-ceiling mirrors in the entire bathroom.

"Did she look knocked up?" he asked in a quiet tone.

"My guy said it was hard to tell because of what she was wearing. She checked out of the hotel this morning and went into a bank a couple of blocks from Grand Central. After that she took another cab, this time heading for the airport. My other man followed the cab to the US Airways terminal at JFK. He parked and then went into the terminal to check the departure boards, writing down all the cities with flights leaving within a four-hour spread."

"I want facts, Jake, not minutiae."

"The facts are going to cost extra."

Chuck struggled not to lose his temper. He didn't want to believe the little cretin was attempting to squeeze more money out of him. "Don't I pay you enough?"

"The money's not for me but for someone with enough skill to hack into an airline database and access their passenger list."

Chuck smiled for the first time since answering the call. "How much?"

"One hundred."

He laughed. "One hundred dollars."

"No, Chuck. One hundred thousand."

Laughter died on his tongue as if he'd tasted bile. "If your person is so good, then why doesn't he hack into a bank and get the money?"

"He doesn't do that anymore. One hundred or no details."

Rage turned his face a dangerous shade of purple. "Since when did you get into the business of blackmail?"

"I'm not blackmailing you. I'm merely telling you what my man wants. Let me know now what *you* want."

Chuck knew he couldn't afford to alienate Jacob Walsh because the man had never *not* come through for him. "Okay. I'll transfer the money before noon tomorrow. Now, tell me what you've got."

"Thank you, Charles," Jake drawled facetiously. "Ms. Collins boarded a return flight to Charleston, South Carolina. There's something else you should know."

"What's that?"

"She's wearing an engagement ring."

"What the hell was going on? She and Emerson...were they both engaged to other people when they were sleeping together?"

"I don't know, boss. Do you want me to pull my people off this case?"

"No, no. Keep on it. I need to find out for certain that she's not pregnant."

"What if she is and it's Emerson's kid and she's trying to pass it off on her fiancé?"

"She wouldn't be the first woman and definitely not the last. Have your men check out her fiancé, find out who he is and when and where they met."

"Okay, boss."

Frowning, Chuck patted his paunch. It was time to go under

the knife again. The next procedure would be a tummy tuck. "Nice work, Jake."

"Thanks, boss. I'll let you know what we find."

He ended the call, leaving the phone on the vanity. Jake's call had come at the right time. Congress had reconvened after the Easter recess, Guilford had resigned, and the governor had announced his intent to appoint Gregory Emerson to replace the ailing congressman. And if it turned out his ex-girlfriend was pregnant, then Jake's people would take care of all the loose ends that would prevent Emerson from winning the seat on his own.

Chuck returned to the bedroom, encountering Heather's light snores. Getting into bed, he pressed his chest to his wife's back and kissed her shoulder. Life was good and was about to get even better once Emerson was sworn in as a member of Congress, because he was to become his latest protégé.

Chapter Twenty-Five

David spotted Devon before she saw him; the terminal was crowded with people waiting to claim their luggage from the conveyors, while friends and family members milled around waiting to greet arriving passengers. He couldn't pull his gaze away from the profusion of black curls framing her face and falling to her shoulders as she looked for him.

Raising a hand to get her attention, he wove his way through the throng. Wrapping an arm around her waist over the raincoat, he steered her to a less crowded area, lowered his head, and kissed her passionately.

"Welcome home, Mama."

Devon buried her face against his throat. "It's good to be back."

He inhaled the familiar scent of her shampoo. He'd admitted that he missed her, but those were just words. Whenever they spent time apart David felt as if he'd lost a little bit of himself. He'd stopped asking himself why Devon, why had he fallen in love with her so quickly, and why had he wanted to share their lives and looked forward to sharing a future with her and the child or children he hoped they would have?

"Do you have any other bags?"

"No. I packed just about everything and sent it down with the movers."

David took her carry-on and tote, holding them in one hand while his free arm went around her waist. "Speaking of movers, they delivered your stuff this morning. I checked the number of boxes with the packing list and everything matched."

"Did you see something that looked like a large painting?"

"Yes. Why?"

"My former neighbor gave me one of his paintings as a parting gift. His paintings hang in MoMA and the Guggenheim. Private collectors spend millions whenever he has an exhibit. I need to get it appraised before adding it to our homeowners' policy."

David whistled softly. "You believe it's that valuable?"

"I know it's valuable."

"Do you plan to hang it or keep it in storage?" he asked.

"I want to hang it in our home office."

"If that's the case, then we're going to have to install a security system, otherwise the insurance company won't insure it." He steered Devon to an exit. "I'm parked in the lot across the street."

Devon held back. "Please wait. I need to take off my raincoat. I have on too many clothes."

He watched her slip out of the coat to reveal the roundness of her belly under a body-hugging long-sleeved tee. She looked pregnant. "Do you want to eat something before we get home?"

"No thanks. I ate a full meal before boarding in New York."

"I'll fix you something light before you go to sleep."

"Sounds perfect," she said, smiling.

They left the terminal and walked out into the warm humid air, David reaching for her hand and leading her across the street to the parking lot. She was home and she was safe. Not once since he dropped her off to board her flight to New York was Francine's warning of the danger surrounding Devon far from his thoughts. Now that he didn't have to go into an office it would be a lot easier for him to protect her.

The sound of music and David singing at the top of his lungs to Lenny Kravitz's "Are You Gonna Go My Way" greeted Devon when she stood at the entrance to the kitchen early Saturday morning. David continued to surprise her. She crossed her arms under her breasts and watched him gyrating to the driving bass line guitar beat. So, she mused, the buttoned-up attorney could really cut loose. He wore a white tee, jeans, and running shoes. He hadn't bothered to shave because he planned to have a professional shave later on at the Beauty Box.

The song ended and she applauded softly, capturing his attention. It was apparent he hadn't known she was watching his performance. "I wish I had my phone because I would've videoed you," she said with a wide grin.

David didn't appear the least bit embarrassed that she'd seen his rocker side as he executed a graceful bow. "You should see me do James Brown."

"Really!"

David, going to his knees, sang, "Please, please, please," in a perfect imitation of the late, great soul singer.

Throwing back her head, Devon laughed so hard she could hardly catch her breath. "You're going to have to let me take a video," she said once she recovered from laughing.

David beckoned her closer, as the Four Tops' Motown favorite "Baby I Need Your Loving" started playing. "This song is one of my all-time favorites. Come and dance with me."

She walked into his outstretched arms and he spun her around and around in an intricate dance step. Devon marveled at how well their bodies fit together, even with her belly. He sang, danced, and cooked, and she wondered if there was anything he couldn't do well.

"Have you completed the playlist for the DJ?" she asked David, while following his strong lead. They'd debated whether to have music during their reception, and in the end decided music spanning several generations would appeal to their guests.

"Yes. I worked on it while you were in New York. I know Aunt Corrine likes Etta James and Nat King Cole and my parents are Motown junkies. I selected a few doo-wops for myself, and hip-hop and club tunes for Red and Morgan. I'm not sure what Nate likes, but I know Jeff is partial to R and B. You're going to have to let me know what you want, then I'll let you see the playlist once I'm finished."

Devon nodded, resting her head on his shoulder.

David pulled her closer. "We're going to have to select a song for our first dance as husband and wife."

"How about 'Sexual Healing'?" she teased.

David cut his eyes at her. "I don't think that would go over well with the older folks."

Devon searched her memory for songs that had stayed with her long after they no longer had radio play. "I love 'Remarkable' by Jaheim."

"I don't remember that one," he admitted.

"You can listen to it on YouTube. What about Roberta Flack and Donny Hathaway's 'The Closer I Get to You'?" The classic duet was also one of her favorite songs.

"That's a definite possibility. I thought you would've wanted Whitney Houston's 'I Will Always Love You.'"

"Have you ever really listened to the lyrics?" she asked. "Way too sad for a wedding with all that talk of her leaving."

David stopped mid-step, picking her up around the waist until her head was level with his. "You're stuck with me because I don't plan to leave you either. And it doesn't matter if we can't agree on everything."

Like not having chickens, she thought.

"Please, don't even open your mouth to mention chickens."

Her expression mirrored shock. How did he know she was thinking about chickens? Was he, like Francine, also psychic? "What makes you think I was thinking about them?"

"You get this funny little look on your face when you're thinking about something and I just figured you were going to bring them up again."

"So you think you know me that well to read my mind?"

David set her on her feet, but didn't release her. "No, Dee. In fact I don't know enough about you. But I think that's going to be the exciting part of our marriage. Getting to know you, because when couples date they tend to show each other their best side and once married some of the niceties slip away because she may feel that she's got him or he believes he has her. When I saw you standing outside Red's house the first thing that popped into my head was how beautiful you are. Then when I got a chance to sit and talk to you I realized it wasn't just your face and body that attracted me to you but also your confidence. I told myself this woman really has her stuff together and if I want to ask her out then I have to step up my game."

Devon closed her eyes for several seconds. "I really didn't have what you refer to as my stuff together."

"I beg to differ with you," David retorted. "The fact that you challenged the very traditions you were raised to uphold took a lot of courage. Your brother used his own methods of rebelling, but in the end it led to drugs and eventually imprisonment. You may have had your grandmother to help you, and he had you but chose another path. I know you love your brother and I told you before that when it comes time for him to be paroled, he's more than welcome to live with us until he gets his life back on track, and I'll do whatever I can to help him."

A deep feeling of peace swept over Devon as she clung to the man who had unknowingly become her emotional lifeline. She'd stopped questioning why David had come into her life at a time when she needed him most while the love she felt for the incredible man holding her to his heart was something she wasn't able to put into words.

"I love you." The three words were ripped from her heart.

David rubbed a hand over her back, and then released her. "I love you, too." He expelled a breath. "I think it's time we eat before we head over to the Cove to get ready for the Black and White Ball."

"Do people still wear masks?"

"Yes. You'll be given one once you arrive, which you'll put on before you're announced to the assembly. You'll have to decide whether you want to be announced as Devon Gilmore or Devon Collins."

"Collins."

David gave her a direct stare. "Have you decided if you want to maintain your maiden name after we're married?"

Devon was slightly taken aback by his question. "Why would you think I'd want to keep my maiden name?"

"A lot of professional women elect not to change their names once they marry."

"If I'm family, then I'm going to be Devon Sullivan."

He winked at her. "It sounds good." David glanced at the clock on the microwave. "We have to leave around ten thirty so we don't miss our appointment."

She slipped off the stool and gathered plates and flatware to set the table in the breakfast nook. "I can't believe I slept so late."

"That's because this house is filled with good karma."

"How do you get good karma inside a house?"

David crossed his arms over the tee, which was molded to the contours of his firm upper body. "You get someone to bless your home before you move in."

She gave him a look that told him she didn't believe a word he'd said. "If you say so." Devon wondered if it was another Gullah superstition—one of many she'd heard since coming to the Lowcountry. "And I have a bridge in Brooklyn I can sell you for a dollar," she said under her breath.

"I heard that," David called out.

"I meant for you to hear it."

"You're kinda sassy this morning, aren't you?" he teased.

Devon scrunched up her nose. "And you like me sassy, don't you?"

He patted her behind over a pair of stretch jeans. "Sassy *and* hot as a ghost chili."

"Don't play yourself, David Sullivan. You'd never be able to handle the heat of a ghost chili."

He sobered quickly. "You're right about that, because whenever we make love you're so hot that after we're finished I have to examine my—"

Moving quickly, Devon clamped her hand over his mouth. "Don't say it!"

David forcibly pulled her hand away. "Are you blushing, baby?"

She lowered her eyes. "No."

"Yes, you are."

"Please feed me before I faint on you."

He smiled, attractive lines fanning out around his dark eyes. "One of these days you won't be able to use the baby as an excuse to overrule me."

Devon flashed a sexy moue. "That said, I rest my case."

Chapter Twenty-Six

$\sim$

Devon entered the Beauty Box amid a babble of raised voices and stylists' roller setting and blow-drying hair. David had dropped her off before driving around the crowded lot to find an empty spot. She glanced around the busy upscale salon and saw Mavis instructing a young woman how to cut an elderly woman's hair.

"May I help you?"

Her attention swung back to the receptionist, who'd returned to the front desk after adjusting the temperature on a client's hair dryer. She wore a black smock with *Beauty Box* embroidered in white over her heart. "My name is Devon Collins and I have an appointment with Francine for eleven."

"Please have a seat and I'll check in the back to see if Red's here."

Devon sank down into a black leather love seat as she waited, her gaze sweeping around the full-service unisex salon. The design and furnishings of the salon were similar to those of the upscale ones she'd frequented on Madison and

Park Avenues, sans the inflated price list. The first thing she noticed was the absence of hair on the floor and minimal dialogue between stylist and client. She picked up a brochure outlining the services of the adjacent Butterfly Garden Day Spa, which offered the quintessential massages, facials, body scrubs, mani/pedis, and specialized massages for pregnant women.

Two women seated on matching chairs several feet from Devon were actively engaged in a conversation about the Cove's first female mayor. One commented on attending Mayor Alice Parker's first town hall meeting and being impressed at what she heard. Alice had informed those attending the meeting that she'd applied for Community Development funding to improve the downtown business district. She also wanted to expand the police department to include a full-time assistant sheriff and another part-time deputy to reduce the current twelve-hour shifts to eight.

"Mama, I told you she was going to be good for the Cove."

Devon smiled when Mavis noticed her sitting there, rising as the salon owner closed the distance between them. A bright smile split the flawless dark face. "Hello, Miss Mavis."

Mavis hugged Devon. "I didn't know you were in the appointment book."

Devon returned the embrace, pressing her cheek to Mavis's. "I made the appointment last week for a haircut."

Reaching for Devon's hand, Mavis led her over to an empty chair. "Francine had to take her grandmother to Dr. Monroe because she woke up complaining about pains in her legs." She glanced at the clock on the wall. "She should be back soon. Please sit down. I'll cut your hair while you wait, if you don't mind."

"I don't mind at all," Devon replied.

Picking up a cape, Mavis draped it over Devon's shoulders. Francine's mother took off the elastic band holding Devon's hair in place and ran a wide-tooth comb through the raven curls falling over her shoulders. "It's much too long."

Mavis rubbed strands between her fingers. "You have a chemical in your hair." It was a statement, not a question.

She nodded. "I usually get a texturizer twice a year to relax the curls."

"You don't need a texturizer," Mavis said. "You and Francine have the same hair texture, and when she decides to wear her hair natural, she applies a leave-in lotion that will allow her hair to curl without frizzing."

"I can't use any chemicals in my hair now because I'm pregnant."

Leaning closer, Mavis whispered, "Congratulations. And please tell David congrats, too. When I saw the two of you together, my first impression was that you make a beautiful couple."

"Thank you." It was apparent Mavis believed David had fathered her child. What picture, she mused, had she and David presented at Francine's birthday dinner? It wasn't as if they were all over each other like some couples. He'd served her, they'd talked quietly and laughed together, and he'd driven her back to Charleston.

"I was really surprised when we got an invitation to your wedding, and Frank said there's going to be a boatload of disappointed honeys once they find out that David is no longer available."

Mavis echoed what Morgan had said about David marrying her. "I guess you can say their loss is my gain," Devon said jokingly.

She'd begun to accept the fact that being married to David wouldn't be as scary or traumatic as she originally thought. Although she agonized about marrying a man she'd known for six weeks, she recalled a couple in law school who married a week after their initial meeting in a torts class and more than a decade later were still married.

"I'm going to let Brooke shampoo you, then I'm going to cut your hair wet before I blow you out," Mavis said. "How much do you want me to cut off?"

"I want it about a couple of inches above my shoulders."

Devon reclined in the chair in the shampoo area and closed her eyes when Brooke wet her hair and squeezed a glob of delicious-smelling shampoo over her head. Brooke's fingers were magical as she massaged her scalp and temples, and within minutes she gave in to the hypnotic motion lulling her into a state of total relaxation.

Fifteen minutes later Devon sat in Mavis's chair again, watching as she quickly and expertly cut several inches off her hair, layering it to frame her face and jawline. Out of the corner of her eye she saw David sitting in the reception area reading a magazine.

Francine appeared, wearing a smock, as her mother began blowing out the damp strands. "I'll take over, Mama." Mavis handed her the blow dryer. "I'm sorry I wasn't here when you came in," she apologized.

Devon looked at Francine's reflection in the mirror. The redhead had flat ironed her hair, completely changing her look from ingenue to sophisticate. "That's all right. Your mother told me about your grandmother. How is she?"

"She's good. Dr. Monroe said she had a little arthritis in

her knees, which makes it difficult for her to walk. That's why we installed the elevator in the house. After I blow out your hair, how do you want it styled?"

"I'm not sure."

"Aren't you going to the Black and White Ball tonight?"

Devon blinked. "Yes. How did you know?" She hadn't told the women at their luncheon that David had invited her.

"Everyone knows about the ball and that the Sullivans always attend. When you get an invitation you know you've arrived. Marrying David will give you instant access into Charleston's black society. You will receive invitations to fund-raisers and charity events where the price of tickets begins at a thousand dollars a pop. I'm not saying the money isn't for a good cause, but there're times when I can't stomach some of those fake-ass, supercilious women whose aim in life is to make certain their sons and daughters attend elite colleges, marry well, and have perfect little children who will make their grandmothers proud."

Devon pushed out her lips. "That's something I'll never force on my children."

"You say that because you experienced it. If you had gone along with the plans your parents made for you, then you'd probably repeat it with your kids."

"You're probably right. If David and his sister were raised like that, then why are they different from the others?"

"First of all, Leticia has always been what folks call a free spirit. She used to say she couldn't wait to leave Charleston and see the world. And apparently as a flight attendant she's doing exactly what she always wanted. David was always a little quiet and nerdy until he came back from college. And once he graduated law school the girls were all over him like white on rice, but he has always been very selective when it comes to dating. He'd date one girl for a long time, while the others waited for him to drop her." Francine wrapped a section of hair around the large styling brush as she directed the dryer to the spot, slowly unwrapping the hair until it was smooth and shiny. "I would've considered going out with him if he hadn't been so uptight. I much prefer someone like Keaton, who's definitely more laid-back."

"Did you ever think maybe his relationship with Petra attributed to his being uptight?"

"I know it did," Francine confirmed. "I hate talking about that heifer. When are you going to close on the house in the Creek?"

"We're still waiting for a date. I'm not as anxious as I was before, now that David and I are living together. Staying at the inn wasn't bad only because I had my own suite and could cook for myself. However, I couldn't take the communal eating. It was a reminder of the years I spent in boarding school."

"At least you'll have someplace to live while you wait," Francine remarked. "Once Keaton decided to move out of the Cove Inn, I suggested he move in with us, but he said it would cause so much talk because the folks living along Magnolia Drive are so damn nosy you'd think they were on TMZ's payroll."

Devon laughed softly. "That's one of the drawbacks of living in a small town. Everyone's in your business. Speaking of getting into your business, have you decided where you want to go for your honeymoon?" Francine had mailed out wedding invitations indicating she and Keaton would marry the third Sunday in June.

"Keaton hinted at a honeymoon, but he won't tell me where we're going. All he says is that I should have a valid passport and bring enough summer clothes and several bathing suits to last two weeks, so I assume we're going someplace exotic and/or tropical."

"That sounds exciting *and* mysterious."

"All I know is that I'd better bring loads of sunscreen, a wide-brimmed hat, and long-sleeved tops or yours truly will come back looking like a cooked lobster. As a kid, I resented my father because I'd inherited his red hair, freckles, and fair complexion. I'd go to the beach and sit on the sand under an umbrella, swaddled like a mummy, while the other kids stripped down to their swim trunks and bathing suits to frolic in the water for hours. I told Keaton if our kids come out looking like me I'm going to send them back."

Devon covered her mouth, stifling laughter. "I'd like to think a redheaded Keaton Junior would look adorable."

"Don't go there, Devon," Francine said, deadpan. "You wouldn't think it funny if you had red hair and everyone called you Red or Ginger instead of Devon. I take that back. With your complexion you'd look stunning with red hair."

Devon met Francine's eyes in the mirror. "My mother was born a strawberry blonde, but as she got older it darkened to coal black, so there's always a possibility I could give birth to a blonde or a redhead."

"Speaking of hair, do you have an idea how you want yours styled for your wedding?"

Exhaling an audible sigh, Devon shook her head. "Probably pinned up off my neck. I still haven't decided on whether to wear a feathered headpiece or bejeweled hairpins."

"So you're really against wearing a veil?"

"I am," she confirmed. She'd tried on different veils and didn't like any of them, and she wanted to offset her gown's gold platinum embroidery embellishment and sweep train with simplicity.

"You know Mama has offered to do our hair and makeup."

She smiled, meeting Francine's eyes in the mirror. "I really appreciate it. The only thing left on my to-do list is ordering flowers, corsages, and boutonnieres." She'd picked up David's wedding present and ordered gifts for the wedding party online.

"What about the cake?" Francine asked.

"David and I ordered the cake from the Cake Corner the day I checked out of the inn." The Cake Corner, adjacent to the Muffin Corner, had just had a grand opening and the owner gave out samples to everyone who walked through the door. They'd ordered a cake with three heart-shaped tiers with red velvet, carrot cake, and strawberry lemonade filling. The pâtissier recommended decorating the cake with buttercream frosting and handmade edible ribbons and roses in keeping with the heart-shaped romantic theme.

Francine pinned up the sections of Devon's hair she'd blown dry. "I bought Keaton his tie, so all he has to do is dry-clean his tuxedo and he's done." She glanced over her left shoulder. "Oh no. I'm going to flat iron your hair after I rescue David from Miss Bernice, because when it comes to boundaries she doesn't have any. She's an incurable gossip and a troublemaker."

Devon turned in the chair to find an elderly woman in deep conversation with David. Waiting until Francine removed the cape, she stood and reached for her tote. "I'm going over to the Muffin Corner to get some oatmeal cookies," Devon said. "Do you want me to bring you anything back?"

"No thank you."

David rose to meet her as she walked to the door. "I'm going to the Muffin Corner." He stared at her, his expression a mask of stone. Devon sensed his disquiet.

"Is that the only place you're going?"

"Yes. Why?"

The tense lines bracketing his mouth eased when he smiled. "Just asking."

Some sixth sense told her something was bothering him. "There's a reason you're *just* asking, David."

"David Junior, is this the young lady you've been keeping company with?" Miss Bernice asked at the same time she took Devon's left hand, pulling it close to her face to examine the ring. "Where have you been hiding her?"

Devon now knew why Francine had tried to warn her about the woman. She attempted to extricate her hand, but Miss Bernice gripped it even tighter. "I'm sorry, but I have to leave now."

"David Junior. You're forgetting your manners. Aren't you going to introduce me to your intended?"

Devon knew she had to end the impromptu inquisition. "I'm Devon."

Miss Bernice dropped her hand as if she'd just picked up a venomous reptile. "Where are your manners, young lady? I asked him, not *you*."

Mavis, who'd overheard the exchange, placed an arm over her customer's shoulders. "Miss Bernice, I've warned you about annoying my customers. Now you come on back so you can get your hair washed."

Bernice Wagner wagged her head. "I don't know about these young folks nowadays. It's like they have no home training."

David lowered his head and pressed his mouth to Devon's ear. "I'm sorry about that, sweetheart. Miss Bernice can be a bit much."

"It's okay. She meant no harm."

"Yeah, right. She's as harmless as a pygmy rattler. You can't see or hear it until it bites you. Not only is she a troublemaker but also a shit-stirrer."

"David!"

He waved to Francine. "Hey, Red, can you spare us a few minutes to go next door?"

Francine pushed her hands into the pockets of her smock. "No problem."

Reaching over her head, David held the door open for Devon. The Muffin Corner was halfway down the street, but Francine's vision made him a prisoner of his own paranoia—whether real or imaginary. He blinked against the blinding sunlight. Reaching for Devon's hand, he cradled it in the bend of his elbow, grimacing as he felt her fingernails biting into his skin through his shirtsleeve.

"What are you trying to do? Draw blood?"

"What are *you* doing, David? I don't need an escort to walk to the bakery."

"I promised Dr. Ingram I would make certain you eat."

"But you do," Devon argued softly. "This morning you watched me eat a spinach omelet, sliced melon, orange juice, and wheat toast. Now I'm going to the Muffin Corner to have a glass of milk with a couple of oatmeal cookies."

"Please humor me, Mama."

She rolled her eyes at him. "I'll think about it."

They were only steps from the Muffin Corner when David spied someone he hadn't seen in years. He shared a wide grin with Master Sergeant Collier Ward. "What's up, Scrappy?"

Collier exchanged a rough embrace with David. "Not much. I'm now stateside for good after a few deployments."

He stared at the Dwayne "the Rock" Johnson look-alike dressed in army fatigues. "Are you on leave?"

"Nah. I got a weekend pass, so I drove down from Fort Bragg to see my girl." He flashed a sheepish grin. "She happens to own the Cake Corner."

David landed a soft punch to the career soldier's hard shoulder. "Nice." He rested a hand at the small of Devon's back. "Collier, I'd like you to meet my fiancée, Devon Gilmore. Darling, Master Sergeant Collier Ward." They exchanged handshakes and smiles.

"I ran into Jeff a little while ago, and he told me you're getting married in a couple of weeks."

David nodded. "Devon and I are tying the knot a week from today at McLeay's Garden. If you can get away, we'd love to have you come by and help your girlfriend bring the cake."

"I'll see if I can get another weekend pass." He shook hands with David again. "I have to stop at my sister's. She still doesn't know I'm home."

"Why did you call him Scrappy?" Devon asked once the soldier walked away.

"Because as a kid he used to scrap ass."

Chuckling softly, Devon shook her head. "You guys and your nicknames."

He kissed her freshly shampooed hair. "That's how we do it down here."

"Like giving a kid two first names, like Billy Bob and Jenny Lynn?"

"Don't forget Becky Sue and Beth Ann," David teased as they walked into the Muffin Corner. Devon ordered a cup of milk and two oatmeal cookies. They lingered long enough for her to finish eating, then retraced their steps to the Beauty Box.

Chapter Twenty-Seven

David hadn't realized he'd been holding his breath until he saw Devon descend the staircase in a black ball gown, holding up layers of flowing chiffon in one hand as the other gripped a small black evening purse and silk shawl. He took the stairs two at a time, his arm going around her waist as he carefully led her down. Her straightened hair, parted off-center and tucked behind one ear, shimmered like black silk. The strapless dress with an Empire waistline artfully concealed her rounded belly.

He found himself drowning in her eyes, which appeared more luminous with smoky shadow and mascara. His gaze lingered on her glossy lips, silently screaming for him to devour them in one bite as if they were a frothy confection. His gaze slipped lower to the swell of breasts rising and falling under the revealing décolletage. When she came home with the dress she'd refused to let him see it because she said she wanted it to be a surprise. Well, it was more than a surprise.

Draped over her ripening body, it was innocently wanton—if that were possible.

David smiled. "You look tall and very beautiful."

Devon pulled up the hem of her dress to reveal a pair of black silk strappy stilettos. They'd lingered long enough at the Beauty Box for her to get a mani/pedi, the red color on her toes matching the shade on her lips. "I don't know how much dancing I'm going to be able to do in these, but I have a pair of fold-up flats in my evening bag just in case."

"So you intend to bust a move tonight," he teased.

"I don't know about busting a move, but I don't intend to sit around watching others dance when in a couple of months I'll probably look ridiculous shaking my behind with a big belly on the dance floor."

"If you feel uncomfortable dancing in public we can always have our own private party."

She stared up at him through her lashes. "As long as I don't have to swing around a pole or twerk it's all good."

David shook his head in amazement. He never knew what to expect to come out of Devon's mouth. "No twerking and definitely no pole dancing." Reaching into the pocket of his dress trousers he took out a small velvet box. "I didn't know what your dress would look like, but I think these will go quite nicely with it."

Devon stared at the box on his palm. "What is it?"

"Open it and see. It's an early Mother's Day gift."

Her hand shook slightly when she took the box. "But... but I'm not a mother."

"Not yet, darling." He heard her intake of breath when she opened the box to find a pair of diamond and cultured pearl bow earrings. "The woman in the jewelry store said the design was popular during the Belle Epoque, whatever that means."

Devon handed him the box, her purse, and her shawl, and then removed the pearl studs from her ears. "It means 'beautiful era' in French and they are truly beautiful."

David had forgotten that Devon spoke fluent French and Spanish. He watched as she inserted the earrings in her pierced lobes, fastening the butterfly backs. Against her skin the pearls took on a pinkish glow. They were the perfect backdrop against her long, slender neck.

She touched her ears. "How do they look?"

"Perfect. Just like you." Extending his arm, he smiled when she looped her bare arm over the sleeve of his tuxedo jacket. "Let's go, princess. Your carriage awaits."

"Don't you mean my pumpkin?"

"No, baby. It's a carriage until midnight, then it turns back into a pumpkin."

Devon stared up at the antebellum mansion ablaze with light showing through every window. She felt flutters in her stomach as she mounted the steps, holding on to David's arm to keep her balance. There was a steady stream of limos and luxury cars maneuvering up the winding path as red-jacketed valets moved quickly to drive the cars to an area set aside for parking.

Prisms of light from hundreds of bulbs in a massive chandelier sparkled like jewels on the marble floor. A woman handed David a Venetian carnival masquerade gladiator mask in black and white with black satin ribbon ties. Devon smiled when she was given a white mask elegantly crafted with black feathers and matching ribbon ties. A couple in bottle-green livery helped them with their masks.

An elderly man in full livery took a deep breath and announced in a loud voice, "Judge Geoffrey and Dr. Victoria Phillips." A smattering of applause followed his announcement. The couple in front of Devon and David paused at the double doors leading into the ballroom before entering.

David handed the elderly man, who'd snapped to attention like a soldier acknowledging a superior officer, a card with their names. The man studied the card for several seconds, then announced loudly, "Mr. David Sullivan, Jr., Esquire, and Ms. Devon Collins, Esquire." Those standing close to the entrance to the ballroom turned to stare at them.

Devon moved closer to David. "I guess he's talking about us, Counselor," she said sotto voce.

"Wait until we're acknowledged by applause, and then we'll go in."

She successfully curbed the urge to laugh. Francine was right. The people who attended the ball were vain and supercilious. Were they so insecure that they had to engage in mutual admiration for one another?

They entered the ballroom, which was filled with couples wearing the requisite black or white, most holding flutes of champagne while white-jacketed waitstaff circulated among the assembly with trays of hors d'oeuvres. Bartenders mixing and pouring at four open bars were taking drink orders from those milling around their stations. Prerecorded music playing a contemporary love ballad could hardly be heard above the babble of voices as attendees greeted one another with excitement.

"Can I get you something to eat or drink?" David asked in her ear.

"No thank you. I think I can wait until dinner." David had prepared an antipasto chef's salad with kale several hours ago. Though low in calories, it was very filling. "I don't think you want to see me popping out of my dress."

"You're already popping out of it, darling. Your breasts are magnificent." The heat that began in the pit of her stomach spread upward to her face. "And you're even more magnificent when you blush." Devon lowered her eyes, the demure gesture not lost on several men staring at her.

"I think I'm going to need something to drink. Could you please bring me a glass of bubbly water?"

David smiled. "Of course."

She watched him wend his way through the throng, admiring his ramrod straight physique in the tailored tuxedo. "Miss, may I take your wrap?" Devon turned to see a young woman with several shawls and shrugs draped over her arm.

"Yes, of course." She gave her the shawl in exchange for a numbered ticket stub.

She glanced around the ballroom, searching for David's parents. Recognizing them wasn't easy because of the masks. A waiter holding a tray with tiny meatballs approached her. "Miss?"

"No thank you."

Another came over with a tray. "I have toasted flatbread topped with baked prosciutto, blue cheese, mushrooms, figs, and fried onions." He handed her a cocktail napkin. "Try one. They're delicious."

She picked up one of the triangles and bit into it. The sweet and salty textures exploded in her mouth. "It is delicious." David returned with her water and another glass filled with a dark liquid. "Taste this." She fed him the flatbread, watching for his reaction.

"Excellent. I'm going to make some the next time we entertain."

"Do you recognize the ingredients?" she asked. He repeated what the waiter said. "You really know food, don't you?"

David handed her the glass of water. "I'm a foodie."

"What are you drinking?"

"A black dog."

"Say what?" she questioned.

"It's made with bourbon, dry vermouth, and blackberry brandy."

Devon touched her glass to his. "It looks dangerous."

"What looks dangerous?"

A smile spread across the lower part of her face that was not concealed by the mask. "Mother, you look gorgeous." Edna wore a white silk surplice blouse with a long black silk skirt. A black-and-white cummerbund accented her trim waistline. The diamond studs in her lobes matched the graduated strand draped around her neck. "David's drink looks dangerous."

Edna pressed a kiss to Devon's cheek, then her son's. "Devon, you look incredible. I can't believe you're carrying my grandchild."

"It's the dress. It conceals a lot."

"Hold on to her tonight, son, because the wolves see her as new prey."

David looped an arm around Devon's waist. "You worry too much, Mother. Where's Dad?"

"I left him talking to Judge Phillips."

David took a sip of his drink. "It looks like a nice turnout."

Edna rested a hand over her necklace. "The committee managed to sell every ticket." She blew them a kiss. "I'll see you later. We'll be seated together for dinner."

With wide eyes, Devon watched as a buxom woman came up behind David and wrapped her arms around his waist. Everything about her was lush. The seams of her black beaded gown were challenged because it definitely was a size too small. "Where have you been hiding yourself, love? You know you still owe me a dance from prom, handsome."

"Savannah, please let me go."

Savannah dropped her arms; then, as if a lightbulb had been switched on, she noticed Devon for the first time. She stared at her left hand. "So, what I heard is true. You *are* getting married."

"Yes, I am," he confirmed. "Devon, this is Savannah. Savannah, Devon."

Savannah pushed out her lips. "Did you know David was the senior class president and I was homecoming queen when we were in high school?"

Devon affected a saccharine grin. "No, I didn't." She wondered how many more times she would have to watch women come on to her man. Edna had warned David about men hitting on his fiancée, while Savannah hadn't attempted to be subtle when she came on to him. The morals of Charleston's elite were very questionable.

A short man with a comb-over sidled up to her. He stank of alcohol. "Did anyone tell you that you're gorgeous?" he asked. Swaying slightly, he reached over and touched her breast.

David caught the man by his throat, shaking him like a pit bull would shake a Chihuahua. "Don't touch her!" he said between clenched teeth.

Savannah grabbed David's wrist as the man's face turned red, then blue. "Let him go, David. I'll take Mr. Overland to his wife."

Devon watched, stunned, as the man she'd promised to marry finally released the man's throat. It was as though he'd turned into a different person. She took a step backward when he held out the same hand he'd used to choke his defenseless victim. David was at least twenty years younger and a full head taller than the obviously intoxicated man.

"Don't," she pleaded. "Please don't touch me."

A sneer twisted his mouth. "You prefer him touching you?"

"I didn't say that."

"Then what the hell is it, Devon? Either I touch you or you let other men touch you."

Rage washed over Devon like a powerful ocean wave when she replayed his words. Had he just accused her of preferring another man's touch to his? Is that what he'd been thinking all along? She was so enraged she couldn't form the words to defend herself.

Placing her drink on the tray of a passing waiter, she turned and headed for the exit. She hadn't taken more than three steps when David caught her arm. "Where are you going?"

She stopped and he bumped into her, causing her to lose her balance. Devon saw the floor coming up at her and she instinctually cradled her belly, but a strong grip stopped her fall. David had caught her in time.

"Take me home."

Devon consciously blotted out what happened from the instant he retrieved her shawl to his helping her into the car and her climbing the staircase to the second floor. What she did recall was walking down the hallway to the bedroom she'd occupied when she spent her first night at his house.

She calmly closed the bedroom door, walked into the bathroom, and undressed in slow motion. The mask she'd worn, along with her gown, evening purse, shawl, shoes, and underwear lay on the bathroom floor. She'd broken her own strict rule of never leaving clothes on the floor.

However, she did remember removing the earrings and ring and washing her face, scrubbing it until it felt raw. She'd managed to find a new toothbrush in one of the vanity drawers and brushed her teeth. Walking on shaky legs, she returned to the bedroom, slipped into bed, and fell asleep.

David hadn't bothered to change out of the tuxedo before getting into his car and starting the engine. He'd called himself the king of fools and a few other coarse words as he drove aimlessly through Charleston. It was a warm spring Saturday night and college students crowded street corners, while many waited on long lines to get into bars and restaurants.

He didn't know why he'd said what he said to Devon, because he knew nothing was further from the truth. Francine's vision had turned him into a crazy man—someone who'd become paranoid because he feared every man Devon came into contact with might want to harm her—if a madman was stalking her. And now he'd turned into a madman, choking a man who was obviously drunk and harmless. And he wouldn't blame Anthony Overland if he went to the police and charged him with assault.

Forty minutes later David maneuvered into a space behind the Cavanaugh Island Sheriff's Department. He knew Jeff was on duty tonight because he'd arranged to take off the following Saturday for the wedding. Every time he thought about Devon calling off the wedding he felt a fist of fear squeeze his heart. He didn't want to lose her. He couldn't lose her. Tapping the Bluetooth feature, he pulled up Jeff's number.

"What's up, cuz?"

"I need to talk to you."

"When?"

"Now, Jeff."

"I thought you and Devon were going to that fancy masquerade ball tonight."

"We did. Look, I'm parked behind the jail. Unlock the back door and let me in."

"Hang up. I'm coming."

Jeff gave him an incredulous look when he opened the door. "For a man in formal dress, you look like crap."

"That's because I feel like crap," David admitted as he walked into the one-story brick building. He walked past two cells, both empty, and into a room where Jeff and his deputies usually bedded down after they'd made their rounds.

"I would offer you something to drink, but I've made it a practice not to keep alcohol in the station house." Jeff pointed to a chair. "Sit down before you fall down." David flopped down on a worn leather chair, stretching out his legs and crossing his feet at the ankles. A frown furrowed Jeff's forehead when he noticed the slight bulge on David's right ankle under the tuxedo trousers. "Are you packin'?"

David pulled up the leg of the trousers to reveal a small holstered automatic. "It's a long story."

Jeff sat opposite him and ran a hand over his head. "Well, I'm going to be here all night, so please tell me why you're carrying a gun."

David had to confide in someone, and he knew that someone had to be Jeff because he was never judgmental or condescending. He told him everything, leaving out the name of the person who'd warned him that Devon's life was in danger. Francine had told him in confidence that only her family and Morgan knew she was able to discern the future and he wasn't about to expose her secret—not even to Jeff.

Jeff sat straight, staring at David as if he'd suddenly taken leave of his senses. "You believe this person, David?"

He nodded. "Yes, because I trust this person. They have no reason to lie or make something like this up." David didn't have to try to convince Jeff that people were born with psychic abilities because he, too, had grown up listening to people, women in particular, talk about voodoo and root workers. He told his cousin about the incident Devon had with her client and his friends who'd moved into the athlete's mansion and were eventually evicted.

Crossing his arms over his chest, Jeff stared at the newly tiled floor. "It is a possibility it could be related to one of her clients. Maybe someone out for revenge on her for making them give up their cushy lifestyle. But I don't think your choking that man has anything to do with him posing a threat to Devon. You've got to slow down and think rationally. Otherwise you'll end up in jail for doing something dumb *and* stupid."

"You think I don't know that?" David spat out.

"Look, David, don't come at me like some rabid dog. I'm not your enemy. I'm going to give you some advice," he said in a softer tone. "First of all, stop carrying the gun. Then I want you to go home and apologize to the woman you hope will marry your crazy ass next week. And third, I'm going to suggest you postpone your honeymoon until after she has the baby. It will be the perfect opportunity for the two of you to spend some quality time together, because right now your lives are over the speed limit. You're looking to move into a new house, so I'm certain she's going to have her hands full decorating it. You're planning to open a new office, and that, too, is going to take up a lot of your time while planning for a new baby. That's a lot of stress under normal circumstances, without your having to worry if someone is trying to take out the woman you love. I'm going to do something on my end that will take the pressure off you to protect Devon."

David knew Jeff was right about all the changes going on in his and Devon's life. He'd looked forward to the honeymoon cruise, but it was something they could take in the future. "What are you going to do?"

"I have a buddy who retired from the Corps a few months after I did. He operates a private security firm employing former military personnel. Most of his men were in Special Forces, so they're highly trained when it comes to surveillance and protection. I'll call and ask him if he would send one of his guys to look after Devon. She'll never suspect she's being followed, and once he's acquainted with her daily routine everything will go smoothly. He'll contact you with his private number and you can update him if she has a doctor's appointment or if she plans to come to the Cove to eat with the girls."

David smiled for the first time in more than an hour. Jeff was former military police. "Let me know how much he charges and I'll send the money electronically."

Jeff waved a hand. "I'm not going to get into the middle of negotiating a price. I'll give him the number to your cell and he'll contact you directly."

Sandwiching his hands between his knees, David leaned forward, giving his cousin a long, penetrating look. "There's something else you should know about Devon."

Jeff massaged the back of his neck. "The baby she's carrying is not yours."

David slumped in the chair. "How did you know?"

"If you'd been dating someone like Devon there was no way in hell you wouldn't have told me. I saw something in you at Red's birthday party that told me this girl was special, so I wasn't surprised when the two of you hooked up."

"I'm not marrying her because of the baby."

"Come on, cuz. Don't you think I know that? And she's not marrying you because she doesn't want to be a baby mama either." Jeff paused, seemingly deep in thought. "We've been talking about possible retribution from one of her client's former associates who was affected when the ballplayer had to downsize his opulent lifestyle, but have you thought about her ex? Maybe he found out that she's carrying his baby and, depending upon who he is and what he does, he can't afford to have a secret baby so he hired someone to eliminate her *and* the baby."

"That sounds crazy."

"Crazy but plausible," Jeff stated. "Has she ever mentioned her ex's name?" David shook his head. "That alone should tell you she's hiding something. You need her to open up to you about him."

David told his cousin what Devon had revealed about her attempts to contact her ex-lover. "We promised each other we wouldn't talk about our exes, and I've done enough tonight to upset her and—"

"She'll get over it once she realizes you were looking out for her. She's pissed off because someone witnessed you acting a fool, but trust me when I say she'll appreciate the fact that her man stepped up to protect her. I did the same for Kara even before we were married and it goes double now that she's my wife. Go home, leave your stiff-neck pride outside the door, and beg. Once you learn to beg it gets easier every time you have to do it."

David's eyebrow lifted a fraction. "You beg?"

"Oh hell yeah. And I've become pretty good at it since realizing it's not all about oorah and once a Marine always a Marine. It's about trying to be a good husband and father and making certain I have a happy home." He stood up, David rising with him. "Now go home and get your life in order, because I'm still planning to be your best man."

David hugged his cousin, thumping his back. "Thanks for the pep talk."

"No problem. You've talked me off the ledge a few times, so I'm just returning the favor."

David left the station house, got into his car, and headed in the direction of the mainland. Jeff had recommended he beg—something he'd never done with a woman. But he was amenable to begging and groveling if needed.

The house was as silent as a tomb when he climbed the staircase to his bedroom after locking his gun in a wall safe behind a painting in the home office. The light in the hallway between the bedroom and bathroom provided enough illumination to see the outline of Devon's body under the blanket she'd pulled over her head. He went into the bedroom across the hall to undress and brush his teeth so he wouldn't wake her. When he returned to the bedroom he discovered she hadn't moved.

Easing back the blanket, David slipped into bed next to her, luxuriating in the warmth and silken feel of her naked body. "Please forgive me, baby," he whispered in her mussed hair.

"You're forgiven." She sighed.

"I thought you were asleep."

Shifting, she turned to face him. "You thought it would make it easier to apologize if I was asleep?"

He touched his mouth to hers. "No. I was prepared to beg, grovel, plead, and kowtow to get you to forgive me for what I said and for embarrassing you. I'm sorry."

She covered his mouth with her fingertips. "You forgot bowing and scraping."

"That too," he mumbled against her hand.

"I'd planned to spend the night in the other bedroom but changed my mind. If we're going to share our lives then I want us to be able to talk things out until we can at least come to an agreement or be willing to compromise."

David didn't want to think of them sleeping under the same roof and not sharing a bed. "I want you to tell me if I'm acting like a horse's ass. And I'm sorry about that remark about you and other men."

She laughed softly. "You were definitely a horse's ass tonight, but it felt good to know I have a superhero willing to protect me."

David couldn't tell her he planned to hire a professional bodyguard to shadow her with the hope he would be able to subvert the danger Francine had seen in her vision. "I think it's time I hang up my magic cape."

"Cape or no cape, even dressed as Bruce Wayne, you were still a superhero."

He gathered her close, burying his face in her hair, and whispered a prayer of thanks. The fact that Devon wouldn't hold a grudge meant they could have the happy home Jeff spoke of. "Would you be upset if we postponed our honeymoon until after you have the baby?"

A beat passed before Devon said, "No. We'll have plenty of time to honeymoon. I wouldn't mind us occasionally taking a three-day weekend to go somewhere for a change of scenery once the baby is old enough to be left with your mother or to have a playdate with Kara's and Morgan's kids."

"I'll wait until Monday to call the travel agent to cancel our reservations."

"Maybe you can regift it."

"To whom?"

"How about Angela? She told me that she's accrued a lot of vacation days and that she was going to start taking them once you left because the policy at your dad's firm is they'll only pay for twenty vacation days once a support staff member leaves."

"Do have any idea how incredible you are?" David asked Devon. "I'll call her tomorrow and ask her if she's willing to accept it."

"Of course she will, David."

He kissed Devon passionately, wondering how he'd gotten so lucky to find someone like her. Both of them had been given a second chance at love, and David intended to do everything within his power to make it last forever.

Chapter Twenty-Eight

~⊙~

Chuck excused himself from the meeting when he heard the distinctive tone of an incoming text. Standing outside the closed door, he read the message from Jake. His people had located Devon Collins in Charleston, South Carolina. She and a well-known local attorney had applied for a marriage license, and his best investigator was working to find out if she was in the family way. Tapping several keys, he answered the text:

Good work. Keep on it.

He slipped the phone into his breast pocket and reentered the meeting room. Nothing in his expression revealed the excitement that he was one step closer to grooming Gregory Emerson to eventually move into the governor's mansion.

*   *   *

Devon felt her life was traveling at warp speed and there was nothing she could do to slow it down. She'd made the move from New York, finally signed the closing papers for the house on Cherry Lane, and spent the last few days finalizing all the details for her wedding. So many changes were all coming so fast she barely had a chance to take a breath.

After the previous night's rehearsal dinner, Devon had gone back to the house instead of staying with Francine because of a tension headache, while Jeff and Keaton left with David to celebrate his last day as a single man. They'd brought him back home around three in the morning unable to stand up without assistance. It had taken all her self-control not to scream at them for getting him drunk. He'd slept most of the morning, stumbling out of bed at eleven craving cold water. If they weren't to be married later that day she would've let him lie there and try to get up on his own.

But now they were here. The big moment had arrived. Although she'd recovered from the headache, Devon tried ignoring the flutters in her chest, but they persisted despite taking deep breaths to calm her nerves. She'd arrived at the restaurant twenty minutes before with Francine and Keaton, and they'd been whisked into a room of the former inn-turned-restaurant to wait for the ceremony to begin. Her soon-to-be mother-in-law stuck her head in to let her know David had arrived before her and he was wearing a hole in the carpet pacing back and forth.

The door opened and Francine swept in with the flourish of an actress coming onstage for a live performance. Francine had placed David's wedding band on the thumb of her left hand. "How is he holding up?" Devon asked her maid of honor.

Francine shook her head. "Not too good. He's pacing and drinking water."

Devon closed her eyes. "That's because he's still dehydrated from last night. Men are such fools about their bachelor parties." She brought her hands up to cup her breasts. "Look at me, Francine. David gets to have these titties every night." Francine pressed her lips together as her shoulders shook from repressed laughter. "It's not funny. You'll get your payback when the fellas throw Keaton a bachelor party complete with strippers."

Francine sobered quickly. "Please don't say that, Devon."

Then, there came three rapid taps on the door. It opened and Keaton stuck his head through the slight opening. "Are you ready to become Mrs. David Sullivan?"

Devon inhaled, held her breath, and then let it out slowly. As annoyed as she was with her fiancé, she was ready to become his wife. She picked up her bouquet of white violets, calla lilies, and roses. "Let's do it."

Francine wiggled her fingers. "I'd better get into place." She walked out as Keaton walked in, looking resplendent in a tuxedo with a black silk tie. He took Devon's hands, brought them to his mouth, and kissed her fingers.

"Your hands are ice-cold. Are you feeling okay?"

"I know I'm definitely feeling better than my soon-to-be husband."

Keaton tucked her free hand into the bend of his elbow. "I'm sorry, Devon. I had no idea David wasn't much of a drinker."

"He'll probably feel better once he eats something."

"He's really a good guy," Keaton said as they walked the carpeted hallway leading to the solarium.

Devon wanted to tell Keaton that David was more than a

good guy. He was her friend, lover, father of the child she carried, and husband for life. They stopped at the carved door. Keaton nodded to the restaurant employee and he opened the door to reveal an indoor rain forest.

Her gaze went to David at the opposite end of the room; he stood on Jeff's right, his body ramrod straight. A slight smile softened her mouth when he winked at her. He wore a different tuxedo than the one he'd worn to the charity ball; this one was double-breasted with peaked lapels. She focused on his dark gray silk tie under a wing collar. He'd opted to wear a pin-striped silk vest under his jacket instead of a cummerbund. Her eyes went to Jeff, whose tie was an exact match for Francine's sea-foam green gown.

The judge in his black robes nodded to the DJ and the familiar strains of the "Wedding March" filled the solarium as their guests rose to their feet and turned to look at her and Keaton.

David clenched and unclenched his hands when he saw Devon in her wedding finery for the first time, unable to believe she could improve on perfection. Overhead light shimmered on her raven-black hair, which was brushed off her face and secured with jeweled pins in an elaborate twist behind her left ear. She wore the earrings he'd given her a week ago. The gown she'd chosen artfully concealed her expanding waistline. No one would suspect she was pregnant.

Keaton led her down the aisle to his side, and any doubt he might have had about marrying Devon was dashed at that moment. Her eyes sparkled like precious jewels, appearing even more brilliant. Mavis had outdone herself styling her hair and applying her makeup.

The music ended, and the judge, a longtime family friend,

cleared his throat. "Who gives this woman in marriage?" His sonorous voice carried easily in the room.

Keaton shared a smile with Devon. "I do." He took Devon's right hand, placing it in David's outstretched left, then turned and took his seat.

The judge motioned for everyone to be seated. He waited a full minute and then began. "We have gathered here today to bring this couple together in the bonds of matrimony." He opened a small Bible. "If a man vow a vow unto the Lord, or swear an oath to bind his soul with a bond, he shall not break his word; he shall do according to all that proceedeth out of his mouth." He paused briefly to look at Devon. "If a woman also vow a vow unto the Lord, and bind herself by a bond, then all her vows shall stand and every bond wherewith she hath bound her soul shall stand." He closed the Bible.

David felt Devon trembling and he watched the natural color drain from her face. He gently squeezed her hand as her eyelids fluttered wildly. He prayed for her not to faint.

Lowering his head, he pressed his mouth to her ear. "Baby?" he whispered.

She blinked as if coming out of a trance. "Yes, darling?"

"Are you okay?"

"Yes."

David met the judge's eyes. "Let's do this quickly." He suspected she hadn't eaten.

"Do you, David Edgar, take Devon Juliana, whom you have promised to love, honor, and cherish, to be your lawfully wedded wife?"

David smiled. "I do."

"Do you, Devon Juliana, take David Edgar, whom you have promised to love, trust, and understand, as your lawfully wedded husband?"

"I do," Devon said.

The exchange of rings was accomplished quickly and the judge told David he could kiss his bride. Cradling her face, he lowered his head and kissed her parted lips, deepening the kiss when her arms curved under his shoulders.

The solarium was filled with applause and whistles as David bent slightly and swept Devon up in his arms. He carried her to a group of chairs near one of the two waterfalls and waved to a waiter. "Please bring me a glass of orange juice."

Edna pushed through those gathering around her daughter-in-law. "Is she all right, David?"

He glanced up at his mother. "Yes. I suspect she didn't eat."

"I'll go and get something."

David waved the banquet manager over. "Could you please escort everyone into the ballroom while I take care of my wife?" The woman ushered the wedding guests into an adjoining ballroom, where they would be served dinner, as he marveled at how easily it was to call Devon his wife.

She pushed against his shoulder. "Please let me go. I promise you I'm not going to faint."

"I'm not going to let you go until you get some color in your face."

The waiter returned with a glass of orange juice seconds before Edna thrust a small dish of sliced melon at David. "Feed her some of these."

He held the glass while Devon took furtive sips of the chilled liquid. "You're embarrassing me," she whispered.

David dropped a kiss on her hair. "You should've eaten."

"I did."

"When?"

"This afternoon."

Picking up the fork, he fed her some melon and within minutes her natural color returned. "What am I going to do with you, Mrs. Sullivan?" he teased. "Hire someone to watch you twenty-four/seven to make certain you eat?"

David's teasing wasn't a threat but reality. He'd taken Jeff's suggestion and contacted the security company to speak to a consultant about providing protection for his wife; several hours later, he'd received a call from a protection specialist who'd scheduled a meeting for the following week to go over the strategies to keep her safe.

"I don't think so, Mr. Sullivan."

"Oh. Miss Sassy is back. Or will I have to call you Mrs. Sassy now?"

Devon laughed. "I'm feeling better, David. Really," she insisted when he gave her a skeptical glance.

"Finish the fruit because we're going to have to take photographs before we get a chance to eat dinner."

Looping her arms around his neck, Devon pulled his head down until their lips were inches apart. "I suspect I'm not the only one in need of food. You still appear a little worse for wear from your titty bar escapade."

"Who told you we went to a topless bar?"

"You just did because you didn't bother to deny it." She narrowed her eyes. "Don't I have enough for you, darling?" she said, not raising her voice above a whisper.

"You have more than enough. Please don't tell me you're jealous."

"Of course I'm jealous. I love you, David, and I swear I will dropkick any woman who looks sideways at you."

David was momentarily surprised by her sudden possessiveness. He brushed his mouth over hers. "I'm not going to cheat on you, Devon. Remember, we both had unfaithful partners." He pulled back when he heard someone clear her throat. "Yes, Red?"

Francine walked into the solarium. "How is she?"

"She's fine," Devon said, smiling. "I was feeling a little light-headed, but I'm okay now." She stood up, as David also came to his feet. "I'm going to check my face and hair before I meet you back here in five minutes."

Devon hadn't realized she was ravenous until she sampled a perfectly grilled lobster tail with avocado and mango salad with citrus dressing. The photo session lasted exactly one hour as she, David, and the wedding party posed for hundreds of shots, using the solarium as the backdrop while their guests enjoyed a cocktail hour replete with open bars and carving stations.

"It looks as if Trevor is quite taken with Kara's former roommate," Devon said, watching the pair lean in close as they spoke.

David set down his water goblet. "They look like Ken and Barbie."

"Are you a betting man, darling?"

"Not really. But I have played poker a few times. Why?"

"How much do you want to bet that Trevor will leave Sullivan and Matthews and move to New York?"

"I think you're wrong. Trevor moved to Charleston because of a woman and he was devastated when they broke up. If anyone's going to do any moving, it's Dawn. She misses Kara and she's godmother to her son. I'm willing to bet she'll give up the bright lights of the Big Apple before the end of the year." He extended his little finger. "How much do you want to wager?"

"Is one hundred dollars too rich for your wallet?"

"I think I have an extra Benjamin lying around some-where." He hooked his finger with Devon's, sealing their bet.

Devon sipped a glass of water infused with lemon. "I like the playlist." The DJ had spun tunes spanning the decades and she and David still hadn't shared their first dance as hus-band and wife.

He leaned closer, their shoulders touching. "I don't know about you, but I'm ready to dance off some of this food."

"Let's do it."

She allowed him to pull back her chair and help her to her feet. Unrestrained laughter and the babble of voices faded when David led her to the area set aside as a dance floor. All eyes were on them when the DJ played Jaheim's "Re-markable," featuring Terry Dexter. Once David had heard the song, he couldn't believe how appropriate the lyrics were for their whirlwind romance. Cradled in his embrace, Devon closed her eyes, curving against the hard planes of her hus-band's body. The song ended with raucous applause. The music segued into the upbeat classic dance tune "Everybody Everybody" by Black Box, and chairs were pushed back from tables as couples practically ran to the dance floor.

Devon found herself twirling around the dance floor with Jeff before Keaton cut in. "Beautiful bride, handsome groom, delicious food, top-shelf wines and liquors, and great music. The night couldn't get any better. You've done very well, Devon."

"I have you to thank for that. If you hadn't invited me to come down for Francine's party, I never would've met David."

"Yes, you would have. Maybe not now, but you and David were destined to meet."

"Like you and Francine?"

"Yes, friend. Like me and Francine."

David's father tapped Keaton on his shoulder. "May I cut in?"

Keaton inclined his head. "Of course."

Devon rested her left hand on her father-in-law's shoulder as he took her right. "You gave us quite a scare when you looked as if you were going to faint just before taking your vows."

"I felt a little light-headed."

"Is the baby all right?"

She stared at the man who still harbored a lingering resentment that his son had decided to establish his own firm. "The baby's okay. I'm okay. And David is okay."

Dark eyes burned with an intense fire that reminded her of David whenever he felt passionate about something. "You're a very strong woman, Devon Sullivan, and my son is blessed to have someone like you. I'm honored that you agreed to join our family."

Tears welled up in her eyes. Not tears of sadness but of joy. "Thank you, Dad."

The frivolity continued for hours with dancing, endless toasts, and a supply of food that included grilled-to-order steaks, seafood, and chicken with accompanying vegetables. The chef had prepared a special dish of Mandarin beef with jasmine rice and Devon ate so much she could hardly move off the chair when David whispered it was time to leave. He'd arranged for them to spend their wedding night in a nearby hotel.

Francine helped her out of her gown and into a loose-fitting sheath dress. "Next month it will be your turn," Devon said, as she slipped her feet into a pair of ballerina flats.

"Although I can't wait to marry Keaton, I'm feeling

stressed about all the pomp and circumstance leading up to it. I keep thinking about eloping, but my mother would never forgive me. Enough talk. I'll take your gown back to the house. Now go and enjoy your wedding night."

Devon hugged Francine, picked up her overnight bag, and slipped out of the restaurant through a side exit. David pushed off the side of the building where he'd been waiting for her. He took her bag, leading her to the lot where he'd parked his car.

No words were spoken as he drove the short distance to the hotel. David had preregistered and after giving the desk clerk a credit card and his driver's license he pocketed the key card. "We're on the third floor."

She moved closer to him when they entered the elevator, the car rising quickly once the doors closed. The hotel, located in the Historic District, was within walking distance of their home. They exited the elevator, their footsteps muffled by the deep-pile carpeting of the hallway. David stopped in front of a door at the end of the hallway.

Slipping the key card in the slot, he pushed open the door with his shoulder before sweeping her up in his arms and carrying her over the threshold. Burying her face between his neck and shoulder, she breathed a kiss under his ear. "Now I know why you wanted to stay in a hotel tonight."

David set her on her feet. He kissed the end of her nose. "If I'd carried you over the threshold the first time you came to *our* home, I know you would've thought me crazy."

Going on tiptoe, Devon traced the outline of his mouth with the tip of her tongue. "Falling in love can make one a little crazy. I'm going to wash this makeup off my face, then take a shower. You're more than welcome to join me."

Reaching up, he removed the pins from her hair and released the elaborate twist until her hair floated around her face. "Beautiful," he whispered reverently. "And all mine."

Devon froze like a deer caught in the headlights. The three words chilled her to the bone. Did he think of her as his partner...or a possession? After the choking incident with Mr. Gropey Hands at the Black and White Masque, she wasn't as confident that she knew the real David. She forced a brittle smile. "I have to wash my face." Reaching for her bag, she walked into the bathroom.

She knew there were times when she tended to overthink a situation, and she didn't want to do that tonight. It was her wedding night, and Devon wanted to create memories she would remember as a very old woman.

She stepped into the shower stall and adjusted the water. Just as she raised her face under the pulsing spray, she felt David get in and move behind her. His hands cradled her breasts as if testing their weight. He shifted until they were facing each other, and he lowered his head and suckled her like a starving infant. Devon moaned as passion shot through her like a lighted fuse. David shifted again, this time behind her as he lifted her hips and entered her. His groans, the sound of flesh slapping wet skin, and her screams created a cacophony of sensual music that pulled Devon under, and she didn't know where she began and David ended. She pushed her hips back against his hard sex, unable to disguise her body's reaction to his raw lovemaking. Heat rippled under her skin, her breathing coming faster and faster until she finally surrendered to the ecstasy tearing her asunder.

David made love to Devon as if it would be the last time. He loved everything about her: her voice, her face, her lush body. Just being with her made him grateful he'd been born male. Ever mindful of the child growing inside her, he made slow, deliberate love to Devon, and as he aroused her passion his own grew stronger, more powerful, and intense.

He felt her inner muscles contract, milking him until he spilled his seed inside her. Pulling out, David rained kisses down the length of her spine before nipping the smooth flesh on her buttocks. He loved her—oh, how he adored this woman he'd vowed to love, honor, cherish, and protect.

"Remind me not to shower with you again because we always end up making love." Devon's soft voice broke into his thoughts.

"What would happen if we share a bath?" he teased.

"We can't, David."

"Why not, sweetheart?"

"Because the bathtub isn't large enough for us to sit side by side."

He kissed the nape of her neck. "We can if we renovate the master bathroom on Cherry Lane and put in a garden tub."

Devon chuckled. "That sounds like a plan."

They washed each other, lingering under the water long enough to rinse the soap from their bodies, and then swaddled in towels, they returned to the bedroom and lay across the bed, holding hands.

A comfortable silence enveloped them before they finally succumbed to the sated sleep of lovers.

Chapter Twenty-Nine

David finally met with the security specialist. It was a
Monday and he'd driven Devon to Sanctuary Cove for her
weekly luncheon with Francine, Morgan, and Kara. He had
the man come to Cherry Lane because he wanted to be
nearby when Devon called him to pick her up. He'd convinced her to turn in the rental car, so now she had to depend
on him to drive her around. He'd promised they would go car
shopping, but he used every excuse to put it off: He had to
meet with the contractor who'd begun renovating the Haven
Creek office or he volunteered to go shopping with her to
pick up something for the house, and he'd even offered to
clear a portion of the property for her to plant a flower and
vegetable garden.

The furniture Devon had shipped from New York was delivered to Cherry Lane after the rooms were painted. David
had pulled up the carpeting on the second floor, revealing
parquet floors that needed refinishing. They agreed not to

move into the house until renovations to the master bath-room were completed and the upstairs bedroom floors were done. The furniture Devon had ordered for the front and back porches, dining room, home office, and kitchen was delivered and with accent pieces like lamps, rugs, and window treatments the house was beginning to look like a home. She'd conferred with Abram Daniels, the interior design partner at Dane and Daniels Architecture and Interior Design, about how to decorate the four bedrooms.

Shifting his thoughts from the activity going on in the house, David stared at the man who'd introduced himself as Carlos. David didn't bother to ask him his last name because he knew he would not reveal it. Carlos was medium height and slender, with a ruddy complexion and cropped light brown hair and eyes. He had no distinguishing features, which helped him blend in with millions of other men who resembled him. David continued to be puzzled by Francine's warning because she hadn't said anything again about Devon's being in danger. They sat on the back porch under one of two ceiling fans.

"Why do you think your wife's life is in danger?"

David knew he couldn't tell him about Francine's warning, so he told him about Devon's client who'd had to evict his friends because of financial difficulties. "I believe one or several of them blame her."

Carlos stared at the toe of his construction boot. "Has she been threatened? Any weird phone calls, texts, or emails?"

"No."

"So this threat is more perceived than real?"

David nodded. "My wife is pregnant and I don't want to run the risk that someone will try to harm her or the baby."

"I usually deal with real-life situations, but if you feel

someone is trying to harm your wife, then I'm not here to discourage you. Does your wife drive a car?"

David told him about turning in the rental car and his chauffeuring her around. "I plan to buy her a car, but I wanted to wait until we talked."

Carlos smiled, minute lines fanning out around his eyes as if he'd spent too much time squinting in bright sunlight. "When you buy the car let me know; I'll install a tracking device that will let me know exactly where she is. I'll follow her, so you can stop playing chauffeur. The only thing I need for you to do is give me her schedule. If she plans to go shopping, then I'll have to know which mall, or when she goes to the doctor. It's my understanding that you have this house and another in Charleston. Where are you staying most of the time?"

"Right now we're staying in Charleston. But as soon as some of the floors are refinished and a bathroom is completely renovated then we'll spend most of our time here."

Carlos nodded. "I'm going to check into a hotel close to your Charleston place and at the inn here on the island. I'll give you a number where you will text me to let me know your whereabouts. If you're going to stay here, then I'll be on the island, and vice versa. And don't worry about your wife knowing that she's being followed because I supervise two other specialists in this area and they'll rotate following her using different cars so she won't get suspicious. Women are a lot more perceptive than men once they believe they're being stalked. When's her next doctor's appointment?"

"She had one last week, so she won't go again for another month."

"Does she have any routines?"

David extended his legs, crossing his feet at the ankles.

"Mondays she has lunch with her friends. But she claims once she finishes decorating the house then she can have them meet here."

"Do they lunch here or on the mainland?"

"Here. They meet at twelve at Jack's Fish House."

"What time do they finish lunch?"

"It varies. I dropped her off and told her to call me when she's ready for me to pick her up." The last word was barely off his tongue when the sound of a car's engine shattered the silence of the afternoon. David stood up and rounded the porch. He stared at Devon as she struggled to get out of Francine's red Corvette. He motioned for Carlos to stay out of sight, but it was too late. Her gaze was fixed on the strange man as she walked slowly to the house.

"Hey, Red," David called out in greeting.

Francine stuck her head out of the open window. "I drove Devon home because she fell and hurt her knees. I wanted to take her to Dr. Monroe so he could check her out but she insisted I bring her home."

David galvanized into action, bounding off the porch before anyone could blink and rushing to his wife. The knees of her slacks were ripped and skin showed through. He tenderly took her abraded hands in his and kissed her forehead, hoping she wouldn't pick up on his heart pounding a runaway rhythm.

"What happened?"

Devon shook her head. "I'm not sure. It happened so quickly that I didn't have time to react. After lunch I decided to run over to the sweetgrass basket shop to look at what they had when some guy on a bike came racing down the sidewalk and ran into me. He knocked me down and kept going. I called Francine to bring me back."

Carlos had asked him whether his fear was real or perceived, and now he saw firsthand that it was real. Whoever
knocked her down had to have read the posted signs that bike
riding and skateboarding were prohibited on island sidewalks.

David's gaze swung back to Carlos. "I'll talk to you later."

The man nodded. "I have your number. I'll call you."

David smiled at Francine. "Thanks, Red, for driving her
home."

She waved to him. "No problem."

Francine drove away and minutes later Carlos left in his
car as David turned and slowly walked up the porch. "Did
you get a look at the person on the bike?" he asked Devon.

"No. I know it was a man but I couldn't get a good look
at him before I was down on all fours."

Francine had mentioned a man shrouded in darkness,
and her vision had become real. His outward calm belied
the rage and fear roiling inside him; he didn't want to wrap
his head around the fact that someone wanted to harm
Devon. He shouldered the door open and carried her into
the living room, setting her down on the sofa. "I'm going
to clean you up, then take you over to Dr. Monroe so he
can check you out."

Devon shook her head. "I don't need to see a doctor. I
didn't hurt my belly because I put my hands down to break
the fall."

"I don't care, Devon. I'm still taking you to the doctor."
He ignored her pouting when she pushed out her lips. He
found the first-aid kit in the downstairs bathroom and gently
wiped the palms of her hands and her knees with peroxide-
soaked sterile cotton. Devon winced and moaned softly each
time he touched the abrasions.

She lay on the off-white sofa, an arm covering her face, as

he dialed the doctor in the Cove and asked if he could bring her in. Once he revealed she was almost five months pregnant, the nurse said to bring her in.

Devon stared up at Dr. Asa Monroe as he positioned an examining light to look at her scraped knees. She'd learned that the resident family doctor had married Deborah, the owner of the Parlor Bookstore, and together they had a preschool-age son. The son and daughter Deborah had from a previous marriage were now in college.

"I don't think I broke anything, Doctor."

The attractive middle-aged physician smiled. "I don't believe you did either. But you do have some ugly-looking abrasions on your hands and a few contusions on your knees. I'm going to recommend you put ice on your knees to prevent swelling. You're going to be really sore in a couple of hours, and because you're pregnant I'm not going to be able to give you anything for pain."

Devon went still when she felt a flutter in her belly. Then she felt it again. "I just felt the baby move."

Dr. Monroe helped her to sit up. "I checked the baby's heartbeat and it's very strong. When are you scheduled to see Dr. Ingram again?"

"Not until the third week in June."

"I'm recommending you call her and let her know you fell, and if she wants my report then I'll fax it over to her."

Devon managed to get off the table without falling again. Dr. Monroe was right. Her knees were on fire. "Please ask my husband to come in and help me." David came into the examining room and carried her out of the doctor's office to his car. Never had she felt so completely helpless. The tears she'd kept in check when the man knocked her down and she feared losing her baby overflowed and streamed down her face after David had buckled her in.

"Hey, hey," he crooned, dabbing her cheeks with a tissue. "You're going to be all right, baby."

She broke down completely with his attempt to comfort her. "I'm just so relieved. The thought of anything hurting our baby was so awful."

He placed a hand over her belly. "Nothing's going to hurt this baby."

She managed to smile despite her lingering fear. "Are you sure?"

David kissed her mouth. "Very sure. Now I'm going to take you back to Charleston, and you're going to sit and put your feet up while I wait on you hand and foot. No more running around shopping or lunching with the girls until you're healed."

"I can't sit and do nothing," she protested.

"You can watch your beloved British dramas while you knit and piece quilts."

David was right. She'd knitted four baby hats and two sweaters and was halfway finished crocheting a crib blanket. She'd returned to Nine Patch Quilt and picked up enough fat quarters to piece a quilt for Morgan's baby. Whenever they retreated to the family room to relax, she kept her hands busy with a needlework project.

"Who was that man I saw you talking with when Francine drove up?"

"He's a potential client. He saw the sign in the window announcing the future law offices of D. Sullivan with my cell number and he called and asked for a consultation."

"Are you going to pick him up as a client?"

David gave her a quick glance. "I'm thinking about it.

I don't want to see clients in our home, but I may have to make an exception in certain cases until we officially open after the Island Fair."

Devon nodded. David had told her that the annual island-wide celebration began July 1 and ended with a spectacular fireworks show at midnight on July 4. The carnival-like events included amusement park rides, picnics, and fun and games for all ages. "You're still projecting opening in July?"

"Yes."

David hadn't realized he'd become such an adept liar, but he'd skirted the questions about Carlos. While Dr. Monroe was examining Devon, he'd stepped out to call Jeff to let him know about the accident. Again his cousin urged him to broach the subject of Devon's ex because, with nearly twenty-five years of experience as a military and civilian police officer, he suspected her ex-boyfriend and biological father of her unborn child.

"What's your ex's name?"

"Gregory Emerson," Devon replied. "Why?"

"You were talking in your sleep last night and I thought I heard you call a man's name." He'd lied again and would do it again and again to get the name of the person who was intent on hurting Devon.

"I don't remember having a dream about him and if I did then it wouldn't be a dream but a nightmare."

"It didn't sound like Gregory or Emerson."

"What did it sound like?"

"Ralph, or it could've been Russ." It was another lie.

"It was probably Ray. My brother is Raymond."

"Yeah. It could've been Ray." David knew her brother's name began with an R. "I'm going to call Mother to let her know we won't be able to come over for dinner tonight after all."

"Please don't tell her about the accident, David, because you know how melodramatic she can be."

"What do you want me to tell her? You know eventually she's going to see your hands and knees."

Devon chewed her lower lip. "I'd hate to lie to her."

Join the club, he mused. "I don't believe Mother is going to have a meltdown if we postpone dinner. I'll tell her you're feeling fatigued and you're going to bed early."

"She knows that I'm no longer dealing with fatigue."

"Don't stress about it. I'll tell her something." Lying and hiding things from Devon was not only stressful but emotionally draining. He had to tell one lie to cover another and he prayed he'd be able to keep the lies straight. "I told Jeff about your accident."

"Why did you do that?"

David met her eyes when he gave her a quick glance. "He needs to know that someone broke the law when it's clearly posted that no bikes are allowed on the sidewalk. He said he's going to look at video footage to see if he can identify the rider of the bike." Downtown Sanctuary Cove and Haven Creek were equipped with video cameras, while the residents of Angels Landings were opposed to having cameras in their town.

"I think you're making a mountain out of a molehill. It was an accident."

"An accident where you could've been seriously injured."

"Thankfully I wasn't seriously injured."

David clenched his teeth tightly. He'd promised himself not to argue with Devon but there were times when he had to work hard to hold his tongue. He just hoped Jeff would be able to glean something when he went over the camera footage on the sidewalk outside A Tisket A Basket.

"We didn't get her."

Chuck glared at his fixer. "What the hell do you mean you didn't get her?"

"My man managed to knock her down but she didn't stay down."

"What did he use to knock her down? A feather? We know she's pregnant, and based on the information your man got from hacking into her doctor's computer system, we know it's Emerson's kid. The date he gave us coincides with the dates in her file. I want you to make certain she loses that kid. I don't care who does it or how it's done, but I want it gone."

Jake used his cane for support as he pushed to his feet. "Your wish is my command," he drawled facetiously.

"Watch your mouth, Walsh!"

Jake turned and glared at the man who was responsible for making him very wealthy. "No, you watch your mouth, Hanson! If I don't tell you how to do your job then back the hell up when it comes to telling me about mine."

Chuck didn't want to and couldn't believe Jake had gotten up enough nerve to speak to him in that manner. Maybe it was time for him to look for a new hatchet man, because Jake was getting soft.

Chapter Thirty

It took more than a week for the bruises on her knees to fade completely, and the second Monday in June Devon decided to host the Lowcountry Ladies Luncheon at the house on Cherry Lane. It would be the last luncheon until the Monday following Labor Day, because they'd all agreed not to meet during the summer months when most businesses traditionally shut down between the hours of noon and two to conserve energy. The Mondays in September were tentative because she and Morgan were due that month. She was in her sixth month and felt and looked very pregnant.

Devon had convinced David to make Cherry Lane their principal residence after all the floors in the house were refinished. A security company had wired the house and installed cameras, a rarity with residential properties on the island, to make sure her new painting would be safe.

Her days began with getting up early and walking with David before it got too hot. They returned home and shared a shower and then breakfast. Devon enjoyed tending the self-watering vertical planters she'd ordered from Williams-Sonoma. David laughed when she purchased flats of herbs to line seven rows of planting areas, each nearly three feet long, but she had the last laugh when he needed fresh dill, rosemary, or cilantro and he didn't have to get in his car and drive to the supermarket to shop in the produce section.

He'd helped her plant a vegetable and flower garden, enclosing the area with chicken wire to keep out critters looking for a free meal. Another section of the property was fenced off for what would eventually become a playground. She and Peggy established an unofficial barter system: fresh eggs for homemade bread. Her new neighbor surprised her one day when she brought over jars of sweet and tangy chow-chow relish, blackberry jam, and strawberry preserves.

Sitting on the porch to watch the sun rise and set; cooking and baking bread on the high-performance stove; and knitting, crocheting, and quilting in between putting up loads of laundry afforded Devon a sense of domestic peace and stability that had always eluded her.

David had boxed up and brought his law books from Charleston to Cherry Lane, and Devon told him she would begin studying for the South Carolina bar after she had the baby. While their daughter slept she would study, and once a week he would give her a test on what she'd retained.

She adjusted the thermostat on the enclosed back porch to offset the buildup of heat coming from the kitchen. A steadily falling summer rain prevented her from cooking outdoors on the gas grill.

"Something smells good," David said as he walked into the kitchen. He'd spent most of the morning on the phone with a client.

"Those are Thai meatballs you smell. I'm going to serve them with a spicy peanut sauce as an appetizer along with crab cakes with horseradish cream."

David kissed her forehead. "What else are you serving?"

"Korean-style barbecue short ribs, cheddar biscuits, a cannellini bean and basil tuna salad, and grapefruit mojito mocktails."

"Wow! Maybe I should stay home and join you ladies instead of visiting Aunt Corrine."

"You'd better not stand her up. Last Sunday she couldn't stop talking about how you don't come around anymore."

"I used to visit her at least once a week before Jeff came back. Now she has Jeff, Kara, and Austin to keep her company. Speaking of keeping company, you owe me a hundred dollars." He extended his hand, palm up. "Pay up, Mama."

Her jaw dropped when she realized what he was alluding to. "Dawn's moving down here?"

"Yep. Trevor called to tell me she's moving in with him. It's apparent he's been flying up to New York every other weekend and he told me Dawn refused to give up what she had in New York unless he put a ring on it." He pantomimed the hand motion in Beyoncé's "Single Ladies" video.

"Did he?"

"Damn skippy he did."

"Kara must be in seventh heaven, because she's been trying to get her to move down here for a while."

"Are y'all going to ask her to join your Lowcountry Ladies Luncheon?"

"Probably."

David speared a meatball with a toothpick and popped it into his mouth. "Hey. These are good without the peanut sauce." He wound an arm around her waist. "I felt the baby kicking this morning."

Tilting her chin, Devon stared lovingly into his eyes. "She's anxious to bust out."

Bending slightly, David kissed her belly. "You're still cooking, so it's too soon to take you out of the oven."

Devon kissed his head. "Do you really think she can hear you?"

"Of course she can. Baby girl knows her daddy's voice. I'm going to hang out here until the ladies arrive, and then I'm heading over to the Cove."

"You don't have to wait for them. Go."

David palmed her face. "You know I don't like to leave you alone."

"And what's going to happen to me from the time you leave till the time the girls get here?"

"What if you go into premature labor?"

She glared at him. "Please, David. I have the rest of June, all of July and August, and at least three weeks in September. As you were saying, baby girl is still cooking."

Reaching into the pocket of his jeans, David took out his cell and punched in a number. "I'm leaving now." He ended the call. "Okay, I'm leaving." Holding her shoulders, he kissed the side of her neck. "Have fun."

"We will."

She stared at the space where he'd been. Devon pressed her palms together as she mentally ran down a checklist. The only thing remaining was baking the biscuits. She wouldn't put them in the oven until everyone arrived.

Ten minutes later she heard the sound of a truck's engine and walked to the front door. Someone from the post office was delivering a package. All island mail was delivered to the small post office in the Cove, but packages were always left at the door.

Devon couldn't make out the man's face. He'd pulled the hood of his slicker over his head. "I need a signature."

She unlocked the front door and before she could open it the man dropped the box and snatched the door handle from her grip. Devon managed to scream once before she felt numbing pain and then fire in her belly. After that, darkness descended, shutting out the world as she knew it.

David saw Carlos's number come up on his screen, then a text message that congealed the blood in his veins: Get home. Got attacker. Call 911. She's hurt.

He executed a U-turn with one hand and dialed 911 with the other. "Cavanaugh Island Sheriff's Department."

"Winnie, David Sullivan. I need you to call for an ambulance. My wife has been attacked."

"I'm putting the call through as we speak. You're on Cherry Lane?"

"Yes!"

"Jeff just walked in. I'll—"

David tapped a button on the wheel, disconnecting Winnie. How could it have happened so quickly? He hadn't been gone more than five minutes and...His mind was a jumble of whys and guilt. He shouldn't have left her alone, but then if someone was intent on hurting her then what could four women do against one man—especially if he'd come armed.

He came to a screeching halt, putting the car in Park and not bothering to turn off the engine. A man in a US Postal Service uniform lay facedown on the ground, hands and feet bound with plastic ties. A trickle of blood pooled from a gash near his temple. Carlos was on the porch with Devon, applying pressure to her belly. Blood stained the front of her white man-tailored shirt.

Carlos glanced back at his hapless prisoner. "Go inside and get some ice. We need to slow down the bleeding."

David raced into the house, snatching a terry-cloth towel off the countertop and filling it with ice from the in-door ice maker. By the time he returned to the porch the EMTs were working on Devon. Jeff's official vehicle came to an abrupt stop, spewing gravel. He jumped out of the Jeep, an automatic pressed to his thigh.

Jeff's gaze shifted from Carlos to the man on the ground. "He's all yours."

David panicked. "What the hell are you doing letting him go? Arrest the bastard!"

Jeff caught his arm, spinning him around. "If I arrest him, then we'll never know who sent him. Let the man you pay the big bucks do his job. I'm going to call Kara and tell her not to come over because Devon had to go to the hospital. I'll park this piece of shit's truck behind the house and send one of my deputies over to get it later. Meanwhile, I want you to lock up your house and follow the ambulance to the hospital. I'll come by later."

David didn't want to believe his cousin was so calm when he was vacillating between rage and fear. Covering his face with his hands, he counted slowly to three and then did as Jeff directed.

He stared at Devon as the technicians lifted her gently and placed her on the gurney. She was so still, so lifeless.

"Is she . . . ?"

The older of the two met his eyes. "We've stabilized her for now. It's the baby. Right now, it's touch and go."

David slipped behind the wheel, staring with unseeing

eyes out the windshield. Shifting into Drive, he followed the ambulance, its siren wailing like an annoying insect buzzing near his ear. I can't lose her. I can't lose her. The plea played over and over in his head until he hit the steering wheel so hard with his fist that pain radiated up his arm to his shoulder. He welcomed the pain because it helped him not think about how he never should've left her alone.

Fifteen minutes after leaving Haven Creek he pulled into an empty spot in the hospital's visitor area. He was out of the Lexus and racing after the technicians who were wheeling the gurney into the Emergency Room. Doctors and nurses crowded around Devon.

David had never felt so helpless in his life. There was nothing he could do but look on as a doctor checked her vitals and a nurse hooked up an IV.

"Are you her husband?" a nurse asked.

"Yes."

"What's your wife's name?"

"Devon Sullivan."

"Mr. Sullivan, what happened to your wife?"

"I don't know. She was alone in the house, and then..."

"How far along is she?"

"Around six months."

"You don't know?"

David's temper flared. "She's due at the end of September. You do the damn math."

"I know you're worried about your wife, but I have to ask you these questions."

He glared at the woman as realization dawned. "You think I did this to her? You think I hurt my wife and unborn child?"

"Mr. Sullivan, please lower your voice."

"David!" He turned to find his parents racing into the ER. "Mother, who told you?"

Edna buried her face against his chest. "Jeff. He called to say some man had attacked Devon and she—"

"Don't say it, Mother. We're not going to lose either of them."

David Senior dropped an arm over his son's shoulders. "We have to stay positive, son."

The attending doctor came over, his expression grim. "We're going to take her up to surgery now. We have to take the baby in order to stop the bleeding."

David's eyes danced wildly, as if he'd ingested a powerful hallucinogen. "You can't!"

"Mr. . . ."

"Sullivan," David supplied.

"Mr. Sullivan, we're going to have to take the baby to save your wife's life. She's bleeding internally. We're going to do our best to try to save them both."

He nodded like a bobblehead doll. "Okay, Doctor."

"Please give the nurse as much information as you can about your wife. We're going to take her up now. There's a waiting room for family members on the surgical floor. I'll be by later, hopefully with good news."

Devon tried opening her eyes, but it felt as if someone had put weights on her eyelids. She heard beeping sounds but didn't know where they came from. Her hand moved down her chest to her belly. Her eyes flew open. Where was her belly?

She sat up as if pulled by a taut wire. Her lower lip trembled once she realized where she was. "My baby. Where is my baby!?" Devon saw movement out of the corner of her eye, a stranger with a familiar face.

"Devon. Baby, you're awake."

She frowned. What was he talking about? Of course she was awake. "Where's my baby? Who took my baby?" Devon began screaming and couldn't stop. She struggled against the arms and hands holding her down as a figure wearing bright green scrubs imprinted with large yellow happy faces injected something into the tube running into her veins. "Where…is…my…" Darkness covered her like a comforting blanket as she fell asleep.

Devon drifted in and out of consciousness for the next twenty-four hours, hearing familiar voices, and a few she hadn't heard in a long time. Each time she woke screaming for her baby someone put her to sleep. Had they drugged her because there was something they didn't want her to know?

Expelling an audible sigh, she opened her eyes, her mind clear for the first time in what felt to be a very long time. A shadow fell over her and then the familiar scent of a masculine cologne. "David?" She hardly recognized him with the beginnings of a beard covering his face.

"Welcome back, baby."

She smiled. "Where have I been?"

"You're in the hospital. You had an accident."

Lines of confusion creased her smooth forehead. "What kind of accident?"

"You don't remember?"

Devon shook her head. "No." She rested a hand on her flat belly. "The baby?"

Sitting on the side of the bed, David traced her eyebrows with his finger. "She's…good. She's in the neonatal unit. Our little girl is a fighter. What's surprising is that she weighs almost four pounds."

"Four pounds? She's not even full term and she's four pounds?"

David adjusted the pillows behind Devon's head and shoulders. "Can you imagine what she would look like at nine months?"

"A little porker. Dr. Ingram was concerned about me gaining weight when it was the baby who was siphoning off whatever I ate." She grimaced when pain shot through her lower abdomen.

"You had a Cesarean, so you're going to be sore for a while."

"Can you take me to see her? I want to see our daughter."

David combed his fingers through her damp hair. "Later. First there's someone I want you to see."

"Who?"

"I'll be back."

Devon watched as he walked out of the room filled with plants, flowers, and a table covered with get-well cards. She massaged her temples, wishing she could remember why she ended up in the hospital.

She didn't have to wait long to see what David meant when her mother and father entered the private room. Her parents had changed, especially her mother. Her once raven hair was liberally streaked with gray and she was a lot thinner than Devon remembered. She looked old, almost frail. Only her eyes were the same—a brilliant blue green framed by long dark lashes.

Devon's gaze shifted to her father. He'd aged much better than his wife. His premature gray hair was full and shiny. There were a few new lines around his dark eyes, while his complexion, which had always reminded Devon of a sweet potato, was radiant.

"Mama. What are you doing here?"

Monique Collins's eyes filled with tears. "Your husband called me. He said it's time we made peace with each other now that I have a granddaughter."

"Make peace, Mama? I always tried to make peace with you but you wouldn't let me. I came home to tell you I was going to become a mother, and when you asked me if I was married and I said no, you slammed the door in my face."

Monique blinked back tears. "I was angry and hurt."

"Angry and hurt, or embarrassed because your daughter was going to be a baby mama? It was always about you and your image. How you tried to mold me into something you wanted. It was never about what I wanted. I wanted so much to love you, but you just wouldn't let me." Devon couldn't stop the tears running down her face. "Why, Mama? Why wouldn't you let me love you?"

Monique's sobs filled the room. "I don't know, baby. I so wanted to raise you differently from how I was raised, but I couldn't. And when your grandmother came to live with us I resented her because she was able to connect with you in a way I never could. If I could turn back the clock, I would..."

Devon wiped angrily at her tears. "What about Ray? Do you know what you did to him? You broke his spirit, so he wallowed in drugs and alcohol to dull his pain. You cut him off and he in turn cut me off. He was the only one I loved and you even ruined him for me."

Her gaze swung to her father. "And, Daddy, you stood by and let it all happen. You claimed you wanted a peaceful home, but your children lived in hell. I wanted so much to hate you both but I couldn't. And now that I'm a mother I can't permit myself to hate anything or anyone, because I'll end up transferring that bitterness to my daughter."

Monique placed a trembling hand over her mouth. "You don't hate me?"

"No. I don't hate you because I can't hate you. If you hadn't had me, then I wouldn't be here where I've been given a second chance to fall in love with an incredible man who I know will be an incredible father to our daughter."

Reaching into her bag, Monique took out a tissue and blotted her face. "I saw her, Devon. I saw my granddaughter. Even though she's tiny, she's so beautiful."

"Who does she look like?"

"It's hard to tell, but she does have reddish hair."

Devon laughed, then thought better of it when she felt a spasm of discomfort in her belly. "You had red hair when you were born," Devon said.

"Monique, stop trying to be modest. You know right well that baby looks like you."

Monique glared at her husband. "Raymond, I thought we agreed—"

"We, Monique?" Raymond retorted. "We didn't agree to a damn thing!"

"Raymond!"

"Enough, Monique. I've spent almost forty years trying to keep the peace, not saying anything because *we* agreed I would be the provider and you would raise our children. I've always provided for my family, but you did a piss-poor job of raising our children. That young man who married our daughter could teach me a thing or two about being a husband and a father. And I'm not too old to learn. I'm going to stay here in Charleston until my grand-daughter is released from this hospital. After that I'm going to take all the time I need to undo the hurt Devon has had to go through."

"What's going to happen to your teaching position?" Monique asked.

"What about it? Are you concerned your uppity friends will think your husband has left you when you attend a black-tie event unescorted?"

Devon blinked in disbelief. It was the first time she'd witnessed her father actually challenging his wife. "Mama, Daddy, please. Not here."

"I'll take this up with your mother—later," Ray promised.

"Where are you staying?" Devon asked.

"We planned to check into a hotel, but David insisted we stay at your house here in Charleston. He told us about the cottage you have on an island and I can't wait to see it."

"I'm still decorating it…" Her words trailed off when Kara, Morgan, Keaton, Francine, and Dawn crowded into the room.

Francine placed a shopping bag on the tray table. "We bought you some food from Jack's because everyone knows hospital food ain't fit for human consumption."

"Word," drawled Kara. "I know my Yorkie wouldn't touch it and he's always begging for table scraps."

Devon held her belly as she tried not to laugh. "Y'all can't make me laugh because it hurts."

Morgan rested her hands at her waist. "Well, look at you, Mrs. Sullivan. You've become a real Southerner because you said *y'all* instead of *you all*."

"Ladies, I'm forgetting my home training. I'd like you to meet my mother and father, Monique and Raymond Collins. Daddy's going to be staying with us for a couple of months."

"I'll be staying too," Monique said. "I'm not leaving here until I get to hold my granddaughter."

Dawn sat on the side of the bed, her blue eyes wide with excitement. "We saw the baby, and she's beautiful. I can't wait to marry Trevor so we can start a family."

Devon picked up Dawn's left hand, nodding. "He really stepped up and put a ring on it."

Dawn rolled her eyes. "I wasn't having it any other way. I told him that I had to give up a nice New York City apartment with views of the river and a dance studio where I teach little girls to believe they can become the next Misty Copeland."

A nurse knocked on the door, capturing everyone's attention. "There are too many folks in this room. Some of you are gonna have to leave."

Devon shook her head. "These folks are my family. My parents and my sisters and brother. And I'd like them to stay." She'd referred to Keaton as her brother.

Jeff, dressed in uniform and wearing his firearm, and Corrine pushed into the room, adding to the throng. "Hey, cuz. Looking good."

"We saw the baby," Corrine said, smiling. "She's gorgeous."

Monique puffed up her chest. "I'm her grandmother."

"Hey, Devon. Have you given her a name?" Francine asked. "She can't be Baby Sullivan for too much longer."

Devon spied David staying outside the room. "David and I decided if it's a girl we would name her Anaïs Francesca Sullivan."

Francine pumped her fist. "That sounds like a stage name."

Devon shared a smile with David. "If she wants to be an

actress we'll support her one hundred percent. Jeff, David, could you please find some more chairs so everyone can sit down?"

Raymond stood up. "Monique and I are leaving. We spent more than six hours at O'Hare on standby and we're a little tired."

Devon stared at her parents. "I don't know when they're going to discharge me, but we'll have a lot of catching up to do." She smiled at her father, then her mother. "I'm glad you came." She'd extended the olive branch, but she knew it would take time for her to completely forgive her parents for the pain she'd endured while growing up.

"Me too," Monique agreed.

Waiting until her parents left with David, Devon peered into the shopping bag. "Hey, you brought enough so everyone can have a little."

Francine reached into the bag and took out plastic bowls, forks, spoons, and napkins. "We missed our Lowcountry Ladies Luncheon, so I figured we'd bring it to you because it's going to be a while before we get together again."

Devon nodded. "By that time you'll be an old married woman, Morgan will be in labor cursing Nate for getting her pregnant, and hopefully Anaïs will be home from the hospital and on her way to becoming the indisputable boss of the house on Cherry Lane."

Keaton closed the door to the room while Francine and Kara opened containers from which wafted mouthwatering aromas. "Why is it every time we get together it's over food?" Dawn questioned.

All eyes were directed at Corrine. "That's because good food is the heart of the family. And everyone in this room is family."

"Even me?" Dawn asked.

"Even you," everyone said in unison.

Devon slumped back into the pillows and closed her eyes. She'd lost her family, found a new family, and because of David she had reconciled with her parents. It would take time to get past the pain, but she was willing to do any- and everything possible to bridge the schism to give her daughter another set of grandparents who were certain to love *and* spoil her.

Epilogue

~~~~~

Labor Day

David whispered in Devon's ear that he needed to talk to her—alone. She stood up and followed him into the home office and closed the door. "What is it?"

He sat on the off-white Haitian cotton love seat and pulled her down to sit beside him. They'd opened their home to celebrate the holiday weekend with friends and family. And they had a lot to celebrate: Anaïs had come home from the hospital several days ago with no lingering effects attributed to a premature birth, David's law practice was doing well, Francine and Keaton had announced they were expecting a baby, Dawn and Trevor were to be married New Year's Eve, and Morgan confessed to experiencing Braxton Hicks contractions.

Devon's parents had approached David, offering to buy the house in Charleston, and he still hadn't given them an answer although he'd told them they could live there for as long as they wanted. Her father planned to retire at the end of the next school year and her mother had elected to live in

Charleston rather than return to Illinois so she could be close to her daughter and granddaughter.

He stared at the side table lined with six terrariums. He focused on the violets in a bell jar that held a thriving tropical rain forest. Reaching for Devon's hand, he laced their fingers together. "I hate to bring this up, because I don't want you to relive the horror of nearly losing your life and the baby's, but you have a right to know who was behind the attack."

David told her about Francine's vision and then Jeff's suspicions about why the cyclist had tried to run her down and then the so-called postal worker cutting her belly. "Jeff recommended a protection specialist who tracked your every move once you left the house. I didn't want to leave you the day you'd invited your friends over, but when I sent a text to Carlos it was to alert him to watch the house. Fortunately he subdued the man who attacked you and was able to do some digging to discover who'd hired him. It was like peeling an onion, first one thin layer, then another, until Gregory Emerson's name floated to the top. Someone feared that you might ruin Emerson's chance of becoming governor. We all know what happened to John Edwards's chance of occupying the White House when the news broke about Rielle Hunter and their love child."

Devon shook her head in disbelief. "But why, David? It would've been different if I'd remained single. But I married you early in my pregnancy and there are still some folks who believe you're Anaïs's biological father."

"I don't know, baby. I suppose they didn't want to chance it."

"What's going to happen to Gregory?"

"He'll remain a member of the House until word gets out

that he fathered twin boys with a woman he slept with in high school. His father paid the girl off and made her sign documents that she would never tell anyone."

"How did you find out?"

"There are no secrets in politics, sweetheart." Cradling the back of her head, David gently suckled her lower lip.

"Let's get back to our guests or they'll think we're working on giving Anaïs a sister or brother."

He kissed her again. "We can try next year."

Devon scrunched up her nose. "That sounds like a plan."

They left the office and walked out into the sunlight to join their family and friends who'd come to Cherry Lane to celebrate the homecoming of another generation of Gullahs.

After a failed marriage, Broadway star Francine Tanner quits acting to return to Cavanaugh Island. But a mysterious newcomer may give her love life a second act...

Please see the next page for an excerpt from *Magnolia Drive*,

Francine and Keaton's story.

Chapter One

⌒

Francine Tanner downshifted, decelerating to less than ten miles an hour as the rain came down in torrents, obstructing her view. The rising wind blew the precipitation sideways. The wipers were at the highest speed, yet did little to sluice the water off the Corvette's windshield fast enough. She maneuvered along Sanctuary Cove's Main Street before turning off onto Moss Alley and parking behind the Beauty Box; she turned off the wipers and then the engine to the low-slung sports car. It'd been raining for nearly a week and she, like everyone else who lived along South Carolina's Sea Islands, wondered when they would ever see the sun again.

Pulling the hood of her raincoat over her head, she sprinted through puddles in the parking lot to the rear of the full-service salon and day spa. It took several attempts before she was able to unlock the door. Her mother had had the locksmith change the cylinder, yet it still jammed. She made a mental note to have him replace the entire lock. Pushing open the steel door, she flipped on the light switches and within seconds recessed and track lights illuminated the newly renovated salon like brilliant summer sunlight.

Francine had come in an hour before the salon opened for business to take down Christmas decorations and pack them away until the next season. After hanging up her raincoat in the employee lounge, she slipped out of her wet running shoes and turned on the satellite radio to one of her favorite stations. Hip-hop blared through the speakers concealed throughout ceiling panels.

She took a quick glimpse at her reflection along the wall of mirrors. A profusion of dark red curls framed her face, falling to her shoulders; it wasn't the first time she realized she'd been so busy styling the hair of the salon's customers that she'd neglected the most important person in her life: Francine Dinah Tanner.

Although she normally didn't make New Year's resolutions, she resolved she would dedicate this year to herself at the same time she pulled her hair off her face, securing it in an elastic band. Several wayward curls escaped the band, grazing her ears and the nape of her neck.

She needed a new look and definitely a new attitude but didn't want to think about all the things she had to do to change her life as she pushed her sock-covered feet into a pair of leather clogs and walked to the front of the shop to check the voice mail. Five days a week Francine helped her mother manage the salon, cut and style hair, and occasionally fill in for the manicurist and/or aesthetician whenever they were backed up. The other two days were now spent helping her grandmother adjust to moving from her Charleston condo to living under the same roof with her son, daughter-in-law, and granddaughter.

Eighty-one-year-old Dinah Donovan Tanner had protested loudly when her son insisted she give up living independently and move into a wing of his house on Cavanaugh Island. Frank Tanner had installed an elevator so his mother wouldn't have to navigate the staircase, converted the west wing to include a bedroom suite with an adjoining bath outfitted for a senior, a living/dining room with a sitting area, and a state-of-the-art kitchen. Once the octogenarian saw her new apartment she reluctantly agreed to move to Sanctuary Cove. Even if Grandma Dinah had initially pouted like a surly adolescent, Francine secretly applauded her father's decision to take control of his mother's life because it meant she didn't have to drive to Charleston to see to her grandmother's physical and emotional well-being. And most nights she ate dinner with her. Dinah, who lived up to her reputation as one of best cooks in the Lowcountry, had settled into a more laid-back life on the island, grinning nonstop because she got to see her only grandchild every day.

Now that her best friend, Morgan Dane Shaw, was married, they had curtailed their early-morning bicycle outings from five days a week, weather permitting, to one or two. She and Morgan had been high school outsiders and had never cultivated close relationships with the other students living in Charleston or on Cavanaugh Island. Even when both left the island to attend out-of-state colleges they never lost contact with each other. She missed hanging out with her friend, but she was glad that Morgan had found her happily ever after with Nathaniel Shaw.

Pencil in hand, Francine activated the voice mail feature and jotted down appointments in the book spread out on the reception desk. There were messages from regulars who wanted a myriad of services. Then she went completely still when she heard the last two messages. The nail technician and one of the stylists had called to say they were experiencing flulike symptoms.

Two weeks after Thanksgiving influenza had swept across the island like wildfire. Hardly anyone was left unscathed. Classroom attendance in the schools in the island's three towns—Sanctuary Cove, Haven Creek, and Angels Landing—was drastically reduced when students, faculty, and staff alike succumbed to the virus. The local health department had declared a health emergency, forcing the schools' superintendent to issue an order to close the schools four days before the onset of the Christmas recess. Under another set of circumstances students would've applauded extending the holiday recess, but most were too sick to celebrate.

The waiting room in Dr. Asa Monroe's medical practice had been standing room only. The island's resident doctor sent his patients home to limit the spread of the virus and made house calls instead. Dinah refused to let Dr. Monroe give her a flu shot, declaring she didn't like doctors or needles, opting instead to take an herbal concoction guaranteed to offset the symptoms of colds and flu. The elderly woman declared proudly that she was healthier than many half her age because of the herbal remedies that had been passed down through generations of Donovan women. Francine and her parents took the shot and were fortunate enough to avoid the full effect of chills, fever, and general lethargy. However, her mother, Mavis Tanner, like most of the merchants in the Cove, closed the Beauty Box for a week because of a rash of cancellations. She'd used the time to have repairs made to the adjacent space that was now the Butterfly Garden Day Spa.

Francine disassembled the lifelike artificial tree, putting it and the ornaments in a large duffel bag on wheels. Coming in early had its advantages. She could listen to her favorite stations on the radio before some of the elderly customers gave her the stink eye about her taste in music. They'd grumbled constantly to Mavis until Francine told her mother she wouldn't be opposed to listening to a station featuring songs spanning the sixties, seventies, and sometimes the eighties because she'd grown up listening to the music from her parents' youth.

She'd just wheeled the duffel into the storeroom when the rear door opened and her mother walked in. "We're down two this morning, Mama."

"Who are they?" Mavis asked as she hung her jacket on the wall hook.

"Candace and Danita have come down with the flu. Don't worry, I'll cover for both," Francine volunteered.

She watched as Mavis shook the moisture from her shoulder-length twists. Physically she and her mother were complete opposites. Mavis, petite with a dark complexion, claimed the distinctive broad features of her Gullah ancestry, while Francine had inherited her paternal grandmother's fair complexion, red hair, and freckles. However, the special gift she'd been born with to discern the spirit had come from her maternal grandmother.

Mavis slipped into a black smock with her name and *Beauty Box* embroidered in white lettering over her heart. "How many customers does Candace have?"

Francine put on her own smock. "Three. She has two cuts and a color. We can't afford to turn anyone away after losing a week's receipts."

"We're going to fare a lot better than some of the other

shop owners who rely on folks coming in from the mainland to keep them out of the red until the spring and summer."

The Beauty Box, the only salon on the island, boasted a thriving year-round business because many residents didn't want to drive or take the ferry into Charleston to get their hair and nails done, while most mom-and-pop stores in the Cove and the Creek weren't as fortunate. They relied on an influx of tourists during the spring and summer months to sample the cuisine, buy local handicrafts, and tour the antebellum mansions and plantations.

"You're right," Francine agreed. She stared at Mavis as she took a large envelope filled with cash out of her tote. Although the salon accepted credit card payments, some of their customers still preferred using cash. "You're past due for a rinse, Mama." The neatly twisted hair was liberally streaked with gray.

Mavis's dark brown eyes met a pair of shimmering emerald green. "Your mama is fifty-nine. And that means I'm old enough to have gray hair *and* at least *one* grandbaby."

Francine rolled her eyes. "Please, let's not start in on grandbabies again, Mama. You don't hear Grandma Dinah talking about becoming a great-grandmother."

"That's because she's already a grandmother," Mavis countered. "Adding *great* to *grandmother* is just a formality. I'm the only woman in the Chamber of Commerce's Ladies Auxiliary who's not a grandmother and that is something Linda Hawkins is quick to bring up every chance she gets."

"That's because she's still pissed off that you took Daddy from her."

Mavis glared at Francine. "I didn't take him from her because she couldn't lose something she never had."

"That's not what she tells anyone who will stand still long enough for her to badmouth you."

"And you know I don't entertain gossip *or* lies."

"I know and so does everyone on Cavanaugh Island," she mumbled under her breath at the same time she took the envelope from her mother. "I'll put this in the cash register for you."

She did not have to be reminded of her mother's pet peeve; beauty salons were usually breeding grounds for salacious gossip, and because of this Mavis had a hard and fast rule that if any of her employees were caught gossiping with the customers or repeating something they'd overheard it would be grounds for immediate dismissal. Mavis ran her business with the precision of a Marine Corps drill sergeant, much to the satisfaction of those who frequented the salon. If someone had an appointment for two, then they were guaranteed to be sitting in a chair at that time or within fifteen minutes.

Francine knew if she didn't put some distance, if only temporarily, between herself and her mother, Mavis would invariably bring up the topic of her not dating some of the men who'd expressed an interest in her. Although Mavis claimed she didn't entertain gossip Francine knew she'd overheard talk about her daughter being linked with David Sullivan.

The attractive Charleston-based attorney had become a very eligible bachelor once his girlfriend ended their five-year relationship because of his inability to commit. Although she and David were seen together at the annual Island Fair, she was aware their friendship would never become more than that. David was a wonderful catch but not for her. Francine knew her mother's wish to become a grandmother was overshadowed by her need to see her daughter married to someone with whom she could spend the rest of her life.

When she married Aiden Fox, Francine believed it would be forever. But, sadly, her fairy-tale marriage didn't end with a happily ever after. Deceit and mistrust had reared its ugly head once she realized the man who'd declared his undying love had only used her to further his acting career. What had shocked her more than Aiden's duplicity was that she hadn't seen it coming. Although she could see someone else's future in her visions, she could not do the same with her own. She still believed in love and happily ever after, although it appeared to have passed her by. She wanted all of the things she and her best friend, Morgan, had talked about when they were teenage girls. They'd wanted to fall in love and marry men who would love and protect them, who'd become the fathers of their children, and with whom they would grow old together. She hadn't given up on love, and she was still hopeful she would be given a second chance at finding her own happiness.

Tapping buttons, she entered the passcode on the electronic cash register, placing the bills in the drawer and then closing it. Staring through the front door's beveled glass, Francine smiled when she saw pinpoints of sunlight coming through watery clouds. The downpour was letting up. Maybe with the sun her mood would improve. Last night she'd had a vision wherein she heard angry voices; the sound grew louder, reverberating in her head. She then saw gaping mouths from which spewed expletives and threats. What she couldn't see were the faces of the people in her vision. She knew it was in Sanctuary Cove because she recognized the marble statue of patriot militiaman General Francis Marion atop a stallion in the town square. The vision had vanished quickly, but the uneasiness that had gripped her persisted. This was the second time the vision had come to her. The first was on Christmas Eve, when she'd returned from Charleston after a day of last-minute shopping, and Francine hadn't thought much of it until now.

She made a mental note to talk to her mother about it. Mavis, who'd grown up with her own mother talking about dreams and visions, had taught Francine how to interpret her visions, but this one puzzled even her. It was on a rare occasion that she didn't or couldn't see the faces of the people in the images and because of that it was more than disturbing. Who, or what, she mused, had set neighbors against one another?

Francine was six when she realized she was different from other children. A week before she was to enter the first grade she could describe what the school's new first grade teacher looked like. When Francine recounted the frightening incident to Mavis, she reassured her Francine had been born with a special gift just like her grandmother, but that the gift would have to remain the family's secret. The second vision didn't appear until she turned ten, and then they became more frequent as she grew older. Morgan was the only person aside from her family that knew she had psychic abilities.

Francine unlocked the front door and turned over the sign to indicate the Beauty Box was open for business. Francine returned to the lounge and found Brooke Harrison, the shampoo girl, and Taryn Brown, the aesthetician-masseuse, brewing coffee and setting out an assortment of sweet breads from the Muffin Corner for the staff. The space contained a utility kitchen with a microwave, cappuccino-espresso machine, refrigerator-freezer, half bath, and a table with seating for six as well as a seating arrangement to accommodate eight. It was where the employees came to relax between customers and to take their meals. A cleaning service came in twice a week to keep the salon and spa spotless. Mavis spared no expense when it came to creating a relaxing environment for her customers and employees.

"The coffee smells wonderful," Francine said as she tuned the radio to a cool jazz station. Brooke smiled and the skin around her robin's-egg blue eyes crinkled with the gesture. They teased each other, saying they were sisters from different mothers, because both had red curly hair.

"It's a hazelnut blend."

Brooke, a recent cosmetology graduate, had offered to assume the responsibility for brewing coffee. She still worked part-time as a Starbucks barista. "Candace and Danita have called in sick, so we're going to be a little tight today," Francine informed the two women.

"Do I have any cancellations?" Taryn asked Francine.

"No. You're good." Taryn, who'd worked at a spa in Atlanta for more than fifteen years but wanted a more laid-back setting, had applied for the position of masseuse when she'd read that the Beauty Box had expanded to include a day spa. Offering spa services had attributed to a steady increase in the salon's overall profit margin.

The chime on the front door echoed and Francine went to greet their first client of the day.

Keaton Grace knew he couldn't meet with his attorney and business manager looking like the Wolfman. He hadn't shaved in more than two weeks and hadn't cut his hair in four. He'd spoken to Devon Gilmore, who'd arranged to meet him in Sanctuary Cove so he could sign the necessary documents to dissolve the partnership between him and his investment banker slash brother-in-law. At forty-one, he now wanted complete control of his projects: writing, directing, and producing. The dissolution had caused a rift between Keaton and his sister Liana, but he was willing to risk their close relationship in order to control his own destiny.

Opening the binder on the boardinghouse's bedside table with listings of shops and services on Cavanaugh Island, he perused it. Reading the advertisement for the Beauty Box, he noted the hours of operation. He smiled. They welcomed walk-ins and that was exactly what he was going to be this afternoon.

Keaton had spent the past week cloistered in his suite at the Cove Inn because of the rainy weather. He'd ordered room service instead of eating with the other boarders because he'd found himself in the zone when revising a script. His first visit to Cavanaugh Island had been last summer, to survey the region. At that time he'd checked in at a Charleston hotel and driven to the island under the guise of tourist when in reality he was looking to purchase property.

Cavanaugh Island was one of the many Sea Islands ranging from South Carolina to Florida that Keaton had explored. The price of an acre of land on some of the better known islands like Hilton Head, Myrtle Beach, and Jekyll were either exorbitant and/or the zoning laws wouldn't permit him to erect a movie studio.

Once he'd found the perfect property on Cavanaugh Island, he knew this time he intended to stay. Keaton had arranged a proxy purchase of a twelve-acre lot with an abandoned farmhouse because he'd been unable to leave Los

Angeles. He was involved in wrapping an independent film that was already well over the initial budget and it was important that he remained on the West Coast to complete the project. He planned to live in the renovated farmhouse and utilize ten of the twelve acres to build a studio and sound stage for Grace Lowcountry Productions. Thankfully Sanctuary Cove's zoning laws did not have the restrictions he'd encountered on many of the other islands.

Living at the Cove Inn suited Keaton's daily needs. His furnished suite had a private bath, mini-bar, TV, and radio, and his laundry was done on the premises. He'd had little contact with the other boarders because he coveted his time. Relocating from Los Angeles to the small island off the coast of South Carolina was definitely a culture shock. He didn't have to deal with traffic jams, bright lights, smog, and wailing sirens. And then there was nightlife. It was virtually nonexistent. The exception was the Happy Hour, a nightclub in Haven Creek. The quietness and slower pace was something he hadn't known before and had come to look forward to. It was as if everything around him was slower, serene, and at times appeared surreal.

Pulling on a bright yellow slicker over his sweatshirt and jeans, he picked up his keys and left the suite, closing the self-locking door behind him. Taking the back staircase, Keaton walked to the parking area. The cars and SUVs in the lot bore license plates from as far away as Michigan. His BMW sedan with Pennsylvania plates was parked between two minivans from Illinois.

Snowbirds. He'd discovered many of those at the boardinghouse were spending their winter in South Carolina to escape the snow and frigid northern temperatures. If they thought him a snowbird Keaton wasn't about to correct their perception. He'd come from L.A. to Sanctuary Cove via New York and Pittsburgh, which many of his family members still called home. In his heart he was still a son of the Steel City and a rabid Steelers fan. He'd joked to a reporter during an interview that if stabbed he wouldn't bleed red but black and gold.

The rain had slackened to a drizzle and after starting up the engine he turned the wipers to the lowest setting. Although he'd heard some people complain about the incessant rain, he didn't mind the inclement weather. Keaton discovered years ago that he did his best work with the sound of rain hitting the windows; he'd always found it soothing. It was akin to being in a cocoon where he was able to shut out reality to escape into a world of his own choosing.

He'd also noticed there were no posted speed limits, traffic lights, or stop signs on the island, prompting him to drive slower than twenty miles per hour when he saw other motorists driving slowly, as if they didn't have a care in the world. The adjustment hadn't been easy after years of zipping along California's freeways. However, the topography was something he never wanted to get used to. The primordial swamps and forests teeming with indigenous wildlife, ancient oak trees draped in Spanish moss, the fanlike fronds of palmetto trees, the stretch of beach and the ocean were unlike anyplace he'd ever lived. The rain had stopped completely when Keaton entered the business district and maneuvered into an area behind rows of stores that had been set aside for parking.

Leaving his slicker in the car, he set out on foot for a leisurely walk along Main Street, while glancing into the quaint shops so integral to the viability of everyone living and working in the small town. Shopkeepers were cleaning plate-glass windows and sweeping up the palmetto leaves littering the gutter. Keaton smiled. It was as if the island were waking up from a weeklong slumber. He noticed the woman in the Parlor Bookstore placing a sign in the window indicating a 15 percent discount on best sellers, and a couple of doors down a man in the Muffin Corner was filling a showcase with trays of muffins and doughnuts. His stroll ended when he pushed open the beveled glass door to the Beauty Box.

When he saw the woman at the reception desk, a line from one of his favorite films popped into his head: *Of all of the gin joints in all the towns in all the world, she walks into mine.* But he wasn't the Humphrey Bogart character referring to Ingrid Bergman, and the Beauty Box wasn't Rick's Café from *Casablanca*. What were the odds he would walk into a hair salon in a town on a remote sea island and come face-to-face with Francine Tanner?

Dark red curly hair framed a face he could never forget. The last time he'd seen her she'd been on an off-Broadway stage basking in thunderous applause as she took an infinite number of curtain calls. He'd been living in New York City, working as a scriptwriter for an Emmy Award–winning daytime drama, while completing a graduate degree in theater at New York University. When not working or studying he'd spent all of his free time going to Broadway and off-Broadway plays or catering parties.

When he went to see the play in which she'd played one of the lead characters, Keaton had sat close enough to the stage to see the vibrant color of her emerald-green eyes. He knew it was rude, but he couldn't pull his gaze away from her beautiful face. What, he mused, was she doing in Sanctuary Cove? And why was she working in a hair salon?

"May I help you, sir?"

Her beautifully modulated voice, with traces of a Southern drawl, shattered Keaton's reverie. "I don't have an appointment, but I'd like a haircut and a shave."

Francine smiled. "You don't need an appointment. Please, Mr...."

"It's just Keaton," he supplied.

"Mr. Keaton, please have a seat in the second chair."

"No. Keaton's the first name," he corrected in a quiet voice.

He sat where she'd directed him, the salon's sleek black-and-white color scheme reminding him of the upscale establishments in tony New York and L.A. neighborhoods. The mirrored walls, track lighting, white marble floor, and soft jazz were sophisticated as well as inviting. Keaton's eyes met Francine's in the mirror when she draped a black cape around his neck and over his shoulders and chest. The scent of her intoxicating perfume wafted to his nostrils, and he thought the scent perfect for her.

"How short do you want it?" she asked, running a wide-tooth comb through tightly curling hair sprinkled with flecks of gray.

Keaton couldn't stop the smile finding its way over his features. "I want it cropped close to my scalp."

Francine rested her hands on his shoulders over the cape. "I'm going analyze a few strands before I cut it. After the cut I'll wash your hair and condition your scalp because it looks a little dry. I'd like to warn you that you'll have to sit with a plastic cap on your head while I shave you. Do you have a problem with that?"

Smiling and exhibiting a mouth filled with straight white teeth, Keaton shook his head. "I don't think so."

A slight flush suffused Francine's face. "I said that because there are some men who don't want to be seen sitting in a salon wearing a plastic cap."

He smothered a chuckle. "I'm not one of those men." And he wasn't. If there were two things Keaton was secure about it was his masculinity and his work.

Settling back in the chair, he succumbed to the touch of the woman who had him intrigued the second he recognized her. Rather than stare at her, he closed his eyes and crossed his arms over his chest under the cape. Keaton remembered Francine's performance in the off-Broadway play *Sisters*; he had been profoundly disappointed when she hadn't been nominated for an Obie. Years later he'd recalled her acting ability when he wrote a script with her in mind. He contacted her agent, who told him she'd left the business. The news stunned Keaton, because he didn't want to believe someone of her incomparable talent would walk away from a career to which she'd been born. He opened his eyes when someone tapped his shoulder.

"You're new around here, aren't you?"

Keaton stared at an elderly woman with white hair set on a profusion of tiny multicolored plastic rollers. She stared back at him over a pair of half-glasses, dark eyes in an equally dark face narrowing slightly. There was something about her face that reminded him of his grandmother, but knew his prissy relative would never be so forward as to approach a stranger to ask a question without first being introduced.

"Yes, I am."

"Are you keeping company with anyone?"

Francine returned from the back, where she'd analyzed several strands of Keaton's hair. She knew he wanted it cropped, but she had to cut it short enough for the strands to lay flat. Her steps slowed when she saw Bernice Wagner engaged in conversation with him. As a first-time customer she didn't want Keaton to get the wrong impression about her mother's establishment. Miss Bernice, a former seamstress, had been an incurable gossip for as long as Francine could remember. There was never a time she came into the salon that Miss Bernice didn't start up a conversation with someone. And there were a few times when she'd become embroiled in a verbal confrontation and ended it only before it escalated into something short of a physical altercation.

"Miss Bernice, let me check and see if you're dry."

"There's no need to check," the older woman snapped angrily. "I was under that dryer so long it's a wonder I didn't smell my hair burning."

Affecting a smile she didn't feel at that moment, Francine counted slowly to five. She loved doing hair, but there were times when the folks who came into the Beauty Box tested her patience and she had to bite her tongue to keep from trading barbs with them.

"If you're dry then it's time for you to be combed out." She beckoned to Brooke. "Please come and comb out Miss Bernice."

"Not her, Red. You know your mother always combs me out," Miss Bernice said loudly.

Francine gave her a saccharine smile. "Do you mind if Brooke takes out your rollers?"

"Yes, I do mind. She can wash my hair, but I draw the line when it comes to setting and combing me out."

Cupping her elbow, she led the recalcitrant woman to Mavis's chair. "Please sit down and my mother will comb you out as soon as she finishes in the back." Her mother was busy mixing colors for a customer who'd wanted to lighten her hair to conceal the gray.

"If you say so," Miss Bernice said loudly. "What I cain't understand is why Alice Parker thinks she's going to be a better mayor than Spencer White," she said loudly when a customer walked in wearing a campaign button. "She and her husband look like dem Ken and Barbie baby dolls. Ain't dat enough one of dem is a politician?" she asked, lapsing into dialect. "Why cain't she stay home and raise her babies instead of runnin' round trying to git votes."

"Quit jawing, Bernice," admonished a woman who'd just sat down to wait for her hair to be blown out. "If it hadn't been for Congressman Parker we wouldn't have the newly paved road between the Cove and Landing."

Francine agreed, but held her tongue. Before the road was built the residents of Sanctuary Cove had to take the ferry to the causeway, then the rutted, unpaved road connecting Haven Creek to Angels Landing. Few were brave enough to navigate the swamp, quicksand, alligators, and poisonous snakes on foot or in a vehicle, which made travel very difficult.

Bernice pushed out her lips. "I ain't saying her husband didn't do good, but why does she want to pit folks against each other by running agin Mayor White?"

Francine wanted to tell Miss Bernice that becoming mayor wasn't the same as being confirmed to the Supreme Court. It wasn't a lifelong position. And Spencer White had become complacent when it came to a number of issues affecting the Cove. Alice Parker's decision to challenge him in the up-coming election was certain to light a fire under the popular politician with matinee-idol looks. Alice had come out the frontrunner in a special fall election to have her name placed on the ballot in order to oppose the incumbent mayor. Francine thought it would be nice for the Cove to have its first female mayor.

She managed to ignore her mother's client, who continued to engage the other customers in conversation, as she picked up a pair of clippers and began cutting Keaton's hair. As a trained actress she'd learned to hide her innermost feelings behind a façade of indifference. Although she wasn't as blunt or prying as Miss Bernice, she wanted to know what had brought the incredibly handsome man in her chair to Sanctuary Cove.

The first thing she'd noticed about Keaton when he'd walked in was his height and broad shoulders. She'd estimated he stood several inches above six feet and his sweatshirt and relaxed jeans did little to camouflage a toned, slender body. His dark olive complexion, high cheekbones, lean jaw, and large, deep-set dark brown eyes made for an arresting *and* unforgettable face. When asked if he was new to the Cove, he'd said yes and Francine wondered if he meant new as in visiting the island or if he'd come to spend the winter.

Forcing her thoughts back to her task, she cut his hair, clumps falling to the cape around his shoulders and onto the floor. Once Francine had given up her acting career she'd returned to Sanctuary Cove and enrolled in cosmetology school. There weren't many employment opportunities on the island for a former actress but working with her mother at the Beauty Box had become a perfect fit.

She passed all of the courses and with a license in hand she worked as a floater at the salon, filling in as a shampoo girl and manicurist. It wasn't long before she could roller set faster than any of the other stylists, and like her mother, she excelled in cutting all types of hair.

If she'd felt she was born to act, Francine discovered doing hair was more than a satisfying substitute for what had been a lifelong dream. For as long as she could remember there'd been two barbershops in the Cove, but now there was only one. In order to take in the overflow she decided to go to barber school. The old-timers still frequented the barber shop on the side street between an auto body shop and shoemaker, while many of the younger men frequented the salon. Besides haircuts and hot towel shaves they also requested manicures, pedicures, and eyebrow waxing. Once Mavis opened the day spa, men and women lined up to make appointments for facials and massages. During prom season the Beauty Box offered student specials. There were also packages for brides, grooms, and wedding parties.

Francine picked up a blow dryer and blew the remaining hair off the cape. "Is it short enough?" His cropped hair lay close to his scalp.

Keaton's eyes met hers in the mirror. He nodded. "It's perfect."

"Come with me and someone will shampoo you."

"You're not going to do it?"

"No. We have a shampoo person."

There came a pregnant pause as they stared at each other. "Okay," he conceded.

Francine didn't realize she'd exhaled a breath until Keaton rose to tower above her. She didn't want a replay with Keaton that she'd just had with Miss Bernice. Customers who insisted on having one particular stylist do their hair occasionally caused problems when the stylist was either out sick or on vacation. Despite her worry, she couldn't help her excitement at the possibility of seeing Keaton again. She glanced up at him and realized it wasn't often that she had to look up at a man. He was a full head taller than she was. Standing five-eight in bare feet, and at least three or four inches taller in heels, made her height somewhat intimidating for some men.

Even in high school, Francine had been taller than many of the boys. She and Morgan had become best friends because both were tall and had been rail-thin. It wasn't until just before they left the island to attend college that their bodies had begun to fill out. And with her red hair and freckles, Francine had become the brunt of more jokes than she cared to remember. She was Red to everyone but family members and Morgan. She escorted Keaton to the shampoo area, instructing Brooke which shampoo and conditioner to use.

After his wash and treatment, the next thirty-five minutes were spent with Francine shaving Keaton. She skillfully wielded the sharpened straight razor while struggling not to react to the warmth of his body and cologne. Each time their gazes met she felt as if someone had punched her in her midsection, causing a shortness of breath. The beard had concealed attractive slashes along his lean jaw and strong square chin. After Brooke rinsed out the conditioner, Francine applied a light hairdressing, plucked a few stray silky eyebrow hairs, and gently massaged a moisturizer on Keaton's smooth face before realizing everyone in the shop had been watching her.

There were audible sighs and she overheard someone mumble that Keaton made Denzel Washington look hideous. Murmurs of agreement and protests followed the declaration. Francine hid a smile when she escorted him to the reception desk to total his bill.

Reaching into the back pocket of his jeans, Keaton took

out a credit card case. "I'd like to make an appointment for a haircut in two weeks."

She took the card, glancing at his name, swiped it, and then handed him the card and a copy of his receipt. "We're closed on Sundays and Mondays, so you'll have to tell me when you'd like to come in." He moved closer, his breath sweeping over her ear when he leaned in to peruse the appointment book.

"Make it two weeks from today. Ten o'clock is good."

Francine penciled him under her name at ten. "Thank you for patronizing the Beauty Box and I'll see you in two weeks."

Keaton reached into his pocket again, this time taking out a money clip and a business card. "I'd like you to have dinner with me later this evening. That is, if you're not busy. You can reach me at the number on the card." He paused. "By the way, I'm staying at the Cove Inn, Miss Tanner."

Francine was too stunned to reply when he pushed the card and a bill into the pocket of her smock. Her first name was on her smock, but how did he know her last name? "I can't," she whispered once she recovered her voice.

"You can't or you don't want to?"

"You must be mistaken, Mr. Grace. I'm not who you think I am."

"You're wrong, Francine Tanner. I know exactly who you are."

"But I don't know you," she countered.

He leaned closer. "Have dinner with me and you'll have the opportunity to get to know everything you need to know about me."

Francine knew she couldn't continue to carry on a conversation with the arrogant man without someone eavesdropping. As it was, customers were craning their necks to overhear what they were talking about. "It can't be tonight."

"When, if not tonight?" he questioned.

A shiver of annoyance swept over her. If or when she met with Keaton Grace he would quickly learn that she wasn't someone who reacted positively to being pressured. That was something her ex-husband had had to learn the hard way.

"I'll call you."

The slight frown between Keaton's eyes disappeared. "Thank you, Francine."

Much to her chagrin she gave him a warm smile. "You're welcome, Keaton." He inclined his head.

A woman pushed up her dryer, her gaze fixed on Keaton's retreating back. "Damn!" she whispered. "Where did he come from?"

The woman sitting next to her shook her head. "I don't know, but I'd sure like to sop that up with a biscuit."

Francine successfully hid a smile when the women exchanged fist bumps. She wanted to agree with them but kept her opinion to herself. Keaton was gorgeous. She had to give it to him. There was no doubt he was subtle, waiting until it was time to settle his bill before asking her out. She knew she should've been flattered, but she wasn't about to date a perfect stranger, even one as handsome and charming as Keaton.

Reaching into her pocket she took out the card and the money. Her eyes widened. He'd given her a fifty-dollar tip. Was he a generous tipper or trying to get her to go out with him?

Her gaze lingered on the business card. Keaton U. Grace was an independent filmmaker. The card bore a Los Angeles post office box and e-mail address, and a telephone number. What, she mused, was he doing in Sanctuary Cove? Did he plan to use the island as a backdrop or locale for a film? And how long did he plan to stay? There were so many questions she wanted answers to, which made her more than curious about the filmmaker—curious enough to consider setting aside time to listen to what he had to say.

However, meeting with Keaton would have to wait until after she and Morgan co-hosted a baby shower for Kara Hamilton, the current owner of Angels Landing Plantation. She wasn't as close to Kara as Morgan was, but when her best friend asked for her help she hadn't hesitated. They'd also enlisted the assistance of Jeffrey Hamilton, the island's sheriff, to take his wife away for a couple of days so they could finalize what they hoped would be a surprise for her. All of the invitees were sworn to secrecy, but Francine knew secrets on the island were like the mythical unicorn. And because they didn't exist, she and Morgan knew it was their sole reason for keeping the gathering small and very intimate.

The door opened and Trina Caine bumped into Keaton, her arms going around his waist in an attempt to keep her balance. Trina's eyes grew wider when she stared up at him. "Well, hello there," she crooned.

Francine watched Keaton smile, and then reach around his waist in an attempt to extricate himself from her arms. "I'm sorry, miss."

However, Trina was not to be denied when she held on to his hands. As a teenager she'd earned the reputation as a flirt, and it had continued into adulthood. Twice divorced, she'd made it known that she was on the prowl for her third husband, and there was never a time when she wasn't seen wearing an outfit that was at least one size too small for her voluptuous body.

"Where are you going so fast, handsome?"

Francine had had enough. "Trina, stop harassing my customer, or you can go to Charleston to get your hair done." Trina dropped her arms and Keaton gave Francine a look of gratitude before he walked out.

Trina pulled down the hem of her spandex top. Large eyes framed with thick false lashes fluttered wildly. "I was just teasing him, Red."

Francine leaned in close. "The next time you act up like that you'll be banned from coming into the Beauty Box."

"You tell her, Red," shouted a woman close enough to overhear her admonishment. "What is wrong with you, Trina?" she continued. "I'm certain if your grandmomma, God bless the dead, were here she would skin you alive if she saw you hanging on that young man like some strumpet."

Trina stood up straight, resting her hands on her ample hips. "Well, for your information, my grandmomma ain't here, so there."

"Didn't anyone teach you not to sass your elders?" Mavis asked. She'd returned in time to hear Trina insult a woman old enough to be her mother.

Lowering her eyes, Trina managed to look contrite. "I'm sorry."

A frown marred Mavis's smooth forehead. "Don't apologize to me, but to Miss Chloe."

"I'm sorry, Miss Chloe." The other woman nodded.

Mavis's frown disappeared. "Trina, please sit down and someone will be with you directly."

Francine shook her head in amazement. It was just another day at the Beauty Box.